TOWER FICTION

THE

STUDS LONIGAN TRILOGY

★ ★

Young Lonigan

The Young Manhood of Studs Lonigan

Judgment Day

JAMES T. FARRELL

The Young Manhood of Studs Lonigan

WITH A NEW INTRODUCTION WRITTEN BY THE AUTHOR FOR THIS EDITION

CLEVELAND AND NEW YORK

THE WORLD PUBLISHING COMPANY

Published by THE WORLD PUBLISHING COMPANY

2231 WEST 110TH STREET · CLEVELAND · OHIO

TOWER BOOKS EDITION

First Printing January 1944
Second Printing March 1944

Books in Wartime

"Books are weapons in the war of ideas."
—President Roosevelt

This book is manufactured in compliance with the War Production Board's ruling for conserving paper.

It is printed on lighter weight paper, which reduces bulk substantially, and has smaller margins with more words to each page. The text is complete and unabridged.

Thinner and smaller books will not only save paper, plate metal and man power, but will make more books available to the reading public.

The reader's understanding of this wartime problem will enable the publisher to cooperate more fully with our Government.

HC

MANUFACTURED IN THE UNITED STATES OF AMERICA

TO

MY UNCLE—R. T. DALY

"Your woraciousness, fellow critters, I don't blame ye so much for; dat is natur, and can't be helped. . . . No use goin' on; de willians will keep a scrougin' and slappin' each oder, Massa Studd; dey don't hear one word; no use a-preaching to such dam g'uttons as you call 'em, till dere bellies is full, and dere bellies is bottomless; and when dey do get 'em full, dey won't hear you den; for den they sink in de sea, go fast to sleep on de coral, and can't hear not'ing at all, no more, for eber and eber."

MOBY DICK BY HERMAN MELVILLE.

Introduction

THE story of Studs Lonigan is that of a young man's life. He is a normal American youth, *un homme moyen sensuel.* In *Young Lonigan,* the first volume of this trilogy, Studs was a healthy boy just out of grammar school. He stood in front of the poolroom at Fifty Eighth Street on the South Side of Chicago, associating with those older than himself, imitating them, thrilled when they permitted him to join with them in the perpetration of practical jokes, and viewing them as models for his own future conduct. He confidently told himself that soon he would be older, and that then like them, he would really be "strong, and tough and the real stuff." Here, in *The Young Manhood of Studs Lonigan,* I have attempted to tell what happened to Studs when he did become older, and with this, what happened to Studs' dream of himself.

Studs is far from satisfied with himself. One form his dissatisfaction takes is that of anxiety about his health. A more fundamental expression of his dissatisfaction is a concern over his conduct. In his own conscience, he is faced with moral problems which are occasioned by his behaviour. He wants to be different from what he is. He wants a different life from that which he lives. He hopes sentimentally that he will meet some girl, perhaps Lucy, his childhood sweetheart, and that then, he will fulfill his dream of himself: then, the real Studs will emerge from the recesses of his own consciousness. He makes resolutions, and breaks them: he makes new ones, but again, he shows that he is "human-all-too-human." He drifts. Again and again with his friends, he, or someone else, asks out of boredom—"What'll we do?" In fact, this question is a *leitmotif* in his life. His education, the values which he has absorbed from a spiritually depoverished background, give him no real aid in finding an adequate answer to this question. Time passes, often like a slow and sluggish stream. Rudderless, he floats on this stream.

Most of the action in this novel occurs in the 1920's. Novels and motion pictures have stamped conceptions of this decade in the popular mind. A conception of the gangster type has been established in such novels and films as *Little Caesar, Scarface,* and *Public Enemy.* The gangsters of that time, so celebrated in our popular culture, were *entrepreneurs* of the period: they were business men, engaged in illegal activities for profit. They became the "big shots" of the era: they made the huge profits which were to be derived from racketeering and the sale of liquor. In part, *The Young Manhood of Studs Lonigan* can be described as a novel that seeks to re-create another side of the 1920's. Its characters are representative young men from that large body of customers who bought the gin and whiskey which the "big shots" sold. More or less from afar, young men such as Studs admired these big shots as those who really were "strong, and tough and the real stuff." But only a small percentage of the youths of Studs' generation became gangsters, and those who did generally came from poorer neighborhoods, poorer homes than did Studs. A far greater proportion of this generation paid out money for the products sold by the gangsters. Studs was one such young man. The commodities dispensed by the big shots helped Studs and his friends to find one answer to that question—"What'll we do?"

In this fictionized character, I have attempted to present the story of one young man, of his time and place, as he comes to grips with his destiny. This novel is the second of the three novels which recounts that unfolding destiny. It sets the stage for Studs' final denouement which is described in my novel, *Judgment Day.*

The Young Manhood of Studs Lonigan was completed in Saratoga Springs in September 1933, and it was first published in January, 1934.

JAMES T. FARRELL

Aug. 31, 1943
New York City

SECTION ONE

1917—1918—1919

I

The baby bawled. Lee heard a final sob from his wife. He slammed the door. Cursing in disgust, he walked along Calumet Avenue. He joined the lads in the barber shop, front of Charlie Bathcellar's poolroom, and smiled with a lightened mood.

"Congratulate me, boys!"

"What, did you get a divorce?" asked fat, middle-aged, dour-faced Barney Keefe.

"You sound like you lost your job, Lee," Jew Percentage smiled.

"Nope! I got a one-way ticket to Berlin. Leaving tomorrow," Lee said.

"Say, I see where some guy in Kansas City put a Colt in his mouth, and fired, committing suicide. That's four suicides in the paper tonight," Slew Weber said, looking up from his newspaper; he was slouched in one of the barber chairs.

"Hey, Swede, drop that morbidity!" said Barney.

"Lee, what did the missus say?" asked Percentage.

"What she says ain't nothin' out of my poke. Her old man has enough to take care of her and her goddamn brat. And I don't care if I never see her again," Lee answered spiritedly.

"She must have thrown the rolling pin at you," said Fritz, the poolroom pest.

"She acted like a goddamn bitch. She jerked on the tears. Then, she came petting around. Just like a goddamn bitch, trying to get me hot. She pulled every trick that a bitch pulls on a guy," Lee said in disgust.

"She loves you. She just doesn't want to see her man shot into sixteen pieces," Pat Coady said.

"I ain't afraid of death, and before they get me, I'll chop down a few goddamn sausage-eatin' Dutchmen. I'm glad to go and take my chances. I've been a shipping clerk for a whole goddamn year, and I'm fed up with it and that goddamn bitch of a wife I got and that squalling brat. I'm fed up, and want to see the fun. . . . And listen, lads, don't think that Lee Cole ain't going to sample some nice French chicken," he said, winking.

"Well, Lee, give our regards to Kaiser Bill," said Pat.

"And tell him the boys from Fifty-eighth Street want to throw a party in his honor, if he'll drop around," Slew said.

"Sure thing! And say, boys, since it's my last night, how about having a blowout?"

"You said it. We'll send you off to Berlin in the right way," said Barlowe.

Chapter One

I

STUDS LONIGAN walked north along Indiana Avenue. His cap was on crooked, a cigarette hung from the corner of his mouth, and his hands were jammed into the pockets of his long jeans.

Warm sun sifted dozily through an April wind, making him feel good. He liked spring and summer. There were things in winter that were all right—ice skating, plopping derbies with snowballs—but spring and summer, that was his ticket. Soon now, there would be long afternoons ahead, at the beach and over in Washington Park, where they would all drowse in the shade, gassing, telling jokes, goofing the punks, flirting with the chickens and nursemaids, fooling around and having swell times. Like last summer, only this one was going to be even better. He was a year older now, bigger, and he knew what it was all about. After June, he wouldn't have that worry about school. It sure was a black cloud over his head. Gee, he didn't know what night he would go home to supper and learn that his old man had found out. How would he face it? If only he hadn't done it!

But he'd lied, and had had to go on telling more lies until now he was so damn mixed up in lies about it, that he didn't know what to do. He hadn't wanted to go to high school anyway. Well, it was the old man's fault. And if the old man did find out, all right. Studs Lonigan would let him know that *he* was his own *boss*. It was a black cloud always hanging over his head.

He shrugged his shoulders, because Wilson was going to declare war any one of these days, and maybe the war would get him out of it. He might be able to go. In a few months he'd be sixteen. Next fall, he might be doing his bit for Uncle Sam, and then all his troubles about school would be forgotten kid worries.

Praying in church, at Stations of the Cross, he'd learned something about himself, and about praying. Whenever he prayed for something he really wanted, and he could see the thing he wanted clearly in his own mind, he could pray good, concentrating on God and holy things. But when he just prayed in general, with no particular intention in mind, he just mumbled out the prayer words, and his thoughts wandered over everything, and he couldn't, not even to save his neck, keep them on God and holy things. Today, he'd asked God in his prayers to be on the side of America, if Wilson declared war, and let him fight and be a hero and not get killed or mortally wounded.

He remembered his history lessons from grammar school. We had, America had, the most glorious and bravest and noblest war record in all history. Old Glory had never kissed the dust in defeat. And now, maybe, yes, Old Glory would be flying victorious over the battlefields of the biggest war in history. But what would it be like in war times, because war times were the only important times in history? It was great to think that kids in the future might be reading about the times when Studs Lonigan had lived. They might even be reading of William Lonigan, the hero, just like he'd read about Hobson, the guy who had carried the message to Garcia in the war with Spain when America had set Cuba free from tyranny. He guessed he might still be too young, but he'd get there soon, somehow. He was prepared to fight, and, if necessary, die for his country. He paused under the elevated structure at Fifty-ninth and Indiana, and slowly, solemnly, as if taking an oath in the very presence of God, he muttered:

I pledge allegiance to the flag, and to the republic for which it stands. One flag, one nation, one people, indivisible, with liberty and justice for all.

He turned down the alley between Indiana and Prairie. He was going to be a soldier of his country. Suddenly, he trembled. If he was killed in action, it would be a hero's death, but . . . he thought of the Stations of the Cross in the church, slow, sad, solemn, the story of Christ on the Cross, the sad singing, all the statues draped, death, and dying, people going, soldiers going, never speaking again or seeing anybody they wanted to see and speak to, and leaving the people they loved like he loved Lucy, and he was afraid of war because there was so much dying in it. He hastily muttered a Hail Mary to the Blessed Virgin, asking her protection, and promising always to remember her, pray to her and wear her scapular.

He fell into marching step, as if he were an American soldier going off to war. He imagined himself going over the top with the American Army, not stopping until they captured Berlin. He saw Private Lonigan as the soldier who captured the Kaiser. He saw himself with levelled gun forcing Kaiser Bill to cower into a corner and yell Kamerad, like a yellow skunk.

"Take that, you raping sonofabitch!" he said, swinging on the Kaiser.

"And that!" he followed, massacring the air with a good old-fashioned American right uppercut.

A passing laundry-wagon driver leaned out of his seat and yelled: "Hi there, Jess Willard!"

Shame blushed his cheeks. He walked circumspectly. Well, after war was declared and Studs Lonigan was a brave and gallant soldier of his country, he wouldn't have to pretend, and he would make everybody and Lucy envy him and be proud of him, and recognize he was a somebody all right, and he'd win medals for bravery and have his picture in the papers, and maybe, years ahead, even in the history books.

Studs emerged from the alley and walked down to the northeast side of Fifty-eighth and Prairie. At the elevated station, a half block down, he saw people crowding excitedly around Sammy Schmaltz, the newspaper man. He started to go down there, but heard Red Kelly calling him from the other side of the street. He turned and saw Red waving in front of Frank Hertzog's shoe repair shop, about fifty yards or so down from the corner. Studs dashed across the street, dodging a truck that just missed him. The driver cursed him. Red said war was declared. They went inside the shoe repair shop, and stood outside the counter. Frank, a middle-aged man with a square face and a mustache, was carefully half-soleing a shoe.

"The extras are out now. And we're gonna cook the Kaiser's goose plenty. How about it, Frank? You know we can do it, don't you, because you're from Germany?" Red said, slurring and running some of his words together.

"I'm an American citizen now," Frank remarked without looking up from his work.

"Say, Frank, tell us what kind of a lousy country Germany is," said Red.

Continuing to work, Frank said that he had come to America because it was a democratic country with more opportunity, and because there was no compulsory military service.

"Yep, it's the land of the free and the home of the brave," Red said knowingly.

"We had to do it or the Germans would have come over and attacked us," Studs said.

"We got to save a civilization. You can see what the Germans are doing from the papers. Only they haven't told half of it. Why last week, I was reading a book by a Catholic priest telling what the Germans did in Belgium. You know what they'd do? A hundred or so of 'em would line up, and take a woman, or even a six-year-old girl or an eighty-year-old grandmother, like old Mrs. O'Flaharty, and they'd strip her and rape her one after the other, until she was dead. Then they'd go and do the same thing over again."

"The book says that? Does it describe the rapes?" asked Studs.

"Yeah."

"What's the name of it? I'd like to read it," Studs said.

"I forgot, but I'll take you down to the library and show it to you and you can read it there."

"I'd like to. You say it describes the rapes?" Studs asked.

"The Huns, they're not civilized . . . of course, Frank, you know I don't mean you because you're Americanized . . . but the Germans are brutes. Why, they're destroying Catholic churches, and Red Cross hospitals, and they sink ships without warning, letting helpless women and children drown. Look at the Lusitania! I tell you, they ain't civilized."

Frank's eyebrows rose, and he glanced at the two boys. He thought of other years, back in Bavaria, his fatherland. And friends and cousins, and the children of friends and cousins, boys of fifteen and sixteen like these, being taken off to war and killed. Why? His own brother, shot with Hindenburg's army on the Russian front! The world was calling them Huns, beasts, brutes, savages. These silly boys had picked it up like parrots, all that awful talk. He tried to work rapidly. He had come to America, haven of peace and liberty, and it, too, was joining the slaughter, fighting for the big capitalists. There was no peace for men, only murder, cruelty, brutality. He was choked with feelings and fears. His own name! His birthplace, His fatherland! He loved it, suffering Bavaria. America would be a war-crazy nation. He told the boys he was very busy, and asked them to return and see him another time. He went to the back of the shop to sit down and try and think and assimilate this terror.

"I want to go," Red said.

"Me, too," said Studs, leaning on the fireplug in front of the chain drug store.

Some of the passing people acted as if nothing had happened. Others had their heads buried in extra papers. Groups paused on the corner to discuss the declaration of war. From down the street, newsboys barked:

"EXTRA PAPEE! CONGRESS DECLARES WAR! EXTRY! WAR!"

"Yeah, I want to go," Studs said reflectively.

"I'm going to try and get in."

"But you're underweight and underage."

"I'll say I'm eighteen, and I can maybe put on enough weight by eating bananas and drinking water before I go down to enlist."

"Say, Red, that's an idea."

"What you say? We'll both join the marines?"

"Maybe we'll get all the guys. We'll have a company from Fifty-eighth Street," Studs said.

"It'd be good if we all could become aviators, and have our own squadron," Red suggested.

"We'll have a swell time. And we'll bring Kenny Kilarney along, too."

"Say, he'll be a one-man circus in the war. . . . But did you hear, Kenny's got a job?"

"No kiddin'."

"Sure, he's deliverin' orders for Ortenstein and Vauss' drug store down on Garfield Boulevard. I wouldn't believe it myself if I didn't see him there."

"If he goes to war, he'll probably pull off some stunt like capturing all the rats in our trenches and sending them over to the Huns. That'll be the way we'll win the war," said Studs, laughing.

"And I hear the hustlers are yum-yum in France, too," Red said.

"We won't do nothin' atall with those French chickens," Studs bragged lasciviously.

"If we save civilization and France, I think we'll have a right to."

"You know, I got to laugh, just thinkin' of what a guy like Kenny wouldn't pull in the war. He'd probably go over and cop all the German soup-kitchens, or he might nab Berlin from right under the Kaiser's nose, without the Germans knowing it was gone."

They talked of how they would come home in glory and victory, marching down Michigan Boulevard with their medals and souvenirs. And Kenny Kilarney would probably have the Kaiser's mustache, iron helmet and his iron cross, and he'd hold them up, shouting RAGOLIRON, as he marched out of step.

Kenny happened along, carrying a bottle of seltzer water for delivery, and singing, *Reuben, Reuben, I Been Thinking*. They told him about enlisting. He looked at them in that goofy surprised way of his, waved his arms, and sang, *I Didn't Raise My Boy To Be A Soldier*. It was so funny they had to laugh, because Kenny was a funny guy. They said he ought to go into vaudeville. He said that, all kidding aside, the idea was jake with him. He showed them how he would jam a bayonet up the Clown Quince's.

"Hey, there's that Jew punk, Stein. His old man speaks German. I'll bet he's a German spy," Red said.

Studs grabbed Stein, a neatly dressed, twelve-or-thirteen-year-old, four-eyed sissy. Bawling like a mama's cry baby, Stein asked what he had done. Kenny squirted seltzer water in his face. Stein shrieked to be let alone. Kenny appointed himself judge for a court-martial and told them to hold the prisoner until he came back. He dashed away. While they waited, they tortured the kid with questions. Kenny quickly returned with a small American flag which he'd copped from the nearby five-and-dime store. Stein was sentenced to kneel down and kiss the flag. He demurred, but rough handling changed his mind. He knelt down and pressed his lips towards the flag which had been placed on the sidewalk. He was hurtled forwards by three swift kicks in the tocus. He was still bawling when Kenny grabbed his feet, and Studs and Red nabbed him under the arms. They gave him the royal bumps, slamming his can against the sidewalk. A stranger told them to let the kid alone. Kenny said that the kid's father was a German and that he had just yelled "Down with Wilson" and "Hoch der Kaiser."

Macnamara, the pot-bellied cop, came along, twirling his club. He intruded to halt the punishment. They told him Stein had spit on the flag. Stein, stuttering and tearful, denied the accusation. Macnamara asked him his name. Stein replied meekly. The cop said you could expect anything from one with a name like that, kicked his tail, and told him to get home. He told the guys that they'd done right, but the next time to go back in the alley where they wouldn't cause such a commotion. He flatfooted along twirling his club.

Kenny turned his cap around backwards and sang:

Oh, say can you see, any bedbugs on me . . .

It was funny. Red pointed at the empty seltzer bottle on the sidewalk, and asked Kenny wouldn't he get canned on account of what he did with it. Kenny said no because he'd quit. He struck a Napoleonic attitude, and said:

"On to Berlin!"

They shook on it.

II

After he became a hero, and everybody knew of him, the story of the stunt they were pulling would be remembered and they would all be telling it. . . . Well, he would become a hero. . . . He would!

He casually leaned against a girder in the alley in back of the Fifty-eighth Street elevated station, cigarette drooping from the corner of his mouth, his cap set back on his poll, a mop of darkish blond hair showing.

"I wish Kilarney would shake a leg, wherever he is," Studs Lonigan said, as if he were not excited, and all this that was happening was just ordinary and everyday.

"He'll cop a bike, all right. That boy is a past master," Red said.

"Yeah," said Studs, secretly envying Kenny Kilarney's talents.

Studs itched to walk around a bit and do something—anything. Waiting like this got him. But he couldn't let Red see he was nervous or Red might think he was yellow.

They heard whooping down the alley. They looked and saw Kenny on a bike, coming towards them like a bat out of hell. He clamped the bicycle brake, and leaped off. He was breathless and he laughed.

"How do you like it?" he asked, smiling goofily.

They examined the bike, a new one, with blue bars and mudguard, and a bushel basket tied in back of the seat.

"Jesus Christ!" Studs exclaimed admiringly.

"Where'd you get it?" asked Red, also with admiration.

"Off a back porch at Fifty-sixth and Prairie," Kenny proudly said.

"That near? Maybe we better get away from here. Somebody might be following you," said Studs.

"Hell, no! I stopped in the alley right near there and tied this bushel basket on," Kenny said.

"Well, now let's get going. We got lots to do today," said Studs, nervous.

"You guys got any ideas on how we'll pull the trick off?" asked Red.

"Leave that to Uncle Kilarney," said Kenny confidently.

"Why? We ought to help," said Red.

"If you leave it to me, it'll be pie. I got the bike. All I got to do is to find a banana peddler, and wait till he sells something and leaves his cart. Then, I'll just fill the basket and blow. If you guys come along, it'll be easier to catch you because you'll be on foot."

"But listen, Kenny! . . ."

"Never mind, Red. You guys meet me at Sixtieth and Prairie.

Take a little time getting there, and wait. I won't be long. It's just a matter of finding a Guinea peddling bananas."

He shot off. They shrugged their shoulders, and walked slowly down towards the meeting-place.

"We won't be seein' much of this burg for a *long time,*" said Red.

"I guess not," said Studs, melancholy at the thought of leaving. Did Red feel the same way? He didn't like to ask because he'd never had a friend he could feel sure of in talking about things like that. Everybody might feel that he was soft and yellow. But, gee, he was leaving the burg, and everything. He was game. He wasn't backing down. But he did feel a little, well, sad at the idea of blowing.

"Think your old man will put in a squawk when he finds out?" asked Red.

"Gee, I wonder. I'm afraid he might."

"I don't know about mine. I don't think he will, but I ain't positive."

"If mine does, I'll just raise all holy hell with him," Studs said.

"I guess the best thing to do is not to tell them. We'll just blow, and then, when we're sure they can't crab our act, we'll let them know. Anyway, Kenny's old lady will probably just say good riddance. He won't have any trouble," said Red.

Studs wished he had parents like Kenny's old lady. He seemed to do anything he wanted to without ever having any trouble about it at home.

"Say, Studs, what's happened about school?"

"I won't have to worry about it any more now."

"I know, but has your old man found out?"

"No! But if he does, Jesus! He'll throw cat-fits all over the house. I haven't gone in months, and last winter I got sixty bucks from him for tuition and books and blew it in," said Studs, laughing with a pride of achievement.

"He isn't wisened up then?" said Red.

"Not yet."

"Got any more cigarettes?" asked Red.

Studs shook his head. Red sniped a butt from the street.

"Too bad we can't get more of the guys to go," Studs said.

"Aw, they're yellow! They all said they would, and where are they? Tommy Doyle, today of all days, giving us that crap that he has to help his old man. Say, that bastard hasn't helped his old man or old woman do anything since he was an infant. That crap!"

"Yes," said Studs, thrilling with a feeling of his superior courage.

"And Weary Reilley, the tough guy, saying they can keep their war," said Red.

"His name ought to be Schultz or Hoffman, the way he talks," said Studs.

"Well, let 'em. We'll do our duty, and we'll have our fun, too. With Kenny around we'll have a hell of a time," said Red.

"And if we do get killed, it'll be for our flag, and you know, a soldier dying for his country don't have to worry about going to hell. It's like a martyr's death," said Studs.

"We won't get killed. We'll just kill the Germans," said Red.

"What'll we join?" asked Studs.

"I'm all for joining the marines," said Red.

"Me too, the devil dogs," said Studs.

"There's where that screwy big elephant Jeff lives," said Red, pointing to a three-story apartment building next to a vacant lot between Fifty-ninth and Sixtieth on Prairie Avenue.

"The punks all over the neighborhood are digging trenches," said Red, pointing at trenches which had been dug in the vacant lot.

"It'll be nice coming around on leave in devil-dog uniforms before we go across," said Red.

"Yeah," said Studs, thinking of how he would go to mass in his uniform, receive everybody's congratulations, even be seen by Lucy. And he'd go back and see Battling Bertha too.

"We'll be among the first from the neighborhood to go. Lee Cole was the first. But that'll be something, because after all, we're younger, and not even expected to fight," said Red.

"Yeah," said Studs, a sense of martyrdom and nobility plunging extravagantly within him.

"I'm kind of anxious to get the thing settled, and sign on the dotted line," said Red.

"Me too," said Studs.

They sat on a fence at Sixtieth and Prairie Avenue in front of the home where that punk from St. Patrick's, Morrie Regan, lived.

"Say, maybe we can get in just as we are," said Red.

"We hadn't better take any chances. I only weigh a hundred and ten pounds, and Kenny's lighter. How about you?"

"I'm about one nine," said Red.

"We better eat the bananas," said Studs.

"You're pretty anxious," said Red, as Studs got up and walked in front of him.

"Kind of," said Studs, running his words together.

"I can understand it."

"Suppose he gets caught?" said Studs, glancing north.

"Kenny never gets caught."

"Hello, fellows. . . . Say, got a fag?" asked Three Star Hennessey.

"Go on home and wash your face," Red said.

"Don't be a heel," said Hennessey.

"Why don't you go to school? The truant officer will be nabbing you, and your old man will kick your ears off," said Studs, with the superior sneer warranted by age and size.

"Say, what you guys doing today?" Hennessey asked.

"Nothin'," said Red with obvious mysteriousness, and winked at Studs.

"Hey, punk, blow!" Studs commanded.

"Aw, come on, Studs, what did I ever do to you?"

"I'll give you just about five seconds to remove yourself from sight," said Red.

"This place is free. I don't have to, if I want to stay here."

"No?"

"No!" whined Hennessey.

"For the last time. . . . Blow!"

Hennessey stood there gritting his teeth. Red kicked him in the tail. He bawled.

"Need another invitation?" asked Studs.

"You don't own this sidewalk," Hennessey sniveled, snot running from his nose.

Red slapped his face. Studs booted him one.

"If you don't blow now, I'll kill you, you little. . . ."

Hennessey ran, yelling back wait till he got his gat.

Kenny rode up whooping, with a basket full of bananas. They congratulated him again. He imitated the way the dago peddler had shagged him. But there had been no one on the street so it had been a cinch. They went to Kenny's basement.

"Here goes," said Red, peeling his first banana, as they sat on boxes.

"Well, Kenny, how'll you like it in the trenches?" asked Studs.

"Me, I'll be a general by that time."

"General Kilarney," said Studs; they laughed.

"This ain't so bad," said Studs, starting on his second banana.

"Nope," said Kenny, swigging water from a milk bottle.

"Wait till we get over there. You'll be so funny, the Germans will have to laugh at you. Christ, when we get to Berlin I'll bet you'll steal the Kaiser's mustache," Red said.

"I'll be a soldier of America," Kenny said melodramatically.

"I'd like an iron cross to bring back," said Studs, his face stuffed with banana.

"I can just picture Kenny. When he goosesteps, it'll be better than Charlie Chaplin," said Red.

Kenny mimicked the goosestep.

"How do you feel?" asked Red, after Kenny had finished the comedy.

"All right," Studs valorously said.

"I'm O. K. too," said Red, slowly reaching for another banana.

"I never felt better. These things agree with me," Kenny said, biting off almost a half.

"Me too," said Studs, not to be outdone, as he jammed half of a banana in his mouth.

"Wait till tonight when we go around the poolroom and say: 'Well, boys, wish us luck!'" Red said.

"Christ, will they be surprised," said Studs.

"They won't believe us," said Red.

"Here, have another, Red," said Kenny, tossing him one.

Studs took the milk bottle and filled it slowly at the faucet. He looked at the bananas stacked in the basket.

"Jesus, you certainly got enough," he said.

"Need 'em, I'm only a bantamweight," Kenny replied.

Red took a gulp of water. He set the bottle down and cursed.

"What's the matter, son? Gettin' you already? That's no way to be a soldier," said Kenny.

"I just drank too fast," Red said, biting a hunk.

"Say, Kenny, your janitor will like us, dumping these skins all over," said Studs.

"He's only a Hunky," said Kenny.

"You won't win a war on that stomach, Kelly," kidded Kilarney after Red had belched.

"I'm all right. It's only that I drank that water too damn fast. How about you, Studs?"

Studs nodded, reaching towards the basket.

"Kenny, show us how you're going to bayonet the Clown Quince," said Studs.

"This is serious," said Kenny.

He told a dirty joke. It was a scream. In the midst of laughing, Studs hiccoughed.

"Take a drink, Studs," said Red, fighting his hiccoughs.

"I'll be all right," said Studs, not liking the tone of Red's voice.

"Well, here goes for another," said Red, reaching for the basket, and looking at Studs, so that Studs would notice him. Studs grimly took another also.

"Maybe you better let up for a while Studs," said Red as Studs nibbled.

"No, I just think we've all been eating too fast," Studs answered.

"Jesus Christ. Say, why the hell do we have to eat bananas to go to war?" Kenny suddenly said.

"You got to. You won't make the weight," said Red, nibbling.

"You don't get me, fellow! I just always think of Kilarney's comfort," Kenny said.

"You know what General Sherman said. . . . War is hell," said Red.

"That was General Sheridan," snapped Kenny.

They had an argument over which general it had been.

"Say, is there a can here?" asked Studs.

Kenny pointed.

"I'll bet Studs fell in," Kenny said, after Studs had remained absent for about five minutes.

"It's got him," Red said.

Studs came out in about fifteen minutes, his face white.

"Sick?" asked Red.

"I'm all right," said Studs, taking a banana.

Red went to the can. He took a long time too. Then Kenny.

Studs looked at the basket, over half full. They ate more and more slowly.

"I won't eat any more of those goddamn things," Kenny suddenly said.

"Come on. You want to get in. Well, you gotta have the weight."

"I'll stay home if it means eatin' all that crap," Kenny said.

"Come on, Kenny. We can't go on without you," Red pleaded.

"Jesus, Kenny, won't you do that much for your country?" said Studs.

"My country can have me, but I don't see why it makes me eat bananas till I bloat like a balloon," said Kenny.

"Well, I told you. You have to be a certain weight, or you can't be accepted. Listen, after it's all over you'll be glad. Think of it, going to France. Say, we'll have a hell of a time. And you'll come back a hero," said Red.

"Come on, Kenny. We need you with us. And we ain't beefing," persuaded Studs.

Red handed Kenny a banana. Kenny took it with a pout. They nibbled their bananas, and sipped water, almost by drops.

"Say, it's gettin' late. We better be going," said Studs.

"I was thinkin' that too. Only there's more bananas. And we don't want to get rejected," said Red.

"I'm going," said Kenny.

"Come on, just a few more. We want to make sure," said Red.

"But listen, Red, if we don't get in, we can come back and try it again," said Studs.

"Not this boy," said Kenny.

They sat there, each taking another, gazing at it long. They finally agreed to go. They left the basket, still about half full, and the basement floor was a litter of banana peels.

"How do you feel?" asked Red.

"Ask me another, wise guy," said Kenny; they laughed.

"It wasn't so bad," said Studs.

He saw that Red was white. Red noticed that Kenny was pale. Kenny observed that Studs didn't look so hot. They walked very slowly. It was a job, climbing up the back stairs of the elevated station, to gyp the elevated company. On the train, they did more hiccoughing than talking. People noticed them and suppressed smiles. Suddenly, Kenny lit for the rear platform. Studs and Red followed. They stood by themselves, looking at the tracks as if sightless, while the train sped downtown. They got off at State and Congress and found a marine recruiting station, with a picture of Uncle Sam pleading, and pointing to a Hun in the background. Over it were the words: "He Needs You."

"I guess Uncle Sam needs us all right," Red said.

Studs nodded.

"Kilarney only needs some Pluto Water," Kenny said.

Their smiles were sickly.

"Well, here goes," Red said.

He stepped up to a beefy-faced, hard-boiled sergeant. Studs and Kilarney stood by him.

"We came to join up."

The tow-headed sergeant took one look at them, and laughed. They hiccoughed, almost trembled.

"Sure, we're keepin' a little date with the Kaiser," Kenny said.

The sergeant let fly a gob of tobacco juice.

"G'wan home, children, and get your diapers pinned on!"

They trooped off.

"The bastard," said Red.

"We should have socked him," Studs said, and Red nodded.

"If we did, all he would have had to do was touch my belly. I'd have blown up like a balloon," Kenny said.

"We could have mobbed him, and cleaned him too, only for the bananas," Studs said.

"That's what I thought. As soon as we feel better, I say we come down and lay for him. We'll get him," Red said.

"How about the navy?" asked Studs.

"That's an idea," Red said, without interest.

They started out for a naval recruiting station. On the way they passed a burlesque show with advertisements flaunting pictures of semi-nude girls. Studs had money. They went to the show.

III

Aloof and alone, his stomach like a lump of lead, Studs stood on the sidewalk by the vacant lot near Fifty-eighth and Indiana.

In the prairie, the Indiana punks were in two trenches facing each other, and exuberantly warring with sand-filled tin cans. The nearer trench was a wide hole, partly covered with a piece of tar paper, and protected by earthworks of sand, heavy stones, and grocery boxes. The farther trench was long and narrow, and connected by a communication trench with a shallow reserve trench. In front of it was a deep hole, dug as an observation post.

Studs wondered where they could have collected so many cans. He sneered. Only for that goddamn recruiting sergeant, he wouldn't have to watch punks in short pants have an imitation war. He couldn't forget that lousy, tow-headed marine. They ought to go back and jump the bastard.

"G'wan home, children, and get your diapers pinned on!"

He belched. And last night had been just like a nightmare. They ought to go back, all right, and jump him.

Andy Le Gare and Danny O'Neill rose from the farther trench, holding, between them, a five-gallon oil can that was heavy with sand. They maneuvered into position to heave it. Dick Buckford rose from a nearer trench, and whacked Andy in the arm with a can. Andy let out a yell, dropped the can on his foot, and dove back into his trench amidst a tin-can shower. O'Neill retrieved the trench mortar, and scrambled to safety. Studs laughed. He wished he'd been in the trench and had such a chance to plop goofy Le Gare.

He felt like joining in the battle. But, hell, it was only playing at war, and he wasn't a kid in short pants any more. And they wouldn't take him in the army. A lot of nerve that goddamn sergeant had had.

And then when he'd gotten home, with an awful bellyache, he had all that trouble. They never made any least effort to try and understand him. His old lady still nagging him to study for the priesthood. And Fran, a great big pain she was. And the old man! Let him yell. He'd told them he didn't want to go to school. Now they knew. Father Mahin from Loyola had called up to ask what had happened that he hadn't been to school for so long, and the old man had also learned about his having blown in the tuition money. All the damn yelling they'd done over it. And just when he had that bellyache.

He felt like blowing, going on the bum. He could just hop a freight and enlist in some other town. Then when he went to war, and they'd learned that he'd died a hero's death, how'd they like that? The old man would be plenty sorry, and it would serve him right. And Father Gilhooley would say a solemn high mass for him at St. Patrick's, and they'd all be there in tears, and maybe his old man would even cry. And then, maybe Lucy Scanlan would be proud she'd known him, and maybe she'd cry too.

But he didn't want to die. Well, maybe he wouldn't. Maybe he'd enlist and become a hero, and not get killed but would return as Lieutenant, or Major or Colonel Lonigan with medals all over his chest. And his picture would be in the paper, and when he came back they'd be pretty goddamn proud to see him.

Led by Ralph Borax, the enemy in the farther trench spread out in No-Man's-Land in front of their earthworks, and kept up a steady tin-can barrage, permitting Le Gare and O'Neill to get into position and heave their trench mortar. It smashed sand and wood down in upon the punks in the nearer trench. Andy jumped up and down, yelling with idiotic glee that he was smashing the German line. Dick Buckford plopped him on the ear with a can.

Studs laughed, but he couldn't keep his mind off that trouble at home. Anyway, the cat was out now. That was a relief. The worst that could come would be better than having that dark cloud of fear always hanging over him. The old man would probably cool off. He'd said plenty already about it being dishonorable. And the old lady had cried and babbled that they were disgraced, and that she'd never again be able to hold her head up, and that they'd have to move out of the neighborhood, because she could never again face the neighbors and parishioners. And Fran sticking her nose in too, as if it was her business. If she wasn't his sister, he'd kick her teeth in for her. And when he'd said he never wanted to go to school, and that he'd told them so that night he'd graduated, that hadn't meant anything. It was always the same. They all acted as if they were always right.

The punks argued shrilly. He laughed, forgetting his own troubles. Fat Malloy jumped up from his trench and yelled in his bullying loud-mouthed way:

"All right, you birds! Play square. We said the side that lost the toss-up had to be the Germans. And who lost? Tell me that! Who lost? . . . If we lost we'd have been the Germans. Play square."

"You guys ain't got any sportsmanship," Young Horn Buckford said, wiping his nose with his sleeve.

"You cheated in that toss-up, and we won't be no Germans," Andy yelled.

"If you guys were patriots you'd want to be the Germans anyway because you're getting licked. You wouldn't want the Americans to be licked," yelled O'Neill in a loud, squeaking voice.

"Come on over and try and make us be the Germans," yelled Andy.

They drove him under cover with tin cans. In the midst of the battle, he popped up and shouted:

"You guys would cheat your own mother."

Young Horn tried to rearrange the battered earthworks in front of his trench. O'Neill hit him in the shoulder.

"Hurrah for us Americans!" yelled Andy, again jumping up and down, and laughing like an idiot.

"Hey, Le Gare, watch out for the squirrels," Studs shouted.

No one heard him. The punks didn't even seem to know that the great and tough Studs Lonigan was watching them.

Studs was keen to join in the battle. He couldn't play punk games any more. He wished that Red and Paulie Haggerty and some of the guys would come along. Then they could all get in, and that would be different. It wouldn't be just him, alone, playing. Or else the bunch of them could bust the game up, and that would be fun, all of them kicking in the trenches, and when the punks got loud-mouthed, booting their tails around the block.

O'Neill crawled out from the reserve trench, and yelled that he was wounded and couldn't be hit. He went over by the side fence of the prairie, walked past the baby-buggy where Young Horn had left his baby brother, and came out on the sidewalk, as the battle continued.

"Hey, goof!" yelled Studs.

O'Neill came over to Studs like one in his sleep.

"Where you going?"

"Hospital," said O'Neill, showing a hand bleeding slightly from a scratch.

Studs shook his head quizzically, as he watched O'Neill enter Levin's drug store across the street. But he itched to get into it, or else break it up. He looked at his long pants. He stuck his hands in his pockets, and stood sneering.

Well, before the war was over, he'd be in it, and get the real stuff. And suppose he did get killed. All right, it would make him one of his country's heroes, along with those who'd died in the other wars to make America the great land that it was. And it would only serve his old man right.

Screwy McGlynn, the laundry driver, hopped from his wagon and joined Studs.

"That's why this country's great. These kids exemplify the unconquerable American spirit. They show in their way why this country can lick the world, and why our boys aren't going to stop, once they get started, until they march straight into Berlin," philosophized Screwy.

Studs assumed a mature man-to-man attitude, and nodded.

"Pretty crazy, but it's great to be a kid," a needle-faced stranger said, ranging himself alongside of them.

Studs tried hard to convince himself in his thoughts that he was not envying the punks out there fighting, and, hell, he'd grown past all that kid stuff. But he knew that he couldn't fool himself and tell himself lies, and that when he wanted something, he wanted it, and all the telling himself in the world that he didn't want it couldn't make him get rid of that wanting. The same way he tried to tell himself that he didn't really love Lucy, and that loving a girl the way he loved Lucy was goofy, because a big tough guy should only want to jump a girl, and think that all the rest and the love was crap.

"Kids will be kids," said Screwy.

"Yep, they will," a bakery driver said.

"Yeah," the needle-faced guy said.

"No time in life like when you're a kid," the bakery man meditated aloud.

"You should have seen them bellyaching before it started. They both wanted to be the Americans. I thought they'd end up in a free-for-all fist fight," said Studs, a man in a man's world.

They haw-hawed, Studs the most loudly. Not one punk noticed Studs Lonigan laughing, a man in a man's world.

And smiling-eyed, curly-haired Lucy Scanlan, plump, pretty, flowering beautifully into young womanhood, came along. Studs saw her. She saw him. Studs took out a cigarette and lit it like an expert. He talked and laughed with the other men, as if Lucy might have been in Africa. She paused on the sidewalk, only a few yards away from Studs, watching the battle. She didn't look at him. He tried not to look at her. He watched her out of the corner of his eye. She might be going to the store. He could go along, help her carry the groceries home, go to the park with her, like last summer on the day when they'd sat in the tree, and he'd kissed her, and seen her blue wash bloomers, and she'd sung *In the Blue Ridge Mountains of Virginia,* swinging her legs in the tree, as if they two had been all alone together in the world. He looked at her out of the corner of his eye, at her shapely legs, and her growing girlbreasts, Lucy. Gee, she was even prettier than she was last summer, and growing, too. And she wouldn't bat an eye at him even.

Screwy spoke of playing pirate in Missouri, when he was a shaver living only about a hundred miles from Hannibal, that Mark Twain had written about. The bakery man spoke of barefoot-boy days in Indiana. Studs listened and laughed as they detailed their boyhood pranks. He looked at Lucy cold. She looked back. Their eyes met. She turned away, as if he were a total stranger.

The tin-can battle raged on, and after an attack was repulsed, Andy again went batty, jumping and yelling that the Americans were winning.

And Studs wanted to be a soldier now, marching away in uniform, and become a hero, and then if he died, well, it would serve her right. Because he loved her with the best and deepest part of himself, and what did she care! And if he came back with medals all over his chest, then she might change her tune. He'd walk along Indiana in his major's uniform, sword at his side, and she'd maybe come up and say, very penitent and meek:

"Studs, I'm sorry."

And Major Lonigan would walk past her as if she was a flea.

The battle raged.

Lucy walked on. Maybe on her way back, with her arms full of groceries, she'd talk, and he'd help her carry them. Or maybe he wouldn't. She'd say hello Studs, and he'd say, hello, or maybe not, and then let her go on with all her groceries. And if she dropped them, he'd just laugh. She'd laughed at him, not caring how he felt. He wouldn't care about her feelings. He who laughs last, laughs best, and Studs Lonigan was the kind of a guy who got the last laugh on everybody, and he'd get it on her. He watched her go. She didn't look back. The hell with her. Only the image of her girlbreasts, underneath her dress, stuck in his mind. Lucy!

"Yeah, great sport," Screwy said for the sixth time, with nostalgia aching in his voice.

"Say, I see trenches like this all over," the bakery man said.

"You do?" the needle-faced guy said.

Studs wished the bunch had thought of doing this a couple of years ago. Would have been fun. It still would, if they'd all come around. Nope, punk stuff.

"Yeah, great sport," Screwy said for the seventh time.

In his mind, Private Lonigan, with a steel helmet, and in khaki, dodged star shells, crawled through the shell holes of Flanders Field, and flung a hand grenade into a dangerous German machine-gun nest. And with fixed bayonet, he leaped into the nest, and frightened all the Germans that were still alive into yelling:

"Kamerad!"

He led them back across the shell-torn midnight of No Man's Land, and turned them over to that same sergeant, who'd said:

"Gwan home, children, and get your diapers pinned on!"

The men from Studs' man's-world departed. He watched the punks, alone. He glanced towards Fifty-eighth Street to see if she was coming back yet. Mrs. Dennis P. Gorman, the lawyer's wife, stopped by him, and Studs perfunctorily tipped his hat. She remarked that it was very dangerous and rowdyish and disgraceful for those boys to play that way. She passed indignantly on.

War reigned in the vacant lot. And in the mind of Studs Lonigan. Suddenly, a randomly-flung tin can hit the young Buckford baby. It squawled, with irritating loudness. Young Horn rushed over and wheeled the buggy out on to the sidewalk. The punks gathered impotently around it, accusing each other of having thrown the can, while the baby continued to yell. Studs singled out Young Horn, who was a snotty kid with a head that seemed three sizes too big for his body, and told him he ought to be socked for leaving the baby where it could be hit like that. Young Horn shouted that it wasn't his fault. Women surrounded the baby, and slobbered baby-talk over it. Young Horn turned his back on Studs, and, poking one lady in the thighs, said:

"Hey, what the hell, that guy ain't hurt."

The woman continued to slobber baby-talk.

"Hell, lady, last week I had him down the block and you know what he did, he fell out of the buggy on his bean, right on the stone, and it didn't hurt him none. Hell, lady, you can't hurt that guy's bean."

Dick Buckford dragged his kid brother aside, and told him to shut up and take the baby home. He kicked Young Horn in the tail. Horn shrieked. He got his face slapped, and the cooing women were appalled. Horn wheeled the baby buggy off. He turned, a hundred yards away, and yelled at Dick:

"Wait 'till I tell mother on you!"

The punks continued the battle, but the spirit of fun was gone.

Studs turned and walked down Indiana towards Fifty-seventh. He wished he'd see Dan Donoghue or some of the old Indiana bunch he'd gone with from St. Patrick's. He felt like going over to Fifty-eighth and Prairie to see if any of the Fifty-eighth Street guys were around. But he waited for Lucy to come back, walking slowly down towards Fifty-seventh. He passed and re-passed, and re-passed her house, looking furtively at the gray stone building. And last year, she'd stood on the porch and blown him a kiss. And he'd been a damn fool, and proud, and when someone had scrawled those things about him loving her, he'd been just dumb. She'd stood there as it was getting dark and thrown him a kiss. He belched. His stomach still felt like lead from those bananas. He came back to the prairie, but the punks had gone home for lunch. The twelve o'clock whistles blew, piercing the scene. They made Studs very lonesome. When would she speak to him again? He wanted to kiss her again too. He shook his head, thinking that he sure did have his troubles. He didn't see her coming back either, and there was no one else around, and he couldn't go home and eat. And if he'd only get into the war, he'd be a hero. And he'd sat in the tree with her, and the way she'd swung those legs that were now so pretty and had such shape, and her lips that were now redder, and then, she hadn't hardly any breasts to notice, and now she was like . . . like a growing flower . . . and he wanted to kiss her again. He glanced at the deserted trenches. He went over and looked down into them. He jumped into the nearer trench, and flung a can. He inspected the other trench. His troubles still weighted his thoughts. He was sore, goddamn sore at the world. He'd pay it back too. He got sorer. He kicked in the trench, and tore down the earthworks.

He heard a laugh. He looked towards the sidewalk. Lucy Scanlan stood there laughing at him, holding her head high.

His face a blazing red, he walked out of the vacant lot, past her, and on over towards Fifty-eighth and Prairie Avenue. He tried to think of himself as a hero. He was a hero in his own mind. He was utterly miserable.

II

KILLED IN ACTION, NOVEMBER 11, 1918 . . . LESTER H. COLE.

Chapter Two

A DRUNK in the jammed elevated car sang *The Star Spangled Banner*. Studs tried to join in. The train rocketed along, and the song died feebly in the noise. A souse on the rear platform donged a cowbell. The train whistle emitted a piercing wah-wah. A powerful roar came from the front of the car:

"TO HELL WITH THE KAISER!"

Studs was swayed with the crowd as the train pulled into the Fifty-first Street station. The platform was crushed with people, and when the conductor refused to open the gates and admit additional passengers, they blared protests and loud-voiced jokes. There was another drunken bellow when the train pulled out:

"TO HELL WITH KAISER BILL!"

A female body pressed against Studs. From the corner of his eye, he lamped the woman; her face was wrinkling, and she must be forty or over, almost old enough to be his grandmother. But she excited him as much as if she was a young jane. Perspiration beaded his broad, planed face.

He again tried to sing and was toppled sidewise in a wave of good-natured shoving. A fox-in-the-bush got his place beside grandma. Studs looked at the beard, lace curtains that must be dirty as a door-mat. Hatred of fox-in-the-bush flared in him. He remembered his excited sensation as she wiggled against him. She'd been giving him the works all right, and he didn't care about her age, and he'd liked it. And that goddamn fox-in-the-bush had gotten his place. He wished he was alone with her; he'd bet she knew her onions, and could teach him plenty that he ought to know. Catching a quick glimpse of her ruined face, he was disgusted with himself. But he looked around, to see if he could get shoved against any other woman on the car.

The train passed Forty-seventh Street. He was all nerves to be down-town and off the train. The whistle wah-wahed. Kenny let out a long and funny wahoo that took down the car. Studs glanced around for a woman, wondering how he'd never before thought of the possibilities of getting against one in crowded el trains. Suddenly everybody was laughing. He looked to his right, and saw that Kenny Kilarney had fallen into the lap of a young chicken and didn't want to get up.

He heard the fox-in-the-bush squeaking that the war was over. He imagined himself socking the guy. He was shoved near him, and as fox-in-the-bush said something else to hot grandma, Studs felt like asking why he didn't give towels with his shower baths. A drunk in front of Studs ponderously muttered uh huh the war was over. Two girls near Red Kelly sang *Over There,* making Studs lonesome to be in France. He looked at the young janes, and thought that Red was a lucky guy, and there was gold in them there hills. To attract their attention, he started singing, *We'll Make the Hindenburg Line Look Like a Dime,* very loudly.

The train stopped at the Indiana Avenue station, started, switched onto the express track, took the curve to go north again, and quickly gained momentum. The passengers were thrown every which way, Studs saw that fox-in-the-bush had grandma leaned forwards on him, and he was jabbing to her a mile-a-minute. They meant business, but how could any dame, even grandma, kiss a guy like that. Her tongue would get lost in all the thickets on his map. He edged down towards the janes by Red.

The train whistle wah-wahed. It roared downtown, over the slums and filth of the black belt.

A drunk yelled that America had won the war. A long-faced bozo shrieked that the world was safe for democracy. A cabbage-faced woman with a brogue a yard long hollered:

"Bully for Wilson and Ireland!"

"Six cheers for the Scandinavians," whooped a jag.

"Aw, quit your kiddin'," Kenny innocently shouted back at the jag, and people nearly busted their guts laughing.

They passed the Thirty-third Street station. It was crowded with happy, singing dinges.

A monkey-faced mick blubbered tears, whining that Padraic Pearse was dead, whoever that guy was.

The trainwheels clattered with the friction of steel, rolling over steel rails. The whistle wah-wahed. The car grew more and more rancid with alcohol and tobacco breaths, stale perfume, perspiring human odors.

Studs noted fox-in-the-bush, still barbering like an express train. He was envious, knowing she'd give the guy what he was after. He slowly squeezed nearer to the janes by Red, casually eyeing the train advertisement above the window. Chew Wrigley's Gum! American Family Soap made it cheaper to wash than buy new clothes. The latest war news was to be found in the *Chicago Daily Tribune*. Red, the lucky bastard!

The train rocketed onward. Studs became suddenly oblivious to its strains and jerkings. He thought of France . . . Doughboys marching, fighting, loving the mademoiselles. The Yanks were there rum-tum-tumming up everything. And if he was only one of the Yanks who'd come. He was seventeen, and just ready to try again, after that time he'd eaten the bananas, and everything at home was just grief. If he'd gone, he might be dead now. . . . But no, the Blessed Virgin would have protected him because he would have worn her scapular. And the next war we had, with Japan, or Mexico, or the Bolsheviks, he'd go and be a hero. If he was only a Sammy now, in Paris, celebrating the Armistice!

A fat, gray-haired woman in tears said that her son Allen had been killed, but that she was happy the war was over, because no more mothers would be broken-hearted over their dead boys. A gray-haired man tried to soothe her, saying her son had died saving the world, and everybody had to bear their crosses. Studs edged further towards the janes by Red.

"It hurts me . . . here!" the mother sobbed, pointing to her heart. The train whistle wah-wahed. The jag on the back platform steadily clanged his cowbell. Studs was halted getting near the janes. The crying mother made him think of Death that was terrible, and cold, and all maggots and putridness, and rotting, and awful on the battlefields or anywhere, even when you died after receiving Extreme Unction. And even if he wasn't Over There, he was alive, and might get in the next war. But he'd give any damn thing to be a soldier, laying up with a French broad right now in Paris. But he might have got killed, just before the Armistice whistles blew, and Death was an old man of ice, smelling lousier than the stockyards, or than a stiff pair of socks that have been worn a year, if anybody wore socks that long. And he had a swell time, shadowing soldiers in France, until they were cold and gray and stiffer than branches stuck to the ground in January. Anyway, he wasn't getting Studs Lonigan for a long time now.

The crowd took up singing, and Studs, swaying in the grinding car, edged nearer the janes. He saw that one was giving Red the works. The other smiled at him, and yelled:

"TO HELL WITH THE KAISER!"

Smiling, Studs accidentally on purpose bumped against her and the quick brush against her body went through him like electricity. She said it was all kinds of fun celebrating the war, and he could feel her bad breath on his face, and smell it too. He didn't care. She had everything she owned pressed right up to him, yumyum, and she made him want it like he almost never wanted it before, and he knew he'd be able to pick her up and make the grade.

The train passed Twelfth Street.

"It won't be long now," said Red.

And Studs didn't want it to be long until they hit Congress Street, and she was pressed right into him, and he could feel the whole outline of her body, too, and she seemed to be breathing hot in his face, panting. It made him proud, a manly feeling. He asked where she was going.

"To hell, want to come along?"

"It'll be heaven if you're there."

"You're a kidder."

She twisted against him and he felt that it was all set.

At Congress, the whole car seemed to jam towards the door simultaneously. He and Red lost the janes in the crush; just their goddam luck.

He hoped he'd pick her up again, as he ganged along with the guys over to State and Van Buren. He looked frantically into faces, hurried the going, wanting to get her again, suddenly wanting Lucy Scanlan, but wanting her the more because she had everything a guy could wish for, and she'd go the limit, and what the hell if her breath was bad.

The Chicago Loop was like a nuthouse on fire. The sidewalks were swollen with people, the streets were clogged, and autoists honked their horns, and motor men donged bells in vain. Tons of paper and confetti blizzarded from the upper stories of buildings and sundry noise-makers echoed an insistent racket. People sang, shouted until it seemed that their lungs would burst from their mouths.

Studs followed a guy playing a clarinet. A bag of water dropped on the guy's bean. He played on, and a fellow clamped him on the dome with a banana stalk. He played on. He was caught in a laughing crowd which followed a fat black mammy who paraded down the sidewalk, dressed in a washtub full of clothes, joyously singing:

Oh, Lawd, I'se happy!
No mo' washin' fo' me!
No mo' washin' fo' me!
My two boys'll be comin' home soon!
My two boys'll be comin' home soon!
Oh, Lawd, I'se happy!

He watched a sailor and a marine scrapping. A pretty girl stopped the fight by kissing each of them. He clapped and catcalled with the crowd. If he was only in uniform. Everybody snickered as another sailor rushed forwards and threatened to fight if he wasn't kissed. She kissed him, and the other two demanded second kisses. Everybody laughed.

He was plumped on the head with a banana stalk, and went sick with a sudden thud of a headache. He shook his head, turned, and tripped the guy with the stalk, just as he had lifted it to club someone else. He grabbed the stalk, and circumspectly clubbed a little fellow. Ahead, he saw a guy parting a way by brandishing a blackjack. Somebody spit in his ear, yelling that the war was over. A drunk came up to him, seriously and methodically shook hands, and then seriously and methodically walked on. Another drunk rolled in dt's on the sidewalk, and a girl stuck her high heel in his guts.

Jesus, it was great! he thought.

He suddenly looked up through the noise and falling paper, and there was Old Glory on a flag pole, furled in the breeze, glinting the November sunlight—Old Glory that had never kissed the dust in defeat, and he could see it floating, flying over the trenches, ruins, corpses of the fields of France, again Victorious! Old Glory! His Flag! Proudly he told himself:

I'm an American.

He heard raucous feminine shouting. Turning, he saw a hysterical woman, her gray hair falling over her aging face. She yelled:

"My son didn't die in vain. Thank God, my Willie is not dead in vain!"

He joined a snake dance which sang *There'll Be a Hot Time in the Old Town Tonight*. The snake dance dissolved, when a man on crutches, with two wooden legs, solemnly marched holding a small American flag between his teeth. He was cheered uproariously.

He bumped into the gang while they were gathered around a drunk who insisted that they all would hang the Kaiser to a sour apple tree. They tried to scrouge a drink but he said that now the Kaiser must be hung to a sour apple tree and Wilson must be crowned King of Germany and the League of Nations. They tried to scrouge a drink, and he said they'd get a barrel if they'd bring the Kaiser to him. A soldier dragged him off.

An insane-looking woman passed, holding a sign aloft:

FOLLOW ME TO THE KAISER'S FUNERAL HANS AND FRITZ HAVE THE FITS.

"WAHOOOOOOOOOOO!" they yelled under the leadership of Kenny Kilarney.

Studs lost the gang again. He didn't care. There'd never been a day like this in history. And he'd find her or another girl, and would he get it today!

He went on, head lowering as if he was a fullback hitting the line, feeling like he was a bursting boiler that was liable to blow the whole Loop to smithereens.

"WAHOOOOOOOOOOO!"

He fought his way into a store in a jam, copped a horn, crushed out, and blew the horn for all he was worth. A funny-looking egg pushed a wheel-barrow along, lashing an effigy of the Kaiser in it with a horse whip. Studs got behind the guy, blowing his horn, feeling swell that everybody was seeing him in the midst of things, hoping she'd see him, and rush out and grab his arm, hoping that Lucy Scanlan would see him and think that he was pretty much the real stuff.

He blew the horn out and joined in a mob that was making a center rush. A girl's dress and coat got torn off, and Studs fought to get a look at her. But she flung herself into the arms of a sailor and yelled for him to hurry up and take her with him where she wouldn't need the damn rags. Jesus, it made him hot.

He was jammed to the curb to watch a parade of hearses. The first hearse was black, and carried a sign:

THE KAISER'S COFFIN! KILLED BY THE U. S. A.!

A white hearse following it:

THE KAISER'S FUNERAL!

A third, black:

THE KULTUR INVENTOR DIED AT 2 A.M. HIS NEXT EMPIRE IS HELL!

Damn good stunt! thought Studs, trying to out-bellow everyone else, wishing like hell he had mightier lungs and stronger mitts.

A bunch of sailors came by, and he joined them. They cursed fiercely because they wouldn't get their shot at the Huns. One of them gave Studs his first slug of whiskey. It burned all the way down, made him sneeze and cough, with watering eyes, and they laughed at him. He slunk off, and even when out of their sight, seemed to hear their laughter. Shamed feelings blistered into oaths. He put his cap on at a crooked tough-guy angle, slung back his shoulders, scowled with intent ferocity, and clenched his fists. He saw a little girl with a flag, and, fed up, he snatched it, letting her bawl her eyes out.

He laughed, forgetting, as he spotted a funny drunk leaning against a department store window. Studs gave him a disdainful hello. The fellow mummed his fingers to his lips, drew Studs close, almost suffocated him with an alcohol breath, and whispered that he couldn't move because German spies had undermined the foundation of the building, and he alone was holding it up, and if he moved, it would come down on everybody. He, like Wilson, was a savior of Humanity. Red came along. Studs gave Red the wink. Red nodded. They each cut one of the drunk's feet from under him and he went down, his head snapping and cracking on the sidewalk. Blood oozed from it. A singing bunch of marines stepped on the drunk as he lay there, and Studs and Red hurried away, afraid that maybe they'd killed the fellow.

They followed in the trail of five janes who were singing dirty songs and carrying a sailor on their shoulders. Studs wanted a uniform. Jesus! All the janes would be kissing him, and telling him to come on. He tried to think of himself in uniform, being kissed and grabbed by all the janes, carried about, taken to hotels, loved up by ten of them in succession. Goddamn it! He was nearly knocked down, and that brought him to his senses. Red grabbed him and said look at the funny bloke with the pig.

They went behind a fellow who dragged a pig along by a rope. There was a sign tied on the pig:

THE KAISER.

The fellow kept twisting the pig's tail to make it squeal, and it was funny.

They followed him over to Michigan Avenue, hoping to get near enough to twist the pig's tail. They spotted Kenny Kilarney on top of one of the lions in front of the Art Institute, flinging tomatoes into the crowd, and rushed over. Studs grabbed Kilarney's last tomato, and let it go. He was glad when it hit a soldier in the ear. They dashed down the steps, and bumped square into a girl as she went for a sailor with open arms, shrieking:

"Here I am, sailor boy!"

Studs stood next to them, watching them kiss, the girl's body straining, her lips pressing, her face going taut, tense, her arms and his arms tightening vise-like, their mouths opening, french-kissing in public.

"OOOHHHHHHHH!" muttered Studs.

Kenny grabbed his arm.

"Where to?" muttered Studs.

"We'll brown the Kaiser," shouted Kenny.

"And the Clown Quince too," said Studs, his mind painful with the thought of girls.

They stopped at a fight. It was Tommy Doyle. He knocked a souse out. Red Kelly kicked him in the ribs.

"That's the Fifty-eighth Street spirit," yelled Studs, as they rushed on.

They ate in a restaurant and ran out without paying.

They saw a guy fall through a plate-glass window. He was pulled out, and laid on the sidewalk. They fought in a whole mob, that milled like cattle to look at the guy, as he lay bleeding and moaning.

It got dark. Studs saw the girl from the elevated train again. He rushed to her and said, "Hello," but she didn't hear him, and dove for a passing marine. Another jane copped the marine, Studs grabbed her and kissed her. She slapped his face, and stopped a soldier to kiss him. She simulated moans as the soldier kissed her.

"Come on, girlie!" the soldier said.

Studs watched them quickly disappear in the crowd, and he was hot and wanted it, and gloomy, and just like that his heart seemed to go out of the whole celebration, and he felt that he was only a punk to them, just as the kids around the neighborhood were only punks to him.

It was late when Studs climbed into bed. He was tired, but too excited to sleep, and the refrain of *Pack Up Your Troubles In Your Old Kit Bag* drummed in his head. He tossed in the bed most of the night, wishing the war wasn't over, wishing he was a hero, wishing, wishing he'd had the dough for a can house, or had copped off a broad downtown. He tried to keep thinking of that girl on the train, and of making her, over and over again. His head got drowsy, his eyes heavy, and he tried to think even more of her because then he might dream of her and something might happen in the dream

and

Dough-boy Studs Lonigan

wearing a steel helmet, his bayonetted gun levelled, crossed No Man's Land Over There, one of the rum-tum-tumming Yanks who were advancing. Star shells flared. Shells fell all around him. Machine gun bullets whizzed by his ear. He stepped over corpses. He leaped into the German trenches and suddenly discovered that he was alone, and that the Germans, the whole German Army, brutes, every one of them looking like the fat man with drooping mustaches in the Charlie Chaplin pictures, came at him. They came slowly forwards, goose-stepping, bayonets pointed. He backed into a corner, prepared to pay dearly for his life, terrified into courage by abject fear. And suddenly, all of a sudden in a funny goddamn way that he couldn't understand, there were no Germans, only Old Man Death, wrinkled and creaky, coming at him with a scythe to which there hung a skull and cross-bones. And every time he breathed, ice floated out of his mouth. Studs cowered, prayed to the Blessed Virgin Mary. He turned and ran.

He looked behind, and there was Old Man Death coming, an even steadiness in his tread. He realized that Old Man Death was The Rose of No Man's Land, and he ran the swifter, it seemed for miles and miles, and turned, thinking that he had escaped, and there was The Rose of No Man's Land, still coming, even, steady, breathing chunks of ice, carrying his scythe. Sweating, he turned and ran through fields and towns back to the eighth grade classroom of St. Patrick's Grammar School, and there he found Lucy Scanlan in a nun's garb, teaching the class. He took his seat. Down the hall, he heard the heavy steps of The Rose of No Man's Land

and

then Studs Lonigan was in the cockpit of an airplane, flying over France, surrounded by German planes. He took a nose dive, and headed straight into one German plane, waiting until he could see the aviator's face. It was the face of grandma. He shot once, and down the plane went in flames. He climbed a cloud, and above it, headed for a second plane, saw that the aviator in it had the face of the girl on the elevated train, shot one machine-gun bullet and smiled with ecstasy while it went down in flames. He looped the loop and went for another German plane, controlled by an aviator with the face of Lucy Scanlan. He shot it down in ecstasy with one machine-gun bullet. He shot down another, and another, and another, and Ace Lonigan ruled the sky. He turned around, headed for the landing field, tired, as he coasted downwards, gently bringing his plane to the ground. He was met by Father Gilhooley of St. Patrick's parish, President Wilson, and Abe Lincoln, all of them holding aloft a phallic-shaped medal. He got out of the plane, prepared to accept his glory

and

Studs awoke, and outside it was a gray November morning. He was lassitudinous in a mood of letdown, already lonesome for yesterday. He hummed *Over There* and nostalgia crushed him. The thought that the war was over struck him almost like an unexpected club on the head. All along, he'd thought he'd get into it and become a great hero, and back when it had started, he'd been excited. But after eating those bananas, it had got more natural, and he'd gone along doing all the things he'd been doing, just the same. But it had made life more exciting, and then, in a way, it had all been worth yesterday. Now, he'd have to figure out what he'd do with himself. He could go to work for the old man, or try and get a job, or go back to high school and become a famous football player. He knew he could, but he couldn't stand school. He wondered what the hell he could do for himself. He lay in bed a long time.

Finally he got up, washed and went to breakfast. The old man asked him what he was going to do, and Studs said look for a job. Fran butted her nose into the picture and said she didn't believe him, and thought he'd go and hang around those awful bums in the poolroom. His old man said he didn't want him hanging around no poolroom. The old lady said he should go back to school and get educated and maybe study for the priesthood. They gave him a pain. He was glad when the old man gave him a buck and left. The old lady slipped him a half a buck. He went out at eight-thirty, determined to go downtown and look for a job. When he got to the el station, he couldn't do it. He hung around, hardly able to wait for the guys, so they could talk about yesterday, and maybe find more excitement.

III

*M*RS. LONIGAN *and Mrs. Reilley, each carrying a black prayer-book, walked home from Sunday mass. Mrs. Lonigan observed that there were two cavities in the front of Mrs. Reilley's mouth. Mrs. Reilley perceived that Mrs. Lonigan was thinner and bonier than she had been when they had last met, and that a few of the strands of hair falling from under her hat were gray.*

"And how is your Frank? I never see him about the neighborhood," Mrs. Lonigan asked.

"My Frank has not been feeling up to snuff these days, and he doesn't be runnin' in the prairie with the lads. He does be a quiet boy, and he often comes to me and says 'Mother, sure I don't care to be keeping company with the likes of them that's always at that pool-room on Fifty-eighth Street.' Sure, he's a sensible boy, and he knows full well that the curse of God has been put on the likes of them, the tinkers, that's always to be seen in that poolroom," Mrs. Reilley said, with a pronounced brogue.

"Is he working?" asked Mrs. Lonigan, as the two mothers glanced pointedly at each other.

"Sure, the lad and his father have had a great talk about that only this last week, and the lad's father thinks that as soon as the boy is up to it, we'll be sending him off to learn something technical, because there's money to be got there."

"Of course, you can't place a boy of that age under too great a strain."

"And aren't them the very words I was telling me old man this last week."

"My William went to Loyola for one year, and he made a fine record for himself. But we decided to keep him out this year and let him help his father with the business, because Patrick has so much to attend to. We're leaving him rest a while first, because he is only young and growing. But after Christmas, Mr. Lonigan will be starting him in, and he'll finish up his credits at night school. He's going to start at the bottom to learn the business, but it shan't be just as a common laborer," said Mrs. Lonigan.

"Well, me and the boy's father expect to see the day when the lad is an engineer," Mrs. Reilley said.

"Only recently my husband and I were talking about all the boys our William knew in school, and Patrick was saying that your Frank must be a great comfort to you, he was always such a good boy."

"And sure, only last night, I was saying the same words to me old man, telling him how you and Mr. Lonigan must be proud of your boy, him such a fine upstanding lad, and not at all the likes of them that's to be found at that poolroom, morning, noon, and night."

The women parted, looking at each other in a way that women have. And in each mother's heart was the gnawing of fear and disappointment because of a boy threatening to go wayward.

Chapter Three

I

YOU guys complaining that there's nothing to do ought to just stop and think about all the poor chumps who got to work on a day like this. Think of some goddamn Hunky swinging a pickaxe, chopping up the street with his fanny dragging to the ground, swinging away with that goddamn pickaxe, thirsty, his underwear dripping, wishing it was all over and he was sitting in the shade of the old apple tree," Benny Taite said, tilting himself backwards on a chair in the corner of the poolroom, and looking at the boys seated about in a circle.

"Benny, can that crap. You make us hot and tired, just hearing about it," said Red Kelly.

"I got a job swinging a pick for the city, and I worked one day. Was my can draggin'?" exclaimed Tommy.

"That was your record for work, wasn't it?" said Kenny Kilarney.

"It wouldn't hurt Taite there to try that for a couple of days. It might make a man of him," kidded Studs.

"Sure, Taite, tell us where you got all that pep of yours?" said Red.

"I inherited it from my grandfather. He didn't work for forty years, and I'm out to break his record," Benny dryly said.

"Say, for Christ sake, let's do something," Studs said, suddenly restive with inaction, while the boys were laughing.

"Exercise your tail on that chair you got. That's what days like this were made for," said Taite.

"What time is it?" said Studs.

"Two o'clock," said Red.

"Lonigan's waitin' for supper again," said Kenny; they laughed.

"Let's go over to the park," said Studs.

"Walk a block and a half in this sun? Not this sundodger," Kilarney said.

"Oh, by the way, fellows, I forgot to tell you that I saw Paulie Haggerty," Red said.

"Is he still chasin' that jane of his?" asked Studs.

"Married her. I think it was a shot-gun wedding," said Red.

Kilarney suddenly changed their astonishment to amusement by melodramatically lamenting that poor Paulie preferred double wretchedness to single blessedness.

"You know, fellows, getting your ashes hauled is one thing, and getting married is another. You can joke all you want about marriage, but it's sacred, a sacrament of the church, and when you're married it's serious, for life. Paulie's too young for that, he's only seventeen. He might be ruining his whole life. . . . Well, he can't say that I didn't warn him because I did, plenty," Red Kelly said.

"Hey, Kelly, why don't you hire a hall?" Kilarney said.

"Kilarney, you couldn't be serious about anything, could you?" Kelly said, good-naturedly.

"He must be cured," Studs said, butting in on Kilarney's rejoinder.

"He said it cured itself, but he can't kid me, and nobody can tell me that a dose cures itself without even a doctor. And if you ask me, he's playing a damn rotten trick on Eileen. She was a sweet girl, coming from a decent family and a good home. She falls for him, and what does he do but knock her up, and I suppose dose her. Paulie is a pal of mine, and I'd stick through hell with him, but he certainly did act like a rat with Eileen."

"Hell, Red, that jane is five years older than he is, and don't tell me she didn't know what she was doing. She chased him all over the neighborhood, and now she's got a ball and chain on him. Christ, he'll even have to go to work," Taite said, burlesqueing his last sentence.

"That's not so. It was a lousy trick, and she comes from a decent family and doesn't deserve it," Red said.

"Red, she's a terrible spider, and she spun a web around Paulie, my pal Paulie," Kilarney said, extravagantly.

Weary Reilley entered, with his right hand bandaged. They asked him if he'd been knocking brick buildings over.

"I just tangled holes with some flukey-looking wiseacre down at Sixty-third and the Grove. He thought he was tough, so I sent him home with a handful of teeth and a puss full of blood. But I damn near broke my hand to hell on him and had to have three stitches put in it. Anyway, I learned something. Instead of breaking my dukes any more on some rat's face, I'm getting me a nice pair of brass knucks."

Studs thought of how he hadn't had a fight since hell-and-gone. But once he'd cleaned up Reilley. Nobody else in the neighborhood had. He supposed, too, that he'd have to tangle again with him. Reilley always tried to get even. Well, Reilley wouldn't be as hard this time, with his dukes on the fritz. They kept asking Reilley questions and praising him. Hell, had they forgot what a battler Studs Lonigan was?

"Say, who in hell is going to give me a fag?"

"Kilarney, don't you ever smoke your own?" Red responded.

"O.P.'s satisfy me."

"Some day other people will get wise to you," kidded Red.

"Fellow, you know what Barnum said?"

Studs handed Kenny a cigarette.

"Thanks, chump," kidded Kilarney.

"Hey, Kilarney, think you'll ever amount to much?" asked Taite.

"Sure! Why I even went downtown yesterday to look for a job."

"How was the show?" asked Doyle.

"Good bill at the State and Lake."

"I guess then we'll all have to go looking for a job tomorrow," Red said.

"What about you, Reilley, have you been thinkin' of getting a job and desertin' our cause of late?" asked Taite.

"There's plenty of chumps workin' already," Reilley said.

"That's what I'm trying to suggest to my old man. But he gets on a soap-box every morning at breakfast and threatens not to give me any more dough," Studs said.

"My old man tried that once, and I blew. He knows better than try it again. He's got enough dough and did enough work for the Reilleys for a long time to come. If he cracks wise about it, he knows I'll just tell him all right fellow, and blow. I can get me a gat and pull a stickup when I need the kale," Reilley said, causing them all to admire him.

"You know, boys, sometimes I think it would be a good idea to go on the bum," Doyle said.

"Not me. I know where I can find my pork chops," Studs said.

"If you did go, you might meet Davey Cohen. Hell, he's been gone three years, ever since that time we gang-shagged that little bitch Iris, and she told him no soap because he was a hebe," said Red.

"If somebody hasn't croaked that kike by this time, they ought to. I don't like kikes," Weary said.

Studs finally tired of the gassing and sitting around, so he drifted over to the Washington Park boathouse. It was a long, low, open structure, bounded on two sides by shrubbery. He picked out a cane chair and rocked rapidly. There were few people around, some old men and women who talked too much in loud, cracking voices, Coady, the red-faced, flat-footed park cop who always eyed the lads with suspicion, and a couple of dinges. If the guys had come, they could have ganged the dinges. Niggers didn't have any right in a white man's park, and the sooner they were taught that they didn't, the better off they'd be. He looked around; no chickens.

A coatless fellow rowed effortlessly by on the lagoon. If he had a dollar for deposit, he could get a boat and row around, maybe pick up a chicken by the stone bridge, and fool around with her until it was dark, and then take her over to the wooded island.

Rocking away wasn't his idea of a picnic, so he went outside, and plumped down under a shady tree behind the bushes that stood in front of the boathouse. He fell asleep thinking about girls. Suddenly he opened his eyes, feeling stiff; he didn't know where he was. He heard sounds, voices, the shouts of children, footsteps, the hum of automobile motors as if in a blur. He rubbed his eyes, sat up, and realized that he'd been sleeping.

He was moody, trying to recall something sad that he'd been dreaming about. He couldn't remember it, and started thinking again of picking a chicken up, and making her. The fact that later on he'd have to go home for supper dropped in his thoughts like a soggy towel. The old man would probably be on the war-path again. He didn't mind work, he guessed. It was the looking for it, having to learn things about it and seeming like a goof while he was learning. He mightn't even mind working for the old man, but it was only the idea of it, the old man still trying to be his boss. The old man seemed to understand less and less every day and he couldn't be natural with the old fathead. Treated him just like a kid in short pants. If things got too hot at home, he had that gat he'd gotten from Young Hennessey. He'd take it and blow. Weary wouldn't be afraid to. He could do anything that skunk could. But robbing was dangerous. Jail, getting pot-shotted by cops! It was more fun thinking of pulling off a stick-up.

He pillowed his head in locked hands, and looked driftingly through the stirring leaves at the almost cloudless sky. The wind waved branches, the sun glinted on the leaves, and the sky was big and round and far away. He was lonesome, wanting things, a girl, Lucy, wanting that and something more and he didn't even know what it was. Always these days, no matter what he was doing, he wanted to be doing something else, and he couldn't think of much else for long, but girls, Lucy, and girls too, and he was always wishing, looking at girls on the streets as if they were the thing he was always wanting, thinking every morning he might meet Lucy again, or some girl who would be what he wanted and might help him find out the thing that was always bothering him without his even knowing what it was. Must be going bugs! Doyle, Red and the guys didn't seem to have troubles like that. He looked through the leaves, with wind creeping in them, waving branches in groups. Looking and shuttering aside his thoughts, he felt pleasant and happy. And a girl could make him so much happier!

"Hello!"

It was a big guy, maybe thirty or even older, who had sat down by Studs without his knowing it. The fellow looked like a bag of mush, with soft skin, almost like a woman's, and a squeaky, weak voice. He made Studs uneasy.

"It's a ripping afternoon!"

"Yeah!" Studs said coldly, thinking that the guy was goofy all right.

"You come over to the park to find the girlies. There's plenty of them here, nice buxom nursemaids, you know, who would like a strong young boy like you."

What the hell was he driving at? Something fluky about him all right!

The fellow stretched out, and his thigh, very casually, seemed to touch Studs' knee. This slight contact made Studs want to vomit, just as the sight of oysters did.

"You like the girlies?"

"Oh, yeah," said Studs, feeling more and more uncomfortable, wondering if he ought to blow, or take a chance and sock the guy, even if he was heavier, or what?

"Boys your age generally do. If you don't, there must be something wrong with you. How old are you?"

"Seventeen," Studs answered, not knowing why he even answered the guy.

"You're old enough to play. . . . You know?" the guy said with a wink as he gave Studs a soft but knowing little poke.

Studs knew he must be blushing.

"You shouldn't be ashamed of it. It's only natural to do that.

"Say, what's the idea?" Studs tensely asked.

"Oh, nothing! You needn't worry. I just like to try to be friendly with young boys, talk over their problems with them, give them advice."

Studs glanced aside. The fellow's leg kept rubbing against him. It made him feel like he might if he'd drunk something like toilet water.

"Playing, you know, is safer than fooling around with the girlies, because you can pick up diseases from them. Most of them have diseases."

"Yeah, I know," Studs said, trying to be hard.

"You have to be careful all the time."

Studs felt like telling him a lot of bull, but he couldn't think up any story. The guy clogged up his tongue.

"You know, there's better and safer ways," the fellow said, his hand ever-so-lightly running up Studs' thigh. Studs noticed how queer and tight the fellow's face got. He felt himself being pawed.

"Listen! What's the idea!" Studs said very excitedly, sitting up.

"Now, sonny, be calm! I'm only going to be a friend to you. I wouldn't try and hurt a clean decent-looking boy like you."

"Yeah!" jerked Studs menacingly.

He stood up with his fists clenched, but indecisive. The guy arose, slipped into the bushes and disappeared.

Studs woke up. The guy was fruit, the first one he'd ever met like that. He was sorry he hadn't hauled off on him. He walked into the path, and looked up and down. Then he looked in the boathouse, but couldn't find the guy. He returned again to sit down under the tree.

He was ashamed of himself, of his thoughts, his body, of the way life was. He heard birds chirping and the winds above him in the tree leaves, pure like Lucy, and he looked up at the waving bushes, first one group of bushes flaunting, then another, then all of them whipping back and forth, and through them he could see patches of sky. He felt as if somebody had rubbed him all over with horse manure.

He got up, and walked about, moody, not wanting to go any place, not wanting to go back and sit around the poolroom with the guys, feeling all clammy.

He got home for supper late, and the old man was crabby. He didn't say anything at the table. They noticed that he was acting queer and kept asking him what was the matter.

"Nothing," he said.

II

After supper, Lonigan called Studs into the parlor for a talk. He said all right, a bit surlily, and stopped off in the bathroom to get his thoughts collected. He felt that maybe this was going to be a showdown with the old man, and if it was, he'd let him know that Studs Lonigan was going to be his own boss.

The old man sat in his rocker, an ancient piece with a plush cushion that the old lady had been trying to get out of the parlor for years. Studs entered with a scowl of determination on his face. The old man gave him a sharp look, as if to scare him. He told Studs to sit down, his manner authoritative, and he dabbled away at lighting his stogy.

"You're going on eighteen?"

"Yes."

"I wonder if you agree with me that it's about time that you begin to figure out what you're going to do with your life?"

"Well . . . I looked for a job today."

"Where?"

"Oh, a number of places in the Loop," Studs said, wishing he had told the old man to mind his own damn business.

"Do you want to go back to school or don't you?" the old man asked, nodding ironically.

"I don't like school," Studs said with uncertain firmness.

"Well, what do you want or like?"

"I'll get a job one of these days."

"Yes. You've been doing that for over a year, and it's cost me a buck a day. What's the matter with you? Are you sick? Tonight at the supper table there, you didn't even bat an eye and had a face a yard long. What's wrong? Are you sick, or in trouble?"

"Nothing. I'll get a job."

"Take the chip off your shoulder!"

"I ain't got any on it!"

"I can't understand you. Here I'm willing to give you a hell of a lot better chance in life than I ever had, and you won't take it. You just mope along . . ." the old man stopped short and shrugged his shoulders, a gesture of weariness. Studs waited to see what would come next.

"Well, as they say, you can bring a horse to the trough, but you can't make him drink!"

The old man whewed as if expressing the difficulties of thinking down into disconsolate depths.

"Maybe you're better off without an education, and a lot of book-learning. It might make you into a high-hat snob like it did Dinny Gorman. You don't need an education like that to be a success. I didn't."

Studs wanted it to be over so he could get out of the damn house.

"What you need is hard work, and I'm going to give it to you. Tomorrow you can come with me, and I'll put you to work."

Remembering what Weary had said of his old man, Studs felt that he'd be yellow if he took this. And he felt his courage ebbing.

"I had to work a damn sight harder than you'll ever have to. . . . And I'll be damned if I let you become a poolroom bum!" Lonigan said with sudden energy, banging his right fist into his left palm.

"I'm not a poolroom bum," Studs unconvincingly replied.

"I don't want you to become one!"

"I'm not!" Studs countered like a pouting child.

"I'm your father, and it's my duty to see that you amount to something and turn into a decent citizen. And, by God, I will. You children are all your mother and I got. We worked hard for you, and we don't want to feel that we done it all for nothing. You owe us something in return, and all we are asking of you is that you amount to something, be decent citizens, give us the right to be justifiably proud of you. We don't want to have to hang our heads in shame because of any of our children when we walk down the street. And, by God, I'll see that we don't have to!"

Studs was sore, but words just choked up in him.

"You understand now. You come with me in the morning!"

A dangerous pause.

"I can find a job, maybe tomorrow," Studs said, immediately perceiving that his words had weakly fizzled.

"I told you what you'd do!" the old man half-shouted.

"I'll find my own job!" Studs said swiftly and breathlessly, as he jumped to his feet.

"For once, you do what I say! In the morning, you start turning over a new leaf. . . . And, yes, you might as well stay in tonight so's to get a good night's sleep. You'll need it in the morning."

"I'm my own boss!"

"Why, you goddamn little . . ."

A red flush from the slap he got appeared on Studs' left cheek. Uncontrolled tears welled forth. He wanted to hit back. He was afraid of his father. He sniffled without will.

The old man dropped back to his rocker, held his head in his hands. Studs looked at him, imagined himself smashing the old bastard's face till it bled and swelled. He stood impotently.

"You heard me! Tomorrow! Now get the hell out of my sight before I give you the trimming you deserve, you dirty little whelp!"

"Patrick! What's happened?" the old lady said coming to the entry way, as Studs, still bawling, turned to go.

"William! . . . *William!*"

"I'm leaving here!" Studs said, brushing past her.

"Did you hit him?" the mother demanded.

"And I'll hit again. After all I done for him, the dirty little ingrate, defying me! All right, go on, get out, and don't come back. I don't ever want to see you again!"

"Patrick Lonigan! How dare you! Striking my son, my own flesh and blood! Ordering my precious first-born baby out of my home!"

"Mary, you don't know what you're talking about. Don't tell me what I'm to do in my home! And don't be wastin' your sympathy. What he needs is to get the tar kicked out of him. And if he wants to live here, he'll do what I tell him!"

In his room, Studs was proud of himself for having defied the old man. Glad, too, that his father and mother were having a big blow-out. He cried; well, he was so goddamn sore, he couldn't help it.

"You ought to be ashamed of yourself!" Fran said, stopping in his doorway.

"Mind your own goddamn business!"

"How dare you curse me!" she said, shocked.

"For Christ sake, shut your trap!"

She rushed into the parlor, and shrieked in a high-pitched voice. It was like a nut-house now. He slipped into his old lady's room, and copped five bucks from her pocket-book. He got his rusty old gat from its hiding place at the bottom of his closet. He put on his cap, and went to the bathroom. He saw that his eyes were red from crying. He tried to hide the redness with Fran's powder. He was ashamed of himself.

"My son . . . my son!" his mother muttered, trying to block his path at the front door.

"I'm going!"

"William, your father just lost his temper. Go in and tell him you're sorry and. . . ."

"I can take care of myself!" he said, viciously slamming the door.

"You don't know what you're doing to dad. Come back," Fran begged, pursuing him in the hallway.

"Take your lousy hands off me!"

His parents called him from the window. He didn't look at them. At the corner, he turned, and saw his old man coming out of the building. He ran, ditching the old man by running through alleys and gangways.

III

With dew-soaked feet, Lonewolf Lonigan tramped across the ball field of Washington Park. He suddenly wheeled around, thinking that he had heard approaching footsteps. He looked in back of him; darkness. He gazed all around at the surrounding blackness, the extended shadows of bushes on the edge of the park suddenly losing themselves in an awfulness of night. To his right, and several blocks away, was the illumination of the park refectory. The lights of a passing automobile showed like fleeting electric pinpoints and vanished.

To get rid of the thoughts he was having about himself and the darkness, he whipped out his gat, and pulled the trigger, the hammer clicking.

How could he get bullets? Where did burglars go for their ammunition? He could see himself walking into a joint, looking tough, saying in a hard-boiled way:

Three rounds of cartridges for a forty-four!

Well, soon he would have a forty-four, instead of a twenty-two!

From Cottage Grove Avenue, he heard the muffled echoes of a street car. The air was cut with the inhuman shriek of ungreased automobile brakes that had been suddenly applied. The sounds faded deeply into all the surrounding silence. He heard many crickets.

Lonewolf Lonigan stopped, stricken with indecision. He could see himself captured, shot . . . killed.

If he hadn't gone off the handle! He could have gone to work for the old man and it mightn't have been half bad. Right after graduation, he'd wanted to. And the old man had been right in what he'd said. He had been wasting his time. But it was the way he'd said it, the bossy way, disregarding all of Studs' feeling, treating him the same way as if he was only thirteen or fourteen, that caused it all. If he was working though, the old man couldn't pull a stunt like that, because he'd be independent.

He couldn't remember ever having felt like he did now, with only his feeling of being alone, as if all the loneliness of the night and the sky were inside of him, crushing out everything else. It was a snaky feeling like maybe some one would have, or Robinson Crusoe might have had, being alone on a desert island. He had burned all his bridges, and gone from everything, and he was a man alone forced to fight by himself, an enemy of society, a burglar and robber—well he would be one after he pulled off his first stickup. And he would. He'd pull it off, and make his getaway. His old man might have called the police by now, after going around Fifty-eighth and not finding him there. He guessed he'd been wise not going around. But it had been slow as hell, with nothing to do all night. He'd been so nervous and excited that he didn't even know what picture he'd seen in the movie. It was tough too, that he wouldn't be able to go around Fifty-eighth with his gat, and show 'em what he did and could do.

But it would be dangerous. He'd have to blow town tonight, because his old man might even have his picture in the paper, and dicks might even be looking for him at the railroad stations. He might never come back either, and they'd be searching for him all over the country. Or he might come back sometime, and rob his father and leave a note signed:

THE LONEWOLF!

Fun, thinking of all the things like this that might happen. But it was getting late, and he'd have to get busy. He clenched his fist, emphasizing firmness to himself. He stopped and drew out his handkerchief, and wrapped it around his face. He bent down on one knee, waited with drawn gun. He jumped up with a levelled gat, threatening the darkness.

"Stick 'em up fast. . . . Come on! Hand over your jack quick or I'll drill yah!" he said in a cool, collected voice.

He snatched, as if taking money, and ran, turning repeatedly to pull the trigger. He dropped behind a water fountain, and shot. Suddenly, he dropped his gun, and clutched his left shoulder. He pressed his upper lip over his lower lip, and grunted, fighting off an apparent effort to moan. He picked his revolver up and swung the butt of it down, like he was cracking a copper's skull. He ran, with simulated staggers, turning again and again to shoot.

Suddenly, he remembered that Martin had often played like this in the back yard. But he wasn't playing. He was just rehearsing things, so he would have all his plans down pat, and know what to do in every emergency.

He jerked off his handkerchief, and lit a cigarette. He was calm now, and he ought to pull the job off right away. He walked on across the park. He'd do it, and not get caught. If he did? Even so, he might be let off because it was a first offense, and then, the old man would see he meant business, and if he did go back home, the old man would change his tune. But he wouldn't be caught. He wouldn't ever see his old man either, and he'd let him do the worrying. Studs Lonigan was the wrong guy to monkey around with.

He paused by the bushes on the eastern edge of the park, and looked back across the park to the south west. Out there, in back of the darkness and shadows were all the things he was leaving, his home and family and friends and Lucy. It was his last good-by to everybody, everything, even maybe to all the fellows, the best pals in the world. Good-by!

He put his hands before his face to ward off branches, and dived through the bushes. He came out of the park at Cottage Grove, and started to scuttle across the street. He saw a cop down a little on the east side of the street walking towards him. He had to cross the street calm, not arousing any suspicion. He felt as if the cop could see he was a criminal. He walked across, going slower than he had intended so as not to make the cop suspicious, fearing he'd hear the cop call him to halt, touching his hip pocket to be sure his gat didn't stick out, then touching all his pockets so it wouldn't look fluky to the cop. His shoulders slumped unconsciously after he got across and down Fifty-third out of the cop's sight. A close one, that!

He walked towards a fellow at Ellis, and wondered if he ought to stick him up. He passed him at a swift pace. Too bad he hadn't taken a pal along. It would be easier. But no, he was going to be Lonewolf Lonigan, taking his own chances, pitching his own game in his own way.

He turned towards Fifty-fourth Street, and, spying another cop, went on to Fifty-fifth. Tough luck! He had to go over a block, and on a street with car lines where there'd be more people to see him. He turned south again, and spotting a fellow and girl coming north, pulled his cap peak lower and went by them with his head down, hoping he made them afraid of him. He stopped and, rubbing his hands in dirt, smeared his face a little; made him look more desperate. And goddamn it, he was going through with this stick-up tonight.

He found a place in back of a telephone post at Fifty-sixth Street in the alley between Kenwood and Kimbark. He stood hunched, trying to figure all his plans out clear. He'd step up to a guy with the gun drawn, talk fast, get the dough, blow. Nope, the guy might yell and set up an alarm. Have to tap the guy on the bean with the gun butt, just enough to knock him cuckoo, but not kill him. If the guy was too much trouble, all right, kill him. Before they sealed a coffin lid over him, he'd knock plenty of guys out of his way like that.

The wanting for home blotted his plans aside. But no, he had to be brave. Could postpone it until tomorrow? Yellow? He took his handkerchief out quickly and tied it around his face, leaving only his eyes revealed. He crouched. His heart pounded. His hand, touching the gun in his pocket, quaked. But when the time came, he'd be just as cool as . . . a cucumber.

He heard the sound of an automobile. Far away, there were the dying echoes of a girl's voice. A black cat ran before him. Still he would take his chances. He'd overcome bad luck too. A fellow was coming along . . . the steps got nearer. In a few seconds . . .

"Stick 'em up!" Studs said in a husky, strained voice, as a big fellow stepped into view.

The man stopped short, and his hands went over his head. Studs leaped before him, the gun pointed by a trembling hand. The realization that it was just like a movie holdup flew through his brain.

"Don't . . . m-move . . . or I'll . . . drrrr . . . drill you."

The victim smiled with self-possession.

"Son, you better put that toy away!"

The gun fell. He turned and ran lickety-split down the alley, hearing diminishingly, the echo of hearty laughter.

IV

At two o'clock in the morning, Studs Lonigan walked breathlessly along Fifty-eighth Street. A large man with shoulders bent, and something of a pot-belly, approached him.

"Bill?"

Studs stopped.

"Come on home, Bill," the man said with kindness.

Studs walked beside him.

"Bill, you don't ever want to be doing a thing like this again. Your mother's heartbroken!"

Studs was glad to be going home.

IV

DAVEY COHEN risked his last two bucks in a crap game around the Toledo docks. He stood, rattling the dice in his right hand, holding fifteen bucks in the left one; he had twenty dollars in his pocket.

"Come on, baby needs new diapers!" he said, shooting, trying to act natural and unafraid, when he was goddamn near crapping in his pants; there were plenty of big tough babies in the game. He'd like to get their dough, but if he did, he knew what would happen.

He looked at the dice: seven. He picked up the pot of eight bucks. He threw ten down. If he lost ten or fifteen bucks, it wouldn't look like he had much, and he could slip off. The money was faded, and Davey rattled the dice in his right hand.

"Shake 'em, Jew!" crabbed a big, beefy-faced Lakes sailor.

"I'm shaking," Davey replied apologetically.

Seven again. He picked up five and left fifteen on the ground.

A bruiser complained about the dice. Davey held them for inspection in the palm of his hand.

"I know they ain't loaded. But use these ones. Them damn things is jinxed!"

Davey's first roll with the new dice was a seven. He coughed sharply and laid twenty bucks down.

"You damn kike, you got too many horseshoes," a sore-head said as Davey raked in the pot.

"I'm shakin' fair, brother. They're just hot for me this time. The dice get hot for a guy like this maybe once in his whole life.

"They get too damn hot when I lay my sheets down."

"Want to finish my turn and try 'em yourself?"

"Shake!"

"I was just lucky tonight," Davey said, picking up the winning of the last pot.

They glowered at him. He said so long. He walked slowly away, trying to feel that it wouldn't happen. He'd get away, get a swell meal, have a high-class woman for the night. Then, he'd buy a new suit, and ride back home on the cushions. It would sure be swell, seeing Paulie Haggerty, Studs, Red, Tommy Doyle, all of the old guys, the best gang in the world. Hadn't seen them in three years. It sure would be great.

He knew that he was being followed. As soon as he had a chance, he'd run. He walked along, as if he wasn't quaking with fear. He glanced back. Two of the bruisers were drawing close to him. He started to run. He tripped. They cold-cocked him, and left him unconscious. They weren't letting a runty, hook-nosed kike get their dough.

The two bruisers fought over the dough, and one of them was laid out.

When Davey came to, feeling the bump on his head, he cried like a baby. Christ, wouldn't he ever get a decent break?

Chapter Four

I

HE COULD hear the old man in the parlor, happily telling to the old lady that this summer sure, they'd have to step out a little, and go out to Riverview Park, and have a good time like they'd been planning to for a long time. And Fran was in her room, singing a new song about west-side chauffeurs who kiss 'em where you find 'em and leave 'em where you kiss 'em.

Studs studied himself in the mirror. He tipped his first straw hat at a rakish angle. He felt his face and looked closely where he'd shaven off the down. He stood back, erect, and pulled down the sleeves of his gray suit, holding them with the last three fingers of each hand. He arranged his blue tie. Quite a guy, he thought. But maybe he ought to have a loud purple silk shirt, the kind Pat Coady and Percentage wore. He would have gotten one, only if he had, he'd have had his tail kidded off. Later on, he would, and damn tootin', he was quite a guy.

Pretty well off too at seventeen. Hell, Dan Donoghue and the others from the Indiana gang he'd graduated with from St. Patrick's, were still only high school kids. He was earning his own living, making good dough, and his old man had changed his attitude towards him. He really wasn't so bad, and he'd only been saying the truth in that scrap they'd had. Great, all right, to be earning your own dough. He took his wallet out, counting the twelve single dollars from his first pay that he'd stuffed into it. And, some day, he'd be a full-fledged painter, on a scaffold, spreading on paint just as nice and easy as old Mort Morrison did now. There was a good guy; all the fellows he worked with were white, and treated him decent. And, yes, the time would come when he'd step into the old man's boots; then, though, wouldn't Fran change her tune?

He whistled as he walked towards the front door.

"Have a good time, Bill, old boy, and don't take any wooden nickels," the old man called from the parlor.

His mother rushed to the door, made the sign of the cross before him, kissed him, and told him to be a good boy.

He walked along, whistling. He stopped at the corner of Fifty-eighth and Indiana. If he walked down to Fifty-seventh, he might just bump into Dan or Helen Shires, talk about old times, let them see how he was all dolled up, bowl 'em over by flashing his roll. And he could maybe see Lucy, and speak, and she'd say how swell he looked, and he'd say what are you doing, and he'd say come on, let's take in a show, and he'd have a blowout with her, and not go around the poolroom, and he'd kiss her good night on the steps. Now, he'd have the dough to take her out regularly. Girls liked a fellow to take them out and show them a good time. Swell to be earning your own living.

Hell, he was out of their class now. He took a few steps across Indiana Avenue. He paused, looked down to see the street in a fading spring twilight. Buildings he knew, a few automobiles parked along the curbs, some kids playing across from O'Brien's house. The tumble-down wooden buildings near Fifty-eighth on his right, where Mush Joss lived. The row of two-story gray bricks where Lucy lived. Where they used to play tin-tin on nights like this, and sometimes with everybody giggling, he'd kiss her. He wanted to put his arms around her and kiss her again. Aw, hell, he had the dough to get all the girls he wanted. He turned, and walked slowly down Indiana Avenue on the west side of the street. Maybe he'd see Dan. The last time he'd stopped in, Dan had been studying. Let him!

No curtains in Lucy's house. The lights out. . . . Moved. He looked in. Funny, he hadn't heard from Fran or anybody that she was moving. Where? There was the house empty, and he could remember seeing her around it so often, on the steps at this time of day when they'd come home from the park, and she'd blown him a last kiss, on the steps yelling for him when he fought Weary, looking out the window one day smiling in that way of hers when he had passed by. She had even perhaps moved to another city. Perhaps never, never again would he see her! All his hopes were gone, like they'd dropped into a sewer, and what if he had dough in his kick, and looked swell, and was wearing his first straw katy! Through that window there was growing darkness, no furniture. There were plenty of girls to be gotten, and perhaps he might never see her, or would see her only far far ahead, when it was all too late.

He walked down to the corner, absorbed. Without realizing it, he stood by the mail box, opening and closing it. If anybody saw him, he'd look crazy as a loon.

"Hello, Studs!" said Andy Le Gare, entering the corner building.

"Shut up!"

Studs walked west on Fifty-seventh to the alley, and then turned around. It wouldn't look fluky now, if he just turned back and walked by her house again. Look like it was just on his way somewheres. He didn't want to go anywhere. He glanced at the empty house, desolate. Across the street kids played hide-and-go-seek, their voices and shouts seeming far away. He and Lucy had passed the crossroads of life now, their paths had cut away from each other. In that movie the other night the same thing had happened to the fellow and the girl, only they'd found each other again, in time.

Aw, what the hell! Let it go! He was sitting pretty!

He was aware of it being very quiet, lonesome, the sad part of the day. A dog barked. A horse and wagon clattered by on the rough, unpaved street. There was the noise of automobile brakes. The kids. The dog barked again. Quiet.

He went over Fifty-eighth Street. There was the tailor shop run by Cohen's old man. A dry goods store in place of the old Palm Theatre. A shoe repair shop where Schroeder had had that ice cream parlor they'd raided. The alley. The chain store, and the five and dime. The neighborhood was still much the same, and yet it was different without her. Every block, every store was somehow connected in his mind with her. It was as if she was like God, and her spirit was in everything in the neighborhood, only it wasn't any more. Suppose he had gone to war, and been killed. They would always remember him as a hero, and now maybe. . . .

He stopped to get a drink of water at the fountain in front of Sternberg's cigar store straight across from the drug store at Fifty-eighth and Prairie.

Some punks he didn't know stood at the fountain, and as that snotty, loud-mouth little hebe, Phillip Rolfe, drew near, they squirted water square in his puss. Studs laughed. Phillip shouted irritatingly. They squirted again, and, dodging, Phillip bumped into him.

"Get out of my way!" he said, missing a kick.

"Aw, it wasn't my fault!"

"Shut up!"

An old man limped stiffly along, shouting swear words at the top of his cracked lungs. The laughing punks egged him on, and he cursed them. Studs laughed.

"Hey, grandpa! Button up. You're losing something," Rolfe yelled, everybody laughing; the old man heaped foul curses on them. Funny! Studs watched him struggle along, followed by the punks.

A truck was coming, and on an impulse he dashed before it. Had to cut that out. Might be mashed someday, if he didn't.

He looked at his shoes, and leaned down to run a finger across the right toe. But it had been scuffed. Didn't like that. He noticed the sharp press in his trousers.

He walked on towards the poolroom, wishing he was going out with Lucy, a girl. Maybe they'd all go to a can house. He was afraid to do that; no, he wasn't.

He smiled at Sammy Schmaltz the newspaper man, hoping Sammy would comment on his new lid and clothes. Sammy was too busy selling papers.

Self-conscious, he joined a gang before the poolroom, and smiled deprecatingly when they kidded that he was all dolled up. Then they went back to kidding Paulie Haggerty, the married man, they said, who was too young to stand the gaff.

"Yeah, you guys just ask my wife if I ain't the goods!" said Paulie.

Studs envied him. He could stand up and say there was one girl who was all his, every inch of her. And every night with her, he could get it, as much as he wanted.

"Hey, Haggerty, does your wife wash your diapers?" asked balloon-bellied Barney Keefe.

"Ooph, that's a hot one," Fitz, the poolroom pest, said, as they laughed.

"You know, Barney, you look almost human these days, even with your false teeth," Paulie replied.

"He just bought new knee pads today too," Kilarney said.

"Look at the can on that one!" Slew Weber said, pointing as Elizabeth Burns passed.

"Hey, Haggerty, shield your eyes. You're married," Barney said.

"A married man has more experience."

"Listen, she lays for every punk in the neighborhood. She's a fourteen-year-old bitch," Kelly said.

"But she's all right. I speak from experience," Doyle said.

"I wouldn't kick her out of bed," Slew said.

"Weber, you're age limit is from eight to eighty," Barney said.

"Let's do something," Paulie said.

"Let's!" Studs said, forgetting his moodiness.

"Hey, lads, look!" Pat Coady said, pointing.

They saw Barney tagging after Elizabeth Burns.

They laughed, and when Barney came back, unsuccessful, they kidded his pants off. Barney retorted by kidding Paulie, telling him a married man had to keep his feet from smelling and take regular baths.

"Let's do something," Studs said.

II

Studs glanced around the saloon. He watched a big bloke at the rail spitting into a spittoon. Some of the birds at the bar, like that red-faced guy in khaki at the end, looked tough. Suppose there would be a free-for-all fight? Might get mashed. He imagined himself in a brawl, fighting like a demon.

"Dempsey's too damn small to take Willard," Kelly said.

"My dough's on Dempsey," Studs said.

"Say, Willard's sixty pounds heavier," said Red.

"And that sixty pounds is crap," said Barney.

"A good little man can often trim a big guy," Studs said, hoping they'd think of himself.

He took a sip of beer and ate a pretzel, because the beer didn't taste as bitter with the pretzel.

"Barney, what you gonna do after Prohibition?" asked Coady.

"Become a nun!"

"No kiddin', Barney?"

"Get married like this punk," Barney said, wiping his chin with his coat sleeve.

"Who'd have an old man like you?" asked Paulie.

"Listen, punk, there's plenty of stuff left in Barney Keefe!"

"Horse," said Paulie as they loudly reminded him of Elizabeth Burns.

"Come on, Barney, tell us what you're going to do after Prohibition?"

"What am I gonna do after Prohibition. . . . What am I gonna do after Prohibition. . . . What am I gonna do after Prohibition? Ask me something brighter!"

"Isn't Prohibition a goddamn bright idea," Red said.

"Like hell," Fitz, the pest, answered seriously.

"I'll tell you what I'm going to do . . . I'm going to stay drunk," Barney said; they laughed.

The beer began to make Studs a little dizzy. He didn't like it, didn't want any more. He saw Lucy in his head, and suddenly she spun around, and his head whirled like a merry-go-round. They ordered more, and Studs grunted he'd have another with them.

Slug Mason joined them. He was a bruiser over six feet, broad-shouldered, a leathery, stupid face, and hands like steel cranes. He looked like a brute to Studs.

"After the first of July, they're planning on deporting all you Irish along with the bullshevicky. The bullshevicky kill you with bombs, and the Irish with the whiskey breath," Slug Mason said, changing all his ths to ds, dropping the h from his withs, and slurring the pronunciation of most of his other words.

They laughed.

"Say, Slug, didn't you have a tryout with the Sox?" asked Fitz.

"Long time ago when they had Ed. Walsh. Nineteen eleven or twelve. But I was supposed to be there at twelve, and for three days, goddamn it, I couldn't wake myself up that early," Slug said.

"Early to bed, and early to rise, makes a man healthy, wealthy, and wise," Kenny said, apropos of nothing, and raising his mug aloft; they laughed.

"You punks ought to be home in bed," said Fitz.

"A guy going to bed early never meets a regular guy like myself," Barney said.

"Say, Barney, do me a favor. Lose your head back there in the can," Pat Coady said.

"This Lothario, Haggerty, better be early to bed and early to rise, or that wife he's got will knock his tail off," Barney said, ignoring the crack.

Slug talked about women. Everybody bragged how much he had had. Studs felt out of it, because he hadn't had so many girls like that, only Iris, and that Halloween in 1918, when they had gang-shagged some bum they had picked up on Wabash Avenue. Red Kelly bragged, and Studs, even though drunk, knew Red was throwing bull all over the place. He wanted a girl. But he felt so lousy, he couldn't keep thinking of it. His belly seemed bloated; he was dizzy in the head. He could only sit straight by exerting all his will-power.

Charlie Bathcellar joined them. He told them he'd just closed a deal, selling the poolroom to a Greek. The guys were sorry, and got sentimental. Suddenly Charlie remembered that Paulie's wife had been around, almost in tears, looking for him. They laughed, kidding Paulie. Slug told Paulie he was handling his woman right. They had to be trained, and when they were trained right, they were as meek as a lamb, and if they weren't, they were female tigers. Once you let them wear the britches, they'd never take them off, and you were a goner. Paulie drank on it with Slug.

"But, fellows, you know, my wife is a good kid," Paulie suddenly said.

"She looked awfully blue," Charlie said.

"She'll get over it," Paulie said.

"My old woman did. Just treat her a little tough, and when she squawks, slap her down. They like that," Slug said, in his way of pronunciation.

"You guys drop the skirts. Here's the only solace for mortal man," Barney said, raising his mug aloft.

"Sure, but try and keep it from having the old sailor freeze on a windy night," Slug said.

Paulie's head fell to the table. Barney laughed, and said it was one punk drunk under the table. Slug said Barney didn't have any belly; it was a barrel down there.

Slug suddenly saw that Studs was getting pale and glassy-eyed. He said they better get the kid some air, and, lifting him, supported him outside. The whole gang followed. He helped Studs along, the two of them looking like Mutt and Jeff.

Paulie staggered in the rear. In tears, he said that he loved his wife. He asked Kenny if he didn't think she was one damn swell woman. Kenny answered that she was homelier than Maggie in the Jiggs' cartoons.

"Come on!" challenged Paulie, putting up his fists; tears splattered down his face.

Paulie swung wildly, belaboring the air, while Kenny laughed and shadow-boxed out of his reach.

"Please fight me," sobbed Paulie, dropping his hands to his sides.

"No, but I'll play you a little casino."

"Well, come on then, you bastard!"

They sat down on the sidewalk, and Kenny started dividing rocks between them. Paulie said these were stones, not cards. Kenny seriously said they were cards. Paulie said he'd fight over it. Kenny leaped up, and ran ahead. He watched and kidded while Slug held Studs, who was vomiting over the curb.

"I love my wife," Paulie shouted, as he staggered in the rear, his coat slung over his shoulder, his hat askew, his hair plastered down his forehead.

He caught up with the other guys, and sobbed that he was worried because he thought that he still might have that dose of his, and he was afraid that if he had any kids, it would make them blind, or even nuttier than Kilarney.

"Blah!" mouthed Kenny.

"Say, for Christ sake, will somebody drag that puppy home to his she-bitch," Barney complained.

Paulie mumbled it was no fooling. He was worried because it might even mean that he'd have kids like Kenny Kilarney. He fell down. They had to carry him, and he wouldn't shut up.

III

"I'm drunk!" Paulie said emphatically, as he floundered besides Studs.

"I'm weak," Studs said.

"I'm drunk, Studs."

"Didn't it give you a headache," Studs said, feeling his head, glad he had vomited it up.

"Christ, Studs, I'm drunk!"

Studs belched.

Paulie complained, too, because of that dose and having kids like Kilarney. He said he loved his wife. Studs wanted to mention Lucy, but he didn't get a chance. Paulie talked a leg off him. He left Paulie, and walked slowly home, his head pounding. He felt proud of having been drunk, and sorry, and rotten. He worried lest he would wake up the family. He started walking on a crack in the sidewalk, back and forth, to prove to himself that he could walk straight. And if anybody was up, they might smell his breath.

Getting in, he fumbled with his key, and it seemed like he was as noisy as an earthquake.

"That you, son?"

He stood still, like an apprehended burglar. His mother said she'd worried because it was late. He said he was all right, and had only been talking with some of the fellows. Luck! He quickly tumbled into bed, into its soft whiteness, protection from his headache, and thoughts, and everything.

V

STUDS LONIGAN, *Tommy Doyle, Red Kelly, Benny Taite, and Kenny Kilarney acted slightly aloof, while a gang of bloodthirsty kids swirled and milled about them reiterating the cry of "Let's go!" Clubs and sticks were brandished. Three Star Hennessey gritted his teeth, and slashed the air with a straight razor. Weary Reilley casually and publicly examined a twenty-two revolver. Kenny Kilarney put on a pair of brass knuckles, and permitted the punks to examine them. Studs Lonigan gripped a baseball bat, and swung as if stepping into a pitch. He said that when he cracked a dinge in the head, the goddamn eight ball would think it had been Ty Cobb slamming out a homer off Walter Johnson. Red Kelly unsheathed a hunting-knife, and vowed that he was ready. Andy Le Gare tried to tell everyone that in close fighting they should kick the niggers in the shins. Tommy Doyle said the niggers were never going to forget the month of July, 1919. Studs said that they ought to hang every nigger in the city to the telephone poles, and let them swing there in the breeze. Benny Taite said that for every white man killed in the riots, ten black apes ought to be massacred. Red said that the niggers had caught Clackey Merton, from Sixty-first Street, down in the black belt, and slashed his throat from ear to ear, and plenty of niggers had to be slashed to pay for the death of Clackey. They lamented that Clackey was a victim of the riots. Fat Malloy started telling how the Regan Colts were marching into the black belt and knocking off the niggers. Andy said well the Fifty-eighth Street guys were going to do the same thing.*

Young Horn Buckford suddenly appeared and breathlessly said that there was a gang of niggers over on Wabash Avenue. Studs, Red, Tommy, Weary, Kenny, and Benny Taite led the gang along Fifty-eighth Street, over to Wabash. For two hours, they prowled Wabash Avenue and State Street, between Garfield Boulevard and Fifty-ninth Street, searching for niggers. They sang, shouted, yelled defiance at the houses, and threw bricks into the windows of houses where they thought niggers lived. They were joined by other groups, men and kids. The streets were like avenues of the dead. They only caught a ten-year-old Negro boy. They took his clothes off, and burned them. They burned his tail with lighted matches, made him step on lighted matches, urinated on him, and sent him running off naked with a couple of slaps in the face.

Back around the corner at six o'clock, Studs and Red talked of how they would get a bigger gang together after supper, and go north of Garfield Boulevard until they found niggers. They described what they would do to them. They walked down to the el station and bought a paper. The headlines said that with the militia out, peace and order were being restored in the riot-stricken black belt. They cursed, and said they would get the niggers in spite of even the whole United States Army. They would avenge Clackey Merton, the kid from Sixty-first Street, who had been killed down in the black belt.

Chapter Five

STUDS walked with Paulie and his Eileen towards the park, and he and Paulie gassed about the good old days. But it seemed stiff with her there, smiling politely at everything they said, even the things they kept exaggerating and making more than they actually had been, in order to make her think that they'd been great guys.

They talked about what the boys from Fifty-eighth Street had done in the race riots last month, and she acted horrified, but Studs guessed it was only put on. They told each other that the niggers needed a couple more riots.

Crossing South Park Avenue, Paulie took her elbow. Studs envied him, because she was his girl, his woman, and she slept with him, undressed in front of him, and he could do whatever he wanted with her body. It was something, having a woman all the time. When you walked down the street, with her on your arm, everybody could see she was yours and gave it to you whenever you wanted it. And you could bring her around to meet your friends, and let them see you got it, and they'd look her over, and envy you, seeing she had nice legs, a swell figure, enough meat on her in the right places. Maybe he did kind of wish he had a woman of his own, as nice and as hot as Paulie's with a good figure, and good-looking clothes like the blue suit she had on. Studs fell behind, pretending to pick up something, so he could get a look at her. She was hot-looking all right, with plenty of meat on her, nice tocus, slim ankle, and the fragment of leg between dress and ankle was the stuff too, fleshy and shapely. She was gorgeous to look at, to touch, to. . . .

It was swell out, just cool enough, with the park air smelling sort of cool; and the trees were green and leafy, their shadows falling in solid black now as it got dark. He looked at her again, then up at a tree, and in back of him; she must be catching on that he had to keep looking at her. What a sweet piece she must be!

She told Paulie about the new set of dishes she wanted; he didn't seem to be interested; Studs thought that part of things should be taken care of by the wife, and she shouldn't bother the guy about it. Same way at home, the old lady always had to tell the old man what she'd buy, and he didn't want to hear it.

"Going to have a football team in the fall, Studs?" Paulie asked, ignoring her as she harped about dishes.

"I think so. Looks like it will be pretty good."

Maybe Paulie would say something to let her know he'd be captain and quarterback, and that he was one damn sweet football player. Next fall, she might even come out to one of the games and see for herself how good he was.

"You're not going to play, Paul?" she said, entreating.

"No."

They walked along on the path that led from the entrance, and curved around to the left, past the boathouse.

Studs used to like to talk to Paulie; now, with his wife around, there didn't seem anything to talk about, and it didn't mean much; it was like stabbing in the dark to reach something when there was nothing to reach. Paulie was different.

"Think you'll be getting married?" Paulie asked, and Studs saw that his wife smiled condescendingly.

"No," Studs said, luckily checking himself from putting a "hell" first; he'd just thought that it had its advantages, but then the way it kept a guy from his pals, the arguing, the kids later on, the time to come when your wife wouldn't be a hot hunk any more; there were both sides to it.

"You'll tumble some day," Paulie said in the voice of experience.

"No danger," Studs insisted, dismayed by her steady smile.

"It's always the ones talking like you who fall the hardest," she said, smiling sweetly.

"You'll fall!" Paulie said confidently.

Studs enjoyed being the center of conversation like that. If it kept on, Paulie might say something like, how's Lucy, or, why don't you marry Lucy? Of course, he'd answer he didn't want to, but he didn't know if he did or not. And he'd shrug his shoulders don't-care-like when Eileen would ask who Lucy was, and Paulie would say she was a nice girl, Studs' girl. The whole business suddenly seemed goofy. Still, he waited to hear Paulie mention her name.

"Yes, Studs, some morning you'll just wake up to find yourself married."

He forced another laugh. He tried to think of himself settling down with a wife. Himself getting up in the morning, kissing her, sitting down to be served breakfast, eating supper with her; himself coming home one night and telling the family he was going to be married, looking Fran in the face when he said it. He was glad he wasn't going through that kind of thing yet. But having a woman! Fellows saying Studs' woman. That was all right. Thinking about it, at least, was. They'd kid him, but it would only be fun and half jealousy on their part. Himself coming home in winter, she taking his shoes off, putting his slippers on, sitting and watching him with love while he read, doing things for him, and then, when it was cold out, going to bed, he taking her clothes off, she taking his off, getting all warmed up together. That would be better than hanging around the poolroom. But then, if she nagged! He had time, and there were both sides of it.

"Why so quiet?" asked Paulie.

"Ope, just looking around, and thinking about the team we'll have in the fall," Studs hurriedly answered, feeling, though, as if Paulie had seen right into what he'd been thinking.

They sat on a bench near the circle with the fountain, where the path curved.

Studs noticed a doodish guy on the bench across from them. He was classily dressed, the kind of a bird who'd go over bigger with girls than fellows.

"Gee, it's a swell night," Paulie said.

"I think I'll be dashing along," Studs said.

"Hang around a while," Paulie said.

He sat on the edge of the bench. Maybe they wanted to be alone. He wanted a girl, Lucy, a girl to be sitting with him on a bench, under the trees like this.

"Dear, it's perfectly grand here."

"Swell," Paulie said, looking up at the trees that roofed in the gathering darkness.

"Yeah," muttered Studs abstractedly, raw with thoughts of himself and Lucy in the park, himself all open so that every thought and word seemed like they were touching an open cut inside him.

"Many's the times we had in this park, huh, Studs?"

"Yeah," Studs said, observing that the guy seemed to be looking at her, wishing that Paulie would speak of some of the fights he had had.

He glanced down at Paulie, and saw that his wife had her legs crossed, showing her leg almost up to the knee. No wonder the guy looked. Couldn't blame the guy; hell, her legs were worth seeing all the way up. If he sat alone on a bench and saw a girl like her with legs crossed, he'd look for all he was worth. . . . But Paulie was his friend, and she was Paulie's wife. He liked Paulie and liked to stick with him; it was his duty to a friend to tell Paulie, and, if necessary, help him sock the guy. Anyway, he didn't like the bastard's looks. Some of the guys might be in the boathouse too, if they needed help, but they wouldn't. Studs turned to tell Paulie, but saw that he was on to it.

"See anything green?" asked Paulie.

The fellow didn't answer.

"Hey!" snarled Paulie.

"Paul!" she begged, touching his sleeve.

"Hey, you, I said: 'See anything green?' " Paulie said, rising and brushing his wife's hand aside; Studs jumped up.

"The grass is green," the fellow said, smiling good-naturedly, an expression of almost sick friendliness on his face.

"Buddy, there ain't room for all of us around here!"

"Yeah, fellow, shove on while you're all together!" Studs said.

"Paul, please . . . please, don't go fighting; he hasn't done a thing to you," she pleaded, pulling at his coat.

"Shut up!" he snapped at her.

"It's healthier in that direction," Studs said, pointing with his right hand.

The fellow, taller than Paulie, started to slink away. Paulie swung, catching him unexpectedly in the jaw from the side. The fellow staggered, then made a start to run. Paulie caught him, and jerked him around, for Studs, who drove him a fierce uppercut. The fellow punched and kicked back.

"Oh, you will, will you!" Paulie said, his wife screaming as her husband's fist drove into the bastard's mouth. It bled. He went down, and they kicked him. He went off, holding a handkerchief to his face.

"Brutes!" she said.

"Listen, bitch!" Paulie said.

A fellow asked what was the matter. Studs said the guy had monkeyed around with his pal's wife. The fellow said it was good for him. There was a lot of damn mashers like that, and they all needed a sock in the puss.

"And you listen to me. Any goddamn time you sit like you were then, showing off everything you own, there'll be trouble. My wife ain't acting like a whore in a public park when I'm around. Get that straight, and don't forget it!"

She cried, denying his accusation.

"You're a goddamn liar!" Paulie shouted.

"I'm going to the boathouse," Studs said, embarrassed; he left without them noticing him.

None of the guys were around. He noticed, too, that no niggers were in sight. He spied a lonesome-looking chicken sitting up towards the front. Maybe she wanted to be picked up. He sat near her, and kept giving her the eye. She was pretty, a baby-faced blonde. She sat impassive. He could just go up and talk to her, say let's take a walk, and get her over on the wooded island. And he'd go back to the poolroom, and tell the lads what a lay he had, describing how it all went off, and knock them cuckoo wishing they'd been that lucky. She met his eye, icy, not a hint on her face. Sometimes they were like that in pretence, making it a game where you worked for it. He lit a cigarette, nonchalant, as if he were just as unaware of her presence as she seemed to be of his. He looked out at the water, black, except where the boathouse lights and stretches of moonlight lay over it. He tried to think up something clever that he might say to make an opening. He could just see her smiling at his cleverness, if only he could hit upon some good crack. He watched two couples rowing away from the landing. One of the girls laughed loudly. He arose, and casually sauntered to her side, glanced at her while she looked uninterestedly ahead. He said hello. She didn't respond. He got nervous, and greeted her a second time. She looked up at him, as if he were so low that he crept on the ground.

"Like to go oaring, cutie?"

"I should say not," she said, turning her back.

He felt like he might just go crawl into a barrel, and sink his head. Blushing, he left the boathouse. Just a goddamn bitch trying to be swell! He wandered back on the grass, wondering if he might take in the movie at the Prairie Theatre. Dirty it was, jumping the poor bastard, when you couldn't blame him for looking at something offered to him on a platter; she knew he was looking. If that jane, bitch, in the boathouse had a husband, he'd be the same way and want to start swinging. Just natural to look at a girl's legs. He was sorry, a bit ashamed of himself; but that uppercut he'd given him, it had been beautiful, timed just right. Remembering the thrill of landing it was even swell.

He crossed the bushes in back of the bench where they were. He saw them in each other's arms, and heard her say to Paulie;

"Honey, I love you!"

Made him want a girl! Put his arms around her, draw her tight so he could press into her, feel her hardening herself against him, feeling her quiver and shake with excitement because he touched her, wanted to know her. No girl had ever said she loved him like she'd just told Paulie. The Great Studs Lonigan, the battler. . . . no girl ever seemed to think so. He wanted one, maybe he even wanted to marry one . . . maybe, perhaps, Lucy. . . .

He met Elizabeth Burns crossing the drive from the Fifty-eighth Street entrance.

"Say, aren't you afraid being over here alone in the dark?"

"Nobody would hurt little me," she giggled.

"You need protection," he said, taking her arm.

He walked her around the south bend of the lagoon, and over the stone bridge to the wooded island. They found a spot right near the tree where he and Lucy had been. She didn't offer him any resistance.

He was tired, drowsy, walking back with her, their clothes all rumpled. She was too much for him. Never would get enough. What a bitch! But before he had got so tired that it hurt him, nice, and he'd looked up at the sky, blue, big, so many stars like jewels, feeling perfectly at peace. Only she wanted an army. And what she didn't know at the age of fourteen wasn't worth knowing. They walked slowly towards Calumet, not saying much. At the corner of Calumet, her old man, a big bastard over six feet, jumped out with a horsewhip.

"Get home, you whore!" he said, roughly pushing her aside. He snapped the whip, bearing it down on Studs' shoulder. Studs was so surprised that he stood stock still. The old man lashed him three times, before he ran. Old man Burns followed him down the street, cursing him, lashing him with the horse whip till it stung and burned. Strangers stopped to laugh. He felt that he couldn't run much farther, and he ran, gasping, his side paining sharply. He couldn't stop, and Christ, that whip. He dashed recklessly in front of automobiles and got across to the park side of South Park Avenue. He turned and saw the old man flaunting his whip on the other side of the street, yelling:

"I'll teach you whose daughter you're monkeying with!"

He flung a rock, and ran through the bushes on the left-hand side of the tennis court. Old man Burns didn't follow him.

11. [illegible] Zeppelin came [illegible] only the [illegible] the [illegible]
connection.

[illegible] and [illegible] been [illegible] in the [illegible] as studied. [illegible]

[illegible] connection [illegible] any relation [illegible]

[illegible] number [illegible]

[illegible] Academy, 18[illegible] [illegible]

[illegible] another [illegible]

[illegible] and [illegible] along the [illegible]

[illegible] writing [illegible]

SECTION TWO

1922

VI

HOLY MARY, *the Mother of God, the Virgin of Virgins, Mother most Powerful and Merciful, Morning Star and Health of the Weak, Comfortress of the Afflicted, Mother of God, Mary who had herself gone down into the valley of the shadow of death . . . she, Blessed Mary, she would understand the burden of distress and naked sorrow that lay on the heart of a poor mother whose precious baby son lay at death's door; she, whose only begotten Son had been crowned with thorns and crucified to save all mankind, she would understand, she would sympathize, she would intercede at the throne of God Almighty, the Creator of Heaven and Earth; she would beseech that if it be the will of God, to Whom all things were possible, that He spare the life of Mrs. Haggerty's son, Paul.*

Mrs. Haggerty, stout and shabby, her eyes raw with tears, dropped her tenth dime into the slot by the candle rack before the altar of the Blessed Virgin. She gazed adoringly and with tears of hope at the waxenly expressionless face on the blue-robed statue of the Mother of God. Her face accumulated intenseness, and the lips on the waxenly expressionless face seemed to move, miraculously, in calming words.

Mrs. Haggerty lit her tenth candle and placed it in a holder that it might burn as a prayer of entreaty.

She prayed in a church wombed in quiet. A jangling street car passed outside, and its racket was like a rough, uncouthly handled instrument lacerating the churchly hush. The beat of marching feet thundered on the ceiling. From outside came the shouts of school children, boys and girls. The swinging door in the rear was jammed back and forth; feet scraped on the aisles. A boy knelt before the center altar, and his face became wistful in prayer. Mrs. Haggerty looked at him with maternal eyes.

And only five years ago—life was short—Paul had been a boy like that, innocent; and his steps had mingled with the feet of other boys and girls as they marched out of the schoolrooms upstairs. And he had romped and shouted as the children without were now doing.

HAIL MARY, FULL OF GRACE, THE LORD IS WITH THEE, BLESSED ART THOU AMONGST WOMEN, AND BLESSED IS THE FRUIT OF THY WOMB, JESUS . . .

Mary, please spare me a mother's agony, please, oh, please, save the fruit of my womb, my Paul, my precious baby son. . . .

HAIL MARY, FULL OF GRACE. . . .

Chapter Six

I

MIKE stared out of the poolroom window. His face was a gaze of primal obtuseness. An elevated train rumbled out of the Fifty-eighth Street elevated station. An automobile whizzed by.

"Hello, Mike!" said Slug Mason entering, his smeary-lipped mouth cracking in a smile.

Mike greeted Slug with an idiot grin. Slug lit a cigarette, shoved his hands in his pockets and leaned back on his heels.

"Smoke?" asked Mike, holding out his greasy, sweaty paw.

"Say, it looks like there's gonna be some sun out this morning," Slug said, with faulty pronunciation, as he studied the street outside and the blue September sky that was slowly being shattered with sunlight.

Mike lit one of his own cigarettes.

"Jesus, was we all cockeyed las' night . . . but say, Mike, I fixes the lads with some flaming jazz-babies!"

"Push-push," mumbled Mike, lust, like thick, ugly sweat, oozing from his eyes.

Slug beamed patronizingly.

"Push-push!"

"Yeah, Mike, I'll bet you know your stuff.'"

II

"Wheeeee!" shouted Young Rocky Kansas as he crashed through the narrow entrance door, removing his jacket coat.

"Wheeeeeee!" echoed skinny, toothpick Harry Pochon, following upon Young Rocky's heels past the shoe-shining stand which stood where Charlie Bathcellar had had his barber chairs.

"Time on table number one, Greek!" Young Rocky shouted.

"Come on, time on, you dumb Greek bastard!" parroted Pochon.

Mike's face clenched with hate. Slowly, he turned and went to the counter. He punched a card on the time clock.

"These eighteen-year-old punks need their snouts punched in to teach 'em a lesson," Slug said.

A slow gleam of assent was born on Mike's face. He shrugged, and placed a hat on the cleaning block. He commenced to brush the hat.

Slug watched the youngest Sullivan girl trip stiff-leggedly by.

"Nice," Mike babbled, with clumsy, pawing, emphatic gestures. They laughed in mutual understanding.

III

Bob Connell entered, wearing a loud gray summer suit with bell bottoms. Big Rocky Kansas followed him, walking muscle bound and like a tame bear. He was a bushy-browed lad of about twenty-one, with broad shoulders. He smiled with intoxicating good-nature, and, sticking a cigar in his bucolic face, ranged himself alongside Slug. Slug ignored Bob's cloying salutation; he said Rocky looked like a politician, smoking that cigar. They heard the click of the pool balls. Big Rocky yelled hello to his kid brother.

"Say, last night, Gleen Reaves and me had some red hot mamas dated up. Cost us five bucks at Kling Hing Lo's Chop House. But, boy, did those broads know how to sock. Say, fellahs, I tell you, I never danced with the broad who socked like mine did. Why she dry . . ." Bob said with enthusiasm, cutting off his words, and answering the call from Young Rocky.

"Say, that punk has only got fifty cards in his deck," Slug said, pronouncing his ths as ds.

"Hell, he is only young, sixteen. He hasn't lost his cherry," Big Rocky said.

"Look! Look!" Mike said, pointing at a passing broad.

IV

"Well, Studs, you're a man now," grinned Slug.

"That doesn't mean nothing," replied bleary-eyed Studs.

"Say, you're right there. It's true," Slug said.

"Most things are just plain crap to me," Studs said.

"Ain't they though?" said Slug, saying "though" as if it were "dough."

"My head!" said Studs, feeling his right temple.

"Well, you was polluted last night," Slug said.

Studs nodded agreement.

"Say, Paulie's in bad shape. He was prayed for in church this morning."

"He's a good lad."

"Gee, I hope he pulls through. But he's in a tough spot now," said Studs.

"He's down for the count, huh," said Slug.

"Let's get a coke and take a little walk," Studs said, as they walked out.

V

"And was I blind last night!" reiterated eighteen-year-old Ellsworth Lyman.

"You were soused to the gills," Wils Gillen said, causing Lyman to smile with the pride of achievement.

"Ellsworth was so drunk he went around with tears in his eyes, sobbing the blues, because he couldn't stop breathing," said Darby Dan Drennan; they guffawed.

"I don't remember that, but I do remember a guy getting tough with me around Sixty-third, and I was all set to knock his teeth down his throat. But he was so yellow, I didn't have the heart to lay one on him."

"When Lyman called him, he folded up like an umbrella," Gillen said.

"I can't stand a guy with a yellow streak down his back," Lyman said.

"Well, by God, Ellsworth, you were snaky last night," said Wils.

"I guess I was," Ellsworth proudly said.

VI

"Jeff, you're falling away to a ton!" Red Kelly said.

"Yeah, don't fool yourself! I just dropped seventy-five pounds," Jeff replied, handfuls of fat on his cheek, chin, and neck wiggling into a smile.

He rolled along the poolroom, a lumbrous, slightly limping, waddling barracks of flesh.

"Hi, boys!" he said with excessive good-nature.

"Boys, here's Jeff, the baby elephant!" yelled Pochon.

"Say, Jeff, I thought you'd already joined a freak show," Young Rocky said.

"Say, Hippo, Man Bleu is gunning for you, and promises that he won't do anything at all but lose his fists in your goddamn fat puss," Lyman yelled.

"I ain't done nothing to him," Jeff protested.

"What, another chump you took in?" asked Kelly.

"Man gave him five bucks to get him some punch boards. He ain't seen the elephant since," Lyman said.

"He's not gettin' gypped. He'll get them. They were just delayed at the factory. Just got 'em yesterday. In fact, I came around to see if he was here now."

"B. S.," Young Rocky said, lip-farting.

"Jeff, you ain't got the heart of a snake, have you?'" said Kelly.

"Commere, Red. I got a funny story to tell you," Jeff said.

"Jeff, the first ton is the hardest, ain't it?" said Gillen.

VII

"Arnold, where'd you get the shiner?" Stan Simonsky, nephew of a baseball magnate, asked.

"Oh, a fight last night," Arnold replied.

Stan, plump and medium-sized, stretched on his toes to examine Arnold Sheehan's black eye. Arnold was taller, and well built; his face was crude in features, with heavy dark brows, and a long nose. He wore a loosely-cut black suit with flashy pin-stripes, a checkered gray topcoat, an almost pearly gray fedora, and black tie.

"Drunk again?" asked Stan.

Arnold nodded.

"Every time you get snozzled, you get a break, don't you! Two weeks ago you were maggoty and got your dose, and you're still limping from getting shoved down those elevated steps last week. You better stick to malted milks, Arnold."

"Just hard luck! I was dancing at Trianon, and got in a scrap over a broad I was trying to make. I wasn't so drunk, though. You should have seen Weary Reilley. He was tossing sugar bowls all around Kling's Restaurant."

"Some day that guy's gonna get worse than you'll ever get."

"Say, Arnold, what'll you take for your shiner?" Kelly hollered over to him.

VIII

"You were pretty gone last night," beefy Tommy Doyle said to his cousin Les.

"Yes, I was," Les modestly said.

"Your old man should have seen you."

"Don't worry. He's tipped many a bottle himself," Les said, smiling like a cherubim.

Tommy shook his head in expression of indefinite amusement.

"Hell, I might just as well get drunk. I don't see why I got to rot away in that rut, working on an electric for the Continental Express Company. Gee, I'm never going to amount to anything, and I might as well have a little fun. . . . Say, Tommy, I sure do wish I'd gone to school and gotten an education," Les whined.

"You don't know when you're well off. I'd like to have a job paying the dough you get."

"Well, I wish I had an education. Look at where Joe O'Reilley and Dinny Gorman are. Now if I was a lawyer, I might be getting somewhere's."

IX

"You know Dot Gorman. She's older than us guys, see, but lemme tell you . . . she's keen. *KEEN!*" funnyface Young Duffy orated for his own benefit.

"She ain't so much. She's horsefaced and stuckup," Denny Dennis said.

"Say, your taste is all in your mouth," funnyface Duffy said.

Goofy Nate Klein called Duffy aside.

"Listen, punk. Dorothy Gorman is a friend of mine. She's too nice a girl to be talked about in a joint like this. If you know when you're healthy, don't mention her name in this place again. And don't call her Dot. Get me?"

"I didn't say nothin' against her. I was just complimenting her. . . ."

"I told you that if you don't want your friends taking up a collection for flowers for you, don't mention her name in this joint again!" Nate said, hard-boiled.

X

"You know, I just went into the bedroom with that broad last night, and everything went out like the lights," Studs said.

Tommy Doyle cracked a joke about what should have happened.

"Look at the punks. They ain't washed under the ears yet," sneered Slug, gazing surprisedly around the poolroom.

"They look goofy in their ding-dong pants," said Studs.

"Monkey suits," said Slug; he pointed at the twenty-two-inch bell-bottoms on Phil Rolfe's carefully, precisely, exactly careless black suit. Phil turned his light-complexioned, insipid face towards them and smiled. He was wearing a blue shirt, collar attached, a soft, wine-red knit tie, and a light brown hat.

"Pull up your skirts," said Stan Simonsky.

"Hi, kid," patronized Phil.

"Hey, Rolfe?" yelled Red.

"What you say, Red," replied Phil with aplomb.

"Hey, punk, where's your rubber knee pads?" Studs sneered.

"Did you get that out of a joke book?" he asked, but he blushed slightly.

Phil walked away from them, towards a table in the back.

"Hey, Studs, I haven't eaten today. Can you loan me two bits. After while, I'll shark some guy in a pool game, but Christ, I'm starved!" said TB McCarthy; TB was thin, consumptive-looking, with jaundiced cheeks that seemed to be shrivelling and hollowing away. He wore a spotted, unpressed, shabby, brown suit.

"Get out of here, heel."

"Muggsy mooching again?" said Red.

"Jesus, Red, I haven't eaten today," said Muggsy.

"Well, McCarthy, there's lots of horse manure in the alley," said Slug. All the older guys in the bunch guffawed.

XI

"Thanks, kid, and I'll have the liquor back to you at three-thirty this afternoon. And I guarantee that it's bonded," Jeff said, taking three and a half dollars from funnyface Young Duffy.

"Sure now that it's good stuff?" asked Duffy.

"I wouldn't sell it to you if it wasn't," Jeff convincingly replied.

Jeff struggled and puffed towards the door. Everybody got in his way and he had a hell of a time squeezing past them.

XII

"All I hope is that that dope starts her like nobody's business," Wils Gillen said.

"It did for me when I had the scare about Elizabeth," Ellsworth said.

"Well, if it don't . . . Holy Jesus!"

"You'll either have to join the navy or else . . . marry the pig."

"Marry her, a Midway Garden bum?"

"If it don't, I know a doctor. I fixed up Sadie Prevost with him when she was knocked up by all you guys. She's all right, only to raise the dough she had to go out and hustle. She did so well hustling that she's in the business for good now," Darby Dan Drennan said.

"She sacrificed her amateur standing, huh?" said Ellsworth.

"If it don't, it's the marines and see the world, boys," Wils said.

"Anyway, Wils, no matter how tough a hole you're in, remember that you'll always be better off than poor Paulie Haggerty," philosophized Darby Dan Drennan.

"Now ain't that something," said Wils.

XIII

"Sure, I'm good," Young Rocky said, hanging up his cue.

"You made some good shots," Bob Connell said professionally.

"Hang around with me, brother, and you'll learn how to shoot pool," Young Rocky said. His eyes opened in wide interest. "Let there be light and there was light. Let there be Louisa Nolan's Dance Hall, and there was Three Star Hennessey."

Three Star Hennessey, a pimply-faced runt, wearing a cheap blue suit with flapping bell bottoms, ambled towards them.

"Spats and all," said glassy-eyed Swede Larsen, looking at Hennessey's pearl gray spats.

"Goin' to the jig this afternoon?" asked Connell.

"If he didn't, Nolan's would close up."

"Say, Hennessey, is it true that you go down to Castle Gardens and dance so that you can pinch pocketbooks?" Swede asked.

"I combine business with pleasure . . . but, say, who'll loan me a buck until tonight?"

"Scrouging dough again, huh, Hennessey?" said Young Rocky.

XIV

"What?" Fat Malloy bellowed.

Long-faced Jawbones Levinsky adjusted his horn-rimmed glasses, stuck his hands in his topcoat pocket, and sneered.

"Gypp was overrated."

"For Christ sake!" exclaimed Malloy, belligerent and nonplussed.

"Well, what did he ever do?"

"What did he do? Didn't he make a seventy-yard drop kick?"

Jawbones' right hand pushed outwards in a gesture of disdainful unbelief.

"Listen, Jew! I SAY THAT GYPP MADE A SEVENTY-FIVE YARD DROP KICK AND YOU CAN FIND IT IN THE RECORD BOOK."

"What record book?"

"Why, you damn fool kike, the record book. What the hell record book you suppose, the one on volley ball? What the hell do you go to an A.P.A. college like the U for if you don't understand English?"

"Think I fall for that stuff?"

"Why, you lowdown Jew! Say, get this straight and don't forget it! George Gypp of Notre Dame made a seventy-five yard drop kick," Malloy said, clenching his fists, and shoving a bull-dog mug forward.

"Hell, you're just another one of these synthetic Notre Dame alumni. . . . And you can't even pronounce the name correctly."

"YOU LOUSY KIKE! I OUGHT TO PUNCH THAT FACE OF YOURS FULL OF HOLES. . . ."

Departure became the better part of Levinsky's valor.

XV

"You're exonerated, then?" said big Gannon, a park cop.

"Yeah," Joe Moonan answered; he was a classily dressed, angelic-faced dick.

"How did it all happen, Joe? I never got the story straight."

Joe told how he had caught the kids shooting craps down near Twelfth Street, and had yelled at them. They had run after he called to them to halt, and he pulled out his gun, intending to scare them. He had been aiming to shoot over their heads, but somehow, he didn't know how, and was sorry it happened, he'd hit one of the kids.

"It sure caused a stink, didn't it? But anyway, I'm glad they exonerated you."

"It was all accident. And what the hell, the kid was just a goddamn alley-rat. I don't see why there was so much trouble about it."

XVI

Jim Doyle stuck a fat cigar in his face, and rubbed his right hand over the alderman he was starting to develop.

"Now, Lonigan, remember and always vote Democratic," Jim said, buttonholing Studs.

"Sure, the old man's a good Democrat," Studs said.

"It's only a left-handed mick who'd vote Republican. Hell, Lonigan, if the Irish only would stick together and realize that the Democrats are their party, they could run this city. And if they don't, well, the Jews and Polacks will be stepping all over them."

"Sure."

"Too bad you're not in my precinct. . . . Anyway, a vote's a vote."

"You precinct captain now?"

"No, I just help out Old Rubenstein."

"Oh!"

"Well, congratulations, old man, and so long."

Jim turned back and handed Studs a cigar.

XVII

"Say, Vinc, remember the girl you kissed at Sarah Windlemann's beach party last month, Mary the Wop?" Runt asked.

Vinc Curley, tall with an enlarged and elongated head, and a mouth chronicly opened like a fly trap, gaped at them, visibly remembering and curious.

"I haven't the heart to tell the guy what she's got," Runt said, giving Young Rocky a knowing eye.

"But, Runt, it's only fair to tell him," Young Rocky said after due reflection.

Young Rocky studied a cold sore on Vinc's lip. He looked dolorous, and placed a hand on Vinc's shoulder.

"Vinc, I hate to tell you, but you're my pal. . . . Mary the Wop has syphilis."

"Yeah, the dirty bitch!" Runt said with feigned hate.

"And . . . fellows . . . have I got it too?" Vinc asked after a long pause.

Balefully, they nodded affirmation. He asked what it meant, and what he should do. They answered with mysterious remarks about something gotten in drug stores, called G. O. 45. They told him it was very serious, and made the skin maggoty, caused it to moulder, and might even lead to blindness, deafness, dumbness, and his arms might even fall off, his eyes drop out, and his toes fall apart. Terrible thing! And he had better get it taken care of immediately.

"Vinc, old pal, they'll put you in quarantine, and we'll miss you," Runt said, slowly extending his hand.

Young Rocky sliced Runt's elbow, warning him not to risk contagion by shaking hands with Vinc.

Vince bolted out of the poolroom.

XVIII

"Tough about Paulie Haggerty, my old buddy," Hennessey said.

"Say, just what is wrong with him?" asked Lou Bruner.

"Every goddamn thing. Clap, gonorrheal rheumatism, his heart is shot, his lungs are gone, and he has ulcers of the stomach. The guy has just drunk and jazzed himself to death."

"Jesus Christ!" exclaimed Lou.

XIX

"Yes, I said the Republicans, they went and steal the election from Cox by crookedness," Andy defiantly declared.

"Where did you get all that inside dope?" asked Darby Dan Drennan.

"My father told me. And he ought to know. Doesn't he belong to the Ku Klux Klan?"

"Fellows, his old man wears a nightshirt and burns fiery crosses in empty prairies," said Darby Dan, guffawing.

"He don't neither."

"His old man rides around in bed-sheets on a horse," said Darby Dan.

"Where does he keep the horse?" asked Pochon.

"He ain't got no horse."

"Does he belong to the Ku Klux Klan?" asked Drennan.

"Yes," Andy proudly said.

"Then, he's got to have a horse."

"He don't need no horse," Andy shouted above their laughter.

"If he hasn't got a horse, how can he wear his nightshirt and go riding?" laughed Pochon.

Andy stuttered.

XX

"Whenever you think about girls, you know, wondering if they are all they're cracked up to be, more decent and better than guys, think of this angle! Think of the keenest broad you know sitting down to take a great big healthy . . . ."

"What sweet thoughts you have," Swede said, interrupting Young Rocky.

"Guys talking like you do, just don't rate."

"Is that so, Hennessey? Well, lemme tell you that since I came here from Kansas City two years ago, I've dated up every broad worth dating in this neighborhood," Young Rocky said.

"Horse."

Charley Josephson, a silly-looking runt of seventeen, rushed in and asked what was biting Curley. They told him the joke they had pulled on Vinc. He said he'd been in the drug store at the corner, and Vinc had come in, red in the face and all excited, demanding G. O. 45 right away to rub on his lips.

"Curley hasn't got a marble in his bean," Young Rocky said as they all roared.

XXI

"Well, Conrad's a classic," Mose Levinsky, poolroom intellectual, said.

"What is a classic? Define it," said Big Syd.

"A classic is a book that lives."

"Now take a book like Robert Herrick's *The Common Lot,"* said Big Syd.

"It's a good book, but it isn't a classic," said Mose.

"Say, you guys act like you thought you were too good for the human race," said Red Kelly, passing them on his way from the can.

XXII

"I'm getting along," Hoppy Shanks said, lighting a cigarette.

"The job you got sounds O.K.," said Loeb.

"I make forty bucks a week. My room costs me six and my meals about four or five a week, because I'm cutting down on 'em. I'm salting fifteen and twenty every pay day," said Hoppy.

"That's pretty good. I wish I had a decent job."

"I worked hard for this one. I don't believe in loafing around like some of these guys do. When you're not working, you got time on your hands, and keep hanging around wondering what time it is, and what you'll do. Hell with that for this boy. I'm playin' the game smart."

"Say, Shanks, can you spare two bits? I'm flat, but I'll be able to pay you back this afternoon," Mush Joss asked.

"Haven't got it, Mush."

Mush passed to another group.

"That bastard hasn't worked since Noah got piped on the Ark," said Loeb.

"I wouldn't give him my dough. Him and McCarthy try and scrouge on me every time I see them."

XXIII

"Andy, are the Irish hundred-per-cent Americans?" asked Connell.

"No, because they believe in the Pope," Le Gare answered.

"All right, punk, keep religion out of it," ordered Red Kelly, who had come over to see why they were having such a good time razzing Andy.

"Say, if the Klan is so tough, why doesn't it come around looking for the Irish some night when it's out riding in nightshirts like kids on Halloween?" asked Darby Dan.

"They know when they're healthy," said Red.

"I'll bet Andy's old man has a horse looking like Sparkplug in Barney Google," commented Eddie Eastwood.

"Why don't you come around with the Klan if they're so damn tough?" Drennan said.

"If they did, you would all run home and hide behind your mother's apron string."

"Blah!"

Andy issued a blanket challenge to fight any one his size and age who was present.

"Gawan home, and come back on a kiddy-car, wearing your sister's nightgown and we'll fight you," sneered Drennan.

"Don't insult my sister!" Andy said, knocking Drennan down with a punch.

Drennan sat on the floor holding his jaw; Andy stood over him, defying him to get up and fight like a man. George the Greek told Andy to get out and not come back.

"Keep your old poolroom!" Andy yelled from the doorway in a sulk.

"No, Andy, take it along with you," Hennessey answered.

XXIV

"Paulie's dead!" Benny Taite yelled, rushing in excitedly, disrupting everything.

"Poor Paulie!" Studs said, next to Taite in the center of a stunned group.

"You know, years ago, I warned him to take care of himself, and not be a damn fool with the molls. But poor Paulie, every time he saw a skirt he lost his head and didn't know what he was doing," Red Kelly oracularly said.

"You know, I can't really believe that he's gone," said Studs.

"He was my old buddy," Hennessey said.

"A better lad never walked Fifty-eighth Street," Kelly said.

"Death is a funny thing, all right," Tommy Doyle said.

"We all get called at some time," Les said.

"Yeah, it's a funny thing. You never know who it's going to slap down next, and you never think much about it until one day, it puts your best friend out for the count," Red philosophized.

"It's awful, a tragedy," said Phil Rolfe.

"He had the priest, didn't he?" said Red.

"Shrimp said that a priest named Doneggan was there when he died," Taite said.

"We'll have to take up a collection for flowers," suggested Red.

"Jesus, he's one poor bastard who ended up behind the eight ball," Slug said.

"He can't be dead. Why he was so young, he never lived," said Bob Connell.

"Say, punk, how old are you?" asked Kelly.

"Sixteen," said Hennessey.

"Punks like you should be seen and not heard," Kelly said.

"Poor Paulie," sighed Les.

XXV

"Say let's give the Greek the finger on this game," said Lyman.

"O.K.," said Young Rocky.

Lyman aimed to shoot the fifteen ball for game in slop pool. He missed, and poked the ball in a pocket with his cue.

"Pay up!" he hollered.

"I will like hell," said Young Rocky.

"You lost," said Lyman.

"Gimme! Gimme!" said Mike to both of them.

"See him," said Lyman.

"That bastard is trying to cheat me. I won," said Young Rocky.

"Come ona, you fellahs, what's a the matter?" asked George, coming over.

"I won't pay. He shoved the game ball in with his cue."

"Pay up, you tight heel. I made it fair and square," said Lyman.

"You're a liar!" said Young Rocky.

"Don't call me a liar!" said Lyman.

"No! Well, it's double," said Young Rocky.

"Come on outside," said Lyman.

"Here! Pay, pay, pay!" said Mike.

"I'll brain you guys with a cue," threatened George.

Lyman and Young Rocky grabbed their coats, and dashed to the door, followed by an expectant group. At the door they turned and yelled in unison.

"Finger! Finger Greek!"

They laughed and walked away, arm-in-arm.

XXVI

"Quarter after one!" said Slug, standing with Mike at the window.

They heard the click of the cue balls from the back where Stan Simonsky was practicing. An elevated train rumbled. An automobile whizzed by. A heavy-footed, well-formed girl passed.

"How you like it?"

"Push-Push!" mumbled Mike.

VII

IT WAS *Saturday night. A cardboard picketing sign, letters turned downwards, lay in a corner of the small, disorderly bedroom. Mr. Le Gare looked at it. He felt like a dead man who had returned to life.*

Blacklisted!

No hotel in the city would hire him. He had been a waiter all his life. What work could he do now?

When he had told his family, their faces had dropped. They were discussing it now in the dining room. They had opposed his striking, picketing the Shrifton Hotel, and serving on the strike committee, acting as treasurer for the union. They said nothing; but their silence was more criticizing than anything they might say. He had supported them for years. Now they were irked, lest he be a burden to them. Well, by God, he wouldn't.

But what else could he do?

He had been sold out, and made the goat. Most of the other waiters had crawled back on their knees, begging for their jobs at any salary, under any condition. Yellow Scabs! They had betrayed him, betrayed the cause of the American working-man. They had betrayed themselves. The rankling of defeat and disappointment grew upon him until he cursed, using the filthiest words he knew.

The blacklist meant the dust heap, the garbage can, for a man his age. And his sons, daughter, wife, didn't understand; it was tragedy living with people who couldn't understand what a man was doing. Only Andy stuck by him. But Andy didn't have a very good brain, poor boy. Andy, whose brain was not so good, alone of his children had been loyal. But Andy did not understand either.

He wasn't a fool! He wasn't! He had been right. And they needn't have lost the strike, if only they had all shown unity, courage, heart. But they, foreigners, Syrian bus boys, fat Dutchmen, foreigners, hadn't been interested in strikes. They wanted Shrifton's crumbs. They wanted their tips. They had come over, not to make America their home, but to milk it as well as they could, and go back. They had their stocks, and some of them owned buildings. They served the rich, and tried to think that they were rich. All waiters, almost, did that; aped the rich, and thought that some day they would be rich. Scabs!

Suddenly, he laughed with twisted joy. They had sold themselves for nothing. Girls were cheaper and most of them were on the blacklist too.

He could see it so clear. They could have won if only . . . Some day all the American working-men would strike, and even the waiters would have to then, and then too . . . they would win, and men like himself wouldn't be made goats. He clenched his weak fists, wanting to fight back. But there was no fighting left in him.

Others before him had been blacklisted, and had known his bitterness. Others had been betrayed. But it wouldn't, couldn't, always be thus. All that bitterness and defeat would not die. It would gnaw the souls of men. It would fester. It would spit poison. It was only with bitterness and poison that the working-men, even the waiters, would beat the Shriftons. He vowed that his defeat would not be in vain. He would pass the bitterness of it on, help to make for that day when he would be dead, but when the bitterness of working-men would rise above the brim, and then, the Shriftons would be blacklisted. He felt a brief exultation. It drowsed and died.

"Hello, dad," Andy said.

He looked at his son whose brain was not very good.

"Don't worry, dad. Maybe I'll get a job next week and help out."

Tears grew in Mr. Le Gare's eyes.

Chapter Seven

I

HIS LIFE was much the same as it had been last week or last year. It was a week now since his twenty-first birthday, and his life was much the same as it had been last week or a year ago.

The old man owned a new building on Michigan, near the Carter School, and the Lonigans lived on the third floor south. Studs emerged from the building and walked along, taking loose, easy strides, strides that he considered self-confident.

He had made his decision while shaving. Now, it caused him to have a sense of impending unpleasantness. It would be a wasted evening, and tomorrow he would regret having let a night slip by him. But that wasn't the right attitude to show. Sometimes, he wished that he wasn't a Catholic, and didn't have to meet the responsibilities of a Catholic. But that wasn't the right attitude either.

The Carter playgrounds surrounding the school were rimmed by an iron picket fence. Walking along, Studs had an impulse to touch each picket as he had used to do. But he walked along like a guy of twenty-one who wasn't a clown. He paused at a spot along the fence which stood almost opposite the third base of the indoor diamond in the northeast corner of the grounds.

Remembering, remembering many things, he nodded. And Paulie was dead now. He had never thought that on his twenty-first birthday, first day of manhood, that his old friend, Paulie, would die. Life was funny and unpredictable.

He looked at the rambling, tan-and-gray school building that stood in the center of the grounds facing south. The sky over it was red. It all made him lonesome. The sky red, the empty buildings, the playground he had known so well as a kid, with nobody now in it. He looked at the batter's box on the diamond. Paulie had stood there batting right-handed in a piggy game, cursing Young Coady for twirling the ball on the day he'd cleaned Red Kelly. He could almost hear Paulie's voice:

"Come on, you goddamn punk, or I'll fling the bat at you!"

And right inside the fence from where he stood was the spot where they'd had the fight. Paulie had placed the stick on his shoulder and

Red had knocked it off, and they'd tangled. And the fists of Studs Lonigan had won him respect.

Suddenly, he was lonesome, lonesome to be a boy again.

He looked at his clenched fist. It was pretty big, considering his size. He was only about five six, but he was broad, and he was still tough, and able to spot a lot of guys on weight and take them.

But still he couldn't get himself to believe that Paulie was dead. He had stood right inside the playground, and Studs could almost see him, mushy-faced, a bit fat, big fanny, wearing a red-trimmed, gray baseball shirt. The first to go, and all shot to pieces with clap, and drink, and dissipation.

Poor Paulie.

Studs lit a cigarette. He wondered why the good guys like Paulie went, and the louses like Weary Reilley didn't. He shrugged his shoulders and told himself he ought to snap out of it. But when he looked at the playground, with the sky red over it, and remembered so many things, and thought that Paulie was dead, out in Calvary Cemetery, he was lonesome, lonesome to be a kid again. He walked on towards the corner, along a sidewalk he'd walked with Paulie many times. Even though he was sad about Paulie, he couldn't help being a bit proud, because he was twenty-one and strong, and yes, tomorrow in the football game, he'd show his strength. He'd done his drinking and jazzing too, and still, he was strong and tough. He was the real stuff.

He'd never realized that he was growing up and changing. There had been signs on his body, but they, too, had come gradually. Each day he had grown stronger, bigger, with more hair on him. He had changed, though, slowly day by day, gotten to hanging around the poolroom, worked with his old man, and then, well, he wasn't doing the things he'd done as a kid. Now he was a man. Well, he was! He felt a little goofy, remembering how, before coming out, he'd looked at himself in the mirror, and assured himself that he was a man. But he was. And there were many years ahead of him, drinking, jazzing, poker-games, plenty of things. And he had dough. With the birthday present from his old man, he now had four hundred bucks in his own name in the bank. He was pretty goddamn well off.

A girl came toward him. He liked her looks. He had confidence in his walk. He was well dressed too: gray Stetson, conservative gray topcoat, well-fitting sixty-five dollar Oxford gray suit, good cut, the trousers wide enough so that he didn't look like a hick, but not ringing bell bottoms. The girl passed him. He passed her, and turned over Fifty-eighth Street.

But the evening was all wasted, because he had made his decision and would stick to it.

He walked towards the poolroom thinking about a lot of things. He saw young Cooley, and motioned him over, calling him a dope.

"Droopy, when you gonna let it alone?" he asked, not knowing why he did it, and laughing to see the hurt, shocked look on the kid's face.

He walked along. He had let himself get into the wrong attitude. Well, he didn't have to go tonight. But he did. He didn't like to admit it to himself, but he was afraid. Well, it wasn't yellow. It was a different kind of fear. It was fear for his soul if something did happen to him.

He just felt all off kilter. Maybe afterwards, he would feel different.

II

Studs had what Father Gilhooley always called a feeling of gratification. Red, Tommy, and the guys had kept trying to talk him into going with them, and he had resisted all temptation.

He walked up towards the church, taking his time. There wouldn't be a crowd there. He thought of himself as having already gone to confession. He saw himself saying his penance, saw himself kneeling in the confessional, talking through the screen to Father Doneggan, running through the catalogue of his sins, commandment by commandment. He tried to put himself into a contrite mood. He wanted his act of contrition after confession tonight to be a perfect act of contrition, as if it were his last confession.

Studs walked slowly; nervous, he lit a cigarette.

The thought of Paulie dead out there in the cemetery still hung on him. The thought of another, a waiting grave out in Calvary Cemetery, hung more heavily.

Already this football season, he had read of five or six different fellows being killed in football games. When he had been a kid, he remembered having read about how a fellow named Albert at the U of C had been killed. In Thursday's paper there had been something about a fifteen-year-old kid who'd had his skull fractured.

A voice within Studs, as if it were his conscience, kept assuring him that he was yellow.

He seemed to keep seeing that kid he had read about in Thursday's paper, before him, prostrate, moaning, blood from his cracked head dropping to mix in the dirt, moaning, death-moans persisting, ringing out as if in prophecy of his death, and of the death of everyone that he knew. He seemed to see Studs Lonigan in place of the kid with crushed head. He seemed to hear the deathmoans of Studs Lonigan.

He walked slowly.

The night was crisp. A mist swung down low. It was not the kind of a night to think of death. It was the kind of a night to make one want to live.

He paused at the curb on Fifth-ninth, to let a truck swing around the corner. He had a crazy impulse, that he couldn't understand, to dive in front of the truck.

He crossed the street, walked on lazily.

He tried to examine his conscience. He hadn't broken the first commandment. He had taken the name of God in vain, fifteen, no, twenty or twenty-five times a day, he guessed. Third commandment. He hadn't missed Mass. His thoughts wandered. He realized that he was lonesome. He wondered what he could do after confession. He didn't want to go home. He figured he hadn't better go to a show. It might cause him to have the wrong kind of thoughts after confession. He wondered what the bunch was doing.

He thought of himself, out on the football field for tomorrow's game. The kickoff. Studs Lonigan running the first kickoff back a hundred and three yards. He wasn't going to be hurt either. But suppose he was. Well, he was going to confession so he wouldn't be. He'd be afraid to enter that game tomorrow if he didn't, because he had that kind of a feeling.

He got back to the third commandment, and walked slowly towards St. Patrick's Church.

In the church, a low-ceilinged structure of boxed-in gloom, he took a seat in the rear pew on the left-hand side. He bowed his head, and said a few prayers to the Blessed Virgin in preparation for an examination of conscience. Up forwards, near the side exit door, a woman arose, and waddled a few steps forwards to the plushed entrance of Father Gilhooley's confessional. Behind him, the door of Father Doneggan's box clattered slightly as it was closed. He heard a street car passing, and then the whistle of a railroad engine.

He riveted his eyes in a stare on the altar that was hallowed back in the center. He watched the flickering altar light above it. A man arose from the front, center, and did a St. Vitus dance down the center aisle, coming with twisted and painful slowness, dragging along the ruins of a paralyzed body. It was Joe, the paper-man. Studs knew him. He was all right, and not goofy to talk to, although he looked completely off because of the deadened nerves in the left side of his face. He came to church every morning, and received at least once a week. Poor bastard, he lived somehow on a few pennies made peddling the *New World*. Studs felt sorry for him.

The fellows had talked about going to the State and Congress. He wished . . . but a burlesque show was an occasion of sin. Couldn't be thinking of them and planning to go to confession. Not the right attitude. . . . Oh, my God, I am heartily sorry for having offended Thee, and I detest all my sins. . . . He heard the bang of a door from the confessional box of Father Roney, on the right-hand side of the church, just in front of the choir box.

For no reason at all, he glanced up at the low ceiling. He had to get himself into the right attitude. Feeling contrition was hard. He had to feel it deeply, with his whole heart and his whole soul. Oh, my God, I am heartily, heartily sorry. . . .

He had taken God's name in vain twenty-five or thirty times a day. He had been late for Mass on his own account, but they were only venial sins because he'd gotten in before the Consecration.

He looked behind him. Four and five people in the line before Father Doneggan's box. He turned and glanced off from his right towards Father Roney's box, five and six people in the two lines.

An old man walked down from the altar, where he had been praying, and on back towards the rear, his heels rat-tatting on the rubber aisle.

A feeling of fear came over him, fear of being injured in the football game, fear with a sudden realization that hell was a place of torments, endless torments in a fire that never ended, the monotony of its hissing flames, a sudden fear of life. He wanted to be outside in the fall night. He wanted to get it over with. He couldn't get himself to arise and join one of the waiting lines before Father Doneggan's confessional box. He heard the swinging doors of the entrance, and heels on the marble steps leading from the vestibule. He heard the closing of a door in back of him, then, the closing of a door of Father Roney's confessional. He had violated the fifth commandment by anger towards others, maybe . . . maybe . . . maybe. . . . His eyes were again attracted by the ceaslessly glowing altar light. He had violated the fifth commandment by anger. . . .

Suddenly, he found that he had lapsed into dirty thoughts. He labored through an Act of Contrition, trying to make it a perfect one. A feeling of death was in him, and went from him to the gloomy church, and the autumn night without. He just couldn't seem to be able to get through the commandments.

Suddenly, he just raced through them, estimating his sins, in violation of each commandment, and arose. He took a place in line, his back to the altar, before the left-hand door of Father Doneggan's box. There were four ahead of him. He waited.

The door on the other side opened. Art Hahn, a tall, slim fellow, blond, several years older than Studs, emerged. A woman entered the box. Art smiled at Studs, as he passed him, down the aisle, and Studs pointed towards the exit door. Art nodded. Father Doneggan was quick in everything he did. Studs soon got inside the stale-smelling box. The slide opened, and he saw, dimly, the blond priest inside the wire screen. He confessed his sins, said the Act of Contrition, was absolved and received a penance of nine Our Fathers and nine Hail Marys.

Outside, Studs and Art lit cigaretttes and went north along Indiana Avenue, the street along which Studs had, in his day, always come to and from school. The past came back into his thoughts. The day that Paulie had been licked by Johnny O'Brien. The day in winter that he had clipped a truck driver on the ear with a snowball and they had all been shagged. He felt as if tomorrow he would be going to communion with the boys' sodality at the eight o'clock Mass. But what the hell!

Studs asked Art how he happened to be going to confession.

"I'd never think of playing football without receiving Communion. You never know what's going to happen to you in a prairie football game like that one we've got scheduled tomorrow. And I always play safe."

"Yeah," said Studs, feeling good that he wasn't the only guy who'd felt that way.

"Why did you go—same reason?" asked Art.

"Oh, I just thought it was about time that I'd receive. And then I thought I'd do it for Paulie Haggerty."

"Say, that reminds me, I ought to be offering up my Communion for Paulie tomorrow too," said Art.

Studs suddenly recalled that he had intended to make it a general confession for his whole life. And it had skipped his mind. He was afraid all over again, because of that slip. He saw himself killed in the football game. But he was offering his Communion up for Paulie and Paulie in Purgatory, if he was there, would pray for him in return.

Jesus, what the hell was happening to him, getting like he was.

He went down to the Elevated to get a Sunday-morning paper, vowing to himself that he wouldn't stop at the poolroom. He did, and found Bill Donoghue there. He told Bill he'd gone to confession, and they played several games of straight pool. Studs won. Then they had coffee in fat Gus the Greek's restaurant, between the Elevated and

Prairie Avenue. They talked about the old days when they were kids at St. Patrick's. Studs had a good Saturday night, and got home about a quarter to twelve. He told his old man that he should tell his mother not to get him breakfast, he had gone to confession. Lonigan beamed.

VIII

WORRY did not sit well upon a jolly, red, robust face like Mrs. Sheehan's. But she had a premonition. Last night in a dream, she had seen her Arnold lying dead in a football uniform. Oh, if only sons would heed their mothers, there would be less trouble, fewer broken-hearted mothers in this world. And how much happier a world it would be!

She remembered that Saturday in Rockford; how she had sighed with such relief when Arnold came home and said he had played his last game with the high-school team. She had had her premonitions in those days, too, when he would be playing, and she knew that he would have been maimed for life or killed, but for her prayers. A boy could only trifle so much with the Grace of God, though. She felt it in her that Arnold would be carried home, perhaps dead.

She took a chair by the parlor window, and prayed. She looked out across the street at the leafless trees in the graying October Sunday. Down at the other end of the park, he was playing; perhaps at the very moment, he might be injured, dead. She knew, knew in her mother's way, that something would happen to her oldest boy.

Arnold was her favorite child, her first-born. Her four girls gave her no trouble. They were well-raised, and she could trust them; only sometimes she worried that they couldn't have more clothes. But their father was only a motorman. The youngest lad, Arthur, he was an altar boy, a bright, fine, innocent lad who always obeyed. And Horace, he worked in a gambling house, but he was steady, and brought money home to her regularly, and he didn't drink like Arnold. Arnold, her baby, he worried her. He was the most generous of her children, when he had it to give, with a heart of pure gold. Only he had gotten in with the wrong sort. With the Grace of God, he would settle down.

Her premonitions would not down, and her prayers were not completely self-comforting. Her's was a mother's agony.

Chapter Eight

I

WATCHING himself in the mirror, Studs hitched up his football pants, carefully arranging the cotton hip pads around his sides. Wished he had better ones. Wouldn't be much protection from a boot in the ribs. He touched the schimmels under his blue jersey, and put on his black helmet. Every inch a football player!

He thought of himself going out to play with old street pants, a jersey, and football shoes. Dressed that way, tackling so hard he'd knock them cuckoo; jumping up ready to go on, no matter how hard he was slammed. No use to be senseless and play without sufficient padding. Only it was swell thinking of being reckless that way, having the crowd recognize such gameness.

He flexed and unflexed his arm muscles. Even with the drinking and carousing he'd done these last couple of years, he was still pretty hard and tough. He slapped his guts. They were hard enough, too, and there was no alderman yet, or not enough anyway to be noticed. And there never would be, because he'd take care of himself before that ever happened. He'd never have a paunch like his old man had. Iron Man Lonigan! The bigger they are, the harder they fall. He lit a cigarette and sat on the bed, thinking proudly of his body, good and strong, even if he was small; powerful football shoulders, good for fighting. And this afternoon he'd prove that it was a good body, and that there was heart and courage inside of it.

But there wouldn't be any girls out there for him to be playing for. Other guys had girls. Wished he had a girl, Lucy, a girl coming out only to see him play . . . Goofy! . . . But he still loved Lucy even if he hadn't seen here in about four years. And if she was coming out there to see him play, because she loved him, he would play much better, and instead of being in it just for the fun and the glory, and to show them all what he was made of, he'd be playing for her also. And he wanted to. Christ sake, he was getting like a clown, all mush inside. He tried to laugh at himself; it was forced.

Smells of the cooking Sunday dinner came tantalizingly from the kitchen. His mother came to the bedroom door, and said that she had a bite ready for him.

"I can't! I'm going to play football," he snapped in uncontrolled exasperation.

"I certainly don't think much of a game that deprives you of your food," she replied.

Jesus Christ! Couldn't she understand anything!

She nagged and persuaded. He got up, and walked towards the door, with her following, still wanting him to eat. He said that he couldn't play with a belly full of food, and as she dipped her hand in the holy water fount on the wall, and showered him, he slammed the door. The father, hearing him, called that he wouldn't have such vulgar language used around the home, but Studs was gone.

He went down the steps two and three at a time, thinking why they always had to be like that, never open to reason and sense, wanting you to do whatever they wished in everything. Felt like leaving home, and living in a room by himself; some day he'd have to, if they didn't keep from trying to run everything he did.

It was humid and sunless. He liked the click of his cleats on the sidewalk. He felt so good, and in such condition, that he had an impulse to run. He checked himself, and took his time. Studs Lonigan was going to use his noodle, and conserve his energy. He was a wise guy, and in everything in life he was going to be that way, always with a little stuff left in him for a pinch.

Jim Clayburn's dude father came along, dressed in snappy gray, wearing a derby, and tapping a cane on the sidewalk. With his gray bush of hair, his face looked soft, almost like a woman's. Must have been something of a sissy and teacher's pet in his own day at school, just as Jim had been. He bowed stiffly to Studs, and Studs nodded, hoping he noticed the football outfit. Jim was studying law now, clerking for a measly ten or fifteen bucks a week. Well, by the time Clayburn, with all his studying and kill-joy stuff was in the dough, Studs Lonigan would be running his old man's business, and be in the big dough too.

He saw Tubby Connell and Nate Klein flinging passes in the street in front of the poolroom. Nate muffed one, and Studs told him to get a bushel basket. He lit a cigarette and laughed at Nate's scenery; an old-fashioned square black helmet that must have come down from Walter Eckersall's day; tight green jersey with holes in the sleeves; pants so big that he swam in them; shoes turned up at the toes because of their size. He looked more closely at the shoes; they were spiked baseball ones. He told Nate they'd never let him play in those, because he might cut somebody to ribbons. Tubby said that Klein was wearing them to show that he had the Fifty-eighth Street fighting spirit.

"This ain't tiddledy-winks; the guy I cut up will be a Monitor, and that's his tough tiddy," Nate said, hard-boiled.

He and Tubby disregarded Studs' advice to save themselves, and went on fooling around with the ball. Studs turned his back to them, and let his hands fall on his hips; his helmet was over his right elbow, and his blond hair was a trifle curly. His broad face revealed absorption. A middle-aged guy with a paunch doped along; Studs hoped that the guy had noticed him, wished he was young like he was, and able to go out and play a game of football, still full of the vim and vitality of youth. A quick feeling of contrition came over him. Suppose he should get hurt? Suppose he should never come back alive? His mother would always remember how he had slammed the door in her face. But damn it, couldn't they be reasonable?

"Hell, Flannel Mouth! How's the brother?" asked Studs, as Young Fat Malloy showed up.

"He'll be there, and he was saying that if you guys lose your first game of the season, he was going to kick your tails around the block to hell and gone. And don't think he can't! He may be a little runt, but let me tell you, Hugo was one of the toughest sergeants they ever had in the army."

"I know it," Studs said, thinking that it was another case of a good little man.

"Look at Klein, that crazy hebe! He's liable to break his neck trying to catch that football!" Fat said.

"Yeah, he's that way because he got gassed in the war."

"But he has guts. You know, Studs, you guys ought to have a crack team this year. And with a good coach like Hugo, you oughtn't to lose a game."

Studs nodded. He thought that maybe, this year, they would all get to working together like a well-oiled machine, and then, next season they could join the Mid-West League. He saw himself flashing through that semi-pro circuit like a comet, and getting himself signed up to play in the backfield with Paddy Driscoll on the Chicago Cardinals.

There was excitement; a wild fling of Nate's nearly hit a baby being wheeled along. The father crabbed like hell, but finally pushed his buggy on. Nate told Studs that wise guys like that bird needed to be punched full of holes.

More players came around and a gang of them started over to the football field in Washington Park.

II

Wearing a large white sweater, and his old army breeches, bow-legged Coach Hugo Zip Malloy stood with arms folded, his tough mug intent, as he watched the Fifty-eighth Street Cardinals clown through signal practice.

"Come on over here, you birds, and sit on your cans a minute. That's what they're for," he yelled, regally waving his short right arm.

The players dragged over and planked themselves down, facing him. Strangers collected to gape at them. He glared at the strangers.

"Everybody not associated with the team, please fade!" he commanded; some obeyed; others dropped backwards a few feet, and then commenced to inch forwards again. Courageous gawkers stood in their tracks.

Kenny Kilarney suddenly appeared, and did a take-off on a college cheer leader:

We ain't rough!
We ain't tough!
But oh! . . . are we determined?

"Say, Monkey Face!" Coach Hugo said to Kenny.

"No hope for him," Bill Donoghue said.

"Now I want you birds to listen to what I tell you!"

"But say, Hugo?" Bill Donoghue called.

"That's my name."

"Would you mind taking the cigar out of your mouth so we can see you?"

"Sonnyboy, the playground is on the other side of the drive, in back of me," Coach Hugo replied.

"Another thing, coach? Don't you think we ought to give Klein a rising vote? He hasn't been hurt yet this season?"

"Jesus, wouldn't the squirrels make mince-pie out of you?" Coach Hugo said, darting a no-hope look at Bill.

"Now, when the clowns get finished pulling the whiskers off their jokes, I'll talk. . . . And by the way, can't you guys leave the cigarettes alone for a minute. It takes wind to win a football game, and you don't get wind eating them coffin nails!"

"You tell 'em coach, I stutter," said Shrimp Haggerty, lurching drunkenly into their midst; he was thin and sallow, and dogged out in classy clothes. He wore a black band on his top-coat sleeve.

"Haggerty! The other team needs a couple of mudguards. Go on over there," Coach Hugo said.

"Now that the children have finished throwing spitballs around, teacher will talk. . . . Haggerty, get the hell out of here before I have to throw your pieces away! . . ."

Haggerty saw that Coach Hugo was really sore. He staggered away, singing.

"All right, you birds, keep your dirty ears open! I ain't gonna repeat myself! You're goin' out there now for your first crack of the season, and you're gonna play a man's game. There's only one way to play it. Play hard! Hard! Get the other guy, before he gets you! Knock him down! Let them drag him out! If you don't, you might be the unlucky chump that's dragged out. And if any of you birds are carried off that gridiron, cold, don't expect me to break down and weep for you like I was your old lady! Because you won't get knocked cuckoo if you keep your heads up, and play hard! It's the soft guy that gets knocked silly in this game. And if there's any soft babies on this team, the sooner they get it in the neck, the better off they will be, and we too! You guys got to go in there and hit hard, hit often, and every time you hit, make the guy you hit think he's collided with a battleship. Don't worry about giving the ambulance drivers work; they got wives and kiddies to support, and need it. . . ."

"Hey, Hugo, what undertaker's giving you a rakeoff?" interrupted Arnold Sheehan.

"Sheehan, step into the second grade. You're too bright a boy for first. . . . And now, you birds, you're goin' in that football game in about a minute. If you want to win it, you got to do it yourself. I can't win it for you. That's your job, and if you want this game, you'll have to get it by fighting (he slammed his right fist demonstratively into his left palm). I watched you guys go through signal practice. You stunk! If you go into this game like that, it'll be like the Fort Dearborn massacre. And get me, if you guys don't fight, you can get an old lady to coach you. I won't. All right, snap into it. And, oh, yes, a final word. If any bird on this other team starts dirty work . . . give him the works!"

The team arose. Nate tore forwards. The others walked slowly towards the football field, Coach Hugo making up the rear.

"Say, coach, that's a ripe husky bunch of boys you got there. Tell 'em to try center rushes, and they'll win as easy as taking candy from a baby. Now, when I was a kid. . . ."

"Say, fellow, will you do me a favor?"

"Sure, glad to, coach!"

"All right. See that automobile drive? Well, walk across it, and keep on going until you lose yourself in the lagoon."

Coach Hugo roughly yelled gangway, as he went through a crowd, and stepped over the ropes. He clapped his hands together, and yelled to his team:

"All right, you guys, show me if you got any guts in your veins."

III

C
Nate Klein

LG
Harold Dowson

RG
Carroll Dowson

LT
Red Kelly

RT
Dan Donoghue

FB
Hink Weber

LE
Weary Reilley

LHB
Arnold Sheehan

RHB
Art Hahn

RE
Jim Nolan

QB
Studs Lonigan

waited, while the ball was put into position for the kick. It fell off the little mound on the forty-yard line four times, so a Monitor stretched himself out and held it in position.

Referee Charlie Bathcellar, wearing an astrakhan coat and a new derby, importantly signalled the two captains. Studs felt a thrill of pride as he signalled the readiness of his team; hundreds of people were watching, saw that he was captain. The whistle blew. A thin fellow in street pants and an old red jersey booted the ball on a line. Studs muffed it. The Fifty-eighth Street Cardinals formed disorganized interference. Studs scooped the ball up on the go, and thundered forwards, head down as if he were bucking the line, knees pumping. One Monitor clutched at his left sleeve. Another pulled at his pants from behind. A third dragged at his jersey from the right side. A fourth leaped to make a flying tackle around his ears. The whistle declared the ball dead. Nate Klein and a Monitor player were in the center of the field, bucking each other with arms folded together chest high.

The Cardinals lackadaisically took position in a balanced line formation. The defensive Monitor line crowded together, both tackles kneeling down inside of Dan Donoghue and Red Kelly. Hink Weber told Kelly not to play standing up. Red knelt down. Hink told him to crouch low so that he could charge. Red gave Hink a soreheaded look, but squatted in a weak position.

"Signals," Studs yelled huskily, leaning with hands on knees, eyes on the ground.

Studs tossed a lateral pass to Arnold Sheehan, who went through a mile-wide hole at right tackle. The fellow in the red jersey, Jewboy Schwartz, plugged up the hole. Arnold started to pivot, and Jewboy Schwartz got him while off balance. Three Monitors piled on, and Arnold groaned.

"Watch that piling on!" Weary yelled, rushing up.

"We ain't piling on!" Jake Schaeffer, the big Monitor captain, re torted.

"Well, he was down, wasn't he?"

"He might have crawled."

Hink Weber drew Weary back to avoid a fight.

Arnold limped, his face twisted with pain. Nate angrily asked if they had played dirty, because if they did—the works. Taking short, ziggedy steps, Coach Hugo appeared. Arnold was helped to the side-lines, and as he sat down, Fat Malloy told him that he'd played a swell game.

Weary Reilley switched to left halfback, and Tubby Connell took Weary's end. On the next play, Studs slapped the ball into Hink's guts as Hink thundered at center, hitting like a ton of bricks. He fell over Nate Klein. Getting up, he just looked at Nate and shook his head. Nate said he had been holding out his man, hadn't he? Weary Reilley was tackled by Jewboy Schwartz after a three-yard gain. When the players picked themselves up, Nate Klein was stretched out, ostensibly hurt. Coach Hugo strode importantly onto the field, followed by Fat Malloy, who lugged a water bucket. Fat rushed to Nate, and doused him.

"For Jesus sake!" Nate protested.

"Well, you were out, weren't you?"

Nate groaned weakly, rose to tottering feet, and moved dazedly, with his head hanging as if his neck were broken. But he told Coach Hugo he would stick in the game and get those bastards. Coach Hugo called it the old ginger. Nate floundered into position over the ball, and his face became a mirror of jungle ferocity.

Hink Weber punted down the field, and it was the Monitor's ball.

Studs took a defensive position, twenty yards behind the scrimmage line, and placed his hands on his hips. People in the crowd might notice how collected he seemed to be. He might get his chance to be spectacular. A fellow might break through, and Studs would stave off a touchdown with a flying tackle. Jewboy Schwartz started around the end, outran Tubby, who was boxed in, dodged Weary's lunge with a side leap, graceful as an antelope, and tore towards Studs. Studs dashed forwards a few paces, arms encircled outwards and tensed himself. Schwartz came, fast. Five yards from Studs, Jewboy Schwartz performed a feint with his right foot. Studs lunged. Schwartz would have been free had he not slipped, and Studs, in his lunge, caught Schwartz's foot. Jewboy dragged Studs along, and slipped free, but Dan Donoghue was up to make the tackle.

They patted Studs' back for such nice work. Studs' glow of pride quickly faded. He had been outsmarted, and the fellow would have been free to make a touchdown if he hadn't slipped. He was only wearing street shoes. With cleats, he wouldn't have slipped. Studs waited in back of the scrimmage line. Next time, the guy might make a monkey of him. If he was playing the other half, he might not break through as easily because Jim Nolan and Dan were better than Red and Tubby. Studs' confidence seemed gone. The Jew was too speedy and clever for him. No, goddamn it, he'd leave his feet next time before that feint! Nail him! Studs moved forward a few feet with the pass from center. Dan smeared the play for a loss. The teams lined up and Nate staggered into his place as defensive center.

The game see-sawed through the first quarter, slow, argumentative, marred by fumbles. On the last play of the period, Studs took a punt, ran forwards, swinging the ball from side to side for effect, running forwards, thinking he was making a long run, hearing cheering from the side, and . . . Jewboy Schwartz dove into him, his shoulder smashing Studs in the solar plexus. Studs went down with a thud, and lost the ball. His guts pained; he gasped. He slowly picked himself up, a sick expression on his face. The whistle saved him from having to call time out.

IV

Early in the second quarter, Jewboy Schwartz broke loose, and fleeted down the side line. Studs ran over, left his feet, smashed through the air as Schwartz sidestepped, and picked up speed again, rolled over offside four times in a histrionic effort to show the crowd that his try had been fearless and desperate, sat up and yelled to get him. Schwartz was over for a touchdown.

Studs' shame and disappointment was lessened a little when he heard Tommy Doyle call that it was a good try. The kick for extra point was missed. Hink and Weary walked by Studs, into position. Hink said that they would have to slow the Jew up with some rough tackling. Weary declared that if he got his guts slapped a couple of times, he'd slow down because all Jews were yellow. Nate ran awkwardly to Studs and started bawling him out. Studs told Nate to freeze it. Nate megaphoned to all of them that they had to fight now. Studs waited, hands on knees, worrying himself, forgetting the crowd, thinking that they had to win, had to stop that fast Jew.

The Cardinals pepped up and shouted after taking the ball to the Monitor thirty-yard line on four plays. They were going over now, but on the next play Art Hahn went through tackle, and he was stopped by Red Kelly who stood in his way. Nate yelled to Red that it wasn't a sanitarium, and Red told him shut up while he was all together. Weary yelled to can the beefing and play football. Studs flung a pass. Jewboy Schwartz picked it neatly out of the air, and ran in the clear. Studs, playing safety, went for him without confidence, left his feet in a blind dive, opened his eyes as he encircled the Jew's slippery, powerful thighs, clenched them, tumbled him down. Hearing a cheer, he realized it had been neat work. He jumped up, forgetting that it had been lucky in the glory of being cheered. He walked casually away. The thrill of leaving his feet, rushing through the air, hitting him, dragging him down so nicely, lingered. He wanted to do it again. Weary patted his back, and called it a sweet tackle in the most genuine words he'd uttered to Studs since their fight. Studs felt good again. But, boy, that Jew was built like steel. Light and fast, and hard as nails. They'd need a club, or a tank to put him out. Still, the memory of that tackle, a split second of keen release and thrill, hung with him.

Jim Nolan recovered on a bad pass from the Monitor center. Hink Weber took the ball on the first play, and ran forty yards down the left side of the field for a touchdown. He kicked the point after touchdown. The Fifty-eighth Street Cardinals talked to each other like happy children.

Jewboy Schwartz took the kickoff. His own men got in his way, and Weary tackled him. There was a pile on, and Weary jammed his knee into Schwartz's groin. They got off, and Schwartz lay there, moaning and rolling, with both hands gripping his crotch. Schaeffer rushed to Reilley and told him to cut it out. Weary snarled back that he didn't like people to talk with their tongues; fists spoke a harder language. Hink pulled Weary aside, and again avoided a fight.

Jewboy Schwartz tried to play. When he had to punt, his kick went weakly to Art Hahn. He limped off the field, and at the half, the Fifty-eighth Street Cardinals led 7 to 6.

V

Between halves, Coach Hugo Zip Malloy told his team they weren't hitting hard enough. He promised to buy a drink for every one who laid out a Monitor so that the guy stayed out. He told Austin McAuliffe to go in at quarter and unleash their trick plays, because Austin, a thin, weak-faced, red-haired chap, was a scientific player. Studs took Art Hahn's half, Arnold was to go back in, and Weary was to play end in place of Tubby. Bill Donoghue was to take Kelly's tackle.

Jewboy Schwartz was back and returned the kickoff twenty yards. Weary grouped the team together after the play, and said this time, they had to put that Jew out for keeps. Studs took his position at defensive half, keen to be more in the game, tackling, running the ends, bucking the line, smearing passes. Only they couldn't let the Jew get loose. Austin was a poor safety man. But they'd stop him dead now. He waited for the play, suddenly wishing he'd gone to high school and been a star like Dan had. Studs smashed in with the play, but Dan nabbed Schwartz behind the line. Schaeffer carried the ball on the next play. Arnold Sheehan was clipped from behind, and Schaeffer got twenty yards before Hink sliced into him from the side. Arnold went out with a wrenched knee, and Art Hahn came on the field. Nolan recovered a fumble. Austin called a trick play. The ball was passed from Austin to Studs to Hahn to Nolan, and eighteen yards were lost. Austin called another trick play, a quarterback sneak, and he circled backwards, running wide. Tacklers closed in on him. He outran them to the sideline for a twenty-five yard loss. Hink punted.

Schwartz took the ball on first down and came flying through tackle without interference. Dodging to break into the open, he was hit simultaneously by Studs, Weary, and Hink. He arose groggy.

"They'll be picking up the kike's pieces now," Weary said, walking off with Studs.

Schwartz started a wide end run. Nolan smashed in, and made a flying tackle, catching Jewboy by the heels to dump him on his head. The crowd could hear the thud. He lay unconscious. He was revived and insisted on playing. Jewboy dropped back to punt. Weary and Nate Klein broke through, and piled into him blocking the kick. He got up with a bloody nose, and a hand slightly scratched from Nate's spikes. There was a row, but Hink Weber sent Nate to the sidelines to borrow another pair of shoes.

Hink took the ball through the line. Schwartz dove for him, and was stiff-armed on the chin, his head jerking back as he flopped. Hink scored another touchdown.

Hink kicked off to Schwartz. Five Cardinals hit him. He was out again, bleeding from the mouth, his upper lip crusted with congealed blood from his nose. A Monitor yelled that he was dead. Jake Schaeffer helped carry him off and walked back onto the field in tears, vowing he'd get the sonsofbitches. Weary recovered a Monitor fumble, and Schaeffer piled on him.

"What's the idea?" Weary challenged, arising.

"Play football, and quit squawking. You half killed my buddy!"

"And I'll kill you too, kike!" Weary said, clipping Schaeffer on the jaw. Before he knew what hit him, Schaeffer got two more clouts, and went down.

"Get up and fight, louse!" Weary sneered, hovering over him.

Both teams started swinging. Spectators and substitutes rushed onto the field. The three cops, at the game, struggled in vain. One of them whistled loudly. Another fled to call for reenforcements. Hugo Malloy parted through the crowd with a billy. Three Monitors went for Weary. He laid two of them cold with punches, and picked the third up and tossed him four yards away. Studs caught him as he stumbled, and he went down. A fellow stepped on his face. Nate Klein kicked him, and was smacked in the eye from behind. He slunk towards the edge of the crowd. Weary shoved about, swinging when he had to, trying to find Schaeffer. He caught him, and let him have both guns. A billy came down on his shoulder. He wheeled around, getting force, and belted the guy with the billy, flush in the mouth, closed in, and gave him the knee. He kicked the guy for good measure.

A park cop grabbed Weary. He wriggled loose, slipped behind him, and gave him a rabbit punch. A bruiser, guard on the Monitors, slugged wildly at Studs. Studs ducked, in desperation at the guy's size, and swung blindly, landing in the guts. The ham's guard dropped, and he whittled down to Studs' size. Studs let an uppercut go from his heels and caught the fellow under the chin. The bruiser fled. Slug Mason came into action, pumping with both fists. He caught two guys, and crashed their heads together.

"The cops!" somebody yelled.

The cry was taken up. The mob separated in all directions. Police reenforcements came across the park, and clubs were swung, as everybody ran. Studs, running, passed a group carrying Schwartz.

"You bastards, come down to Forty-seventh Street!"

Studs turned and thumbed his nose. An opened pocketknife zizzed by his ears. He ran.

"Swell work, Studs!" said Fat Malloy ranging alongside of him. Shots in the distance were heard.

Studs came out of the park at Fifty-sixth Street, out of breath, his side paining.

VI

The poolroom was crowded. Rumors spread quickly. Talk went of arrests, broken heads, people dead. Studs passed along from one excited group to another, liking it all, the praise, the talk, the excitement. He came upon Arnold Sheehan, who had a sprained ankle, a twisted knee, and a shiner. He had been sitting down, and when the fighting came close, he had arisen and hobbled along the ropes. It had been just his luck to get sloughed in the eye. Weary tried to stir Studs up to go down to Forty-seventh. Nobody was interested. Fifty-eighth Street had won the game and the fight anyway, they all said. Nate came to tell Studs how he'd gloriously gotten his shiner. Young Rocky Kansas interrupted to tell how he had mashed in a big baboon. Studs knew they were liars. Guys always lied like that about how they fought, how they drank, how they jazzed. He told of hitting the big guy, and lied, too, saying he had knocked the guy cold with a punch. It was like being on a glorious jag, a little bit like it had been on Armistice Day.

He heard Dan Donoghue near him ask Danny O'Neill what he thought of the game.

"Most of them don't know how to play. They tackle high, can't block, don't even know how to play their positions."

"Well, they are uncoached, but don't you think it was a fair bunch for an uncoached team?" asked Dan Donoghue.

Studs frowned when O'Neill superciliously answered yes. Remembered the punk when he ran around with his stockings falling and snot running out of his nose. Uncoached! Ought to slap his teeth! Seemed to think his was gold, droopy punk!

"That Schwartz is a player. I never tackled anybody as hard to get in my high school career with Loyola and I played against some tough men," Dan said.

"He was good. But some of the guys, Kelly, McAuliffe, and Klein, for instance, were jokes."

"What do you think of Studs?" asked Donoghue.

Studs tensed. Waited. Oughtn't to care what the punk thought. Waited.

"A bit slow, but he knows what to do, leaves his feet when he tackles, and handles himself well."

"Studs is a natural-born football player," Donoghue said.

O'Neill wasn't so bad. Heard too that he was a high school star. Studs sidled to them.

"Now that you're a star on the team at the Carmelites high school, what did you think of our . . . amateur game?" Studs asked, fatuously.

Before O'Neill could answer, the rumor spread that Schwartz had died on the way to the hospital. Everybody gabbed and shouted at the same time.

"Will anything be done about it?" Studs asked Kelly.

"They might hold us for manslaughter."

"Why? We played a fair game. The fight was afterwards."

"Well, they might, only, of course, we'll get out of it, and anyway, besides, we were in the right. We can get drag through my old man, who's sergeant down at Fiftieth now, and your old man knowing politicians, and some other guys the same way," Red said.

"We can get enough witnesses," said Studs.

The rumor was still being discussed when Studs left for home. If they did throw them all in the jug! He saw himself in the pen for a manslaughter charge. But they couldn't get him. He'd played a clean game.

He realized how tired he was, and his shoulders drooped. But it had been a great game, and a great fight, and he could feel proud of his part in both. He'd showed them all. He remembered that first clean tackle he had made, leaving his feet, the way he smashed into the runner, that sudden rush of his body through the air for a split second, and bang, the guy was down. Hundreds of people, too, had seen it. He was nostalgic to be still playing, making tackles like that.

Dumb, too, not to have gone to high school. If punks like O'Neill could make the grade, what couldn't he have done? He cursed, though, realizing that they would lose their permit to play in Washington Park, and that they couldn't get up a good team to travel, particularly after a fight like this; because if they traveled and didn't have a big enough mob along, they'd get the clouts plenty somewhere. Damn Reilley! And just when the scrap had started, he had been getting into top form, he felt. But the fight, too, had been a wow. The way he had hit that big yellow bastard. Only, gee, he might have been a bigger star in the game than even Schwartz, if it hadn't started.

He stuck his shoulders back, and forced himself to walk briskly. Proud of himself and his body. In his prime right now.

He became aware that it was dark, and an autumn mist was settling over Fifty-eighth Street. Street lights were on at the alley between

Indiana and Michigan. There were lights in windows. He heard the scrape of shoes in back of him, and the rumble of an elevated train. Down at State Street a street car was going, the bell donging. An automobile passed. The lonesome part of the day.

If Lucy had seen it, him! Well, what if he did admit to himself; he had played and acted like a hero!

That poor bastard Schwartz, game, had to grant that, lying dead in a hospital or morgue. It could have been him, perhaps. No, he knew he wouldn't die that way; he knew that he had some kind of a destiny to live for, and that he would live until that destiny was fulfilled. Maybe he would be a damn important guy later on, politician or something. That poor Jew bastard in a morgue. On the impulse, he mumbled a prayer for the guy!

The street around him seemed gloomy, and he was gloomy too. He couldn't get the thought of that dead Jew out of his mind. He didn't feel so cocky. He felt now like he wanted something in life, and didn't know what. That game and fight now, it had been swell. But there was something more he wanted than the glory of it, and he didn't even know what it was. Funny that he kept coming back to thoughts like this.

IX

MONEY's *pretty tight right now,"* Lonigan said.

"I know, Paddy. I wouldn't come to you if I could go anywheres else. I'd borrow on my insurance only I can't, because I had to do that when Ann had appendicitis," Lonigan's brother, Joe the motorman, said.

"How old is Tommy?"

"Twenty," Joe said deferentially.

"You say he stuck this guy up and spent the dough, and you got to make it good?"

Joe nodded.

"He can't get off on first offense?"

"The Jew is sore, and threatens to press charges if he don't get his money back. You know these Jews, always wanting their pound of flesh."

"Joe, you should have watched him."

"I tried, Paddy, but I was working every night on the cars. I did all I could, and it was a great sacrifice sending the boy to high school. But now, Paddy, I think the kid has learned his lesson. And I can't stand by and see my boy go to the pen. That would ruin his life sure."

"A bad business! You should have watched him more. You know, Joe, when a boy goes wrong, it's not only his fault. It's also the father's. I tell you that, Joe, because it's the truth, and we got to face the truth even though it hurts."

"I know, Paddy," Joe said with almost miserable weakness.

Lonigan meditated. Joe waited. Both brothers looked alike, but their difference in economic status was written into their countenances. Lonigan was stouter, his face full. Joe had a frustrated, harassed look.

"All right, Joe. I can do it this time. But I can't if anything happens again, because I got lots of expenses, with my two youngsters still in school."

"Thanks, Paddy. The kid's learned his lesson, I'm sure."

"I'll give you a check for a hundred bucks. But take it from me, what you ought to do is pound some sense into him with a horse whip."

"Paddy, I think he's learned his lesson. . . . But how is your oldest boy?"

"Oh, Bill is a fine kid, working with me, learning the business, a clear-headed, ambitious lad. Bill is all right; he's turned out fine, and I'm proud of him."

Chapter Nine

I

"Now, William, please come to our December formal," Fran said.

"Bill, I'd give anything to see you in soup-and-fish," Lonigan said, boisterously spraying Martin with saliva as he laughed.

A blush spoiled Studs' effort to appear noncommittal.

"A lot of fellows you know, Dan Donoghue, Johnny O'Brien, scads of them will be there, even that awful brother of Geraldine Malloy's," Fran said.

"Now, Frances, you needn't go bothering William. There's time enough for him to be getting a girl. Nowadays, all a girl wants is to get a fellow and have him spend all his money on her. William works hard for his money, and he'll have time enough for girls. He's young yet," the mother said.

"Mother, please don't be so ridic," Fran said.

"My goodness mercy, the language you use. I was saying to Mrs. Reilley only the other day, that the way our young ones are talking, we soon won't be able to understand a word they say," the mother said.

"Bill, don't let 'em fool you. I'll bet you'll be a real sheik, and have a winning way with the ladies. Chip off the old block, you'll be. Now when I was young . . ."

"Father, please!" interrupted Fran in a tone nasty with boredom and disgust.

Lonigan looked hurt.

"Yes, to hear him talk! IF I hadn't married him, he'd still be a wall-flower," the mother said.

"Is that so?" said Lonigan.

"I'll bet Martin will be a sheik and not need any encouragement when he gets a little older," Loretta said.

"Aw, go hop in the bowl," Martin said.

The family paused from its supper to look aghast at Martin.

"Why, the idea!" said Fran in dudgeon.

"Martin, where do you hear language like that?" Lonigan sternly asked.

"He won't get a girl ever if he talks like that," Loretta said amused.

"Now, see here, young fellow! I never want to hear you talking like that inside this house, and above all at the family table, blessed be God," Lonigan commanded.

"You children are the life of me! I don't know where you get your talk and your ideas," the mother said.

"If you would send him to a refined private school, like the one Catherine Hovey's brother goes to, he wouldn't talk like he does," Fran said.

"I won't go to that dopey school," Martin protested.

"Listen! If you want to sit at this table with your mother and sisters, you're going to use civilized, refined language," Lonigan said.

"All right, but gee, can't all of you let me alone?"

"He takes after him," Fran said, pointing at Studs.

Studs was inwardly proud. He was always being told his kid brother was just like he'd been, and plenty tough.

"Nobody asked for your two cents' worth," Studs said.

"Why, William Lonigan, you're not going to talk to me in that tone of voice!"

"Children, please!" interjected the mother.

"I give him up. I don't care what he does any more. I don't want him at our dance, disgracing me. If he chooses to be a bum, let him! I wash my hands," Fran said like a martyr.

"You've been doing that for years. I hope it's final," sneered Studs.

"Don't worry. It is. You have a positive hatred of acting like a gentleman. Go your own way! You might wake up some day and be sorry," she said.

"Swell," Studs said sarcastically.

"That'll be about enough," Lonigan boomed.

The table lapsed into a hostile silence. To break it, Lonigan asked Loretta how she was coming along at school.

"Fine, dad."

Studs ate quickly. Hell, he didn't want to take his time, and listen to all the talk that went on.

"What are you studying?"

"Oh, Latin, and Advanced Algebra, and Christian Doctrine, and History, and . . ."

"You're going to be a smart lady, I see."

"Martin! Haven't you been told before not to set your knife against your plate like that. Put it on your plate. You're not eating with African cannibals," Fran said.

"Oh, all right!" Martin pouted, putting his knife across his plate.

"I thought I said there's to be no more of this!" Lonigan said.

"Well, there wouldn't be, if someone would teach him some manners," Fran said.

"Aw mind your own business," Martin said.

"Fran, please!" said Loretta.

"Well, he could at least eat in a civilized fashion," Fran said.

"Martin, who do you ever see eating like that?" Lonigan asked.

"Him!" Fran said, pointing at Studs.

"Say, keep your trap shut."

"You're not going to snarl at me," she said. She jumped up, and flushed out of the room. Lonigan impotently looked from one to the other.

"I do wish you'd treat one another like brother and sister," Mrs. Lonigan said. She arose and followed Fran.

"Bill, you know your sister's a little nervous and you got to make allowances for her," Lonigan fatuously said.

Fran returned with the mother, frowned, and sat down, preserving an air of armed truce.

"Well, I had an offer of ninety thousand for the building today," Lonigan said.

"You took it?" asked Fran.

"I should say not."

"But, father, this neighborhood is deteriorating all the time. The best people in it are moving over to Hyde Park or out in South Shore. Soon I'll be ashamed to admit I live around here."

"Young lady, you're wrong. The niggers will be run raggedy if they ever try to get past Wabash Avenue. This is a good, decent neighborhood full of respectable people, and it will always be so. Didn't you hear Father Gilhooley talk about the new church he was building on this street. What did he say? Didn't he say Michigan was going to be a boulevard straight through. Then, this building will be worth twice as much. Why this neighborhood hasn't even commenced to grow yet, the way it will, and property values have hardly started to rise in it.'

"But, father . . ."

"Young lady, this is my business."

They finished supper with little talk. Studs left the table and washed his teeth. He put on his hat and coat. He looked at himself in the mirror. He wasn't a bad-looking guy at all. He heard footsteps in the hall, and turned away. He remembered how Fran had once caught him at the mirror, and had razzed him about being conceited in a snotty, superior way that she had.

"Bill, come here a minute!" Lonigan called as Studs turned the knob of the front door.

He was smoking in his rocker. Studs noticed that his belly seemed to stick out more and more every day. He plunked down on the piano stool.

"Bill, you know, Father Time is beginning to catch up on your mother and me. You kids are all we got, and . . . we'd kind of like to see more of you, have you all stay in and spend a quiet, happy evening with us. That isn't asking a whole lot. You're young and want to go out and be a regular fellow, and we don't object. Only there's always another night. And you know, Bill, you'll never have another mother. She sits up night after night worrying about you. It would just tickle her heart pink if you would, now and then, go up, kiss her and say, 'Mother, I'm going to stay in with you tonight'."

"I'm just going to a show. I'll be in early."

The phone rang. Studs was glad it was for him. He went out of the parlor and Lonigan picked up his newspaper to read about the Grand Jury quiz of some alderman implicated in a school board graft. It was Dan Donoghue calling to say that he had found out for certain that Jew Schwartz would be all right, except that he had been ruptured and wouldn't ever be able to play football again. Studs asked Dan about a show, but Dan had a date. He noticed Martin sitting by the crystal radio set with the ear phones on, keeping time on the floor. Loretta came out of the bathroom with a copy of *True Story* magazine in her hands. She stopped, shaking her shoulders and doing a little dance when she saw him. He left, shouting good-by.

II

Off the drear and rock-bound coasts of Alaska, that frigid land where men gamble their lives and souls with the dice of death, and sin for love and gold, the good ship *Mary Ann* braved all the monstrous terrors of the deep. Rolling, tipping, tossing, swaying, swerving, straining through the black and mysterious night, it tacked against a pelting rain, a howling wind, and huge waves that washed over it like evil spirits from out of the bowels of the unconquerable seas.

Captain Arnold, of the good ship *Mary Ann,* was a bulky man with cruelty stamped on a vicious, unshaven face, and a heart more ruthless than the stormy seas. He commanded his seaman with the iron hand of a tyrant. With each order, he gave them a curse, a kick, a blow. One of his sailors was Morgan, a smaller man, with the milk of human kindness in his soul. He gave Morgan an order, and slapped his face, sneering like a fiend out of hell. Morgan received the slap unflinchingly, but defiance struck the kindliness from his eyes.

Captain Arnold turned, and staggered across the rolling deck, with waves washing foamily past him, into his cabin. While the door was open to admit him, wind and water gushed in, a flickering candle almost died, and a whiskey glass tumbled off the table, to crash. In a bunk, Captain Arnold's timid Indian wife cowered like a small and frightened rabbit, her baby girl in her arms.

"Christ, he's a mean-looking brute," Studs Lonigan whispered to Slug Mason, as Captain Arnold's scowl revealed his fangs.

"You said it."

There was conversation, glowering hatred on the Captain's face, naked fear on the countenance of his wife. With wild animal ferocity in his eyes, Captain Arnold pointed demonstratively at the cabin door. The little Indian wife strained her baby girl more tightly to her bosom, huddled herself into a corner of the bunk, and shook her head. Her mouth opened in a scream as he approached her. He clutched her arm, and brutally yanked her out of the berth. He tore the baby from her, and dropped it in the berth, flinging her aside with such force that she catapulted against the cabin wall. Wrenching her arm, he pulled her out of the cabin, dragged her through the high, icy waves, and shoved her amongst the crew of outcast sailors who worked like demons amidst falling spars. A wave knocked her down, and she rolled to the edge of the ship. He struggled towards her, pulled her to her feet by the hair, and forced her back amongst the men. A falling spar cracked her head, and she fell. He commanded his sailors, while she lay unattended in a puddle, prey of the washing waves. Morgan staggered back to the cabin with her in his arms. He gently placed her in a berth, gave her whiskey, and carefully covered her with warm blankets. Through the long and stormy night, he tended her.

And came the dawn, calm and peaceful over the waters by the rock-bound coast of adventurous Alaska. The Indian wife lay at death's door. With her last forced words she begged that Morgan save the baby daughter from its heartless father. Captain Arnold entered the cabin, tore off his sou-wester, and guzzled whiskey. With a face as unfeeling as the sea, he watched his wife die.

"He's a bastard all right!" Studs muttered.

Morgan shook his head sadly as he gazed upon the tragic face of the dead woman. Gently, he covered it with a blanket. He turned and looked into the animalistic eyes of Captain Arnold, and saw a fiend in human form. An overpowering rage stirred him. He punched

Arnold's jaw. Taken by surprise, the captain's head snapped back. He stumbled backwards to the wall. Arnold rushed at the brave, impetuous Morgan and stunned him with a blow. He grasped Morgan in his arms and hurled him into a corner. The baby cried. Captain Arnold, his powerful arms threatening, heavy-footedly approached. Morgan saw a murderous intent written on that beastly face. He clutched a club from the floor and when Captain Arnold was upon him, he leaped up, and crashed it on Captain Arnold's head.

"The little guy has guts," Slug said with his mispronunciations.

Captain Arnold staggered backwards in a daze. Morgan clubbed him, until he toppled like a heavy, dropped sack of potatoes. He looked at the prostrate form of Captain Arnold, fearing that he had killed him. He took the baby, hustled out of the cabin, and escaped in a lifeboat.

Years passed, and much water ran under a crumbling wooden bridge. Seventeen years later, Morgan, now known as Jerome because he feared that he had murdered Captain Arnold, owned a general store in Flamingo, Alaska, where men still gambled their lives and souls with the dice of death, and sin for love and gold. Tenderly reared and named Gloria by Morgan, the baby girl had become a beautiful wild flower of Alaska. Not the faintest suspicion that she was a half-breed clouded her pure and innocent mind. She had been sent away to school and on the day of her expected return, the Law came to Flamingo. The commanding officer of the contingent of soldiers was Lieutenant Ames Dubois, a cynical Southern aristocrat and Don Juan.

Morgan, now Jerome, feared that the soldiers might discover him to be the murderer of Captain Arnold. Morgan's friend, the half-breed Durer, feared them because he was engaged in fur-trading enterprises which they might halt. Durer loved Gloria, the wild flower of Alaska, but she reciprocated only with the affection she would have borne a brother. An even greater fear developed for both men when Lieutenant Ames Dubois captivated Gloria's innocent heart. For they perceived that the officer was only a trifler. And Gloria was young, and as lovely and as innocent as the flowers and sunshine of the springtime.

Then one day, a strange ship put into the harbor, apparently for repairs and supplies. When the captain strode into the general store like a self-confident bully, Morgan, now Jerome, recognized him. He recognized Morgan, now Jerome. Morgan, now Jerome, was relieved of the fear that he was a murderer only to have it supplanted by the fear that Captain Arnold might demand his daughter, and tell her that she was a half-breed. Smiling, and just as innocent, she ran into the store, and back of the counter to the rear, girlishly pecking a kiss on the forehead of Morgan, now Jerome. The captain asked who she was, and Morgan, now Jerome, replied that it was his own daughter. The captain nodded his head sceptically.

But he bided his time.

And one day while Morgan, now Jerome, lived harassed with his new fears, gold was discovered. Gloria quickly persuaded Ames to go out with her and stake some promising claims. As they journeyed, Ames attempted to climax his pursuit of Gloria, and ruin her. She resisted girlishly, suddenly touching the deeper and better chords of his nature.

"Pretty broad, all right," Studs mumbled.

"If the guy gets her, he's gettin' something," Slug said.

Ames changed from a trifler and a Don Juan into a genuine lover. She promised him her hand. They sacredly sealed their newly awakened love by a kiss under a snow-laden spreading chestnut tree. Happy as two larks, they staked some of the best claims.

In the meantime, Morgan, now Jerome, and Durer had gone out to stake ground. On their return, the happy news of love was broken. In the midst of the congratulations and new-found joyousness, Captain Arnold nefariously revealed to Gloria that she was a half-breed.

"He's a rat, all right!" Studs whispered.

His interest was completely absorbed. He was, and he wasn't and he was Ames. He felt, that that rat, Arnold, would crimp up all the plans. Ames had to get the girl. Usually in the pictures the hero did. But it was exciting, and wracking waiting, and he was strung tight.

Ames and Gloria walked moodily off by themselves, their faces saddened with this new rift that had been cast, like a menacing cloud, between them. He pleaded with her that this new revelation, that no revelation, could chill the ardor of his love for her.

Just like Studs had so often pleaded with Lucy in his mind.

She was stunned, and it did matter to her. One small tear crawled from her eye, slid down her cheek. And another. Gloria wept. Ames' tender solicitations and persuasions were vain. She turned and walked slowly away, and Ames' face gleamed disappointment as he watched her disappear beyond the snow-laden spreading chestnut tree where they had sealed their love with a sacred kiss.

Gloria returned home, and quickly packed a few belongings, determined that duty demanded that she go off with her father, no matter if he were a vicious brute. Durer, discovering her note, followed. Ames returned to the general store, and he too set out to apprehend and save his beloved. In a threatened icefloe, Captain Arnold set sail with his daughter. The ship was jammed in an ice field. The crew deserted. Captain Arnold and Gloria were alone on the ice. Separately, Durer and Ames stumbled and fought their way over the slippery ice. Heavy, blinding Alaska snow fell. Ames slipped into the water, and clung tenaciously for life to the precarious ice.

In the cabin of the ship, Arnold looked with eyes of lust on Gloria. She was his daughter. But he was a brute.

Like a bastard, Studs watched, hoping that Arnold would be successful, and rape her. No, he didn't. He thought of himself as Ames, coming to the vessel in the nick of time.

Arnold trapped her in a corner, and imprinted a long and filthy kiss upon her unsoiled lips. She squirmed free. He trapped her in another corner. She dodged under his arm, her sleeve ripping, and fled behind a table. He faced her with eyes of lust.

Studs could just see him grabbing her, flinging her on the bunk, and . . .

Outside, in an Alaskan blizzard, Ames crawled back onto the ice, inch by inch. Durer reached the ship, staggering from his exertions. He busted into the cabin, just as the powerful arms of Captain Arnold encircled the girlish waist of Gloria. Arnold flung her aside, and her left breast almost, but not quite, fell out of her torn dress. The dent where her breasts commenced, and about half an inch of warm bare flesh were revealed.

Durer punched Arnold. Arnold fell. He rose and drove Durer to the other side of the cabin. Durer charged, and with a punch knocked Arnold back three feet. Arnold lifted the table, and brought it down on Durer's head. Durer toppled.

His shirt torn, his unshaven face a mask out of hell, his hairy arms and chest visible, he moved, like a gorilla, upon Gloria. Ames regained the ice, and staggered into the face of the Alaskan blizzard with the courage of desperation, borne of the flames of a powerful love. He fell, arose, fell, arose, rushed undauntedly onwards. Arnold drew the exhausted, dishevelled Gloria near to him. Ames staggered through the cabin door, snow flying from his clothes. He leaped upon Captain Arnold, and the men fought, knocking each other down, driving each other back and forth across the cabin, while Gloria stood trembling with her hands flat upon her cheeks. The men clinched, and Captain Arnold attempted to gouge Ames. Ames knocked him into the wall. Rebounding, he grasped a club. Ames dodged low, and twisted his wrist. The club dropped to the floor. The men went down, and rolled over and over, punching fiercely. They arose. Arnold hurled a chair at Ames. Ames ducked, and the chair broke against the wall. They staggered at each other. Ames warded off Arnold's blow, and connected with a last punch, into which he put all of his ebbing strength. Arnold fell unconscious. Durer shook his head, regained consciousness. They bundled Gloria in warm blankets, and carried her back across the ice, in the Alaskan blizzard. Arnold remained to die a villain's lonely death in the ice-jammed ship.

Back at the general store of Morgan, now Jerome, the three friends enjoyed a happy and delicious dinner which Gloria had prepared. After dinner, she sat on Ames' knee, and the men smoked. Suddenly, Durer arose and said good-by. He walked out and away to a new village, singing, but with a heart painted in the deep dyes of sorrow and unrequited love. Ames and Gloria saddened as they looked out the window to see him disappear. But love overpowered their sadness. They walked out into the glory of an Alaskan twilight, with the fading sun glowing over the snow. Under a tree, in the snow, before the setting sun, they kissed.

And under an Alaskan sunset, Studs Lonigan kissed Gloria, and kissed Lucy.

He made his exit with Slug, wishing there were more of it.

III

In front of the Michigan Theatre Studs guessed that he'd get coffee an' with Slug near the show, and then go straight home. Slug wanted to go down to Fifty-eighth first and see if the lads were around. Studs said all right he'd go along, but he didn't want to be out late because he needed rest; hadn't had a decent night's sleep all week. They crossed Garfield Boulevard, and walked south on Indiana Avenue. Studs felt close to Slug, as if Mason were his best friend. They seemed to understand each other, and when they were alone, they didn't say much; but there seemed to be something deeper than words could express between them. Studs wondered did Slug have the same kind of thoughts that he had.

Exciting picture, full of action; peachy fight at the end, it was. And the broad had been a knockout. When Arnold went at her, her boobs had almost fallen out. If they only let the boobs really fall out in scenes like that. If they could show everything in movies. Wished that she had gotten her clothes wet; they would have stuck to her body, and it would have been the next thing to seeing her stripped. Would be plenty of delights marrying a jane like that. He kissed her; married her; went to bed with her . . .

"Good picture," Slug mumbled.

"Yeah."

"Have one," Slug said, offering his pack of Camels to Studs.

Studs wondered what it would be like, hunting gold in Alaska. Yukon Lonigan in the gold fields. Taking a roulette game in Flamingo, Alaska, for a buggy ride. Shooting his way out to keep the gold he'd won. The picture made him want things like that, big dough, travel, broads as gorgeous as Gloria. The things he did, had no comparison with such a life, hanging around the poolroom, now and then a small-time crap game or round of poker; benders on Saturday night, and maybe a couple of times during the week; sometimes a can house. Nothing like it. And he could see himself returning from Alaska, with endless stories to tell, and his jeans sagging with dough. Knock everybody for a row then!

There were lots of things in life he'd been missing. He was doing a lot of the things he dreamed of doing when he'd been a kid. He wanted more and felt that somewhere there was something else for him in life, and it was the ticket that would satisfy the feeling he always got from the movies, from seeing a nice jane on the street, sometimes from walking in the park in summer and maybe looking at the sky, sometimes when walking home from work in the sunset.

Maybe if he married Lucy, it would turn out happy. Or some one like Gloria. If she and Lucy were the same girl! But what about when she would get old, and he'd want younger broads, and she had him tied home like a trained monkey in a zoo, and there'd be regiments of squawling brats coming along; he hated kids. He could just see himself parading the hall in the middle of the night, carrying a bawling baby, and maybe having the baby let go in his arms. But having a decent girl, who was your wife, must be different than being with whores or bums you took over to the park. Slug said all broads were the same. There had to be more to it than that, more than it was like in a can house, hurrying through with it and being disgusted afterwards. But was it worth having a jane sink the hooks into you, and handcuff your dough? He didn't know, but on summer nights when he saw guys out with their broads, he felt different about it than he pretended when he was with the guys.

"Like the broad I fixed you up with last Sunday night after the football game?"

"Yeah."

"Nice, huh?"

"Yeah."

"Say, wouldn't I like that broad in the picture," Slug said with all his mispronunciations.

Hell, what right had he to think of a broad like her? She wouldn't even spit on him.

They passed the white-tiled Methodist Church at Fifty-sixth and Indiana. At Fifty-seventh, Studs kind of wished that Slug would not turn but that they'd walk down to Fifty-eighth past her old house. But he didn't have any special reason to give for wanting to go that way, and walked with Slug when he turned east of Fifty-seventh. They turned by the Crerar Presbyterian Church on the corner of Fifty-seventh and Prairie, and Studs remembered one Sunday night when they'd been kids; how they'd gone to services there, put slugs in the collection box, and laughed until a sappy-faced usher kicked them out. They saw a group on the corner. Studs determined he wouldn't hang around long. He wondered too, if he didn't marry, would he be an old soak like Barney Keefe. He wanted to be something big in life. But look at what his fat, loud-mouthed old man was! Or Dinny Gorman, the high hat windbag of a politician! It got him all right.

"Lonigan!" Barney Keefe exclaimed with drunken exuberance.

"Keefe!" Lonigan replied with pumped boisterousness.

"Lonigan, you pig-in-the-parlor mick!"

"Keefe, you drunken flannel-mouth."

Slug complimented the boys for being polluted. Baby-faced Mickey Flannagan faced them, stupefied, swaying like a reed in the wind.

Studs told them that Schwartz from last Sunday's game would be all right. They said good.

"Flannagan has his guts pickled in gin," Keefe said.

Mickey mumbled. Slug caught him as he fell forwards, and set him against the fire plug.

Barney pulled out a bottle, and held it aloft;

Past the teeth, . .
Down the tongue,
Look out, stomach,
Here I come!

They laughed. Kelly grabbed the bottle. Barney beefed like hell. Taite and Les tried to get a sip from Kelly, but it was all gone.

Mickey mumbled for them to watch his match trick. He fumbled through his pockets and came out with a box of safety matches. He hiccoughed. He lit a match. It went out. He lit another. The flame quickly died. He repeated until they asked him where the trick was. He pawed out a match and lit it. It went out. That was the trick.

"Look out there, Flannagan, you're guts are rising!" Keefe said.

Mickey belched.

"Here's the Bad News Twins," Studs said, seeing Mush Joss and TB McCarthy approaching.

Muggsy, looking like the con, round-shouldered, a cigarette drooping from the corner of his mouth, tried to scrouge two bits off Keefe.

"So long, boys. I'm going home and sleep," Studs said, yawning.

"Hang around. The Alky Squad is here, and something might happen," Slug said.

TB tried to hit Studs for a quarter. Studs told him to get away.

"Flannagan, you lousy paper salesman, give these mooching bastards a quarter. I can't stand their sight," Keefe said.

Flannagan fell on his face, mumbling incoherently.

Kelly suggested a poker game at his house. Studs said he had to go home. He went with the boys. Flannagan was left draped around the fire plug. Muggsy and Mush rolled him, and had a meal. Stepping out of the Greek restaurant, Muggsy wished now that they could pick up a bum broad and take her back with them to the basement where they slept. Muggsy said it was the best meal he'd had all week.

Studs left Kelly at three o'clock. He walked along with his eyes heavy. He bumped into a building, and realized that he was asleep on his feet. What a chump he'd been! He'd be pooped tomorrow, and only have a couple of hours' sleep. And he'd lost eight bucks.

X

*D*AVEY COHEN *pulled up the collar of his thin overcoat. He climbed a hilly street of Jamestown, New York, in the rain. He spewed up a racking cough, and spat. He entered the public library for shelter. A girl looked askance at him, and he felt as if he were an interloper. A blue-covered book lay before him. He read the title.* The Collected Poems of Heinrich Heine, *translated by Louis Untermeyer. He opened the book, just to pass the time, and read the preface. He read the facts of the poet's life, saddened at his fate, proud that he had been a Jew. A quotation from one of Heine's letters excited him:*

"When the harvest moon was up last year, I had to take to my bed, and since then I have not risen from it . . . I am no longer a divine biped: I am no longer a joyous though slightly corpulent Hellene, smiling gaily down on the melancholy Nazarene. I am now only an etching of sorrow, an unhappy man—a poor sick Jew."

Words that might have been tortured from Davey's own consumptive being. For what was he, too, but an etching of sorrow, a poor, sick, and homeless Jew.

He turned the pages and came upon Monolog From A Mattress. *He could visualize the Jewish poet, twisted in body, unhappy in mind, expressing crucified thoughts from his mattress grave. The deepest poignancy of his whole life trembled within him.*

For the rest—
That any son should be as sick as I,
No mother could believe.

It washed gloom into him. Might he not die on a mattress grave from con in the charity ward of a hospital if he did not die in a prairie or doorway. Just like Heine, who suffered so many years ago in Paris, exiled. He was like an exile from Chicago. He thought of Heine, "who has all the poet's gifts but love," Heine, "a twisted trunk in chilly isolation." Day after day he lay:

Slightly propped up upon this mattress grave
In which I'v been interred these few eight years.

So unhappy that he envied a dog! How many times hadn't Davey Cohen, hungry, cold, knowing he was useless to the world, walked along the streets of strange towns, envying the dogs that people owned, knowing that the dogs were better fed than he, that some people thought more of them than any human being did of him. He thought of dusk coming upon the poet on his mattress grave, another day of life robbed from his twisted body. Outside, in the rain, dusk came too, robbing Davey of another miserable day. He read and re-read Heine's monologue, and then, other poems. The library closed, and the hours had seemed like minutes.

Davey slipped the book under his coat, and left. Rain slapped his face. He was back in the world now. He felt himself an "etching of sorrow, an unhappy man—a poor sick Jew." He coughed, a sharp sword-like pain slicing through his lungs. He spat blood.

He was hungry.

Chapter Ten

I

STUDS LONIGAN arose with the ringing of the alarm clock, and rode to work on a crowded surface-car which ran backwards. As if through a mist, he saw the familiar unremembered faces of the other passengers. A man with an indistinct face and the sleek uniform of an army officer stared at him with contempt. Studs tried to recall that somewhere he had seen that face before. He crossed the aisle and eyed the man with an expression that was both questioning and conciliatory.

"Say, Chauncey, we're going backwards, and I got to be at work."

"All the cars in Alaska go this way."

In a shock of surprise, Studs saw from the window of the moving car that they were passing through expansive, flat fields of snow.

He returned to his seat, and his disappointment dissipated when he realized that he was an adventurer, journeying to fight for love and gold. And the army officer was Lieutenant Ames Dubois. With the pride of ingenuity, he outlined a plan of action. Ames would be returning to Gloria. After seeing her, he would lead his soldiers out on an expedition to shovel snow. And Gloria would be awaiting her lover, Studs Lonigan, in a little Alaska love-nest. She would be prepared for him, without a strip on, and she would give herself unto him, body and soul, until it hurt. Then she would show him where the gold was in them there Alaska hills, and he would become a billionaire. He would return to Fifty-eighth Street with his fortune, and he would go round to the poolroom of George the Greek, escorting glorious Gloria, who would wear pearls in her ears, diamonds on her fingers, and rings on her toes. And every night for a century, glorious Gloria, stripped, would give herself unto him, body and soul, until it hurt. He glanced across the aisle at Lieutenant Ames Dubois, thinking what a chump that boy was.

The car jolted as it was jammed into an unexpected halt. Studs looked up into the face of Ames Dubois, and the countenance of the conductor; he knew that he knew the conductor and hated him like poison.

"Lonigan, take your goddamn tree off the tracks!" they jointly demanded.

"My tree?" Studs asked in surprised apology.

To the amusement of all the passengers, he was ejected from the car, and landed in unwet snow. He found no tree on the tracks, and when he looked up, the car was in motion, and Weary Reilley, the conductor, stood on the rear platform thumbing his nose.

Studs ran, flagging after the car, and pleading in shouts for them to wait. He was outdistanced and he stopped to catch his breath. A sense of loss swept him with oceans of sadness, and he was more sad than any man had ever been. He peered around him, and saw the same monotonous desolation of snow on every side, with neither sight nor sign of a human being. He had lost glorious Gloria forevermore, and he was poor, and miles upon miles from his home in Chicago that he should never have left. And when he did return, after walking the whole distance without shoes, he would have neither love nor gold.

You're no good! You're not a man. You never will be, you yellow Lonigan louse, a voice within him, as if it were the voice of conscience, sneered.

He dropped a dejected head, and set out upon that thousand-mile journey back to his home, without any shoes on his feet. He already could hear the crackling, sarcastic laughter with which he would be greeted. Suddenly, he was amongst buildings which resembled the houses and apartments in the 5700 block on Indiana Avenue. And in the sky, like a rising sun of the spring time, he saw the beaming face of Lucy Scanlan. In a voice as sweet as candy, she sang to him that she still loved him in a cosy Morris chair, and that if he wanted her, he must go and touch the tree. He confidently strode through a recognizable gangway, and came out upon a street which was fronted with a park of huge oak-trees. He crossed the street, but the trees receded and disappeared with his approach. He chased the vanishing trees across fields of grass, encouraged and hopeful, only because the face of Lucy Scanlan still shone in the sky like a rising sun of the spring time. He came upon a bent, gnarled oak-tree, and knew that it was the one, because the face of Lucy Scanlan blew kisses down upon it, and it sang *In the Blue Ridge Mountains of Virginia* with the voice of Lucy Scanlan. He touched the tree gently with the second and third fingers of his right hand

and suddenly . . . .

the boy Studs Lonigan

sat nervously in the eighth-grade room of St. Patrick's school, wishing that school would let out, because he had just touched something that was the secret of love and happiness and he couldn't remember what it was, or where it was, and he had to go out and find it again before it was too late.

"William Bastard Lonigan, you were late for school this morning," Sister Battling Bertha said, wrinkling the toothless face of a crone.

"I wasn't. The bell rang before I got here," the boy Studs Lonigan, replied, and a six-foot-four pupil in short britches named Slug Mason guffawed.

"Sister, he played poker last night and lost eight dollars and when I asked him for a penny because I was starving, he wouldn't give it to me," TB McCarthy said, turning a sickly yellow face upon the schoolboy, Studs Lonigan.

"All I did last night was go to bed with Lucy, only we didn't sleep much. Ha! Ha!" the schoolboy Studs Lonigan said.

William Bastard Lonigan, by your gambling and immoral thoughts, words, deeds, acts and wishes, you have spilled the consecrated blood of the Sacred Heart of the Crucified Jesus, and you have put gray hairs upon the heads of your father, mother, God the Father, Son and Holy Ghost, and all the communion of saints in Heaven and on earth. You will go to the gallows for your sacrileges, and God will send you special delivery to hell to burn forevermore in a lake of brimstone!

She descended on him like a cyclone, and vigorously shook his head.

"Oh, how I hate to get up in the morning," he sang.

"Get up!" she commanded, slapping his face, while the entire class laughed at Clown Lonigan. . . .

and . . .

Studs Lonigan opened his eyes that were heavy with sleep to find his mother gently shaking him. He sat up in bed, yawned, rubbed his eyes with the sleeve of his pyjamas.

"Goodness, didn't you hear the alarm, son?"

"Gee, mother, it was the funniest darn thing. I dreamt I got up with that clock, and was riding to work," he said boyishly.

She suddenly flung her arms around him, pulled him to her thin bosom, and kissed him, declaring that he would always be her baby. He was embarrassed.

"You must hurry now, son. Breakfast is all ready."

He sat on the edge of the bed half asleep, tiredly stretching. He opened his eyes; he'd fallen asleep sitting there. He looked over and saw that Martin was up, and in the bathroom washing. It got him sore. Martin returned to the bedroom.

"Say, what the hell's the idea? You know I have to be out of here earlier than you. You're just too damn wise a punk, ain't you," Studs said, arising, and raising his hand as if to slam his kid brother.

"I'm going to communion this morning. It's first Friday," Martin whined, drawing back.

"You could have waited until I was washed. I got farther to go than you. Why didn't you wake me?"

"Yes, wake you! The last time I did, I got a clout in the ear."

"One of these days, I'm going to slap some of that wiseness out of you, punk!"

"You do, and I'll . . . kill you," Martin shrieked, almost in tears.

Studs advanced a step.

"Don't touch me, you big bully!" Martin hollered.

The mother rushed into the bedroom, and enfolded Martin in maternal arms.

"Is he hurting my darling little child?"

Martin fought to break free. He blushed. Studs busted out laughing.

"If I wasn't going to communion, and it wasn't a sin to lose my temper, I'd tell you what I think of you, you big bum! You just wait until tonight, and I'll tell you."

The mother pressed a wet determined kiss on Martin's cheek.

"Can't there ever be any peace in this home?" Lonigan futilely protested, as he stood in the doorway with his suspenders hanging from his trousers, and his belly falling out.

Studs felt more awakened after he had doused his face in cold water. Shaving, he wished the day was over. He knew how pooped out he would feel in the afternoon, and how he'd only be able to get through his work by doping himself with cigarettes and coffee. Tonight he'd get some decent sleep.

A plate full of pancakes and a cup of black coffee were set before him on the kitchen table. He gulped the coffee down black and asked for another.

"Son, I don't want to nag you, but I'm worried about your health. You never get enough sleep and every morning you gulp down black coffee like that. Coffee is not good for your kidneys. You know the human body can stand only so much, and no more. A boy your age, doing the kind of work you do, has to get his proper rest. If you keep on like this, you'll be getting into consumption at twenty-five."

Studs hadn't listened to her, and with his mouth stuffed with pancakes, said that he was all right.

"Bill, always remember that the wise guy knows that he can always have another night, and doesn't try to do everything in one evening," Lonigan said.

The mother looked at the clock, and dashed in to awaken the girls.

"Bill, a man's health is like Humpty Dumpty. Once it is gone, nothing can repair it, not with all the money in the world, or all the king's men and horses. It can't be repaired like an automobile."

Studs felt like throwing the plate of syrupy pancakes at his father.

An uproar started in the girls' bedroom, and Fran was heard threatening to pull Loretta's hair out if she ever again wore her stockings.

"This family will put me in the nut house yet!" Lonigan said, wincing. He arose and went to stop the quarrel.

Studs was almost finished when Lonigan returned.

"Bill, you know, girls and women have to be handled with kid gloves and jollied along. So when Frances comes out to breakfast, kid her a little. You know, say, Good morning! How is the charming slim queen on this bright and sunny morning?"

Studs' face sank. He arose from the table. His father told him that if he'd wait, he could ride to work with him in the Ford. Studs said it was no use of having to go out of the way, he could take the street car. He was glad to get out. But he was damn tired.

II

"Kid, I'll be damned if my old lady didn't go and get sick again," Mort said, from the other side of the small vacant dining-room in an apartment building where they worked.

"Yeah," said Studs, brushing over the cream-colored paint with measured strokes. He yawned.

"You know, a young chap like yourself who's footloose as the winds don't know how well off you are," Mort said.

Studs yawned. He dipped his brush, tapped it against the side of the pail, drew it down the center of the wall.

"Sometimes when you get married, you don't know what you're being let into. You see a girl, a nice sweet kid, and she's cherry. You think, now I'll be happy with her, and we're just cut out for one another. Well, one thing and another happens, and first thing you know, you're married. You take her on a honeymoon, and there's nothing at all in life like those first nights. Now, take my wife. She was just as pretty as a picture. I'll show you a picture of her took when we were just married. And then our kids came along, and we thought things was going to be nice and smooth, and that we'd find comfort in the kids and someone to take care of us in our old age. And then eight years ago when our last youngster was born, my wife, she gets what they call a milk leg, you see, that's some kind of a clot that makes your leg swell up, all out of shape, and her heart goes back on her, and now the doctor says that she's got to be careful and any kind of excitement might be the finish of her.

"That's tough," Studs said, feeling that he had to say something.

Mort had told him the same story before, almost every day that they'd ever worked together. He went on painting, evening off the last coating. His arm was tired. He wasn't at all interested in the damn work. He liked to look at it when it was finished, and see that it was a good job, and he always took pains to do a good job because he couldn't stand to slop on paint and leave it any old way. But goddamn it, he hated to think of going on, painting walls day after day after day, risking lead-poisoning too, until he got old and a big belly like his old man, and then to go around bossing other guys who painted walls day after day after day. Goddamn it, yes, there was something more to life. There had to be. He jerked out a watch: a quarter to three.

"Every night when I go home, I don't know but maybe I'll find my wife dead. I tell you, kid, married life ain't all it's cracked up to be, and don't let anybody kid you that it is."

"No danger," Studs muttered with over-exaggerated confidence. He yawned.

"It's not that I'm complainin', because I ain't. My wife has been the best in the world, but it's just that life doesn't turn out the way you want it to."

Their brushes swished and slapped as they worked. Studs yawned. Ten to three. Would it or wouldn't it be a good idea to get married? Everybody did, and had kids. He guessed that maybe you couldn't help yourself about it when the right broad came along. That was what love was. Five to three. Love was B. S. Suppose now he got married to Lucy and the same thing happened to her that had happened to Mort's wife. But it wouldn't. Things weren't going to happen to him that way. He had luck, a lucky star, four aces stacked for him in the cards. Well, he did. He had to have them. He did. Three o'clock. He yawned. He whistled.

"As I was sayin', I don't know why the Lord should of visited us with all the misfortunes He did. Sometimes, I fear maybe it's because I sown my wild oats when I was your age, or else because I drank now and again. Oh, sometimes too it's maybe, I feel, because of something I done in a previous life. Say, kid, do you believe in reincarnation?"

Studs didn't hear, and Mort repeated the question. Studs thought it was all crap, but hell, he was too damn tired to argue, so he said he didn't know.

"Well, I sometimes wonder if that's why we were punished. But I tell you it isn't fair. I done the best I could. . . ."

Studs yawned. Seven minutes after three. He was going straight home for supper, and then, maybe, he'd read his newspaper and turn in early.

"But I always come to this conclusion. No matter how bad off you are, there's always somebody in a worse boat. Now take my brother. He's lived in poverty all his life, and would you believe it, he still has a place with the can in the backyard. I always tried to help him out, but charity begins at home. That's what I always figure, no matter how bad off you are, there's always somebody who's worse off. Now take him. About six years ago he was living in a place down on Bishop Street, and one night a rat bites the baby and it dies. Maybe I shouldn't be complaining. But goddamn it, when any night you come home to supper, and you might find a dead wife, it gets you."

Three-fourteen.

"That's why I always say to a young fellow, look before you leap. You never know what's gonna happen, and when you got a wife and love her and got to sit day after day and see her grow old and lose her looks, yes, sir, look twice before you leap."

Three-sixteen. Studs went to the can and smoked a cigarette. It knocked off twelve more minutes. He worked slowly. Mort's voice went on in an unpleasant drone, complaining that it wasn't enough for his wife to get sick, but that damn it if he didn't go and get lead-poisoning because he knew he had it.

III

"Well I hope the old lady is feeling up to snuff," Mort said, as he, Studs, and Al walked to the street car line.

"Tonight all I'm doing is sleep. I was playing poker till three this morning and I'm all pooped out," Studs said.

"I know what I'm going to do tonight," smiled Al.

"You ought to. You're a newlywed."

"Wrong again, Mort. You guys noticed these crossword puzzles in the papers. They got a contest, and they give real dough to the winners, thousand bucks first prize. Well, I'm working them and trying to get me them prizes. They'll fix me up jake with a nice new Ford and something to spare," Al said.

"They're goofy," Studs said.

"Now wait a minute, Lonigan. There's money in them. And I won't be losing out. Suppose I don't get a sou out of it. Look at the self-improvement, the words and things you learn. Say, when I finish all the puzzles in this contest, I'll be knocking you guys for a row with tongue-twisters and the things I know. Take all I learned already. Now do you know the name of a battle fought in England in the year 1086. Well, there was one and it was called the Battle of Hastings. All kinds of things like that, knowledge, you learn. These puzzles are an education in themselves."

"Well, I leave you boys here," Mort said.

"Poor devil!" said Al, after Mort had gone his way.

"He got some tough breaks all right."

"Yeah, he gets my sympathy."

"He's white too," said Studs.

"Don't I know it? I worked with him for five years now. You ask your old man. He knows Mort. Mort's worked for him for years. But, Jesus, he's a tank. He's got a crying jag on all the time. But then, with all his trouble, you can't blame the guy. He's got to drink to forget . . . but here's my car. So long," said Al.

"Don't swallow that dictionary," Studs yelled.

IV

The street car was crowded with home-going workers, a swaying mob of begrimed Hunkies, foreigners, who jabbered in broken English and their own tongues, and smelled of garlic. Studs was relieved when he alighted at Fifty-ninth and State. On his way home, he paused at the corner of Fifty-eighth and Michigan, and decided that since he was a little early for supper, he might as well take a stroll over to the poolroom. He met Red Kelly at Fifty-eighth and Indiana.

"Tired, Studs?"

"I feel like a rag."

"We played on after you left 'til daylight. I cleaned up twenty bucks."

"I would have been better off going home."

"Say, I'll be damned, Studs, if you ain't getting an alderman," Red unexpectedly said, giving Studs a friendly poke in the belly.

"Only a little," Studs said apologetically.

"Better look out, Studs, or you'll be getting like Barney Keefe."

"I'll get it off before that happens," Studs confidently replied.

He felt his belly; just a little bit fat, not any more than Kelly himself had. He was just afraid of getting fat himself. Studs knew he'd be able to watch himself and exercise the fat off before it got serious.

A noisy, excited crowd was talking in front of the poolroom. Studs saw a squad car parked at the curb, and a cop standing importantly by the doorway. He started to move out of the crowd and see what was up, but noticed Joe Thomas, dressed in his bricklayer's clothes, step before the cop and ask what was the matter. The cop grabbed Joe, and called inside. People edged forwards, and the cop told them to get back, while Joe crabbed that he hadn't done anything. A tough-mugged dick appeared from inside the poolroom and talked with the cop. He grabbed Joe by the arm and dragged him inside, heedless of Joe's protests. Studs guessed it must be serious, and edged back in the crowd. He kept asking what had happened, and nobody knew, people saying it was a raid, a murder, a fight, a stabbing, a shooting, a chase after a robber. If it was serious and he tried to get in, he might be held for questioning, and he might, by accident, find himself giving one of his pals away. But none of them ever violated the law, except by drinking or going to can houses. He wondered.

With an air of mystery and authority, six lantern-jawed detectives emerged from the poolroom, putting their guns away in holsters beneath their coats. Talking, they clambered into the car, and shot off. The cop walked on. Studs rushed with others of the curious crowd into the poolroom. Everybody talked at once, and amidst all the gabbing, he finally pieced together the fact that nothing had happened. The dicks had just suddenly showed up with drawn guns, and lined everybody against the wall, and asked them useless questions. Then they had left. Most of the guys took it as a joke. George the Greek crabbed, because he said his business was getting a bad name. He declared, with many reiterations, that from now on, no more drinking, and rough-housing would go in his poolroom.

When the place quieted down, Studs shot a couple of rounds of poker dice with George. He won six bits' worth of chips, good in trade. He moved away from the counter, and stood in a group of punks who were raking Rolfe over the coals. He looked at Rolfe's outfit, a darkish gray topcoat, opened to reveal a blue herring-bone suit with blue-bordered handkerchief showing from the pocket, a blue English broadcloth shirt with collar attached, brown tie and black brogans.

"Phil, is that so that the only thing you read in the paper is Gallicoe's column on what the well-dressed man wears?" asked Swede Larsen.

"Phil, they tell me that with all the sheiking you do, you still don't know what it's for." Ellsworth Lyman said.

"Bug House Fable Number 999; Phillip Rolfe giving a penny to a starving blind man," said Young Rocky.

"I just see you boys shoveling out dimes like you were John D.," Phillip sharply retorted.

"Studs, it's nigger date night tonight. *It* has a date," Tommy Doyle shouted, passing along.

"It wouldn't do a lot of you guys any harm if you invested a dime in a second-hand joke book," Phillip said, walking off.

Skinny Joe Thomas asked Studs how about a game of pool. Studs said he thought maybe he could take Joe.

"Always ready to give you the chance. We'll play fifty straight pool, and I'll spot you ten. And just to make it interesting, we'll play for half a buck, if you say so?"

Studs nodded, hating to take the handicap and admit that Joe was better than he was. But Joe had it on him with the cue, and if he refused the spot, he'd just look like a stuck-up sap. Joe reached with his cue, and set off ten beads on Studs' side of the marking wire stretched above the table. Lagging for break with the ivory, Studs lost, and had to break. He chalked his cue, and took careful aim, planning just to graze off the eight ball on the right of the last row of the racked triangle of balls. He hit the ivory too hard and with poor aim, cracking seven balls loose from the rack-up. Joe sank three shots, and missed an easy one, but left Studs sewn up.

"That was just luck," Joe said, his buck teeth showing in a good-natured, chinless smile.

Automatically chalking his cue, Studs studied the table, roving slowly around it to survey the balls from varying angles. He frowned in concentration. He heard Tommy Doyle remark that it was Studs' can. He bent over the table, and took careful aim, calling the three ball in the left-hand side pocket on a sharp cut. He was aware of a silence amongst the spectators. He shot, the three ball rolling straight into the pocket. He smiled, with a sense of relief. He made a run of ten, and as he sank his shots he saw himself as a careless, chance-taking pool shark. He missed a set-up before one of the lower end pockets. He set the balls back on the table in a line up from the spot, and pushed ten beads more on his side of the wire. He could not check a smile when he heard Doyle tell Joe that this time Studs looked like he might give him a run for his dough.

Three Star Hennessey sauntered in and oozed out a greeting to the gentlemen present. Doyle hopped on him about his spats and bell bottoms. Hennessey replied that they kept his feet warm, and everybody haw-hawed. Joe kidded with Hennessey as he made a difficult bank shot. He knocked six in and left Studs seven up. Studs nettled his eyebrows and called a double bank.

"So, you're smoking Melachrinos now, Hennessey?" Joe remarked.

"The best is none too good for Mrs. Hennessey's son, John," Three Star said.

"Robbing the broads again," Studs remarked, trying to pull Joe's stunt of kidding while he made difficult shots; he fizzled the shot, and left the table open for Joe.

Joe ran off twenty and was ahead of Studs. Studs nettled his brows. He felt his confidence ebbing away. On his next inning, he slammed the eight ball into the side pocket. He had position on an easy shot, and hoped the guys would think he played for it, instead of getting it by accident.

Hennessey and Rolfe started ragging each other in their loud-mouthed punk manner. Studs, unconscious of everything but the balls before him, ran the table, feeling a sense of skill and power as he made ball after ball, planning shots ahead, putting english on the ball to get position, feeling a complete mastery. Joe set the balls back in a line up from spot.

"I only need to make two more to break my high-run record," Studs said to Tommy Doyle, as he chalked his cue.

"You're hot tonight, there, Hoppe," Stan Simonsky said.

"Looks like he's got my number," Joe said, undismayed.

Studs bent over, and pushed the cue through the crooked index finger of his left hand, aiming at the end ball that was frozen against the back rail. The ball seemed suddenly unclear to him. He was nervous. He felt like a mechanical man without control over the cue. He wanted to break that record.

"Well, anyway, louse, I don't snatch pocketbooks," Rolfe shrieked.

The punk's voice drummed in Studs' ear. He stood up, and re-chalked his cue. He took a puff from the cigarette which he had placed on the wooden edge of the table, trying to steady himself. He bent over, and again took aim.

"Any goddamn time you catch me snipping purses. . . ."

The damn . . . Studs miscued. His shoulders dropped in a droop of relaxation, relieved from the strain, even though he was disappointed. Those two snotty drug-store cow-boys had taken his mind off his game.

"Hey!" Studs yelled at them, sore.

"Gwan, rat, frisk some more nickels off working girls," Rolfe yelled.

"Say, Rolfe, you goddamn Jew, if you don't close that trap of yours, I will," Studs barked, throwing everyone into a waiting silence.

"Jesus, Studs! I'm sorry if I disturbed you," Phillip apologized, blushing; Hennessey quietly smirked at him.

"One more bat out of you while I'm shooting, and it'll be curtains for you, punk!"

Studs couldn't regain his form. Joe walked away with the game, and won a second game with ease. Studs handed him a buck, and paid for the time with some of his chips. Joe said it was tough, going so good, and then suddenly losing your form. Next time, he might have better luck. Studs smiled weakly, but a sudden hatred of Joe stirred in him. Joe was almost chinless, not good-looking, a nice guy, but he had nothing on his side except his ability with the cue. No reason for jealousy and hatred. But Studs hated him for winning, hated to lose or be second fiddle at anything. He was even glad when Joe remarked that his rheumatism was bothering him again.

He started out and met Arnold Sheehan limping in the doorway. He asked how tricks were. Arnold said he had a job with a construction gang for the city, and was on the wagon. He was going to start working as soon as his knee, twisted in the football game last Sunday, was better. Studs said swell.

He walked along amidst the six-o'clock confusion of Fifty-eighth Street, with people pouring out of the elevated station, elevated trains rumbling almost continuously, kids barking as they sold the *Saturday Evening Post,* Sammy Schmaltz yelling his latest papers, people hurrying in front of and by him. It made him nervous. And he thought how he had just been going so good, ran the table for the third time in his life at straight pool, had been on the verge of breaking his record run. He remembered the feeling of power he had had, running the table, his eye, brains, arm, all of himself concentrated on the balls, all clicking together like a coordinated machine, and the thrill that went with each shot as the balls were smashed, cut, banked, eased into the pockets. A feeling that, in its way, was like the one he'd had making that first clean tackle of Jewboy Schwartz in the football game.

He saw the dumpy figure of Helen Shires ahead of him, and caught up with her. She looked mannish, with a shingle bob, a simple felt hat, almost like a man's, a plain blue suit with shirt waist and blue tie.

Not good-looking any more. She'd been almost like a pal with him when they'd been kids. Some of the old feeling for her came back. But she hadn't turned into much. Wouldn't be a bargain in bed now either.

"I'm glad to see you again, Studs; haven't seen you in ages," she said.

"How are you, Helen?"

"Fine. Working in an office, stenographer. I hear you're still working for your dad," she said, and he nodded, lighting a cigarette.

"I saw Loretta the other day and she has certainly grown into a sweet young girl."

Not much for them to say to each other. It made him sorry they had changed and drifted apart, because he could remember how she had been such a pal, just like a guy you liked a lot.

"Seen any of the old bunch?" she asked, after the silence between them had grown uncomfortable.

"Bill comes around once in a while and we go to a show together. He has a pretty good job, repairing adding-machines."

"And how's Fran?"

"All right."

He wanted to talk about old times, and have them just naturally talk about themselves, and maybe Lucy.

"I saw Jim Clayburn. He's studying law," she said.

He told her about last Sunday's football game and the fight.

"You're just the same as ever, aren't you? Haven't changed, even to the fighting," she said in a complimentary way; he was pleased, and looked at her out of the corner of his eye. Might date her up at that and make her; she probably could be made, and every jane a guy made was another notch in his belt. But he liked her and wished they could be as they used to be.

"What's your sister doing?"

"She's in high school. She's a flapper now," Helen said.

"You haven't changed either, Helen," he said, but it was a lie. She wasn't the old Helen. And she looked sort of whipped, too. Maybe it was because she wasn't good-looking or something.

They stood awkwardly at the corner of Fifty-eighth and Indiana. Finally they said they'd have to be trotting along. Studs said they'd have to get together some time, and she replied vaguely. He watched her walk mannishly along, her dumpy figure swaying a trifle. He wished. . . . He went in the drug store and bought copies of *Snappy Stories* and the *Whizz Bang* to read after supper, since he wasn't going out.

He felt moody over having seen Helen, noticed the way she seemed whipped, and wasn't the old Helen. And then losing that game too. He yawned, tired. He remembered what good times he and Helen and the old bunch used to have roasting marshmallows and baking potatoes in a bonfire nights over by the foundation when the Prairie Theater was just being built.

XI

A HOLLOW ROAR, *like heavy thunder splitting the sky in a storm, boomed over the neighborhood. People near Fifty-ninth and South Park Avenue heard falling glass, and in some cases, their buildings, and the very bedrooms in which they slept, quaked. Inside of five minutes, a crowd was collected in front of a low, two-story, red stone house between Fifty-ninth and Sixtieth on South Park Avenue. Two policemen stood before the crumbled steps, and the long wide porch before the building was splintered and half-wrecked.*

The crowd was steadily enlarged by people of all ages who displayed the signs of hasty arousal from sleep; men with trousers and coats pulled on over pyjamas, kids with tousled hair and sleep still in their eyes, surprised and half-dressed women. There was much talk and speculation, and amongst them there was a general consensus that the bomb had been placed there through the machinations of real-estate people who desired that Abraham Clarkson, the leading colored banker of Chicago, should sell his property and cease living in a white man's neighborhood. Most of the excited and gaping people present also eyed the wreckage with approval, wishing that it would have a proper and fearful effect. But they knew that the bomb would teach no lessons and inspire no fear. For Abraham Clarkson had been bombed before, and he had stated defiantly that he would move from his home to another one only in a casket. It was nerve for the nigger to say that and go on ruining a white man's neighborhood, living amongst people who didn't want him. Secretly, many of those present wished that he had been killed. Some of the Catholics wished only that it had wounded him, un-mortally, for didn't he always give Father Gilhooley a hundred dollars in the annual Easter and Christmas collections. The crowd increased. After about three quarters of an hour of gaping, it slowly dispersed. Red Kelly walked off arguing with Tommy Doyle, Red insisting that it was the fifth time that the jigg had been bombed, Tommy contending that it was only the fourth time.

Chapter Eleven

I

PAPEE! Box score!"

Studs Lonigan laughed at Sammy Schmaltz like a drunken apparition.

"Which one?"

"There ain't no box scores on Christmas Eve," Studs said, continuing to laugh.

"Papee! Latest papee!"

"Merry Fourth of July!" Studs bellowed, with an uncontrolled wave of his hand; he staggered over to plaster himself against the bellied front of the Fifty-eighth Street elevated station. He saw Phillip Rolfe and bellowed a command for him to come over.

"Say, are you a fag?" Studs sneered.

"You're drunk, kid," Phillip replied, taking Studs' arm. "The boys said you've been home laid up with the flu for several weeks. Do you feel all right now?"

"I'll bet you are a pansy," Studs said, brushing Phillip's arm aside, and eyeing him with curiosity, as Rolfe inched backwards.

"Why do you punks wear those goddamn monkey suits? You can't keep them pressed when you get on your knees," Studs said, studying Phil's bell bottoms.

"They're the rage, kid," Phillip said, walking away.

Studs fell back against the building. He coughed. He saw people passing as in a dream, and imagined himself just walking up to them one by one, and laying them cold.

"Hey, Jew, commere!" he commanded.

Smirking, Jawbones Levinsky halted a respectable distance from Studs.

"So you're the goddamn Jew who's prejudiced against the N. D. football team."

"Yeah," said Levinsky, quickly dodging a right haymaker.

Studs chased him half way across the sidewalk. Strangers watched with amusement. Levinsky stopped on the other side of the alley, which ran parallel to the station, and laughed. Studs floundered like a listing ship, and again plastered himself against the station bricks. Mr. and Mrs. Dennis P. Gorman, passing, saw Studs and clucked.

"Everybody's a bastard!" Studs mumbled to himself.

"William!"

"Thought Studs Lonigan die influenza. Plenty left in Studs Lonigan, get that, you bastards! Whoops!"

"William!"

The sharp, aggravated feminine pronunciation of his name slowly wormed itself into his drunken consciousness. He looked in the direction of the voice. He saw Fran leaning from the front of a closed car that was parked at the curb. He lip-farted.

"William! . . . Come here!"

He threw his shoulders back, and almost toppled sidewise in his effort to walk straight. He stood before her, swaying, his leering face smudged, his clothes spotted with dust.

"The idea! You're a perfect sight; you ought to be ashamed of yourself, disgracing the whole family by your drunken boorishness. And you just out of a sick bed!"

"Whatjahsay?"

"It's shocking, disgraceful!"

A slick-looking Tuxedoed young man, with a talcum-powdered shaven face, leaned sidewise from the wheel.

"Fran, we'll have time to drive him around for a spin in the park and let him get some air."

"Huh!" Studs nastily exclaimed.

"Then, a cup of black coffee might help sober him up."

"Who in the name of all holy hell wants to get sobered up. . . . Sobered up, huh there, Droopy Drawers? Christ is born, and I'm celebrating," he whooped.

"William Lonigan, you'll stop that uncouth, blasphemous talk this minute and get in here!"

"Whoops!"

"Fran, he's drunk. Let me handle him!"

"What's that, Charley?"

"William, don't be so disgusting! You're not funny."

"Sure thing, Charley!" he said with an insulting laugh; he almost fell on his face.

"William. . . ."

"I'm just about ready to haul off on a skunk that I see!"

"William!"

"You're the bastard I'm talking to!" he said, stepping forwards.

Fran slammed the car door, and it shot off. Studs stumbled after it, cursing. He fell in the street. A traffic jam was caused, while he struggled to his feet, and staggered back onto the sidewalk. Slug Mason grabbed his arm, and said, with his familiar mispronunciations:

"Studs, you crazy bastard! Here we all hears that you was in bed with the flu, and what does I do but find you trying to take a nose dive in the gutter."

"Like tuxedoes?" asked Studs.

"What's that?"

"Sure," Studs said, trying to light a cigarette.

Slug lit it for him.

"Say, who took your stick of candy away?" Studs asked Les Coady, as Les lay crying against the poolroom window with tears running down his bucolic face.

"Studs, I'm no good!" Les said heavily.

"You need another drink," Slug said, pronouncing it "anoder."

"I'm only a common ordinary wagon man for the Continental Express Company; I never got a chance. I'll never amount to nothing. I'm rotting away like I was dead, a common ordinary wagon man."

"You better come with me tonight, and get yourself a fast and furious jazz," Slug said.

"Slug, go down to the drug store, and buy him a lolly pop!" Studs said.

Les ran a gloved hand across his teary face, streaking it.

"And I almost went and studied to be a priest. I'm no good," he whined.

Inside the poolroom, a crowd was gathered around the telephone booth, where Red Kelly was cursing his girl. The gang laughed boisterously. Slug took Studs and Les to the can, where they secretively had a drink. When they came out, TB McCarthy tried to scrouge a nip and two bits from them. He was so insistent that Studs handed him a quarter, but said that if he ever asked again, a certain louse named McCarthy would get his consumptive face pounded full of holes.

"Yeah, up your back, Charley," Red yelled, slamming the receiver.

He came out, and led Vinc Curley to the rear of the poolroom, telling him, as a friend, to stand there a minute. He returned to the first pool table, where Funnyface Duffy, and Swede Elston, were shooting a game of pool. He grabbed the balls from the table, wound up like a baseball pitcher, and hurled them at Vinc's bean. They missed Vinc, and crashed into the wall. Red was grabbed. Vinc stood dumbfounded. Studs ran down, and pulled the dumbsock aside. Vinc, blushing, misunderstanding, asked Kelly why he would do such a thing to a good friend of his; and they roared. George the Greek nearly went into a fit of apoplexy, sobbing about his business. Vinc, still perplexed, drew Studs aside, and asked him why Kelly would do a thing like that. Studs told Vinc to soak his head. He drifted off, and saw Mush Joss stemming a buck from Les; he asked Mush if he and Muggsy were making the rounds again. Slug insisted that they go to Burnham. They all went to the can and killed the gin they had. Slug again suggested that they go to Burnham. It was a good idea.

As they crowded towards the door, Vinc clutched Studs' arm, and asked him if he wanted to go to confession.

"Got your car?"

Vinc nodded. Studs said sure they were all going to church. He told the guys and they shoved Vinc out to his car. Some of the guys crowded into Vinc's car, and the others got into Nate Klein's taxicab.

"All right, Vinc, you bastard, drive."

"But I got to go to confession. Are you guys going?"

"Sure, but listen, Vinc, we're goin' to have a nice little harmless party, and we're going to confession out in South Chicago."

"But that takes gasoline."

"Vinc, you crazy idiot, drive and shut up!" Studs said.

Nate honked for them to get going.

"But listen," Vinc said hesitantly.

"Get going, Curley, or we'll throw you out of the car," Tommy threatened.

Vinc was cowed, and he started up, following Nate's cab over to South Park Avenue, and then south.

"Hey, Vinc, look out or you'll get run in for blocking traffic," Mush Joss said as the car crept along.

"I'm driving all right. They can't arrest me," Vinc replied about a minute later.

"They don't allow parking on this street, Curley," Studs said.

"Say, Curley, for Christ sake, move!" Benny Taite yelled.

"Benny, I wish you wouldn't talk like that in this car on Christmas Eve. It might make bad luck and cause an accident," Vinc said.

"His old lady certainly must have dropped him hard when he was a baby," Red said.

"Come on, Vinc, for Christ sake, we don't want to get run in for mopery," Tommy Doyle said.

Two minutes later, he said: "Tommy, what did you mean by that last thing you said?"

"Whoops, we passed another block," Studs shouted.

"For Christ sake, chloroform that idiot," Doyle said.

"Step on it, Vinc," Studs said.

"Why, Studs, I never drive over fifteen miles an hour."

"Hey, Vinc, let me drive!"

"Why, Red, I couldn't. Didn't you know I wouldn't even let my grandmother drive this car?"

"Cheer, boys, we passed another block!" said Mush Joss.

"Hey, Vinc, I'll give you a stick of candy if you'll go twenty miles an hour," Studs said.

"I don't like sticks of candy, Studs," Vinc laconically replied.

"Let's take the car away from him, and throw him out on his ear," Red said.

"We hadn't better. The goddamn fool will yell so much we'd all get pinched," said Taite.

Studs whispered that it would be too good just watching Vinc with the whores out at the Cannonball Inn.

Vinc shot the car up to twenty, and after two blocks of silence, asked if he was now going fast enough to satisfy them, because it was the fastest the car had even been driven.

"Vinc, you're Dario Resta," said Studs.

"Say, Curley, does your mother love you?" asked Mush.

"Why, Mush, I thought you was my friend, and I never thought you'd talk about my mother."

"Christ, I never saw an idiot like it," Doyle said.

"What was that you said, Tommy?" asked Vinc.

"I was talking about the bald-headed sailor."

"I don't think I know him. Does he come around Fifty-eighth Street?"

"Hey, Vinc, please don't drive so fast. You'll make me seasick," Studs said after they had guffawed.

"Is that so? I was afraid, Studs, that I was going a little too fast," Vinc replied, slowing the car back to about fifteen an hour.

"Yes, Vinc, you better be careful so we don't have an accident," said Tommy.

"That's all right, Tommy. Don't worry. I had this car a year now and I never had an accident."

"Say, you horse's ass, drive!" Studs said.

"Why, Studs!"

"Whoops, another block," said Taite.

II

"We're here," Studs whooped, as the car drove into a dreary parking yard.

To the left, there was a low, rambling structure, lit by a small electric sign: CANNONBALL INN.

"But, fellows, what place is this?" Curley asked, still sitting at the wheel after all the others had gotten out.

"Church," Doyle snickered.

Studs and Slug pulled Vinc by the shoulders. He yelled. Slug told him to shut up and get out of the car, if he didn't want a foot jammed through his teeth. Vinc got out, and followed them, as they lurched towards the narrow doorway of the inn.

"Studs! Studs. Just a minute," Curley yelled.

"Shut up!" Studs replied, looking back at him.

"Jesus, Studs, see what he wants," Doyle said, when Vinc continued yelling that he wanted to ask Studs something.

Studs waited. Vinc put his hand to Studs' ear, and whispered:

"Studs, there ain't anything wrong in going here, is there?"

"No! Come on in, Vinc," Studs said, in fake friendliness.

"Well, Studs, if you say there's nothing wrong or sinful about going in, all right."

They entered a narrow saloon. Four tough-looking eggs leaned against a long bar.

"Merry Christmas, Spike!" Slug said to the beefy-faced, burly bartender.

"Same to you, Mason. I see you brought the boys along to have a good time," he replied.

The gang lined up for a drink. Vinc asked for pop. The bartender's thick lips popped open with surprise. Slug gave him the wink, and he nodded.

"Well, here's how, boys!" Slug said, lifting his small gin glass.

"And may it never get weaker," Studs added, downing the stuff.

"And here's to you, Vinc, you fuzzy wuzzy," Red said.

Vinc drank. He coughed, sputtered, lowered a face of boiling redness, hiccoughed. The bartender gave them the wink as they laughed.

"Say, are you sure that was pop?" he asked, when he was again able to talk.

"Sure thing, Charley."

"This guy's a friend of ours, Vinc. He wouldn't fool you," Benny Taite said.

"Well, it's awfully strong pop. Maybe I better have root beer."

"Don't handle it."

Vinc asked for a glass of water. They paid up. Vinc laid a dime on the bar. The bartender sneered, and said it was a half a buck. Vinc drawled that was awfully expensive for pop. He asked Studs if it was right. Studs nodded. Curley paid reluctantly.

Slug led them to a door in the rear of the saloon, and rapped three times. A slide opened, and an eye peered out. The slit closed, and the door was opened. A greasy, pimply-faced fellow with hollow cheeks wished them a Merry Christmas out of the side of his mouth, and told them to have a good time. They heard music as they crossed a dim hallway, and entered another door which led them into a gaudy cabaret with colored lights. A miscellaneous assortment of males were scattered around the tables or belly-dancing with girls in teddies and chemises. They saw the guys who had come with Nate and there was confusion and kidding while two ham-faced waiters placed two tables together. Girls quickly clustered around.

"Say, let's see the snake room first," Slug suggested.

They ordered drinks, and Slug talked to one of the bouncers. He told the girls to wait, and they all said yes, dearie.

They followed a bouncer with cauliflower ears along an aisle of tables, out a doorway, and down a narrow, dim hallway. They heard a mingled echo of moans, curses, indistinct sounds.

"It's as soundproof as we can get it," the bouncer said.

He opened a door. They were struck by an alcoholic stench, and drunken exclamations. The lights were shot on and they saw a bare room where drunks were crowded all over the floor.

The gang laughed at one drunk who snored in a corner, his belly rising and falling, his mouth wide open. Other drunks rolled on the floor, raved and one sat playing with his toes, his shoes beside him.

"Like a booby hatch," Slug said, with a smile.

"Say, are they sick?" drawled Vinc.

"Don't mind that chump," Slug said, when the bouncer looked curiously at him.

A thin guy crawled towards them on his hands and knees, bumping others, falling over one bloated fat fellow. He told them he had to crawl because he was having a terrible time with his feet; every time he tried to walk, his left foot got ahead of his right one. He braced himself along the wall, and with effort. He walked in zigzags, and then turned, and told them to judge for themselves if his right foot didn't always keep getting ahead of his left one.

"Siddown!" the bouncer said.

The guy crawled away. A fellow who had been sleeping suddenly lifted himself from the hips, and heaved; he fell back in his own vomit. Two guys in a corner tried to drown out the room by singing *She's My Lulu.*

"Jesus, let's go. That odor will kill me," said Studs.

A blond boy of about eighteen let out an insane shriek, and dashed towards them, stepping on the face of an unconscious drunk. He fell on his knees before them, and loudly begged that he be saved from the snakes. It was funny. He arose, clapped his hands to his ears, and yelled. He fell before the bouncer, and repeated his entreaties to be saved from the snakes; pointing dramatically in back of them. He crawled to the wall, still shrieking. The bouncer jerked out a blackjack and neatly put him to sleep. His face was pale and sickly in the artificial illumination.

A husky fellow rolled over to them, and yelled he'd been rolled.

"Fade!" the bouncer commanded.

"Give me my money back, you sonofabitches or I'll. . . ."

The bouncer cracked him in the jaw; he fell on top of a sleeping Polack.

"Mother! Mama! Your little boy needs you. He's sick. Mama in heaven, Mama," a fat fellow moaned on his knees in a corner.

"Jesus, they're blind," Slug said with a laugh.

"We got to do something with them," the bouncer said, turning off the light, and shutting the door. Two bouncers, with padded shoulders, passed, carting a drunk along the hallway.

"Boys will be boys!" Red said.

"Makes you want to puke," Studs said.

"Say, Studs, why do they do that?" Charley asked, innocently.

"Shut up!"

"Say, Red. . . ."

"Curley, you talk too goddamn much," Red interrupted.

The bouncer explained, in answer to Red's question, that they dumped them out in the morning.

"Say, most of the guys who work here look like they bought their faces at a second hand auction," Studs said.

They returned to their tables. The girls were there. Slug whispered to a big, angular-faced, high-cheeked, blond Polack in pink teddies.

"Gimme the dough now," she said, pronouncing her words as Slug did.

He whispered to Studs, Doyle, and Red. They handed him some change. He slipped two bills to the Polack broad.

"Hello, Vincent," she cooed, draping herself on his lap.

"Say, how did you know my name?" he asked, as drinks were set down on the table.

"Vincent, a little love-bird whispered it in my ear."

Vinc turned from the girl and called to Shrimp. Haggerty was busy telling the girl on his lap that he got tired of his wife, and needed a change. Vinc yelled to him. He turned.

"Do you want to go to the Michigan with me tomorrow afternoon, and see the picture?"

They roared. Studs told his girl that the goof had water on the brain; born that way, and no hope.

The jazz blared. Arnold, Studs, and Shrimp belly-danced with their girls. The Polack led Vinc onto the dance floor. He protested that he couldn't dance. She said she'd teach him. She rubbed against him. His face looked as if it were on the verge of being consumed by flames.

When he came back, he was kidded. He couldn't understand them. He suddenly called Mush Joss to say the other day Mush had said he had lived in the neighborhood a long time. Vinc said well he would bet ten cents he had lived in the neighborhood longer than Mush.

"You wouldn't bull me," said Mush.

"Come on, big boy, kiss me!" the Polack said.

"And kiss your maidenhead good-by, you, you goddamn fathead," Studs said.

"But, Studs. . . ."

"Daddy, don't you like to love?" the girl asked him.

"Don't do that," Vinc protested, feebly, as she placed his hand on one of her wobbly breasts.

"Dearie, you don't know what loving I'll give you," she said.

"Take your hand away. Why, I wouldn't even let my mother touch me there," Vinc said, convulsing them.

She made a little moan. He threw her off him; she landed on her can. Two bouncers grabbed Curley and they carted him to the door by the seat of the pants and the collar. He got a clout in the jaw, and landed outside.

"For Christ sake, what the hell kind of a fluke is he? Does he want me to beg him," the Polack said.

"That's all right, girlie, come on over here," Slug said.

"I never had one as goofy as that. All kinds of crazy people come to me, and want all kinds of things done to them, but I never had any guy as goofy as that."

"You know, I got four sisters, and they're all the most decent girls in the world. You know, my four sisters are as pure as a lily," Arnold Sheehan bragged drunkenly, and the girl on his lap curled her lips.

"Sing 'em, Sheehan!" Slug said.

"They're as pure as a lily. I shouldn't even walk on the same side of the street with them, after I come here. And anybody that says my four sisters ain't as pure as a lily has gotta fight me," Arnold said, pounding the table.

"My two sisters are as pure as yours," Studs said.

"Say, are all these guys queer?" the Polack asked Slug.

"Polluted. The boys is out for a good time," Slug laughed.

"Well, why don't they shut up talking and prove themselves upstairs. A man only proves himself in a bed. No girls are pure and those that pretend they are are just yellow. They all want it, and they get it too, and they pretend like hypocrites," the girl on Arnold's lap said.

"Sally!" the girl with Shrimp remonstrated.

"I don't care. I'm sick of these guys coming here and telling me I'm a whore and not as good as their goddamn wives, and sisters, and sweethearts."

"Sally had a fight because she wasn't getting enough towels. She's cranky tonight," the girl on Shrimp's lap said.

"Hey, cut it. The show is starting," Slug said.

XII

Los Angeles, Cal.
Dece. 25, 1922

DEAR DAN:

I thought I drope you a few lines to let you know how we all are, and what a very fine Xmas we had an I hope yours was just as marry as my. Well Danny you know we are all settle out here now and it seem different from are last when my father was living. But you know when he lose his job because he was a union man and they give the double + it break his heart and he was a man of sixty year and you know how that just kill him of broken heart. And we miss him but we had a marry Xmas like we know he would want us to and we had sun shines only we all miss my dad lots and it was very hot it was 81 not so bad is it for Dece. I gest its kinda cold in old Chi today but I gest you enjoy it anyways. It looks grate to see all the flower in bloob in Dece and the trees and grass as green as ever. We had lots of rain a cupple of weeks ago and it sure did come down hard when it rain here it is in Nove or Dece. And Dan. but after that seson is over we don't see any rain all summer untill the nex rainny seson. Well Dan in one of your letters you send me you told me some
one said in about two mor month you won't get letter frome me but
me
don't let that wurry you because you will always hear frome the only one that won't get a letter from me is the one that don't answer letter I send them. You my bes pal Danny O'Neill you are and a cupple other are the only one that have send me at all. I have sent a gril a number of letters to and I have got only one answer to them and I dont know what is the matter with him I mean Hoppy Shanks. I thought he was one of my best Pal, but Dan I gest you are the only true Pal I got and I'm sure glad its you. I've been writing a gril in Chi. I gest you know her. Her name is Catherine Heving and she sure is a fine gril and I got quiet a number of letters frome her. Well Dan I gest your getting ready for bed while I'm writing this little letter but I gest I can't think of any mor so good night. Your Pal.

Andy Le Gare

Happy New Year

P.S. Dan and please tell Stutz Lonigan that Andy Le Gare wish him a Marry Xmas and a Happy New Year Tell hime I wanted a send him a card but Dan I couldn't send him one wishing him a Marry Xmas and a Happy New Year when I never know his address because Dan I am always ready to say Stutz Lonigan is the bes whitest guy of the older guy who hang around that pool roome den of iniquieties and the only one of them guy who treat me decent when I was a kid and I like hime and want him to know that I wish hime a Marry Xmas and a Happy New Year and so Dan you please dont forget to tell hime that.

Chapter Twelve

I

Now, Mary, compose yourself! No news is often good news," Lonigan said feebly to his wife who sat with her bowed head lowered in tears.

"He's not worth crying over, getting drunk and acting like a pig!"

"Frances, after all, Bill is your brother, and this is Christmas Day," Lonigan said in a conciliatory manner.

He stared out the window at the snow flurrying lightly through the sunless Christmas Day. There was a catch in his throat; the whole family had received communion at five o'clock mass, except Bill.

"A curse must have been put on him," the mother exclaimed between wails.

"Mother!" Lonigan muttered, unable to say any more. He arose and patted her head. She sobbed that he was her boy and she had suffered a mother's agony bringing him into this world.

"Oh!"

"Don't worry, nothing has happened to him except that he's probably drunk as a pig!" Fran said; she strode nervously back and forth across the parlor.

Mrs. Lonigan drew some rosary beads out of her apron pocket, kissed the crucifix attached to them, blessed herself with it and commenced whispering her rosary.

"Well, maybe I had better notify the police, at that," Lonigan said, continuing to remain slumped in his rocker.

"Dad, he has his name and address in his wallet. I'm sure that if anything serious happened to him, we'd have heard about it," Loretta said.

Lonigan looked gratefully at his youngest daughter.

"I warned you all along to make him go to Loyola and get in with the right kind of fellows instead of with drunken poolroom bums," Fran said; her father winced.

"God, what can we do? If people we know saw him, I'll never again be able to set foot in St. Patrick's Church with my head up," the mother mourned.

"And what will I do? Shamed and disgraced before Michael so that

I couldn't look him in the face last night. My whole evening was ruined. I was so disgraced that I could have wept," Fran complained.

"Fran, please!" Loretta exclaimed.

They were thrown into silence as the key clicked in the front door.

"Now, folks, let me handle this!" the father said, showing a sudden sense of confidence and control.

The mother rushed to the hall as Studs was heard walking to the bathroom. She flung herself on him, and sobbed:

"My son! My son! My precious first-born baby son!"

"Mother!" Fran indignantly called from the parlor.

He heeded their summons and walked into the parlor, limping, with his clothes filthy, his face bloated, his eyes bloodshot.

"Well!" he exclaimed, with a slight shrug of the shoulder.

"Bill, isn't this a fine how-do-you-do on Christmas Morning?" the father said accusingly.

"Yes, William, Merry Christmas!" Fran said sarcastically.

"Jesus, Mary and Joseph, what did Satan do to my son!" the mother cried, throwing her arms dramatically over her head, looking vaguely at the ceiling with haggard, red eyes.

"Please, mother!" Loretta pleaded, showing presence of mind.

Lonigan looked from son to mother, pain in his face. Fran's lip turned with contempt. Martin quietly entered the parlor; he was ordered out, and stood listening in the hallway.

"Mary, most holy Mother of God, what did I do to earn this misfortune?" the mother yelled.

Loretta looked hopelessly from one to the other, striving to calm them with her glances; she smiled weakly but with sympathy at Studs.

"Never as long as I live will I feel towards him again as a sister, or recognize that he is my brother!" Fran said with appropriate melodrama.

"After all I've done for my children, and suffered!" the mother exclaimed.

Fran went to her bedroom, and returned with Studs' Christmas present of six pair of silk stockings.

"Till my dying day I'll hate you . . . you . . . you brute!" she said, returning the present.

Studs accepted them without a word. He was tired and pooped. His head ached. He could taste vomit all the way up from his guts. He could hardly keep his eyes open.

They looked at Fran, shocked, hurt. In a wearied voice, the father asked her please not to do a thing like that. She retorted that her ears still burned from the vile, unmentionable things he had called her and Michael last night. The mother pulled a faint. Fran blamed Studs for it. Loretta ran for water. Studs stood helpless in the center of the parlor. The father excitedly told everyone not to get excited. He patted the mother's pale cheeks.

"Close your trap!" Studs finally barked, tired of Fran's accusation that he was murdering his mother.

"Jesus, Mary and Joseph!" the mother cried, coming to and sitting up, her words drowning Fran's querulous voice.

"Are you all right, mother?" Loretta solicitously asked.

"Don't worry about me. I'm only a mother!"

The father asserted that he would take charge of things, and asked Bill to wash up and have a talk with him. He drank a cup of coffee, and sat in the dining-room trying to read his crumpled copy of the morning newspaper, while Studs washed up and changed his clothes. He drifted into thinking of what he would tell Studs, and was quickly precipitated into nostalgic memories of how he had gone on benders in his own day; and how, once, right after he had popped the question and Mary had said yes, he had gotten blind as a bat and almost kicked over the apple cart trying to start a scrap with a whole room full of her relatives. He had made his mistakes, plenty of them. Ah, some of those Saturday nights. But that was no excuse for Bill. He had had no chance in life. His father had been poor and a heavy drinker, and he and his mother, Lord have mercy on their souls, had always quarreled and bickered. Bill had a good home, a good example set for him, a place made for him in life, all that a young man could ask for. His own mistakes should serve as a beacon light to guide the boy, Bill, along the right way. That solid old maxim: Do not as I do, but do as I say, it was sound sense. And he hadn't drunk stuff like young fellows drank nowadays. It was rat poison, that killed people like flies. If the young fellows kept up drinking stuff like that, they'd all be dead by the time they were twenty-five or thirty. And then too, except for a few times, he'd always known how to keep his liquor under his belt. Ah, yes, he must point out to Bill the vanities and pitfalls that beset a young man, make it serve as a lesson to him. He had to guide Bill so he wouldn't make the same sorry mistakes that all the young fellows in this jazz and Prohibition age were making.

Studs entered, smiling sheepishly; he was cleaned up and had on a fresh suit and shirt. Lonigan's planned talk faded from his mind, and he was only aware that there was a deep common bond between him and his son; after all, he and Bill were the men of the family, and when he dropped the reins of responsibility, Bill would have to take them up. And Bill was the one who took after him the most. A real Lonigan. The others took more after their mother.

Melancholy misted his thoughts. Ah, he was growing old and life was moving along, he thought: he glanced towards Bill. Father and son faced each other with averted eyes.

"Bill, it was too bad, too bad this unfortunate thing had to happen," Lonigan mourned, shaking his head in sadness, and then emitting a drawn-out and soft sigh of regret.

He stuttered and hesitated as he tried to say that he didn't mind a young fellow drinking a little and having a good time, but that there was a limit, and he hoped that it wouldn't happen again. He told Bill what great confidence he was placing in him. He hoped Bill would not destroy that confidence completely; last night he had shaken it severely, yes, severely.

He stopped talking. Father and son sat in silent misery. If only they could get a grip on the right words. They couldn't, and were keenly aware of their smokes.

"Yes, Bill, it's a great disappointment and it's nearly broken your mother's heart," Lonigan said, arising.

He asked Studs to be more careful in the future and said that they would forgive this mistake, but that it shouldn't happen again.

II

In Nomine Patris, et Filii, et Spiritus Sancti. Amen.

A street car grated by. The swinging doors of the church were shoved to admit influxes of worshipers. The new arrivals clustered about the two tables near the holy water founts at the end of the center aisles, paying their ten cents pew rent, causing coins to be weakly clinked together. The ushers led a few lucky persons to the last vacant seats towards the rear of the aisles, while many others joined those who stood in the back and down the side aisles. Those parishioners who had rented pews by the season or annually marched proudly to their reserved places towards the front. Feet were scraped on the rubber floor covering. A man coughed.

Father Doneggan, clad in gold vestments of joyousness, bowed profoundly before the gilded golden altar with joined hands, and sing-songed:

Confiteor Deo omnipotenti, beatae Mariae semper virgini. . . .

Studs Lonigan knelt crushed in a pew towards the rear on the Blessed Virgin's side of the church. He was aware of the perfume scent and presence of a girl beside him, and her squirrel coat was brushed tantalizingly against his knee. He bowed his head to pray, and thought that the Mass was sacred, the unbloody sacrifice of the body and blood of Jesus Christ, Our Lord, the symbolic repetition of His Holy and inspiring life, and he would have to hear Mass in the right and proper spirit. He shook his head to ward off the threat of sleep. He mumbled the words of the Our Father by rote, and looked forwards as Father Doneggan bowed down over the altar, and prayed rapidly:

Oramus te, Domine per merita sanctorum tuorum quorum

Unwittingly, he wished that the Mass were over. He had let himself in for it, coming to high Mass. Anyway, Father Doneggan always hurried through his Masses, and it wouldn't be as long as if Father Gilhooley or Father Roney were celebrating it.

He heard the swinging doors, the scrape of feet, and then, another street car. He glanced around to his right, and saw Young Rocky yawning. He watched Mr. and Mrs. Dennis P. Gorman proceed down the center aisle to their rented pews, past Austin McAulliffe, the usher who stood in the aisle and smiled as they approached. Over to his right and a couple of pews down, he saw Arnold Sheehan's twin sisters, and he thought of how Arnold had bragged of them last night. They weren't as good-looking, or as well-dressed as his sisters. He smiled, seeing the Nolan family marching down the center aisle to their pews: they were built like steps, first the old man, then the mother, then the three boys in the order of their sizes. He smiled again, remembering that joke he always sprung on Jim Nolan; "Every time your old man saves a couple of hundred bucks, he brings another Nolan over from the old country, and gets him a job on the railroad."

He heard the choir singing:

Kyrie eleison!
Kyrie eleison!
Kyrie eleison!

He had to keep his mind on the Mass particularly because he had acted like such a bastard last night on Christmas Eve. He prayed. He watched Jim Clayburn go by him, tall, erect, dignified in a conservative black suit. Jim turned and pointed to a pew seat a couple of yards in front of Studs, and Studs stared at Jim's thin, white face, set above a high stiff collar. A man genuflected and took the pew seat pointed out to him. Jim strode back, smiling a weak recognition at Studs.

Studs looked at the lighted altar. Standing in the middle of it, extending his hands, then joining them, Father Doneggan intoned:

Gloria in excelsis Deo, et in terra pax hominibus. . . .

Studs knew that he was singing the praise of Almighty God, but couldn't remember just what this part of the Mass was called and what it symbolized. Hell of a Catholic he was. He mumbled Hail Marys. Again he listened:

Quoniam tu solus sanctus. Tu solus Dominus . . .

After his prayer, the priest bowed down to kiss the altar, and again turned to face the people and chant:

Dominus vobiscum . . .

The choir replied:

Et cum spiritu tuo.

Studs closed his eyes, opened them. Covertly, he rubbed spittle on them in order to remain awake. He shuddered with a sudden shock, as if of electricity, when the squirrel coat of the voluptuous blond next to him rubbed against his leg, just above the knee. He started saying another Hail Mary, but his thoughts were distracted before he concluded, and he wondered what had happened last night. There had been that raid. Jesus Christ, he'd been afraid. He had been so goddamn shaky that he'd jumped from the second-story window, spraining his ankle. It hurt now. But he was proud of his stunt, escaping from the law, perhaps being the only one who had. It was something they'd remember around the poolroom and the corner for a long while.

He gazed around the church to see if any of the boys were present. Seeing none of them, he guessed that they must all have been picked up, and were enjoying Christmas Day in the can. He knelt forwards and slumped his shoulders, because kneeling erect was tiring. He grimaced with a sudden pain in his ankle, and had to maneuver his right leg. He felt that she was looking at him, thinking he was a clown. His expression became serious and circumspect. He felt her eyes upon him. He would impress her. From the corner of his eye, he saw a finger on her rosary beads, a soft finger, soaped in whiteness, the long nail polished and shinily pink. He side-glanced and saw her thin face, powdered, neatly rouged, a long straight nose, wide lips, an expression of calm sophistication. The squirrel coat touched his leg. Imperceptibly, he let his body edge a fraction of an inch towards her. He heard the mumbling sounds vaguely as Father Doneggan bowed over the altar and silently uttered the prayers in preparation for the reading of the holy Gospel. He yawned. His mind returned to last night. He almost fell asleep, and as if he were coming to his senses, he heard Father Doneggan swiftly chanting:

Sequentia sancti evangeli secundum.

He felt a sudden elation as if he had realized one of his dreams, because he was, he knew it, on the verge of doing just that. He always, each day when he got up, and every time he went to church, had the feeling that maybe he might meet a girl, the girl he knew he would some day meet. And now this girl next to him, maybe she was the one. He quickly palmed his hands together, and tried to pray, and to look like he was praying, with proper seriousness. More aware of her than of the ceremonies, he pattered out the unthought words of the Our Father. He arose with the people, and stood like one in a dream. He sat down, hoping now, maybe, he and she would sit with their thighs against one another. He saw, in surprise, that Father Doneggan stood by the altar rail with a black book in his hand. He arose for the reading of the Gospel, determined to listen:

The shepherds said to one another: Let us go to Bethlehem, and see this thing which is to come to pass, which the Lord hath showed us. . . .

He leaned his weight on the back of the pew in front of him. He tried to keep her face in his mind, but he forgot what she looked like, and had to side-glance to recall the features on her thin handsome face. He stared straight ahead at the priest, whose reading made disturbing indistinguishable sounds to him, and the image of her face thinned out, and then, it suddenly bloated with fat, as if he was seeing her in one of the crazy mirrors at the Fun House in White City. He looked at her again. There was an icy quality about her, too. It made him afraid she was too proud for him to make her love him, but no, it would be different and she would go for him as he did for her. Me for you, baby, he told himself. He determined once again to put exterior thoughts from him and hear Mass in the right way. He forced himself to listen:

And the shepherds returned, glorifying and praising God for all that they had heard and seen as it was told to them.

After the Gospel, Studs sat down with the other people and perfunctorily blessed himself as the sermon began. The sermon seemed like a drone to him. He recalled the phrase from the Gospel, "glorifying God," and a mood of repentance struck him with a sorrow that was almost abject. He said an act of contrition, trying to make it rise from a penitent heart. This was the first Christmas morning since he had made his first Holy Communion upon which he had not received. Glorifying God. Doing what he had done on Christmas Eve. Drunk, in a whore house, watching a filthy performance by two of the lowest women there could be, going up with a whore. . . . Oh, my God, I am heartily, heartily sorry for having offended Thee, I am not worthy. . . . He had come home stinking from drink, looking like a sow, worse than the prodigal son, spoiling everybody's Christmas day at home. Oh, my God, I am heartily sorry. . . . and he had been in bed with the whore. The noise of the raid, the disappointment in that moment of discovery, came back, and recalling how it had just been before the moment, hot desires flushed his thoughts, and he wanted a woman, and her presence next to him made it worse, and if only the raid had been pulled off two minutes later. . . . Oh, my God . . .

He listened to Father Doneggan's description of the manger, where the Christ Child had been born, that conception which was the most important single event in all the crowded history of mankind.

His mind floated and he thought of her next to him in a way that decent girls shouldn't be thought of, and he wished that there was one more person in the pew so that he and she would be squeezed together, and Jesus Christ, he felt like a plain low-down ordinary sonofabitch.

"And there was the Christ Child in that humble manger, a child of poverty. Christ, our Lord, could have come unto man, a king in proud kingly robes, a monarch greater than all other earthly monarchs. But no, HE came as the foster-child of a poor and humble carpenter. He came unto man in humility. And, my friends, that

humility of Christ, our Lord and Savior, is one of the many lessons that we should learn on this great and joyous feast day that is celebrated throughout Christendom."

She was sitting straight up. Was she listening? Did her mind wander? Did she think of him, want to meet him, know him? Had she ever heard of him? Perhaps she had been maybe to a dance and had met Dan Donoghue there, and had heard Dan say something about Studs Lonigan, and she had asked who Studs Lonigan was. And after Dan had told her, maybe she had said, or at least thought, that she would like to meet Studs Lonigan. And now she was kneeling next to him, and afterwards, going out of church, maybe they would talk, and then he would walk home with her, and arrange to take her to a show this evening. He quickly covered a yawn with his right hand. He put his hand down because he didn't want her to notice the nicotine on his fingers. He glanced about him with an air of put-on seriousness, and saw Tommy Doyle's mother in a pew across the aisle to his left. He looked to the rear, and saw the people standing, and by Father Doneggan's confessional, the beaming red face of Father Gilhooley. Father Gilhooley was probably happy, thinking of what a collection he would get, and of how so many parishioners had received Holy Communion. So many, but not Studs Lonigan.

Father Doneggan blessed himself at the completion of the sermon, and turned back towards the altar.

Studs determined that he would be more attentive. He would have to be, or it would be just the same as not having heard Mass, and that, after last night, would be flying too flagrantly in the face of God Almighty. His belly was upset. His head throbbed. He was almost overpowered with thirst. His back was heavy. His ankle pained. He had just about ruined himself . . . like a goddamn fool. He had to smile, remembering Vinc Curley, and that snake-room full of drunks.

Credo in unum Deum. . . .

Somehow, somehow inexplicably, her thigh seemed to brush against him, and it seemed to remain pressed an instant longer than it would have if she had done it without intention, and maybe, maybe it meant she wanted to break the ice. A nervous tremor signalled through him, an exultation flowed from nerve to nerve, and that pressure, like a deft finger, made him feel as if he were on the verge of great happiness and excitement. The pressure relaxed, and a sense of sin came into his thoughts like vomit. He silently muttered an Our Father.

The future seemed opening up to him like a new land, and he could see himself and her going together, making each other happy, surprising everybody who knew them, making the guys all jealous, and he could hear them saying, she must have been stewed when she picked him, she's the keenest girl in the parish, she's hot, boy, Studs got himself a woman and I don't mean maybe.

And he would take her places, and the future was before him like a new land, and he felt like Columbus might have felt when he discovered America.

Father Doneggan kissed the altar. He turned and saluted the people:

Dominus vobiscum.
Et cum spiritu tuo.
Oremus.

The choir sang the appointed psalm. A sense of solemnity came upon Studs. He bowed his head as Father Doneggan took the host, to be consecrated, from the paten, and solemnly consecrated it. Studs' head remained bowed. A vision of Heaven, with God enthroned in red on a golden throne, came to him as through a mist. He was unaware of the sacred progress of the Mass, and he knelt with his head still bowed, filled with vague thoughts of adoration, until he heard the choir:

The shepherds were watching, the whole night through,
Under the starry sky. . . .

As a boy, he had sung the song in the children's choir at five o'clock Mass on Christmas Morning. The feeling of Christmas, a feeling of joy and reverence suffused upon him, and he remembered boyhood Christmas Days, with the snow coming down as he dashed to five o'clock Mass, wearing high, laced boots like those lumberjacks wore in movies, kicking chunks of ice with them, hoping to meet Lucy, meeting Dan and Bill, hunching his face forwards and hurrying into a raw wind. He remembered himself, Dan and Bill running to church to be there on time. He remembered them singing, with Lucy, standing with the girls, singing, now and then seeming to dart a glance at him, and TB McCarthy in front of him, goofily singing:

The shepherds were guzzling the whole night through,
Under the beery sky. . . .

Jim Clayburn came towards him with the collection box, a small, square, wooden container attached to a long pole. Jim pushed it by Studs, smiling a trifle, and Studs dropped in a Christmas envelope, containing five dollars. Studs noticed that the box was packed with bills and envelopes. He hoped she'd noticed that he was making a good offering. She put in a dollar bill.

The offertory bell sounded a warning that the Canon or Sacrificial part of the Mass was beginning. Heads bowed, and hands beat on chest.

Sanctus, Sanctus, Sanctus. . . .

Studs muttered the words of the Act of Contrition over and over again. He wished last night undone, like he had almost never wished for anything. The bell, the sudden feeling of change in everyone at Mass, the knowledge that he was to witness the greatest of mysteries, the changing of bread and water into the body and blood of Jesus Christ, the memories of other Masses, other Christmas Days, catechism lessons, all converged in him. He was lonesome, and contrite, and adoring. He felt himself a part of the great and powerful Catholic Church, built upon the rock of Peter, a member, however unworthy, and he vowed to be more worthy. He thought of how, ever since the Last Supper, the mystery of the Mass had been celebrated, and God, through Jesus Christ, Our Lord, had given himself to the faithful for their redemption. In ancient Rome, in catacombs, in the middle ages in great cathedrals, in Ireland in caves when the priests were hunted, and the British had put a price on their heads, today all over the world, this same Mass, this same sacrifice was being celebrated, and pride in the Church mounted in equal proportion with his cumulative feeling of shamed unworthiness. . . .

Vere . . . Quia pere incarnati Verbi mysterium . . .

The Latin words blended into the mystery, and Studs would have given anything to have received Holy Communion on this Christmas Day. He prayed sincerely, saying Our Fathers and Hail Marys, his mind filling again and again with visions of heavenly rejoicing about the shining thrones of the bearded and powerful Creator of Heaven and Earth, of other Masses, of the Church through the ages, the Popes celebrating Mass in Rome centuries ago, missionaries celebrating in far off heathen Asia. . . . I believe in God, the Father Almighty, Creator of Heaven and Earth. . . . Envy flashed in his thoughts, and he wished that he were in Father Doneggan's place, celebrating the Mass, exercising the greatest and most mysterious powers that man could have, and that only could be exercised by him who was consecreated in the priesthood. He thought that perhaps his mother had been right, and that he had had a vocation, and that he should have studied for the priesthood. Perhaps he had scorned a vocation, and that was the reason why he was always feeling that there was something more in life that he could never seem to get, and couldn't even name. Perhaps his heedlessness to the call from God Almighty meant that he would be unhappy all his life.

Adeste fideles! Adeste fideles!
Regem angelorum.
Venite adoremus, venite adoremus
In Bethlehem.

The tune of the Christmas song ran through his mind, again drawing it back to boyhood, and boyhood Christmas Days, and that Christmas Morning that he had come home from five o'clock Mass, and had been given a ten-dollar gold piece by his old man, and in the afternoon, he and Dan Donoghue had gone to a show and seen Salome, and in the picture, Theda Bara as Salome had done the dance of the seven veils, stripping off veil after veil, and the scene had suddenly changed before the last veil had come off, and they had been so damn disappointed. He was sad because he had grown up, and because the years passed like a river that no man could stop. Oh, come let us adore, oh, come let us adore, Christ, Our King. He had all the old feelings he had used to have on Christmas Day, feelings he could not find words for, feelings that ran through the songs sung in church on Christmas. . . .

Pater noster, qui es in coelis. . . .

Again, the bell knelled through the hushed church. Studs bowed his head in unison with the people, and tapped his breast. His thoughts were vague. His body and mind seemed separated, his mind swimming away free and in a sea of melancholy, his body heavy and sluggish like a dragging weight.

He listened to the choir singing, a sweetness and strength in their voices and in the song:

Agnus Dei, qui tollis peccata mundi. . . .

He watched Father Doneggan bowing his head low and silently reciting the prayers in immediate preparation for the reception of Holy Communion. Through his mind there ran a communion song;

Oh, Lord, I am not worthy,
That Thou shouldst come to me.
But speak the words of comfort,
And my spirit healed shall be.

He felt like a plain, ordinary low-down bastard. He vowed that he would receive Holy Communion next Sunday. But he knew he would always be sorry for having done what he had last night. And he thought of her next to him, and tried to wish she and he were engaged, and going to Communion together this morning, and. . . . He bowed his head as the bell rang for the Domine non sum dignis.

Mass would soon be over. He wanted it to be, and he didn't want it to be over, because maybe if he didn't work fast now, he would never see, or never get a chance with the girl who was next to him. And he was tired. The church seemed to get more and more stuffy, and he was almost falling asleep. He kept side-glancing at her, and he wanted her more and more with every glimpse. He faced the altar, all his confidence shattered, and wondering whether or not she was thinking of him, or even secretly laughing at him. He tried to regain his confidence by assuring himself he was Studs Lonigan, and that Studs Lonigan had done things, was real stuff, and tough, too.

He arose for the last Gospel and people commenced leaving the church. He heard her whispering pardon me, the voice striking him will-less. She had to repeat it. He turned. She smiled, and he didn't know what to make of her smile, whether it was friendly or sarcastic or what. She passed him, and was gone. It was like a toppling of thrones, a toppling of something inside of him. Maybe she was gone out of his life, just like Lucy. He tried to remember her voice, with its quiet but confident tones. He tried to remember her face. He tried to feel he would see her again, and that with her everything would be different, and there would be no more jazzing around, drinking, can houses. Maybe next Saturday night when he went to confession, she would be there and remember him, and he'd be reformed by her, and . . . He yawned. Felt rotten, goddamn it. He had been a complete, undiluted, unadulterated, all-around chump. And he was sorry, very sorry.

Deo gratias. . . .

He walked out of the church, while the choir sang:

Oh, come, let us adore Him! Oh, come, let us adore Him.
Christ, our King. . . .

He shoved forwards, passing people, but when he got outside, he couldn't find her in the crowd. People wished him a Merry Christmas and he hardly heard them. But he would, he would, by Christ, he would see her again, and she would know him, the real Studs Lonigan that nobody had ever known.

He met Tommy Doyle, and they looked at the people pass until Tommy got tired. Studs dragged along with Tommy, still wanting to wait as a last hope that she might be outside, that she might even be waiting for him. Tommy told Studs how they had all been thrown in the can, and asked how he had gotten away. Studs told him. Tommy marvelled. He said Red's old man had gotten them out. Studs felt lousy, but hurried Tommy along, despite his sprained ankle, because he was hoping they would pass her on the street. They stopped for a coke at Fifty-eighth and Indiana Avenue, and then went over to the poolroom, because Studs wanted the fellows to know how he had escaped during the raid. But he didn't think that he had ever felt so low in his whole life.

SECTION THREE

1924

XIII

IT WAS *dreary February weather. The children were all out, and Mrs. Lonigan had the dinner dishes finished. She rearranged a few chairs. She emptied an ash-tray. She straightened her sons' dresser. She pottered about until there was absolutely nothing to do. Then she picked up the* New World *and read the news. Lonigan laughed over the funnies. Cigar ashes dropped onto his shirt, and some fell on the floor. Mrs. Lonigan cautioned him, and hustled in with the carpet sweeper. He said she should not worry because ashes kept moths away and were good for a rug. She said ashes did nothing any good. She put away the carpet sweeper, returned, and looked through the society section of the* Chicago Daily Tribune. *He glanced at his watch. She asked the time, and he answered that it was a quarter to four. She remonstrated aloud with herself that it was too late to go to Benediction. She suggested that they take a little walk and get a nip of air. He yawned and said he was too tired and thought he would take a nap. She picked up the funnies and arranged them neatly with the other sections of the Sunday paper. When Lonigan awoke, it was dark out. Mrs. Lonigan was preparing supper, and Martin was in the parlor playing* The Sheik of Araby *on their two-hundred-dollar electric victrola. Lonigan went out to the kitchen, his face wide with a yawn, and remarked that spring would soon be bursting forth, and that he would have to be taking his sweetheart out a lot like the good old days. He pinched her cheeks. She told him not to be bothering her while she was fixing the meal.*

Chapter Thirteen

I'M YOUR buddy, Hink. I'll take care of you," Shrimp Haggerty drooled; he tottered forwards to clutch at Hink Weber's arm as Hink reeled by the curb edge. Mush Joss feebly grabbed for Hink's other arm, Hink strained and muttered incoherently, while he dragged them about.

Nate Klein alighted from his cab and joined Studs, who stood in front of the poolroom with his hands sunk in his overcoat pocket.

"Weber is aiming to take a nose dive in the gutter," Nate said with a silly laugh.

"Yeah. But say, Nate, I thought Mush Joss was in the navy?" Studs asked.

"He deserted, second time, the boys were saying."

Hink shook free of his caretakers and floundered into a precarious balance. He swayed as helplessly as a baby in the center of the sidewalk, with his shoulders bent and his nodding head lowered.

"How goes the cab racket, fink?" laughed Studs.

"Well, Studs, I ain't got no complaints. I wasn't working for a long time, and then I got me this job, and now I'm also lined up with a can house, and get my split on anybody I bring there. That reminds me. The next time you boys want a girl, let me bring you there. The girls are all young."

"Sure. How about you? Ever take part of your split out in trade?"

"Do I? They got a seventeen-year-old blond there who's as low as a broad could be, but say, Studs, she knows her stuff," Nate said, lasciviously.

Studs watched the blind meanderings of the three drunks. Nate laughed and wisecracked.

"Nate, it looks like hell to see a guy like Hink so goddamn helpless. Christ, look at him, and he's such a powerful fellow, with a beautiful physique. Say, they could make a statue out of that boy's body," Studs said reflectively.

"Hell, Studs, we all get that way now and then; he'll get over it."

"Say, and you know Shrimp is looking bad these days. He's getting skinnier than a rail."

"Yeah, he's hitting it up."

"His wife takes plenty from him. Christ, he's drunk every day, and she goes out and works for him, and they got that kid. I wonder why the hell Shrimp married her. He doesn't seem to give a damn for her," said Studs.

"You know how it is, Studs. A broad won't come across and a guy gets hot for her, so he marries her to get it. Then after he gets it a while, he gets tired and wants something else to change his luck. It happens that way in the best-regulated families," Nate said.

"I guess so, but how come you're blowing so quickly?"

"Work, my boy. I ain't booked a thing tonight yet," Nate said, leaving.

"I see you're sober tonight, Studs," well-dressed Phil Rolfe said, stepping out of the poolroom.

"I got to lay off the stuff. I drank too much of it already. Got a heartburn, and I want to watch my guts."

"Doctor's orders?"

"No, I just figured I better cut the stuff out for a while."

"That's the smart thing to do; it makes a pig out of you when you get blind."

Studs watched Shrimp and Mush laboring to lift Hink from where he had fallen on his face. Studs assisted them and then returned to his post by the window.

"It's chump stuff, drinking that way, and it doesn't pay a guy no-how," Phil said; he trotted on.

Hink broke loose from his buddies and wandered towards Calumet Avenue, babbling; pedestrians give him a wide berth. While Shrimp and Mush laughed, he let out a big heave, and some of his vomit splashed the silk stocking of a passing girl. She walked on indignant, muttering that it was perfectly disgusting, while Shrimp and Mush flirted with her. Studs looked at her leg.

They dragged Hink back, and got him inside the poolroom. Studs walked off towards the park. Like a pig in a gutter. It was queer all right, the way people always drank. You were calm and sober, and wanted something to do, excitement, wanted to cut loose. So you warmed your belly up with a few drinks, and it made your head a little giddy. Everything seemed suddenly rosy or funny, you were happy, you forgot everything that was bothering you. People laughed at what you said, and you laughed at your own jokes too. Everybody looked at you. You were proud of yourself, proud because you couldn't even walk straight. You weren't afraid of any sonofabitch and his brother—sometimes, not even of Johnny Law. You didn't care what you did, told everybody what you thought of him, kicked in windows, raised all holy hell. It was a glorious feeling, but you kept wanting more to drink, and kept wanting to talk more and tell the world who you were and what a great guy you were, make everybody just pay attention to you. And soon, the lights went out. Everything was black, and all you knew about was a kind of torment the same as when you went under gas to have a tooth pulled. You acted like a clown, became so helpless that you couldn't walk, puked, sometimes got puke all over yourself, made a pig out of yourself. Pig Lonigan. A wave of self-disgust swept through him. It wasn't worth it. The stuff was generally strong enough to corrode a cast-iron gut. It was canned heat, rot-gut, furniture-varnish, rat-poison. When you drank it, you took your life in your hands, and even if it didn't kill you, it might make you blind, or put your heart, liver, guts or kidneys on the fritz for life. And after you went on a bat, you woke up the next morning with a hangover. You were so jumpy you couldn't be satisfied with anything. You had sweats, a general feeling of tiredness and were ashamed of yourself for having been a fool. Your head throbbed with lines of pain running clean through it, and you had to put ice packs on it. Your guts were upset and heaving, and you couldn't eat. You were so damn thirsty that you couldn't drink enough water. You had to dope yourself with bromos, bicarbonate of soda, black coffee, aspirin, and cokes. It ruined your whole goddamn day, and you tasted bum gin and moonshine for three days.

He crossed over into Washington Park. It seemed funny to him now, how it was something to brag about, like copping a cherry, and how back in the sixth grade, he and most of the kids had thought drinking was a horrible disgrace. He didn't know why he had drunk so much of the world's liquor in his twenty-two and a half years. He had just started drinking because all the guys did. But he was on the wagon. Yes, and for good . . . maybe.

Suddenly, he sensed that spring was in the air. He could smell it. He breathed deeply, changed his slouchy walk into a brisk one, and looked about him at the dark shadows, the naked shrubbery and trees. He crossed the park drive, and walked around the patch of shrubbery on the right-hand side of the walk that curved to the boathouse. He could see the lagoon, steely, dark, glittering here and there with the moon and stars. The world, the night, the park, spring that was going to come, it was all new. He felt as if he were discovering them for the first time in his life, as if the sense of budding things, of leaves coming out on the branches, the gradual warming and laziness in the air, the grass bursting green through the cold, hard, wintry earth, as if all these were inside of him. He wished that it were spring already. He determined that it was going to be a different spring and summer for him. He was fed up with the old stuff, and he had let himself go far enough already.

He stood by the lagoon watching while trifling waves swished into the thin line of pebbled shore. He glanced up at the sky and was quickened with surprise and elation because it was so clear, with such clean clouds, and a moon which seemed like frothy ice or frozen snow. And he had never realized there were so many stars in the sky, some of them blue like signal lights far, far off. They were all over the sky like jewels flung on a dark carpet and they made him wonder about life, and what it was and why people had such curious feelings. But he guessed that God had made life and the stars just as they were so people would wonder like that, and marvel at His handiwork.

He had a feeling of freshness and cleanness, even if he, too, had often been drunk like a pig. Pig Lonigan! And the thought of the spring that was coming made him happy. He thought how he would walk about in the park, with the trees and smells and sky and shadows and people, young girls in summer clothes, looking like Lucy had looked just so soon after graduation. Spring was like new life to the world, and he was going to be a new person in this coming new spring. And that girl. He had seen her a couple of times at church, but she had not batted an eye; she didn't know who he was, or if she did, she didn't show it. But he knew, he had faith that she was going to be the center of his new life in this coming new spring, and he was going to be a different Studs Lonigan, not a pig, stinking with lousy gin, and rolling helplessly in the gutter, like he'd seen Hink Weber doing. Some day he'd see her, meet her, speak to her, tell her how he had been in the park this very night, and of the things he'd thought, and how she had been in them so much, as if she were the trees and flowers of the new spring growing inside of him. He suddenly remembered Lucy. Hell with her! This other girl was keener. Lucy had had her chance. She could be sorry when it was too late. But he would learn from losing Lucy, and he wouldn't sulk with foolish pride and bashfulness, and be afraid of this girl. He would even every so often treat her coldly, acting as if he didn't care, because the minute a girl was too sure of a guy, she'd tire of him like Lucy must have gotten to feel. He'd learn from experience, learn about women from Lucy. He wondered what her name was.

He walked on and sat on a bench by the stone bridge around past the south bend of the lagoon. He pulled up his overcoat collar, and thought of how it was funny that a guy never took time off to think of what he was doing, and think about life. When he was home, he never did, but always listened to the radio, played a Victrola record, read a story in some magazine like the *Argosy,* or looked at the newspaper. Once in a while he would lie down, but then he would think of something he wanted to happen, getting girls, drinking. Often, since he had knelt beside her at Mass on Christmas Day two years ago, he'd thought of her, of knowing her and loving her. And when he went out, he hung around so goddamn much, restless, wondering what to do, and hardly ever satisfied when he did do something, gassing, goofing clowns like Curley and he always kept wondering what time it was. And all along, he had known there was something missing. But this spring it would all be different and he would be better off from every viewpoint, all because he was going to meet her, and, yes, go with her. He remembered when he had licked Weary Reilley, that other day when he had sat with Lucy in the tree, and that day when he had gone home from work with his first pay, how on all those times, he had felt that life was going to start being different for him. This time, though, it had to be. It would. He looked across the lagoon at the wooded island which was on a small hill, half hidden in shadows, with bare trees ranged backwards at intervals from the bank.

He tossed aside the cigarette he was smoking. Most painters smoked and drank too much. He guessed those heartburns he got were from too much smoking. He was going to cut down. Under no considerations would he smoke more than a package a day. He was suddenly afraid that he had a bum heart. Suppose he wouldn't live long, and even a long life was short. He was going on twenty-three now, and look how quickly time seemed to have passed. He thought of himself being cut off early.

He slowly calmed his fears, because he was sure that it was not too late for him to start taking care of his health. He'd exercise, get the fat off, because if he let it go, he'd have too much on and fat would be dangerous and maybe make his heart worse, and you looked like hell with an alderman. Everybody kidded you. And she wouldn't want a guy who stuck out in the front like a balloon. He would exercise every day, go on the wagon, even watch his eating. Many a guy had dug his grave with a knife and fork, just as that writer in the *Examiner,* Brisbane, had said. The hell with boozing, whoring. It was the crap. Didn't pay. Ended you up behind the eight ball.

He felt chilly, and started back to Fifty-eighth Street. He looked at the trees which spread before him, like corpses, with the wind saddening through them. Nice. He was glad, too, that he had taken this walk. And he was going to stick to his determinations, fight not to break them. By God, he wouldn't! He shot his butt, realizing that he had determined to cut out smoking. Well, it hadn't been breaking his intentions, because he hadn't realized that he was smoking. He felt more different than he had ever felt before. He felt that he had will power, and will power was the main asset needed in every walk of life. Over near the drive, he was again aware of the wind sweeping through the shrubbery. It was a sad song, and it seemed to sing through him. It made him sad, but it was a pleasant sadness, because he knew he was different from all the mopes at the poolroom, he was going to do different things and be more than they. He could see himself, meeting them thirty years from now, himself thin, in the pink, not looking his age, them fat, red-nosed, failures, like Barney Keefe, envying him, and saying Studs you haven't changed a bit, you look swell, say how in the name of Christ do you do it? He was glad he had seen Hink. It had been like having ice-water thrown in his face to wake him up. It had made him think. Pig Lonigan! Not any more. It had made him learn his lesson in time, before he ruined himself like poor Paulie Haggerty had done, and his brother Shrimp Haggerty was doing.

Kelly came out of the poolroom as Studs slouched along. He asked Studs about doing something. Studs shook his head, and felt superior to Red. It was the first exercise of his new will power.

"Hell, Studs, if you go home now, your old man and old lady might have a fit of apoplexy or heart failure, they'll be so surprised," Tommy Doyle said.

"I'm turning in and getting some sleep."

He went towards home. At the corner of Fifty-eighth and Michigan, he saw a nigger and black girl ahead, walking arm in arm. He thought of how in this new spring time, the new man Studs Lonigan would be walking about in the evening with her on his arm. Suddenly, he sneered, thinking that the goddamn niggers had their guts, invading a white man's neighborhood, and sooner or later they'd have to be run out.

Lonigan was glad with surprise. He and Studs talked about business for a half hour. He turned in with the mother. Studs and Fran talked, and he promised to go to the Wednesday evening Lenten services at St. Patricks' next Wednesday. In bed, the father said to the mother that he was gratified because Bill was getting some sense now, and settling down. He took the credit for it.

XIV

PHIL ROLFE was one of the best-dressed cake-eaters at an afternoon dance given on Washington's Birthday at a hall near Englewood High School. A sizeable, lively crowd was in attendance. Amongst them were a number of fellows and girls who rated in the south side high school fraternity and sorority world.

Phillip spotted Loretta Lonigan. He thought that she was pretty, with her dark hair, and small but compact figure, and her gray serge dress, trimmed with collar and cuffs of hand-drawn handkerchief linen. Damn keen girl, even if she had a big nose like her brother, Studs. She smiled as he approached her between dances.

"I see you haven't forgotten me?" he said, smiling with all his talcum-powdered, stacombed charm.

"Why, Phil Rolfe, how could I forget you, ever?"

"Shall we dance?"

"I'd be delighted to."

Phil placed his right hand with effective masculine firmness in the small of her back, and crooked his left arm with his palm flat against hers. He held his head high, his thin shoulders straight and erect, and danced in calculated and precise rhythms.

"Say, Loretta, you're a swell dancer. Where have you been all my life?"

"And, Phil, you are too. And you have a nice line."

They talked about the music, dances, the people present, places to go. As they glided into a corner it seemed that Loretta let herself go tensely against him. He thought maybe she would sock it in. But he had to be careful. She was a nice girl. She might get sore. Had to handle nice girls with kid gloves that way, until you broke down the resistance. And her brother was tough. They turned gracefully in and out of the moving crowd, and Phil whistled the tune of Frivolous Sal as the orchestra played it. She smiled up at him with white, even teeth. He commented again on some of the people present and she laughed. He strategically manipulated his body until he had it against her. Her curly bobbed hair brushed his cheek. She wondered would he think her awful, and try to get too fresh if she shimmied. Fellows often did. But he was so cute. And a girl had to do something about *that, and if she didn't shimmy, she might do something worse. In a corner, she took a chance. Phillip figured she was a nice sweet girl, and he'd have to date her up sometime.*

Chapter Fourteen

GOOD-BY, Arnold! Studs silently thought.

Amidst exuding flower odors, Studs and Tommy Doyle blessed themselves, and knelt down. Their eyes suddenly met and their heads bowed in a mutual expression of surprised regret. They muttered prayers to themselves for the repose of the soul of their dead pal, while behind them, they could hear a choked feminine sob, and the loudly whispered remarks of Mrs. O'Neill that it was God's will, and that Arnold was in Heaven, and that we must all resign ourselves to the Will of the Almighty.

They arose, and looked lugubriously down at the unbelievably dead body; the prominent ashen face with the beard marks apparent despite a close shave and talcum powder, the black hair, thick and wavy, the stiff arms folded in front with a white pair of rosary beads draped between them, the well-built torso sedately clothed in its black death-suit, black tie, white shirt, black socks, and black patent leather pumps. And, pressed against the white satin lining of the coffin lid, they saw their card, statement of the spiritual bouquet they had all chipped in to send. And as he gazed abstractedly, Studs found himself expecting Arnold to smile, hear him tell a funny story, ask if anyone wanted to get a bottle, laugh and say that it was only a joke he was playing on everyone because he wasn't really dead after all. But Arnold would never again speak, never again tip a bottle to his lips, never again make a broad he had picked up at the Midway Gardens dance hall. The finality of Arnold's life made a sudden gash upon Studs' thoughts. He wanted to talk to Arnold, get to know him better than he had, take in a show with him; and, knowing that he never could do these things, he had the vaguest kind of a feeling that whenever anyone you knew and liked died, a part of yourself died with him. It made him think of church on Good Friday, with the statues draped in sorrowing purple, with the odor and feel of ashes everywhere like a pall, and of Ash Wednesday, and the priest's words when he thumbed your forehead with ashes:

Remember, Oh, man, that thou art dust and to dust thou shalt return!

They heard another muffled sob, and turned to face Mrs. Sheehan, who sat on a camp chair near the gray casket, dressed in black with her robust face paled and compressed.

"I'm very sorry," Studs muttered, feeling helplessly inarticulate.

"Mrs. Sheehan, I am very sorry for your great misfortune," Tommy Doyle said, as if learned by rote.

"I know, boys, I know," she gasped, dropping her head and permitting them to stand awkwardly before her. They edged, self-consciously, passed a double aisle of crepe-hanging women who sat on camp chairs. Mrs. Dennis P. Gorman grabbed Studs' sleeve near the edge of the parlor, and whispered that he should remember her to his dear mother.

They saw Mr. Sheehan standing, lost, by the front door. He was a ruddy, full man, with stooped shoulders, a clipped mustache, and a half-bald gray head. They expressed condolences. He seemed not even to see them, and they smelled his rancid whiskey-breath.

"God, it's sad," Studs said, as he and Tommy walked through the hall to the rear.

"Poor fellow, it's knocked him groggy," Tommy sorrowed.

They passed through the dining-room where a small group was gathered around one of Arnold's twin sisters, a pretty black-haired girl who was distraught.

They heard the guys talking in the kitchen. Horace, Arnold's grown brother, stood in the doorway.

"Jesus, I'm sorry, Horace," Tommy said.

"I know! It's tough, Tommy. You know I think it's broken dad. He acts just like a broken man, interested in nothing, hardly ever seeing anybody. I doubt if he'll ever get over it," Horace replied, emphasizing his feeling with slow shakes of the head.

"And Arnold was getting on so well," Studs said.

"Well, all we can do is make the best of it and call it life," Horace said reflectively.

A thick veil of tobacco smoke hung over the kitchen. Jim Doyle stood by the kitchen sink, a cigar pasted in his round, jolly face, and he greeted them, calling them hoods. They saluted in return, and sat down near Red Kelly. Studs noticed a girl in a corner, shabby, faded, blowsy, looked like a two-bit whore; her face seemed familiar. He frowned, and wrinkled up his forehead trying to think; he realized that she was Paulie Haggerty's widow, Eileen. What a bitch she had turned out to be!

"Well, Studs, what's new?" Red Kelly asked.

"Not much."

Horace passed around cigars. Biting off the end of one, and lighting it, Studs remarked with a certain air of importance and maturity:

"Well, Red, I never expected to be here on an occasion like this."

"Studs, when I heard it, you could have slapped me down with a feather. It's very sad, too. It's hit the poor mother hard, very hard. Arnold was her favorite, and he was always a little reckless, you know, a nice guy but a crazy bastard too when he was drunk, and that always caused her worry. And think of it, here he was sloughed off in the very prime of life."

"Poor Arnold, the guy did run in bad luck," Studs said.

"Like that time he was pie-eyed, and got stabbed by a shine; then he no sooner got his wounds healed up than he gets a dose."

"Say, was he oiled when the accident happened?"

"No, he was on the wagon again. He had gone back to work for the city. Remember how he got canned from the job for being oiled and then went back?"

"Yep, that's right."

"He was riding home from work last Saturday, on a city truck, standing on the tail gate, and hanging on to a rope. The rope broke, and Arnold fell off. He cracked his skull. They took him to the County Hospital. He never came to, but in a coma he kept muttering for his mother. By luck a priest was gotten and he received Extreme Unction before he passed away. But when his mother got there he was dead. You know, Studs, it just goes to show that some people are born lucky, and others always live under an unlucky star," Red said to Studs, who hadn't been listening to him, but had rather been looking about from face to face, and smoking his cigar as if it were a ceremony.

"Jesus!" Studs suddenly exclaimed in expression of his reaction to the whole situation.

"Yep, that's the way it is; you're here today, and gone tomorrow," Tommy Doyle said.

"And just think, I saw him at church last Sunday, feeling so swell, and dressed up like a lighthouse," Red Kelly said.

"Life is sure funny," Tommy remarked.

"And it always seems to get the guys who are white, and not the sons of bitches. Take a bastard like Weary Reilley. He's a rat clean through, and he couldn't do a decent trick if he tried. He goes around smashing guys he can lick in the mug, smacking girls to make them come across, and he's even hit his helpless father. Well, now, nothing ever happens to him. I tell you, it's one of the oddities of life and one of the mysteries of the Will of God that a guy who's white almost never gets the grapes," Red said.

"Reilley's a skunk," Studs said, kind of hoping that Red would mention how he had cleaned Weary as a kid.

"Too bad!" said Tommy.

"Where was the fire sale, Muggsy?" asked Studs as Muggsy McCarthy entered the room. He was more slumped and hollow than ever; but he wore a new dark gray suit.

"Muggsy, you look prosperous," Doyle remarked.

"Boys, I'm working for the city now," Muggsy said almost unnaturally exuberant.

"So you got in the political game, huh, Muggsy?" Tommy Doyle asked.

"Yeah, my old man took me back home and got me the job. I'm off that damn crap. There's nothing to it, hanging around all the time with not even a sou in your jeans. How you like the suit, boys?" Muggsy asked.

"I think I'll get me into the political game," Tommy said, while the boys examined Muggsy's suit, and kidded him.

Like an apparition, Barney Keefe stood in the center of the room, and pointed at drunken Irish Mickey Flannagan; everybody laughed.

"And you, bitch! The last time I saw you, you passed out in a saloon over at Twelfth and Halsted, and the boys all took you on while you were dreaming of the birdies of the springtime," Barney said, pointing at Mrs. Haggerty; she smiled feebly and apologetically.

"Yeah, Tommy, you never know when you're called," Studs said, profoundly feeling the uncertainty of life, sensing a sudden fear lest he be the next of the boys called, buoying himself up with the feeling that he was strong and well and taking care of himself and wouldn't need to worry about death for a long, long time.

"Hey, Barney, where you think you're at," Red said, sore because Barney was keeping up the horseplay.

"I thought I came to a wake, but seeing all you flannel-mouth Irish here, I guess it's a saloon or a poolroom," Barney said. They laughed.

"Hello, Studs," Phil Rolfe ingratiated, while the boys still laughed at Barney's wit. Phillip rolled the cigar in his mouth. Studs acted as if he hadn't heard the greeting.

"Yeah, too bad, but we all got to go sometime," Phillip said, finding a chair in back of Studs.

The room snapped into rigid quiet with the appearance of Mr.

Sheehan. He ignored the remarks politely directed at him. Red arose and offered him a chair. He looked around and walked out.

"Just like a ghost," Red dolefully said.

"Hey, Barney, you rat, when you going to sober up?" Mickey asked from the fogs of inebriation.

"Can it, Flannagan, before we toss you on your ear," Red said.

"I'll sober up when I put a lily on the grave of every pigs—t Irishman here," Barney said.

"Come on, you guys," Red repeated.

"Say, Studs, you know, isn't it a shame. You know, Arnold, he was my friend," Vinc Curley said.

"Say, Goof, dry up," Studs said. Vinc looked at Studs, hurt.

"I remember the time that Arnold and I got pie-eyed in a black-and-tan joint. You know he went for a high brown, Georgia Brown, and, boy, I thought we'd get our throats slashed from ear to ear," Benny Taite said.

"Hey, Benny, is that the only thing you can think of now that Arnold is dead? You can't think of anything else, can you—the time you might have seen him coming home with a present to his mother or something?"

"Gee, Red, I didn't mean anything," Benny said.

"Well, those aren't the kind of breaks you want to be making at a time like this," Kelly snapped.

Everybody laughed as Kenny Kilarney came in with that goofy, boyish smile on his thin face, just as it always was.

"Boys, this is Timothy O'Shea," he said, pointing his finger at the character with him.

"Hi, boys!" Timothy O'Shea said like a prizefighter accepting well-earned applause. He swam in a huge, flowing overcoat, and had a rough, wide, surly face. He pushed his dirty fedora on the back of his head, and smiled.

"Say, boys, excuse me a minute!" Timothy O'Shea said, going to the sink; he relieved himself.

They were too surprised to speak. He took a seat. Horace came with the box of cigars. Timothy O'Shea and Kenny each took two.

"Hell, you guys are all hoods. I'm going," Jim Doyle said.

"Sit down, Jim, and tell us about the political outlook for next fall," said Studs.

"Democratic landslide."

"What do you think of the mayor, Jim?" asked Red.

"He's a Sunday school mayor," Jim said.

"Bill Dever, oh, he's all right, Bill is, if you know how to take him," Timothy O'Shea said.

"You know him?" Jim asked hostilely.

"Sure, him and my old man is like that," Timothy O'Shea said, crossing the second and third fingers on his right hand and holding them up in indication of closeness.

"Say, Jim, say?" Curley called.

"You in the political game?" asked Doyle.

"Sure! Me, I'm in everything. Christ, yes," Timothy O'Shea said.

"Listen, Jim, I wanted to ask you if you wanted to go to the Tivoli with me some night this week?" Curley said.

"Hey, Curley, did anybody ever tell you that you were a pest?" said Jim; they laughed.

Fat Malloy arrived and glad-handed all the boys. Studs said he acted like he was a pupil of Jim Doyle's.

"You know, fellows, I hate it, having to think that Arnold's gone from us like this," Les said.

"Yeah, Les, you'll have to drink more to make up for what he won't, huh?" said Tommy.

"Say, Kenny, where in hell you been keeping yourself?" asked Studs.

"Out of the pen," Kenny said.

"Same old Kilarney. But tell me, are you working?" Red said.

"Sure, everybody."

"Say, any drinks in the joint?" asked Timothy O'Shea. No one answered him.

"Hell, come on, Kilarney. I thought you said there'd be some sparkling waters here. Come on, this joint is a hell of a wake," Timothy said.

"Brother, we got respect for the dead," said Red.

"Sure, you run a wake like you were all Jews. If I hung around I'd have to drink noodle soup. Come on, Kilarney," Timothy O'Shea said, leaving, his huge coat swinging after him.

Kenny followed him and left a room full of soreheads.

"If it wouldn't have been disrespectful, I'd have socked that ignorant ape of an Irishman," Kelly said.

"Kenny was always cockeyed, and didn't have sense about serious things," Tommy said.

"Leave it to Kenny to find a guy like that for a wake where tragedy has occurred," Kelly said.

"Same old Kilarney," Studs said.

They talked. More came, and some went out. Finally, Studs and Red left, re-expressing their condolences before departing.

"Studs, let's get a drink."

"I'm on the wagon, Red," Studs said.

"How come?"

"I'm taking care of myself these days."

"Come on, one drink won't make any difference."

"Nope, not tonight, Red."

They walked silently towards Fifty-eighth Street. Across the street, the park seemed gloomy with its deserted tennis courts, and the bare, black trees and shrubbery behind them.

"Say, Studs, I think it was goddamn funny they didn't ask any of us to be pallbearers," Red said.

"I suppose his old man is sore. Thinks we were always responsible for his drinking. Notice the old man didn't say much to us?"

"Yeah, and the first time I met Arnold just after his family moved in the neighborhood, he was looking for a bottle," Red said.

"It's fluky, all right."

"I feel sorry and I understand how his folks might be feeling, and I offered them my condolences. But Jesus Christ, we were Arnold's best friends, and we'll miss him too. I tell you, Studs, it's an insult to all of us!" Red protested.

Studs wasn't listening. He couldn't get the memory of Arnold out of his head, and it gave him a feeling of awe and fear. He had just seen death, death with something terrible, final, about it. It made him suddenly leery of even living. He determined all over again that he was going to take care of himself.

"I suppose old man Sheehan must feel bad. You know, he sees us living, and his son dead, and it must have hit him. But we didn't kill Arnold. He shouldn't act that way towards us. But then I suspect it might be Horace. Come to think of it, he hardly ever comes around the poolroom, and when he does, he doesn't have a lot to say."

"Yes," Studs said, not feeling so badly that he hadn't been asked to be a pallbearer.

"Arnold was a prince, though. That's why I'm going to the funeral, even if his family did act that way, and not ask even one of his best friends to stand by him in his last journey," Red said.

"I'll miss him. He was white, all right," Studs said.

"Say, Studs, sure you won't change your mind and have a drink?"

"No, Red, I'm really starting to put myself into decent shape."

"What the hell, you're in good shape, aren't you?"

"But what I mean is get hard, and get this little bit of belly I got off, and then next season we can get the old team together and play football again."

"That's not a bad idea. Remember that fight with the Monitors?"

"Say, that reminds me, remember that kike they had who was so fast and who nearly got killed? I forget his name, but you remember him?"

"I think it was Schwartz."

"Well, I'll be goddamned if I wasn't out to a game in the park last fall and he was playing, and just as fast as ever."

"But we stopped him," Red said.

"Yeah, we did," Studs said, hoping Red would mention one or two of those tackles.

"But come on, Studs," Red said; Studs shook his head no.

"I was thinking I'd join the Y, and go swimming there and fool around the gym a couple of nights a week. What do you think of it?"

"I might, too."

"I'm going over this week, want to come along?"

"Maybe. Pick me up at the poolroom."

They had coffee an' in the Greek restaurant. Studs went home, and turned in early. Lying in bed he felt as if he had again conquered himself, and was already started on the road to making himself as healthy as the guys whose pictures he saw in the physical culture ads in magazines. He thought that every day in every way he was going to get harder and healthier. But he couldn't get Arnold from his mind, and the words of a song the guys sang kept running through his head.

Did you ever think, when a hearse goes by,
That some day you and I will go rolling by. . . .

XV

I HATE to see the evening sun go down. . . .

Mickey Flannagan's head fell onto the table, and a glass, half full of gin and ginger ale, almost toppled. Slug Mason looked at the high-brown singer; she was dressed in a shimmery blue gown with a slit down the side, and she rolled her abdomen with agonizing slowness as she sang in the center of the glassy dance floor. Slug whispered that he'd take a baby like that on, even if her skin was purple. Red Kelly countered that he personally had too much self-respect to go monkeying around with low niggers. Barney Keefe sneered that Red was B. S. and that it was always the same, a guy wanted a woman, and everything else was crap.

Feeling tomorrow just like I feel today.

Stan Simonsky said he had to laugh when he thought that Studs and Les had gone tonight to the . . . Y.M.C.A. Slug said he couldn't understand what had happened to Studs. Stan added that he hoped Studs wasn't losing his guts.

Barney told them to shut up while they heard the song. The black girl repeated the chorus, her voice throbbing with a mixture of despair and innuendoed sex. The house applauded.

A six-piece Negro jazz band went into action, producing an evil orgiastic jazz. The dance floor of the Sunrise Café on Thirty-fifth Street quickly crowded, and it became like a revolving wheel of lust, the dancers swaying and turning, every corner and floor edge filled with dancers who moved sidewise, inch by inch, socking their bellies together in quick rhythm and with increasing frenzy. The fellows watched. Their faces went tight with hostility every time a white girl went by with a Negro. They saw one beautiful blond girl with a coal-black, sweating nigger, and they said nothing, only because there were too many shines in the place. Slug said what the hell he was going to dance, too. He left, and soon he was socking with a black girl. The others followed Slug's example, and Red Kelly sat boiling sore, alone with Mickey Flannagan, who slept peacefully, with his head on the table. Red looked about at the empty tables. Then at the dancers. He saw Stan socking with a skinny yellow bitch. He thought the jazz would drive him nuts; the thick-lipped singing and shouts of the niggers grated until he was ready to jump. And the place was like the stockyards; he thought they ought to use a little perfume anyway. He called over a nigger waiter, paid his share of the bill, and got up while the dance was still going hot. As he walked towards the exit, he noticed the snottily suspicious glances he got from niggers, and Christ, how he'd have loved to have gotten a couple of them out on Fifty-eighth Street. At the door, there were four dicks, their faces drawn, waiting, as if they were expecting trouble. As he left, two white girls entered, laughing, with loudly-dressed buck niggers. The doorman told him to come again. Yes, he thought, he'd like to come with a machine gun. He took a cab to a white can house.

Chapter Fifteen

I

STUDS' eyes were attracted by a framed picture of the Sacred Heart of Jesus, around which was written the verse:

Heart of Jesus, my true friend,
Make me faithful to the end.

He wanted to substitute the word healthy for faithful. He looked at his feet where he had just dropped the evening's copy of the *Chicago Evening Journal* that he'd been reading. He'd come across a squib telling of how a thirty-seven-year-old man had dropped dead of heart trouble at the ball game. He thought that he had been having pains in his heart, and down around his stomach of late, and he was gloomy and worried, because maybe he'd be having heart trouble and dropping dead, or having to have an operation for appendicitis, or be suffering from ulcers of the stomach or something like that. Maybe his plan to condition himself was just too late, and it was too bad for him. Health was the greatest gift and wealth that any man could receive or have, and when health was gone, all was gone.

He might be dead any day. He might drop dead in the street. He might have already torn all the lining out of his stomach with rotgut gin.

He wanted to live to be a hundred. He could see himself celebrating his hundredth birthday, with everybody he now knew dead, and his great-grandchildren and his great-great-grandchildren surrounding him. He could see himself at a hundred, hale and hearty, having his picture in the newspapers and telling the reporters, while they took his picture, that he attributed his health to careful living, and explaining how when he had been twenty-two he had laid out a plan of careful living and exercise for himself, and he'd followed it conscientiously for years. He could see himself, a hundred years old, walking erect without a cane, not fat either like his father was, coming back to the old neighborhood, looking at all the old buildings where Lucy and Helen Shires and Dan Donoghue and Red Kelly had lived, going over to Washington Park and sitting by the lagoon, or in the boathouse, walking over to the wooded island, looking at the trees where he and Lucy had sat, or at the spot, if the tree was gone, going all around to see the old sights, thinking about all the things he'd done as a kid so long long ago, and the things he was doing now, thinking about Lucy and Helen Shires, and the girl who sat next to him at Christmas Mass and who maybe would be his wife. And maybe when he was a hundred and did that, he might still be having as much as ten years to go. He wanted to live longer than any man in the whole world had ever lived. And goddamn it, he would.

He wanted to be strong and healthy and never turn into a weak-kneed, unhealthy guy. And he would. He got up, and shadow-boxed clumsily around the room. He tensed his stomach and felt it to see if his exercises and training had hardened up his guts. He couldn't tell. He still had something of an alderman. Well, that would go. And he would have a long time to live. He'd only worried unnecessarily about his heart and his stomach. He dressed, ate supper, and then left. He was going over to the Y tonight, and Red and some of the guys were coming along. He walked along, confident and happy, feeling, too, that he wouldn't be hanging around, wondering every few minutes what time it was, and what they'd do.

II

"But it's a pretty long walk, Studs," Les said.

"It'll do us good. It'll be exercise."

"I get plenty of exercise wrestling freight for John Continental."

"Come on, a little more won't hurt you. I get exercise, too. And if we go by street car, we'd have to go down to Sixty-first, and then transfer at Cottage Grove."

"It'd be quicker."

"Come on," Studs said, as they entered the park.

"Say, what'll we have to do?"

"Sign up, pay the fee, and then we can use the gym and swimming pool."

They walked across the park, saying little. Studs tried to think of himself as a prizefighter or some kind of an athlete putting himself in condition to come back. It made it appear more interesting and important that way. It was as if he was somebody in the limelight, a celebrity, and the world was interested in his success and failure. And now, suppose he was a fighter, would it be best for him to call himself Studs Lonigan, Young Lonigan, or K. O. Lonigan?

"Say, aren't Y. M. C. A.'s dopey places?"

"I guess they got all boy scouts in them, but we're going there to swim and use the gym and get ourselves in condition physically."

"Then, what do we do?"

"What the hell! Don't you like to be healthy?"

"Sure, I guess so."

"Puddles here," Studs said, skipping and leaping over a stretch of watery ground.

"I knew it would be best not to come this way."

"We're near the hills now. Then we'll be past the puddles."

Les laughed to himself.

"What's the comedy?" asked Studs.

"I was thinking what would the teameos I know at the express company think, if they knew I was going to a Y. M. C. A. . . . Jesus, them turkeys down there would ride the pants off me."

"You don't have to tell them, and if they do find out, what the hell's the difference? Tell them to go to and stay put."

"But they'll find out. Down there at that express company they find out about everything a guy does. They got the best grapevine in the world."

"There are a lot of bastards like that in this world. I'd like to see them all in hell too."

"Cigarette, Studs?"

"No, thanks."

"Jesus, you're doing this thing right."

"If I plan to do something, I don't see any reason to do it half ass," Studs said.

"I wonder why Tommy and Red and the guys didn't come along. They all promised to."

"Hell, they're mopes. And they're going to a goddamn shine cabaret, and maybe get slashed with a razor," Studs said.

"They never think of what's going to happen to them."

"They're mopes."

They crossed the hills on the far side of the park, went over the drive, along a path, and out at Fifty-fifth and Cottage.

"It's only down a few blocks and over on Fifty-second Street."

"That don't irritate me none," Les said.

They turned east on Fifty-second Street.

"Hey, Shrimp doesn't look so good, does he?"

"He's hitting the bottle every day. I don't think he's been sober since New Year's. He's wasting away to a shadow," Studs said.

"Yeah, poor Shrimp's wasting away to a shadow."

"He can drink the whole gang of us together under the table," Studs said.

"He certainly doesn't look any too good. I'll say that," Les said.

"He's ripping his guts out with rotgut," Studs said.

III

Feeling out of place at the Y entrance, they paused in momentary indecision. Studs acted casual. Les was nervous, and blushed.

"Studs, this joint looks phony to me," Les said.

"Yeah."

There was a drugged sanctimoniousness about the sappy-looking birds seated in the lobby. Studs felt that there wasn't a man or a regular guy amongst them. The desk was at the right of the rectangular lobby, and a blond young man, with a pinhead mustache, stood behind it.

"I suppose we should ask this dope," Studs said, approaching the desk.

"All I can say is that I don't like the looks of this joint," Les said.

"Sure, every one in the joint was probably a boy scout when he was a punk. What can you expect? But we came here to use the gym and swim. We don't have to worry about all these mopes."

As they passed a lounge, a small little chap, with a wax-like mustache and stacombed hair, stopped before another guy who was reading the *American Magazine*.

"Hell, old man!" the chap with the wax-like mustache said.

"Why, George! Gee, George, I'm pleased to see you."

"I wonder what museum those eggs came from," Studs quietly said to Les.

"This one," Les answered.

The clerk directed them to the office of the Membership Secretary. As they entered the office, the vacuous-looking, pale secretary rose and said:

"Good evening, fellows!"

He heartily shook hands with them. They took seats at his direction.

"You gentlemen, I presume, are desirous of becoming members."

They nodded.

"Well, we're always pleased to have the right kind of members. And were you intending to reside here with us?"

"No."

"You're Christians, I assume?"

"Irish," said Les.

"And if I may ask, what is it that prompts you to join us?"

Studs said for the use of the gym and swimming. He told them of the salutary effect of exercise and sports, and what fine fellows they had in the organization. They were given membership blanks to fill out, and their dough was collected. They were told they'd have to be examined by the doctor, but the doctor was not around. They went down to the lockers to undress for a swim.

"That guy's clammy," Studs said.

IV

"You know, I don't think I've ever gone swimming before at this time of the year," Les said.

"I did," Studs said.

"I always hate the first splash. Hitting the water for the first time makes me nervous."

"All you have to do is just dive in and it's over with."

"I know, but thinking about it in advance makes me nervous."

They came to the pool, and heard shouting and splashing. Inside, they paused, and looked around, seeing many guys, some completely naked, some with jock straps. A tall fellow made a big splash as he dove from the board at the deep end of the pool. Studs said that guy didn't know how to dive. . . . They moved around to the diving board. Studs said let's go, walked to the end of the board, stood on his toes, rocked a moment, and leaped, turning over as he went down, arms first, making little splash.

"Nice one, Studs," Les yelled.

Studs came up, puffed, and took a few strokes. He about-faced and swam the crawl stroke back to the pool edge. Holding to the railing with one hand, and splashing water with the other, he told Les it was swell, to come on in. Les said he would, he was just standing there a minute. Studs let go of the railing, and pushed himself away from the pool edge. He turned on his back and floated, the pool sounds and muffling shouts sounding vague in his ears. He turned over and swam speedily to the shallow end of the pool, turned around without stopping, and returned swimming as swiftly as he could, but tiring with each stroke, so that his breath came more irregularly, and his arms seemed to grow heavy. He puffed noticeably and his arms were leaden as he climbed up the ladder, and out of the pool.

"Go ahead. Make the leap, and it's swell."

"I will. I was just watching a minute."

"That almost pooped me. I got to get better wind than I got," Studs said.

He patted the fat around his belly.

"This has to come off."

"There isn't much there."

"It's more than there should be."

A big splash was made, and water was thrown up against them.

"Why don't that bastard learn how before he starts diving. He's like Moses parting the waters," Studs said.

"You're a good swimmer," Les said.

"I used to swim a lot as a kid."

"So did I, but you're better than I am," Les said.

"Well, here goes again. Coming?"

"All right."

Studs ran off the board, and let go, again doing a neat dive. Les followed, diving more awkwardly, splashing heavily.

"Nice," Les yelled, coming up, and swimming alongside of Studs.

"Let's race," Studs said.

"You can beat me."

"Oh, come on, anyway."

They raced, Studs let Les gain, then, with full confidence, he took even powerful strokes to draw alongside, and then ahead of him. They stood up in the shallow water.

"I'm glad I came."

"It's good," Studs said, shaking his head.

"Race back?" he added.

"What's the use. You beat me."

Studs turned, jogged out to the deeper water as he moved, dove, swam under water, and came up near the middle of the pool. He turned and saw Les coming towards him. He swam to the deeper edge, followed by Les, and climbed up the ladder. He took another dive, went under water for about six feet, came up and moved swiftly, exulting in a feeling of complete bodily freedom. It was swell. The water was just right, lukewarm, and he took rhythmic strokes, gaining a confidence in his physical powers, feeling removed from the world, clean. It was like losing all the gripes that had been piling up within him. He felt, too, that he still had a good body. After a few months of this, and then the summer, he'd be hard as nails. And whores and whore houses, and booze, all that were like sins of the past. He swam until he was tired and gasping, with his arms again heavy and leaden, and his back weary as if it were crushed down with weights. He was spent. He climbed out of the pool, thinking how it had been fun spending himself. He lay down wet on the slippery tile, covering his eyes with his arms.

"Gee, this is swell," Les said, lying down beside him.

"Uh huh," Studs said.

Guys talked, dove, swam, ran around the tile flooring. It all seemed far away.

"Yes, hell, it's much better swimming this way than with suits."

Studs looked up, as if he were just awakening. He and Les sat up.

"Come on, let's take another dip before we call it quits."

They dove in, swam the length of the pool, and then went down to the lockers to dress and go out.

"I had a swell time," Les said.

"Yeah, and it's good for you."

"The guys don't know what they missed," Les said.

"They're all mopes."

XVI

SAY, Mr., could you help me to get a bite to eat?" Davey Cohen begged, touching the sleeve of a well-dressed bucolic-looking fellow in front of the Circle Monument in Indianapolis.

Davey watched the fellow move away. Hadn't even batted an eyelid. He was so goddamn hungry that he couldn't get any hungrier. And it was the cheapest damn town he'd ever struck. He sat down on the steps of the Monument, and reflected that the old burg was only about a hundred miles away. He could grab a freight, and tomorrow he'd be in Chicago. He hadn't been back home since 1916. It would be swell seeing the old bunch. Yes, they were a damn fine bunch of guys, Paulie Haggerty, Kenny, Red, Tommy Doyle, Studs, all of them. He'd go back and just pop around Charlie Bathcellar's poolroom, if it was still there. He guessed it was a fixture in the neighborhood and would be there. They'd be glad to see him, and he'd be glad to see them, and they'd talk about old times, and about what had happened to him, and to them, since he'd gone on the bum. He ought to go back and maybe get a job. If he did that, and watched himself, his health would pick up. Hell, he was digging his own grave, living like this. And Vinc Curley. He wondered if Vinc was as goofy as ever. But he was too hungry to think of that. He went around and around the Circle Monument, mooching until he finally got two bits. He walked off towards a cheap restaurant singing:

"Gee, but I'd give the world to see
  that old gang of mine,
I can't forget that old quartette,
  that sang 'Sweet Adeline'
Good-by forever, old fellows and pals . . ."

Chapter Sixteen

I

"SAY, Studs, if I knew you were coming around tonight, I'd have had the boys hire a band to meet you. Where you been keeping yourself?" asked Red Kelly.

"Oh, I've just been catching up on my sleep."

"So I heard; the boys were saying that you're living hygienically."

"You must be another one of these guys who's been working crossword puzzles."

"Say, listen, Studs, how about coming along with me tonight to that meeting at St. Patrick's?"

"What's doing?"

"Don't you remember, Gilly announced it at Mass last Sunday."

"Oh, yeah, the club they're going to have for young people."

"I was thinking I might as well go there."

"That'll be all blah. Every damn time they tried that stunt in this parish, it's flopped."

"I just thought I'd see what was going to happen."

"All the church ushers, Larkin, McAuliffe, Al Borax, and maybe even Jim Clayburn will run it and think up some committees to put themselves on. Then they'll pass the plate. And all the punks will be up there, smelling after young broads. You can have that crap for yourself."

"But look here, Studs; I was thinking that if a couple of guys like us went there, we might be able to make something out of it besides a dancing school for the drug store cowboys, or a hall where those goddamn church ushers could try and pretend that they're Father Gilhooley," Red said.

"Say, Red, are you planning to go into politics?"

"Well, if I ever do, an outfit like this wouldn't hurt me none," said Red.

Studs nodded his head, smiling knowingly.

"Come on, Studs."

Up there, he might see that girl, and he was still Studs Lonigan, and all the punks and everybody would treat him with respect. They always did. They knew they had to. Let them try kidding him!

O'Neill had the other day, and he'd shut up when he'd been told, because if he hadn't, he knew what was coming to him. And going back around St. Patrick's made him think of the old days when, goddamn it, he'd had such a swell time.

"All right," Studs said, feigning disinterest.

"I really think we ought to go. This time they're organizing the thing to raise money for the new church. After all these years and all this talk, Gilly's really going to build it. And there's no reason why St. Patrick's shouldn't have as fine a church as any in the city. This is a good neighborhood and a good church. There's plenty of good Catholics, Irish, in it, people like your old man and mine, and we ought to have a church. There's enough dough in the parish, too, and Gilly's the boy to raise it. But it's a worthy venture, and we ought to try and do our share."

"Red, you're getting the gift of gab. If I'm not careful, you'll probably be selling me real estate out in the middle of Lake Michigan," Studs said, starting with Red towards St. Patrick's.

He could feel it in his bones that tonight he was really going to meet her. And there were things about him that nobody knew, and that he'd once thought Lucy would notice, but hadn't, and she would. Well, Lucy could go plumb to—and then stick her head in the bowl. Tonight was going to be his night in a big way. He'd get her, and maybe marry her. Why not? He tried to remember what she looked like. She was blond. She was slender but with enough meat on her. Her face, eyes. . . . He couldn't remember.

"St. Patrick's is a coming parish, Studs. And the new church is going to make it. It's going to stop all this wild talk about the jiggs moving around here and running the neighborhood. Gilly is a smart man, and what he said last Sunday in church is the goods. Michigan Avenue is going to be made a boulevard. Property values around here will skyrocket. The new church will clinch the matter. You watch, it'll make people stay here, and the new ones of the right kind with money will move in and buy property. Gilly knows his stuff."

"That's what my old man thinks. He won't sell the building because he thinks it'll be worth more in a few years."

"He's got a head on his shoulders, too."

"Oh, yeah."

"And a young guy from a good family in this neighborhood, now he's got a good chance here in politics. You know, we all laugh at Jim Doyle and kid him about being assistant precinct captain. But he's got the dope. He's got a good paying political job now on city construction work, and he's going to get along. You see, Studs, we're younger than Jim, and we still got some wild oats to sow, but sometime we'll have to settle down. That's why I was saying a young fellow in this neighborhood can get along in politics."

Studs kind of wished that he'd finished school and studied law. He could see himself as alderman of the ward some day, maybe even Mayor Lonigan. They walked a stretch without talking.

"Say, Weary Reilley damn near killed a guy in a scrap around Sixty-third and University the other night. You know, that bastard is riding for a fall. He's got into the habit of thinking he's tough, and he has to act tough to keep up his rep, and well, you know what happens to such guys. There's always somebody just a little bit tougher."

"He's got plenty coming to him."

"I never was afraid of him as a kid. Neither were you, Studs. You cleaned him, I remember."

Studs nodded with pleasure. They stopped for a coca cola near the church, and then went to the meeting in the basement auditorium of the parish. Upon entering, Red commented that there was a pretty good crowd. Studs shook his head in agreement and remarked that every drug store cowboy in the neighborhood was present. He and Red circulated from group to group, acting superior, feeling that they deserved being noticed the way the punks noticed them. Without realizing the drift of his thoughts, Studs found himself remembering how they all used to come down to the same place when he was a kid, for singing practice for church, and for elocution lessons. A jane named Miss Cobb had been their elocution teacher. They'd all have to recite, and reciting, they'd have to stand up straight, heels together, feet out, the right foot straight, the left foot, half sidewise, a goofy position, and then recite things like:

Where are you going, young fellow, my lad,
On this glorious morn of May?
I'm going to join the colors, dad,
They're needing men, they say.

It was goofy, and he'd always hated the singing too, but maybe because his own voice wasn't so hot. Preparing to sing at five o'clock Mass on Christmas, they'd practice a half hour right after the afternoon bell rang at one o'clock. Christ, he used to hate it. He sang to himself:

Holy God, we praise Thy name!
Lord of all, we bow before Thee!
All on earth Thy sceptre claim,
All in Heaven above adore Thee!

For a moment, he felt as if he were a kid again, and then the song blew out of his mind, and he felt just lonesome and sad in a vague way without anything clear in his mind, and he hoped some of the guys from his class would be there. He realized that Phil Rolfe was talking to him.

"Say, Jew, this ain't a fish peddlers' convention," Studs said.

"I can come down here, can't I? I just met Father Doneggan. He said he was glad to have me," Phil said.

"Well, don't sell him any fish," Studs said.

"Jesus, we better get the doors locked all right," said Red.

"Maybe they got rat traps in back of the stage," Studs said, pointing to the stage up in front, the same stage on which he had received his graduation diploma. Young Rocky called Phil to tell him something.

Big Nodalsky, who had turned into a tall, dark, sheiky guy, with greased hair parted in the middle and sideburns, greeted Studs.

"You're looking good. You haven't hardly changed a bit, Studs."

"What are you doing?"

"Managing a dancing school and taxi dance hall down town, and giving lessons. But I expect to get lined up for a dancing act with Orpheum. But say, ever see any of the old boys?" Big Nodalsky asked.

"Once in a while. Monk McCarthy's brother, Red, is studying for the priesthood, and Monk has a political job and doesn't come around mooching any more."

"Muggsy was always funny. He was smart but he'd never do anything, and he was always getting in trouble. But say, remember Cudahy? He's got a job with Sloan's Deerfield, the mail-order house."

"Yeah, and I see Bill Donoghue once in a while," Studs said.

"How is Bill? What's he doing?"

"He's got a job repairing adding machines."

"Good old Bill, and what about his brother, Dan?"

"Dan runs a movie in his uncle's chain up in Madison, Wisconsin. He gets into town now and then, Bill says, but I hardly ever see him."

"And Tubby?" asked Nodalsky.

"Haven't seen Tubby in a couple of years. The last I heard of him, he was a glazier's apprentice."

"Jesus, those were the days, weren't they, Studs?"

"Yeah, they were. You were in the same room with our class, weren't you?"

"I was in seventh grade when you were in eighth, but, say, I wonder what happened to Battling Bertha?" asked Nodalsky.

"I think she died."

"She was hard-boiled all right; the year I was in eighth grade, I remember one day she got tough with Johnny O'Brien. He was grade behind me. Well, he hauled off on her. Yeah, he socked her."

"I think I remember hearing something about that when it happened."

"There'll never again be days like those."

"Nope," said Studs.

Studs' eyes roved. Plenty of girls, most of them young flappers, Loretta's age. Only a couple of years ago they were kids. Now they were all painted up, and Christ, he'd bet a lot of them knew more than you imagine.

"Say, Studs, remember the time, the year after you graduated, when you, Weary Reilley and some of the other lads from your class came around in the afternoon and ran through the hall like a tornado. It was funny; and Goofy Cudahy yelled out, 'Jesus, the Germans are here!' It was funny. But Bertha gave him the clouts," Nodalsky said, both of them laughing.

Austin came up with a glad hand. Red followed, and asked when the meeting was going to start. He answered right away. He said he was glad to see Red and Studs up to the meeting, because they wanted to make a go of this club, and they needed fellows like Studs and Red. Studs was pleased to have Austin say this, but then, he reflected, what the hell! Austin was still a goddamn boy scout. Austin shot off to greet Dorothy Gorman.

Studs, after considerable hesitation, walked over to Father Doneggan and said hello.

"Well, how are things, Studs?" Father Doneggan asked.

"Oh, pretty good, Father."

"Glad to hear it. And how are Dad and Mother?"

"They're fine."

"Say, Studs, it's good of you to come up tonight! I meant to tell your brother to ask you, but didn't get around to it. I want, you know, to get a few of you older fellows with good heads in this organization to give it stability. We've got to weld a lively club together and still have it sensible, and we'll need fellows like you, Studs," Father Doneggan said.

Studs smiled. Nice to have Father Doneggan say that. But he didn't know what a wild bird Studs Lonigan had been. Well, no, he was right, fellows like him and Red could be useful, if the boy scouts and church ushers or the punks just didn't go ahead and ruin it.

Big Larkin called Father Doneggan, and Studs watched him shoot nervously away. Father Doneggan was a regular guy. Studs would even bet that he'd have a drink with a fellow.

II

Larkin called the meeting to order. The males sat on one side of the hall, separated from the females by an aisle. Larkin leaned on the table, and jutted his mushy, red, almost womanish face forwards.

"Now, fellows . . . and . . . ah . . . ladies," he commenced.

There were a few titters and smiles. Vinc Curley let out an unexpected horse laugh. Everybody looked pityingly at him.

"We are . . . ah . . . here to form a St. Patrick's Young People's Society for various . . . ah . . . reasons. First and foremost, we want to . . . ah . . . get behind Father Gilhooley in his effort to raise funds for getting this parish . . . ah . . . a church, a beautiful church that will be second to none in the city and that . . . ah . . . none of us need be ashamed of. And then again, we want to . . . ah . . . establish a permanent organization. But . . . ah . . . before we do that, discuss our plans and procedures . . . ah . . . we'll hear a few words from Father Doneggan."

He smiled respectfully at Father Doneggan who rose, and, with swishing cassock, walked forwards. There were a few perfunctory and self-conscious claps.

"I am here to speak for Father Gilhooley, and to deliver to you his message, expressing his fondest hopes that this organization of the young people of St. Patrick's parish will be a most gratifying success, as I know, and as he knows, that it will. He asks me to state, in his name, that he promises to cooperate with you in every way that is feasible. Now, you people all know that for years it has been the fondest dream of your pastor to give the people of this parish a church of which it can be justifiably proud. When he came to this parish in the very first year of this century, there was not even a church, and he celebrated his first Mass in a store building down the street that had been kindly donated to the purposes of God by a generous parishioner. He has built this present church building, housing the church, school, and the auditorium in which we are now gathered; and he has also built the sisters' home and the priests' house. All of these buildings are now free of debt, thanks to his diligence, energy, and intelligent handling of church moneys. Now, he is prepared to open the drive for funds which will enable him to realize his dream, the dream of every good parishioner of St. Patrick's. If all the parishioners support him according to their means and ability, as I am confident they will, he will continue with his present plans, and in the space of a few short years, St. Patrick's new church, bigger than the present, one of the most beautiful houses of worship in this city, will be not merely a plan or a dream, but a living actuality. And one of the principal reasons that your pastor sponsors the formation of this proposed young people's society is that he solicits your aid in the realization of these plans."

Studs saw her, and Father Doneggan's words became a distant hum of distraction. She sat quietly, confidence in her manner, keen, with blond bobbed hair. He could see that her face was thin, proud. She looked like she'd be a hard dame to make. He didn't want just that. She would be hard to win. But there was a broad made for every guy, and she was the pattern cut out for him. He looked at her, unobtrusively, trying not to give himself away, as she sat, still, straight, wearing a green and red plaited flannel dress. He was hot for her, hotter than he'd been when he knelt beside her. He wanted the meeting to be over, so he could have her notice him, notice how people spoke to him. Hoped Fran knew her and would be talking to her, and he could just go up to Fran as if to ask her some question.

He looked back at Father Doneggan, heard him say that the organization they were forming would be a chance, also, to cement old friendships, and establish new ones, and to provide for a decent, satisfactory social life for the young people, with clean dancing and fun.

Father Doneggan was applauded at the conclusion of his talk. His face touched with redness, he sat down. Larkin arose and stood behind the table, leaning clumsily on it with closed fists.

"Now the first thing that concerns us is to get organized. I think we all agree to that," he said dully, speaking first quickly and then pausing to hem out "ahs" as if he were struggling to catch his breath.

"And then the first task in getting organized is to elect a permanent chairman who will conduct meetings until we have our constitution with duly elected officers under it."

Her silk-stockinged legs were crossed, showing up to the knees. She seemed bored. He acted bored, but he wished that some sort of a debate would start so he could say something and make her see he was different from Larkin and the church ushers.

"Mr. Chairman, I have one suggestion and one motion to present to the house. First, I would suggest that a temporary secretary be appointed to keep the minutes of this meeting," Red Kelly said arising.

"That's an excellent suggestion, Mr. Kelly," Larkin replied.

"And I would suggest in order to save time that the chairman we elect appoint this secretary. Later on, when we have a constitution, we will elect one. Now I move that nominations for a permanent chairman be placed before the house."

"I second Mr. Kelly's motion," said Austin McAuliffe.

Larkin was nominated and elected chairman, and he appointed McAuliffe as temporary secretary. A pencil and several sheets of paper were procured, and Austin took a chair at the table beside Larkin.

"Now, the next thing that we need is a constitution," Larkin said, without omitting the "ahs."

"Mr. Chairman, I think that it would be wise before we made any definite move about the constitution to have a little discussion so that we could be clear in the purposes and aims we wish to embody in our constitution."

"Well, I think that we all have that in mind and know more or less what we want, but if anyone wants to say anything about it, he can have the floor."

"You got a line like a Philadelphia lawyer," Studs said to Red in amazement and admiration as Red sat down.

Adele Rogers, who had turned into a flapper, arose, swung her shoulders from the weight of a raccoon coat and said she thought they ought to run a dance. Larkin said of course they would, but that that would be worked out after they got the organization settled. Dick Buckford proposed a baseball team, and that likewise was tabled.

Austin McAuliffe, smiling and polite, asked for the floor, and said that if he may, he would like to say a few things.

"We know, in general, what we want in a constitution. There must be provision for the way to conduct meetings, elect officers, the payment of dues, the minimum number of meetings each month, the organization and conduct of social affairs and such things."

"How much will we have to pay?" Vinc Curley interrupted.

Austin concluded his suggestions by proposing that there be a committee appointed to draft a constitution, and a time limit be set upon them so that they could get going. Red asked that the floor be left open for a brief period to solicit suggestions on the constitution before the chairman appointed a committee. Studs saw through Kelly, realizing that Red just wanted to shoot his mouth off. There was a debate on whether dues should be twenty-five or fifty cents a month. Studs tried to think of something to say so he could pitch right in and impress her. His mind empty of ideas, he watched her from the corner of his eye. He hoped he would be put on the committee. Finally, the committee was appointed. Red was on it, but not he. He was sorry, and yet glad, because he didn't want to be bothering with a lot of crap, and having to meet Larkin and McAuliffe and draw up a damn constitution. But an appointment might have made her realize who Studs Lonigan was.

III

"Let's go!" Studs said to Red, while chairs were being folded up and piled along the walls, amidst confusion and a pretentiously affected masculine show of energy. Studs wanted to hang around, but he was losing his nerve.

"Hell, Studs, there's no hurry. And there's a lot of nice girls here. We might as well dance."

Martha Curley played *Frivolous Sal* on the out-of-tune piano. Studs watched the dancers spread over the large floor. He saw her standing alone. He took a step to go over and ask her to dance. He decided he wouldn't be too much in a hurry. Making them wait was a good technique. He was interested only in her, dancing with her, so he acted as if he was interested in everything. He moved from spot to spot and watched Larkin waltz with Dorothy Gorman. Larkin kept almost a yard between them and acted as if he were being reckless. And Dorothy had always been plain, almost homely. Her face looked muddy. He guessed that because of her old man she had forgotten how to laugh, and only smiled in a half-interested way. He wondered if Larkin was too thick to realize that any regular guy would be laughing at him. He saw Phil Rolfe and Loretta going as if they were dancing slow-motion. The kike could dance, though, and he guessed that was what pleased young kids like Loretta. He didn't like her dancing with the Jew, felt like telling her. But after all it wasn't his business. He minded his business, and felt it was the place of everybody else in the family to mind theirs about him. Austin came by with Lillian Stone, taking short, choppy, graceless steps, keeping over a foot away from her. All church ushers danced alike; if a broad just danced close to them, they'd die of stage fright. Danny O'Neill whirled past him with one of the wild Dolan girls. Both of them were good dancers; it was nice to watch them. But Christ, any guy could waste his time learning how to dance.

She was still standing alone. Funnyface Duffy approached her. He got turned down. Hell, she wasn't a wet nurse to punks. He felt as if her refusal of the goof established a bond between them. He wanted this dance to end, because he knew that he'd dance the next one with her. Red winked at him as he and Fran Reilley stepped along. Fran Reilley was a hot girl. Aggravating. Just like his own sister. Whatever you said about them, the two of them could get about anybody they wanted and wind him around their fingers like a piece of old string. And Loretta was going to be the same way. He felt proud that he had two such good-looking sisters. And they could take care of themselves too. He saw Weary's kid sister, Jane, almost laying against that loud-mouthed Young Rocky, who turned frequently, and placed his thigh between her legs with each turn.

After the dance Red said:

"It's hell dancing with a broad as tantalizing as Fran Reilley. She knows she's got everything and it just teases your pants off. She eggs you into thinking you can get away with murder, and then pulls herself away and goes right on talking as if she didn't even think of what she was doing. Then she starts it all over again. Christ, Studs, she drives you into utter misery."

"Yep, Red, she's luscious."

"The guy who gets her is getting his jack's worth. Only nobody will do it without the ring. She knows how to play her game," Red said, half in tribute.

"Hello, fellows," Larkin said, offering a limp, sweaty hand that made Studs feel as if he was grasping a chunk of contaminated meat. He greeted Larkin with condescension.

"Gee, I'm glad you came, because we all want to get behind Father Gilhooley in the drive to raise funds for the new church."

Studs and Red gave each other the wink.

"Studs, how's it going?"

"Nothing to complain about," Studs replied disinterestedly.

"Well, I hope that now we'll be seeing a lot of you, and Kelly, too."

"That goddamn fat slob," Studs sneered, as Larkin walked away.

Another dance started. Studs hesitated about asking her. Fran came up to him and demanded that he dance with her. He saw that she was with a sappy-looking guy he didn't know. The bird was taller than he, but he'd take him on. He saw himself meeting the guy out on the street, asking him, Are you tough? and letting him have something he wouldn't forget very easy. He danced a bit woodenly, and Fran made it worse, because she kept leading him. She made a dirty crack about Fran Reilley. Studs guessed good-looking broads were that way about other broads. After the dance, she told him he wouldn't be a bad dancer at all, if he got more practice. She went off to join Fran Reilley and some other girls. He looked around until he saw the girl walking towards the other wall with the sappy-looking egg. He felt she'd notice him if he kept looking at her, and he might seem like a goof. He watched Austin join the group around his sister, Fran. Austin talked. He heard them laugh. What the hell could they see to laugh at in anything Austin said?

"Hello, Studs! Say, I'm glad to see you, just like old times," Johnny O'Brien said, smiling, shooting his arm up as if a button had been pressed, and giving Studs the collegiate handshake. Studs remembered that Johnny had been a fat, husky kid. Now he was thin, pale, a bit lifeless. Johnny asked him what he was doing. Studs told him.

"I'm over at the U. Belong to Kappa Psi now. Come on over some time, and I'll introduce you to the boys. Fine bunch of brothers, they are."

"Say, I hear they're anti-Catholic at the University. First thing you know, you'll be losing your religion," Studs said, kidding to make talk; he saw that the sappy-looking guy was walking away.

"Well, some of the professors are. You know, they believe in evolution and teach it in their classes, and say things against the church, but, of course, that doesn't affect me. And the fellows in my frat, say, Studs, they're all swell fellows. I'd like to have you meet them."

"You're all dressed up like Joe College," Studs said, letting his glance wander. She was dancing with Larkin, smiling at something the mush-face said. Somebody ought to take a picture of the guy. Johnny continued speaking.

"Now, you take this suit. As I said, it's new, first time I wore it. Had it made to order at Jerrems, seventy-five bucks. That's the way I believe in getting clothes, if you want to be really well-dressed. Pay for them and get clothes that fit properly and make you look distinguished. You can always tell what kind of a guy a fellow is, and how he rates, from the clothes he wears. A lot of guys you know have enough suits to change every day in the week, and they pay nothing for them. You can't take them out in the rain. Not me, I'd rather have a few suits, but good ones like this one I'm wearing."

Johnny excused himself and shambled over to Big Nodalsky. Studs watched him give the college handshake, and thought what a heel O'Brien had turned into. He wondered if Lucy would hear about the society here, and come out to a meeting. He could see the other girl, himself with her, dancing, everybody taking it for granted that he and she were going together, and Lucy seeing it. Himself treating Lucy with cold formality. He'd dance with her once or twice, and talk about general things. That would be all. See how she'd like it. He wondered what her name was. He could find out from Larkin. He knew he wouldn't ask that mush-face. She was dancing with Austin, and they seemed to be getting along all right. An old, not-belonging feeling came upon him. He felt like going. He felt that it was just nerve, expecting to make the grade with her. Let her go. If Austin and Larkin were her speed, well, she wasn't his kind. He'd go. He watched them dance. He accidentally caught the eye of Martha Curley and she smiled. He turned towards the piano and saw that Dorothy Gorman was playing.

"Don't you dance?" asked Phil.

"Why?" Studs asked, snottily.

"I just noticed that you hadn't been dancing. I wondered because I heard you were a pretty good dancer."

Studs guessed it must have been Loretta. They must have talked about him. He wondered what Loretta really thought of him. He didn't really know her. He looked at her on the floor, young, pretty, lively. She had grown that way, into a pretty girl, without his even realizing it, as if one day she was just a kid, and then the next, she was the kind of girl he saw dancing.

"I suppose you're selling dancing shoes," Studs told Phil.

"Studs, I'll bet the hebe is the kind that takes St. Patrick's day off," Red said, joining Studs.

"And Jewish Easter too," Studs added.

Phil went off to dance. Studs saw that she was again alone. He ambled slowly towards her, hoping no one would spot him, because he became suddenly as shy and speechless as a boy. With a forced effort of courage, he asked her if she'd like to dance. She thanked him but said that she was very tired. He walked away, sore. He tried to whistle. He felt he had to do something. He motioned to Martha Curley. She came towards him. They danced. Martha had used to be a nice girl, and full of life. She seemed tired and faded, and she was only about a year older than he. Girls had to grab their husbands off quick, he guessed. Martha said well, well, and they asked how each other were. She said she hadn't seen Studs in quite a long time. Studs said he hadn't seen much of her either. She guessed they must attend different Masses on Sunday. He asked her if she was working. She said no, she was just a home girl. He danced past the girl; she was dancing with Young Rocky. He couldn't miss seeing how close their bodies were pressed against one another.

After the dance, he told Red he was going. Red was unable to persuade him to stick around. Walking along Indiana Avenue, he thought that if he had danced with her, she might have remembered him, remembered that she'd smiled at him at Mass. If maybe she'd gotten a good look at him, she'd have remembered. But he never could have told her all that he'd thought of her since then. But maybe, maybe, if he had danced with her and things had gone right, maybe he might have, at that. He would maybe have said something like:

I never thought I'd find you here!

No, well, you never know what you can expect, she might have answered.

You're more than I could hope to expect at a place like this, he might have added.

They would have talked, told their names, laughed at jokes he would have been able to think up, and he would have walked home with her. At her door, he would have said, how about a show tomorrow night, and tomorrow he'd be taking her to a show. And they would, yes, go together. What the hell did he care if the gang would try and kid him. He wasn't just a hood, and just going to turn into another Barney Kelly, or Mickey Flannagan.

It was all a goddamn pipe-dream. He was just filling himself full of the stuff. Only if the thing had turned out different! He'd missed his chance. He thought of her in her green and red dress, and her cold aloof face and expression. Haughty jane. And he wanted her. He thought of going with her until finally she'd say yes and no one would be home, and he'd kiss her, and they'd. . . . All a goddamn pipe-dream!

"Jesus Christ, here comes the Fifty-eighth Street Alky Squad," he said with a laugh as he met Slug, Mickey, Barney, Tommy Doyle, Les, and Shrimp at the corner of Fifty-eighth and Indiana.

"We need another recruit," Slug said.

Studs chipped in with them. They bought paregoric in the drug store and drank it. They formed a drugged and stupefied line against the side of the drug store building, Studs was so helpless that Red Kelly had to take him home.

XVII

MARTIN HUSK *Lonigan poked Crabby Kentchy's books out of his arms.*

"Pick 'em up?" Crabby commanded.

"What? Huh! I don't know what you're talking about."

"Well, you will know, if you don't pick up the books you knocked out of my arm."

"What's he sayin'?" Husk Lonigan said to his pal, Pete McFarland.

"What you say, Koney?" kidded McFarland.

"I said pick 'em up!"

"He said to pick something up," Pete said.

Husk Lonigan looked up and down the street.

"There ain't no girls around to pick up."

Pete laughed.

"Gonna pick 'em up?"

"Who was your servant last year?" asked Husk Lonigan.

"You knocked 'em out of my arm."

"What?"

"You did."

"You're a liar," Husk Lonigan said, sneering and looking quite like his brother Studs.

"Who's a liar?"

"You, if you said I knocked your books down."

"Aw, smack him, Husk," said Pete McFarland.

"Try it!"

"Oh, you want to fight?" said Husk, again sneering.

Crabby punched Husk's nose. They fought, and Crabby gave Husk a bloody nose and a shiner. Husk picked up the books.

Chapter Seventeen

I

"I'LL get you a girl if you want me to," Fran said, taking the three bucks from Studs for the ticket he was buying to her sorority's dance.

"I'll get a girl."

"All right. Only if you want me to, I'll arrange a nice date for you," she said, sitting cross-legged on the piano bench.

"Yeah, I suppose with some fishface."

"Why, William Lonigan!" she exclaimed, and he smiled so she wouldn't get sore.

"You'll have a good time. And if you don't think you can dance well enough, you can practice with me."

"No, thanks."

He left and went over towards the poolroom.

Christ, now he'd let himself in for it and where would he get a girl. Lucy? Hell with her. The girl from the parish. How could he? He didn't want her. Let the punks have her. If she wanted punks and guys like Larkin, let them have the bitch. To hell with her! To hell with them all! He didn't have to go because he gave Fran the three bucks for a ticket. He could get out of it by just not going.

But he could see himself at the dance, togged out in new raiment, knocking them all dead, with a broad as keen as that blond. Everybody would wonder who he was, and everybody who knew him would be cockeyed with surprise, realizing that they had been totally wrong when they thought that Studs Lonigan was just one of the hoods in the Fifty-eighth Street Alky Squad. He could see himself at the dance, getting blind and tough, asking all the goddamn boy scouts and sweet boys in the place if they thought they were tough, and then laying one on them. Walking up to some bastard who had a Joe College handshake, messing the dope's manly vaseline locks, twisting his nose, and if he batted wise, giving him the works. Himself cleaning out the goddamn dance, with the blond seeing it. Lucy seeing it, and the blond and Lucy walking up to him, protesting.

And he would look at both of them with his lips curling into a sneer, and say:

"That for you, sister!"

Fran would be sore, and go up, Jesus, like a balloon. But it would be funny. He saw Phil coming along, singing.

Oh, I loved her in the morning,
And I loved her at night,
But last night on the back porch,
I loved her best of all.

"Where the hell you singing?"

"Sunday school."

"You look it."

"No kiddin', Studs, is Fritzie ready yet?"

"I don't know. She was dolling up. Why, you going out with her?"

"I'm taking her to the Tivoli."

"Oh!" said Studs.

"Fritzie is a fine girl. She's the nicest girl in the neighborhood. And don't think I don't appreciate it."

"Should I pay you for that?" Studs asked.

"I'm serious. I mean it, Studs."

"She must be stewed going out with you. You must have sold her the whole line."

"Studs, I'm serious in saying I respect her, and I'd fight anybody who doesn't."

"Who the hell could you fight?" Studs asked, bursting into laughter.

"Say, Studs, who you got against me?" asked Phillip.

"No kiddin', aren't you going to sing in some Sunday school?"

"Honest, Studs, I want to be friends with you."

"Sure, shake!" said Studs, a veiled note of sarcasm in his voice. They shook.

"Well, I better hurry. I don't want to be late."

"So long, Dopey Dan," Studs called.

Loretta could find better pickings than that kike. Well . . . he shrugged his shoulders.

He supposed Phil would be taking her to the dance. He didn't want to go to the goddamn thing. But he could see himself there, and surprising the whole damn bunch of them. Hell, he could do anything they could do.

He wondered how Lucy had turned out, and was she pretty and keen. She was a hell of a lot nicer than that blond. Christ, maybe that blond was only a bitch after all. Maybe she put out even to the punks. Come to think of it, she looked a little hard-boiled. The kind of a broad who knew a hell of a lot. She could probably be plenty hot all right. He thought of how funny it might be, say, in a couple of years, if he and the boys all went to a can house, and who should he see and pick, but her, the blond.

Lucy. He repeated the name, Lucy Scanlan. Lucy Lonigan. Mrs. Lucy Lonigan. Mrs. William Lonigan. He ought to call her up and see her, take her to the dance. He would telephone and act as if he thought, hell, he might as well see her again for old time's sake, and if she wanted to, why they'd go to Fran's sorority dance. Make it just natural.

He'd take her in a cab, and they'd walk through the hotel lobby, he in a new suit, she dressed up like the nuts, and people would spot him, and think there's a guy who's got a hot woman, and the punks with their seventeen- and eighteen-year-old broads, they'd all look at the woman Studs Lonigan rated. And he'd maybe see Dan Donoghue. Hadn't seen Dan since Hector was a pup. And then let the guys around the poolroom give him the horse laugh for going to a swell dance. Slug would look queerly at him, and feel his head, wondering if it ought to be examined. He'd say they better get Studs a bottle and bring him to see a new whore to change his luck. Let them. He liked them, but they would never be anything but hoods. They were all right, but he was cut out for better stuff than being a hood. Damn tootin' he was.

He bought a slug from the cashier in the chain drug store at Prairie and walked back to the telephone booths. He found her number in the directory. He dallied, turning the directory pages to figure out what he'd say. He felt as if everyone in the store were watching him, and knew what was going on in his mind.

He'd sure let himself in for something. He took a booth and was relieved when he got the busy signal and his slug came back.

"Wasn't she home?" asked the pretty cashier, when he set his slug down.

She handed him a nickel and smiled.

"Better luck next time."

He felt a sudden pride, because it was as if he did have a girl all his own, his. It gave him a feeling he'd never had before. She thought he had his girl, a girl who cared only for him, turned down other guys, waited for him to telephone her, went out only with him, his girl. Lucy would be his too. She'd always liked him. She still must. She knew what he really was, and she'd told him she did, and Helen

Shires had said, after they'd quit speaking long ago, that Lucy still did care. He laughed at himself, defensively. Studs Lonigan of the Fifty-eighth Street Alky Squad, talking like that.

He joined Slug and the boys in the poolroom.

"We was just gettin' some Jamaica ginger," Slug said.

"Count me out."

"Say, after that night las' week, I thought you was still the same old Studs," Slug said.

"Yeah, listen, that goddamn paregoric made me sick and jumpy for three days."

"You just got to get used to it."

"Say, Studs, I'll bet some flossie's got you," kidded Tommy Doyle.

"No, I just got to work tomorrow."

"I admire Studs. He's got more will power than I got," Les said.

"You singin' the blues again?" asked Slug.

"Well, he has. Jesus, there's nothin' in drinkin' all the time," said Les.

"Les, hire a hall," Shrimp Haggerty said wearily.

"We'll have to be shippin' you over to that Bug Club in Washington Park," Slug said.

Studs was tempted to get drunk, but finally determined that he wouldn't succumb to temptation again. Not after that paregoric hangover he'd had.

"Come on, let's take in a movie," he suggested.

"Hell, I saw three this week. Come on, we'll get Jamaica ginger and we'll be a movie," said Slug.

"You'll have to count me out, boys," said Studs.

"Desertin' us?" said Doyle.

"I don't feel like it tonight."

They gave Studs up and left.

He kind of wished that he'd gone along. Stan Simonsky came in, and they played rotation pool. Studs won. He and Stan went to a movie. He was determined he'd call up Lucy, too, tomorrow, and take her.

He went home around twelve, feeling confident.

He was going to show the boys something! He counted the days until the dance.

"Hello, Bill."

"Hello, dad."

"Say, I hear you're going to your sister's dance. I'll bet you cut a swath there. Now when I was your age, I never missed any of the big shindigs. That's why your mother fell for me. I was a dandy, even if I do admit it."

"Maybe I won't go. I thought I'd buy the ticket to help her along."

"You don't want to be a stick-in-the-mud. And there you might meet some fellows who can be valuable to you. You know, meeting the right kind of friends, useful ones, is what counts in this world. And the fellows who will be there, now they're the kind that will count later on. They'll be having their homes, their businesses, their buildings. You'll know them and when they'll want a decorating job, right away they'll think, I'll let Bill Lonigan do this for me."

Studs picked up a newspaper and casually glanced at it without knowing what he read.

"I hope you'll be taking that Lucy Scanlan girl. I remember her. She was a fine girl, a fine decent girl, just like your own sisters."

Studs left the room. The old man looked hurt.

II

Studs had a feeling of uncertainty as he got off the elevated, and walked towards Louisa Nolan's, a dancing school over a store near Sixty-third Street. He resigned himself. Only twenty days to the dance, and if he did a little dancing before then, he'd make a better impression on Lucy and everybody. And the punks always seemed to get something here; he could too, and broads were always broads. He spied a group of fellows before the place, and as he passed them to go through the wide-doored entry, he felt that they were giving him the once-over. He started up the broad stairs with slow casualness. The way the gang of guys had looked at him, made him wonder would he get into a fight. It was a windy March Sunday, and the gang would be around the poolroom, because they had nothing else to do. If he got in a real jam, a punk would call them up and it wouldn't take long for them to get here. And Studs Lonigan could take care of himself. Only whenever a guy went to a place where he wasn't known, he had to be ready for anything.

He paid fifty cents and entered, handing his ticket to a bald-headed, narrow-faced man who looked as if he belonged ushering in a Protestant Church. A mixed, talkative crowd was spread over the shabbily-carpeted lounge. Studs was ill at ease because so many of them were strangers to him who were known here, while he wasn't. Strangers coming into the Greek's poolroom and seeing him and all the fellows perfectly at home, would have felt the same way. He saw a sign pointing up a stairway to the check-room. He went up and checked his hat and coat. Two kids with familiar faces looked at him with a glimmering recognition, but he was unable to place them and did not speak. He perceived that the upper floor was a bare balcony and returned to the lounge.

"Come up here to ankle around?" asked Wils Gillen, his face brightening with surprise.

"Oh, I thought I'd look the place over and watch you punks."

"You want to watch the lads strut their stuff, huh, Studs?"

"Christ, most of them here look like kids," Studs said, glancing around.

"Sure, we get the girls from Park High in first year, and train them. After we break them in, there's nobody can complain of their style and technique. Right now we're putting them through their spring training, so that when summer comes they can all do their stuff over on the Wooded Island in Jackson Park."

"So that's what you guys do! Ruin nice girls," Studs kidded.

"Leave it to us."

"What, do all the girls up here put out?"

"If you don't succeed, try again. But there's Elizabeth and she's easy stuff."

Studs smiled as Gillen hastened towards a mushy-lipped kid, with a ravishing figure. Music started and there was a crush towards the dance floor. He saw Hennessey with a luscious blond in wine-red, and after them, Young Rocky leading a baby-faced thing. He moved to the edge of the rectangular dance floor, and watched the couples pass. In the center, he saw a group of six couples doing the Polack Hop, holding partners by the shoulders, skipping contortedly from side to side, and then skidding on one foot sidewise. He shook his head. That wasn't dancing! He saw Three Star Hennessey, and the blond in red, wantonly socking it in, in a corner.

"Hello, Studs," said Ellsworth Lyman, interrupting him from watching.

He watched Lyman move away and grab off the dance with a dark-haired Irish kid, who looked like a knockout. He approached a homely but husky Swede. They walked to the dance floor. From their first step, her big feet got in his and her own way.

"Do you come here all the time?" she asked with an accent.

"Me? No," he said.

"Nice music," she said.

He nodded. He felt as if everyone in the place knew him and were watching him, perhaps laughing behind his back, and thinking that all he could get for a dance was a dumb Swede pig. An expression of lust settled on her face, and she socked with him shamelessly.

"Hello, Studs, how come you're here," yelled Three Star passing him.

Studs did not reply. The Swede had got him hot, and she had her uses, even if she was so damn clumsy.

"Like it?" she said.

After the dance, they walked off the floor.

"So long," he said.

He felt like dancing with her again, but hell, she was easy meat. Maybe he'd get something better. If not, he could always try her again.

"Hello, Studs, Hydrox. How you Ben Turpin?" Noel Morton said.

"Oh, hello," said Studs, looking up at Noel, who was about six foot one, and loose-jointed. His baboonish, loose lips broke into an unassuming and friendly smile. Studs looked his outfit over and kidded him because his suit coat hung so low that most fellows could have worn it for a top-coat.

"Gee, I never expected to see you here."

"I thought I'd see what the place looks like."

"Well, how you like us? Think we're swell people?"

"Half of the broads here look like jail bait."

"They are. But sometimes, when they're young, they're sweet."

"Yeah, and it's sweeter too, laying in a can after you make 'em," said Studs.

"He who hesitates is lost, as I said to my old boy friend, Jess Dempsey," said Noel, dashing off.

"Hello, Studs."

"Hello, Weary. How goes it?"

"Oh," said Weary, shaking his shoulders in a gesture indicating that there was nothing to say.

"How come you're here," asked Weary.

"Hell, I heard the punks around the poolroom gassing about the place, so I thought I'd see them in action."

"Listen, we'll have a crap game in the can in a little while. Come on and get in. Buddy Coen and the guys will be around. You know him, don't you."

"No, but I heard about him."

"Well, the lads probably know you by name too."

Studs felt more at home now. He was not talking with punks.

"I got this hop. See you later."

Studs watched Weary go over to a sexy-looking dark broad in a black velvet dress. They moved among the dancers. He envied Weary because the guy danced so well. He wanted to meet the lads. They probably heard that he was the guy who'd once licked Weary Reilley. He wished some of the broads who knew Reilley knew who he was.

A tall girl, with long blond hair and a purple dress that made her figure sylph-like, stood a few feet away. Studs was wordless looking at her. She turned. It was Helen Shires' kid sister, Marion. And only a few years ago she hadn't known enough to wipe her nose, and one summer, too, they'd thought she was going to die from infantile paralysis.

Like Fritzie. Hell, she was practically a woman, she had everything. She was young, girl-like and woman-like, full of spirits and fun, and gay, with small straight breasts you almost ached to touch, nice figure, pretty as a picture, nice to see, like sunlight, like spring, like a flower blooming, like Lucy had been just before she'd moved from the neighborhood. He saw the same thing in Marion Shires that he'd seen in Lucy that day when the punks had been having their fight with tin cans in the prairie. He perceived that she was gazing at him.

"Say, aren't you Helen Shires' sister?"

"Why, yes. You're Studs Lonigan."

"You've grown into a fine-looking lady. I hardly knew you."

"Thank you."

"How's Helen?"

"She's fine. She's working downtown."

"I haven't seen her in a long time."

"Times change," laughed Marion Shires with disconcerting self-possession.

Studs figured the punks must break their necks over a girl like her. He felt suddenly proud, though, of his sister Fritzie. She didn't come to a hole like this. She was too decent.

"I never expected to see you here," said Marion.

"Oh, I don't come here regularly. I was just looking the place over."

"So am I. Like it?"

"I suppose the kids have a good time."

"Mr. Experience. But aren't you going to ask me to dance, or am I one of the . . . kids?" she asked as the music started.

"Why, it'll be a pleasure," Studs said, trying to be gentlemanly.

They walked to the floor, and danced. She lay against him with her head tilted back. He tried to hold himself in, because, after all, she was Helen's sister, and she was only a kid. Hell, he'd expect a guy to be white to his sisters, and if they weren't, he'd sock them. After the second piece, he couldn't do that. He gave her what he guessed she wanted. Suddenly she drew back, and her face seemed to go cold.

"You still live on Indiana Avenue?" he asked, figuring that she was a damn little teaser trying to make a monkey out of him.

"Yes."

"I suppose you're going to high school?"

"Englewood. I'll graduate this year."

"So is Loretta."

"Yes, I see her a lot at dances."

He was glad when the dance ended. He told her it was very nice to have danced with her, and asked to be remembered to Helen.

The little teasing bitch, somebody ought to cold-cock her, he thought. He looked at her surrounded by four cake-eaters. He saw O'Neill go up to her and he could tell by the sudden disappointment on the punk's face that she had refused to dance with him. He smiled. The Swede pig he'd danced with edged towards him. He moved off as if he hadn't seen her. He watched a guy with a bald head and pince-nez glasses shine up to a wrinkled-faced Polack. Made him realize that the joint looked like a freak show. Next to them, a kid, she couldn't be more than fourteen, was oogle-eyeing a high school punk.

Young Rocky rushed up, glad to see Studs. He remarked about all the keen janes there were for the dance. Phil Rolfe joined them, saying it was a surprise to see Studs Lonigan present. Studs was condescending. They toddled off after a jane. The punks sure felt their oats, and strutted their stuff. He felt that he'd come to the wrong place. He should have gone to the Midway Gardens or Trianon where the bunch was older. It was robbing the cradle here. Hennessey tried to mooch two bits off of him. He told Hennessey to try it on some of the broads. Hennessey said he was known here and didn't try to pinch pocketbooks. Studs realized that Hennessey was goddamn proud of being skillful at robbing pocketbooks; he hated the louse.

Studs stood, posing and watching with a smirk of superiority on his face. He liked to see them pass, see their faces. The youngest Bleu kid, dark, tall—hell, almost six feet—went dancing by, his nose up in the air as if it were severed from his face; he kept glancing all about him as he danced, looking, Studs guessed, for everyone to notice him. The kid he had only came up to his shoulder, and she looked damn young. Christ, he'd be robbing the cradle here. Weary winked as he went by, crudely socking it into a plump girl.

A fake collegian, one of these guys who bought college boy suits on the installment plan, danced by like a whirlwind. Noel Merton followed, turning in a speedy succession of circles, his coat tails flying behind him as if they were affected by strong winds. The jazz was fast and full of sex. Stud's blood thumped. His feet worked. He turned, and saw a kid, she couldn't have been a day over sixteen, making eyes at him. An awfully sweet-looking kid, with large black eyes. It was pretty just to look at her, her body half-formed, thin, so touched with energy. She smiled as he took a step towards her. They walked to the floor. She clung close, followed every step with lightness, and it would have seemed as if he were dancing with himself, if she had not held herself so tight against him. She chattered steadily, telling him about a movie she had seen. Then she said that her name was Nellie, and explained that it was her first time up here. She described a crazy woman with an accent who taught her history at Park High, and talked all the time about ouija boards, so funny. When they drew into a corner, she heated him up with a twisting little wiggle. It made him feel like a bastard. Christ, she was younger than Loretta, and seemed so damn innocent. A kid coming into it all. He tried to draw away from her, but she squeezed more tightly, and her breath came down hot on his cheek. He looked down at her, and her responding smile was tight and forced, almost painful. He felt like a bastard, but he couldn't control himself, and they danced sidewise, socking and shimmying the whole length of the floor. At the end of the dance, she was limp and perspiring. She said she was going to hold the eleventh dance open for him.

He bumped into Weary again, and Reilley asked him to come on back to the crap game. Weary stopped to talk to some guy a minute and Studs waited. They walked back. The music began and dancers passed them. Weary suddenly stopped, frowned.

"Why, that sonofabitch!" he said, standing with hands on hips. Studs saw June Reilley, dancing with a slim fellow, who was about two inches taller than Weary. She seemed to see her brother, and a look of fright came swiftly on her pretty dark face. She seemed just like the kid he'd danced with. It made him wonder, was something happening to girls with this jazz age. Weary motioned for June to come to him. She said something to her partner, and they danced over towards Weary and Studs.

"What are you doing here?"

"Why . . . Why, I was dancing. There's nothing wrong with my dancing. . . . You come here and dance, don't you?"

"Nobody told you you could. You go on home, and do it quick. If you ever come back here, I'll slap your little face. You've got no right here. Hear me!"

A great big baby tear rolled down her cheek.

"Go on!"

"I won't. You have no right to make me, or tell me what to do. You're not my boss and I don't have to do what you tell me to. I won't go."

A crowd gathered. Her tall dancing partner edged out of sight. June broke into uncontrollable tears.

"I'll tell you once more to leave or get dragged out of here!"

"I won't," she said, sweet and cute, as she cried and stamped her right foot.

He took hold of her right arm. She walked off, crying.

"Where did Bain, that bastard, go?" Weary said.

"Who's that?"

"The louse who was dancing with her."

Weary ran about, looking, followed by a small crowd. Finally he gave it up.

"I'll get the bastard," Weary said.

He and Studs went to the can, in back of the stage. Twelve guys stood in a circle shooting craps. Buddy Coen, a wiry little guy with a snotty face, said hello to Weary. He and Studs were introduced. The game went on with a big ox shooting.

"Come on. Shake them dice!" Buddy said.

"I'm shaking."

"Well, shake 'em harder!" Buddy said.

The guy looked at Buddy and shook. He won his pot. Buddy, running the game, took a ten-percent cut on the dough. The guy handed Coen five bucks.

"Five. Five bucks. Who'll fade. Come on, you cheap skates!"

Studs handed him two dollars.

"Three bucks!"

A little fellow, whom Weary had called Razz, faded another dollar. Somebody else took the last two. The fellow shook and made his seven. He shot the ten. Studs took five of it. The guy won. He shot fifteen.

"Shake 'em this time, you!"

"I'm shaking."

"Well, see that you do!"

Weary frowned at the guy, and faded ten of the fifteen. Studs took the other five. The guy made his point.

"Now, let's see them dice!" said Buddy, holding the pot.

"They'll be all right!"

Buddy took a step forwards. Weary crowded in. Three husky micks stood by the ox who held the dice. Weary grabbed the dice from the guy. He, the big ox, and three other fellows edged backwards.

"You sonofabitch! Loaded!"

Weary pumped his right into the ox's eye. Two fellows jumped Weary. Buddy Coen swung and brought his knee into a groin. A fellow went down moaning. The ox swung at Studs. Studs ducked. He hit the wall and winced. Studs swung. The ox dropped, and Buddy kicked him in the head. He moaned, and crawled towards the door. Studs jumped on the back of a guy tackling Weary and got a stomach hold. Studs followed the group out, chasing the bunch who'd cheated in the crap game. The dancing stopped and everybody swirled about, a milling crowd. Girls screamed. Studs ran downstairs with Weary and Buddy, but the guys got away. He learned that they were from Sixty-third and Halsted. Buddy and some of the other lads shook hands with Studs, told him he was white and had guts. Studs felt good, like a hero. Coen gave him ten bucks back from the pot he had held just before the fight started. They chipped in for a bottle, and Studs went back to dance. He found Nellie. She said the fight was terrible.

"They were rats. They got what they deserved. Every one of them should have had his teeth kicked in," Studs said.

"My, what language!"

"Thataboy, Studs," said Phil Rolfe, passing him.

Studs felt like he belonged there, and it made all the difference in the world.

"You must be a terrible fighter."

He shrugged his shoulders a trifle. He didn't want to brag or talk about it a lot, but he was pleased with what she said. He started talking, against his will:

"Well, what I do is keep in good condition, and then, if any trouble starts or I have a fight, I can take care of myself."

"That's very sensible."

"There's a lot of things I can take care of," Studs said in innuendo.

"Yes," she said knowingly.

"Sure."

"For instance?"

"Well, girls and. . . ."

"I'll bet you could, at that."

"You can't keep a good man down," he said.

She smiled an invitation.

After the dance he left her, and decided that he wouldn't, couldn't be the bastard to take her cherry. But he was tempted. He'd never been first with a girl. He wouldn't, and anyway, she was just jail bait and he could get into all kinds of trouble.

The liquor came, and he went back to the can with Weary and some of the boys. He took a swig. It was pretty strong, and he had to fight to get it down.

"Good stuff," he said.

"Sure it is," said Weary.

"To those bastards we cleaned! May they walk under a street car and forget to wake up," Buddy said, raising the bottle.

He drank and they laughed.

"Say, Lonigan, where do you hang out, Fifty-eighth Street?" asked Coen.

Studs nodded.

"Well, drop around and see us any time. We can always get a bottle, and maybe some janes, and can have a little party, or else a game. You know! We got a white bunch around here, and we always like to have more white men with us."

Studs thought that Weary glowered a bit at him. If he came, he supposed he'd have to tangle again with Weary sooner or later. Anyway he would. Goddamn it, he'd take Weary again. He was in condition, and he'd stay that way.

After the dance, he found Nellie waiting for him. She took his arm and started walking away with him. It was too much. If he was a bastard or not, he couldn't help himself. He looked at her. He was proud he was going to get something so sweet, even if he was a bastard for doing it. If he didn't, somebody else would.

XVIII

WHY, Marty O'Brien, how are you?" Patrick Lonigan asked, seeing Mr. O'Brien in front of church after ten o'clock Mass. Mrs. Lonigan and Mrs. O'Brien greeted each other.

"Hello, Pat. Glad to see you," O'Brien said, shaking with Lonigan.

"What are you doing back in the old neighborhood, Marty?"

"Oh, we just thought that we would come down here to church today. You know, it's nice to see the old sights now and then," Marty said.

"Yes, I suppose the old place is the only place for many of us," said Lonigan.

"I'm sorry I cleared out, but glad, because I see what's happening."

"Well, Marty, I don't know if I would be so pessimistic. To be sure, the jiggs have got on Wabash Avenue, and a lot of Polacks and Wops have come in along the southwestern edge of the parish, but still I wouldn't be so pessimistic. I got a building now on Michigan and I think it's going to be worth plenty more than what I paid for it. Particularly since Father Gilhooley is going to build the new church."

"Pat, I don't want to sound discouraging, but if you ask me, I'd say this: the whole neighborhood is being ruined, and quicker than you think. You mark my word, it's going to be so full of black clouds that a white man won't belong in it. Fifty-eighth and Prairie is going to look like Thirty-fifth and State with them.

"Golly, I don't think so, I hope not, Marty, but if it does, well, I'll be out. I'll turn a neat profit when I sell my old building. But if that does happen, it'll be a crime."

"Crime or no crime, those kike real-estate bastards are getting in, and what for? I'll tell you: to sell to niggers, that's what for."

"That will be a crime. We ought to do something about it."

"That's what I thought, but what can you do? That's why we moved."

"That will be a crime, and what with the new church Father Gilhooley is going to build. Goddamn it, Marty, they'll never get Michigan. We won't let them!"

"Well, mark my words . . . but how's business, Pat?"

"I can't complain; things are running smooth enough. I'm worried about unions. You know, them damn unions are robbing me, twelve

and fifteen dollars a day. Why, no painter or plasterer is worth that, but they got to get it; but how's business with you, Marty?"

"Fair."

"Say, you'll have to come up and see us some time," Lonigan said.

"And come and see us, Pat!"

Marty gave Lonigan a card with their new address printed on it. They went to their car and drove away.

Chapter Eighteen

I

STUDS observed that the Scanlans had a lamp in every corner, floor-lamps, table-lamps and lamps on the piano. The parlor contained so much furniture that it seemed overcrowded. He wanted to light a cigarette but restrained himself for fear that he might spill ashes. He looked at a rose-green pottery lamp set on the table near the heavy blue velvet drapes. He moved over to sit on a large overstuffed davenport that was upholstered in dark blue velour. He touched it, studied it. The Scanlans must have spent more dough than the old man on furniture. They'd always been well off, but the old man wasn't tight. He'd been awfully decent, too, slipping him a ten-dollar bill just before he had left to come out here and call for Lucy. He looked about the parlor again, wishing that Lucy would shake a leg. Doggy house all right! Mrs. Scanlan entered. Studs jumped to his feet, smiled, and asked her how she was, simultaneous actions performed with the feeling that he knew the book of etiquette by heart, and the determination that he was going to carry the evening off. Mrs. Scanlan shook hands with him. He saw that she had changed, and it made him feel a little bit sorry. She was gray, and much stouter, and she didn't seem to have any pep. When she commented on how pleased she was to see him, and on what a fine young man he had grown up to be, it seemed almost as if it was only a tired voice without any body behind it. She sat down. He sat down after her. She asked if his mother and dad were well, and he said they were. It was hard trying to talk to her. But all girls were the same, didn't care how long they made a guy wait. Thought it was their privilege. Fran and even Loretta were that way. It was hard to think of anything to say to Mrs. Scanlan. He hoped Lucy would hurry up.

"Lord have mercy on me, I suppose I wouldn't even recognize the old place, if I was to go back there now. Five years is a long time, the way the world does change nowadays," Mrs. Scanlan droned monotonously.

"It hasn't changed so awfully much. Some of the old people, like the O'Briens, have moved away, but many of them are still in the parish."

"Have the Shires sold their house yet?"

"No."

"Ah, they were fine people, even if they were on the other side of the fence. What I always said to my girls, and what I still say, is that if many Catholics lived as upright lives as the Shires family did, they would need have no fear of meeting their Maker on the Day of Judgment. That oldest girl, Helen, she was a bit of a wild one, but a fine, decent girl. I suppose now she's settled down."

"Yes, she's working downtown," Studs said.

"My Helen was saying she saw the O'Brien boy downtown, and he was saying the niggers were getting in there. Isn't it a shame?"

"There's some on Wabash Avenue. That's where my father sold his building, and got one on Michigan. But they won't get any farther. Father thinks property values will go up and the property will be worth a lot more after Father Gilhooley builds the new church."

"You know, William, I never felt the same about any place I've lived in as I did about our home on Indiana. I wouldn't have sold it only for the girls. That neighborhood, there, it was just like home. I lived in it for over twenty years, and raised my family and buried my husband from it. But after he died, I did feel kind of sad like he was always coming back, and I felt it was bad luck to stay living in a house when one of yours has died in it. I've always heard that said."

Studs smoothed his hair back. He wanted to look groomed when Lucy walked in.

"Your sister, Loretta, the one that always played with my Helen, she must be a grown girl now, too. I can remember when they were just tots together, and my Helen had such long red curls. I used to braid her hair every morning. But you know, my Helen, she had scarlet fever, and they had to cut off every inch of that lovely hair, and it's never grown back like it used to be. It's bobbed now. Loretta, she must be the young lady, and the youngest boy—what was his name?—he must be a big strapping lad too. My, my, how time flies."

"Martin, you mean, he's a little bit taller than I am," Studs said.

"Well, life is strange . . . but here's my Lucy now."

"Well, well, so we meet again. How are you, Studs?"

Studs arose and smiled sheepishly as he shook hands with her. His old feelings arose so strongly that he saw her as through a mist. No use kidding himself, his feelings hadn't changed a bit. He'd always like Lucy.

"You haven't changed a bit," she said, standing before him, with a self-possession that dismayed him and aroused envy.

"You have. You look even sweller than you used to," he gulped.

"I'm wrong. You have changed. You've picked up the blarney," she said, smiling and pointing a finger at him in the old teasing manner.

He was only gradually able to see the attractive, sweetly plump young woman before him. He perceived the same devilishness in her eyes. He noticed how her lips and cheeks were still red. And she knew how to dress.

She wore a green crepe, low-waisted dress, the semi-full blouse forming a broad, tight band around her hips; and the skirt fell about three inches below the knee. The ensemble effect was flaring and there were silver rose-buds on the shoulder straps, which were matched by high-heeled silver pumps.

"No kidding, you do look swell!" he said with embarrassment.

"Enough of that, now," she said in a tone which was almost maternal.

"You know, it seems only like yesterday that you two were only children. Now you're a grown up young man and young woman. Ah, 'tis strange, life," the mother said.

Studs came out of a feeling of paralysis sufficiently to suggest that maybe he'd better call a taxi. She said they could pick one up outside.

"You know, Lucy, I'm right. William does take after his father. All of the children, except maybe the youngster, what's his name, do," Mrs. Scanlan said, studying Studs.

"Oh, mother!" Lucy said impatiently.

The mother's face dropped. Lucy got her wrap, a large square silver and gold cloth shawl with black thread through it and bordered in white fox. She threw it over her shoulders. She looked like a knockout. The mother muttered maternal benedictions upon them as they left.

"Poor mother," said Lucy as they walked along a street of apartment buildings, toward Sheridan Road. They heard a Victrola record from an open window, and Lucy started snapping her fingers, and singing:

Don't mind the rain,
It's bound to come again,
For when the clouds go rolling by . . .

It was like a picture that Studs wanted never to forget. The warm spring evening, the promise it offered to him, a mist in the lush air, Sheridan Road ahead, with traffic lights, people crossing the streets, automobiles going by, the Victrola, Lucy singing, so pretty that he wanted to look at her, touch her, kiss her, love her, take her arm, say something to her of what it all meant, and of how all along he had really wanted nothing like he had wanted her. And he couldn't say anything, because it all stopped him. He guessed that when you felt like he did, you just had too many feelings to tell them to anybody. And it made him feel like a louse, him still not completely cured from the dose that little bitch from Nolan's had given him, taking Lucy out when he had a dirty disease. He wasn't at all worthy of her. He felt as if he wanted to crawl before her on his hands and knees, and kiss the hem of her dress.

"Poor mother, she's never been happy since we've moved," Lucy said.

"My folks like the old neighborhood. I suppose they would feel the same as your mother if they left it."

"How about you?" she said, looking at him as if she could see through his mind.

"One place to sleep is as good as another," he said, indifferently shrugging his shoulders.

"Cynical," she said in a dismaying tone.

He hailed a Yellow Cab on Sheridan Road, and helped her in, the mere touching of her arm affecting him like electricity. He tried to give directions in an assured and suave manner and felt like a clown. He sat beside her, liking the perfume smell, and the clean new smell of her clothes.

"You know we sold our building and moved over to Michigan. There's niggers on Wabash now," he said, trying to make conversation.

"Yes, isn't it awful . . . those niggers."

"I suppose there'll have to be more race riots to put them where they belong," he said.

"That would be just perfectly horrible . . . but exciting."

They became silent as the cab rolled along. The silence grew upon Studs. He guessed he better talk, not give her reason to think that he was so damn dumb that he couldn't even open his mouth.

"The O'Briens and some of the other old parishioners have moved out," he said.

"Yes, I saw Johnny. He's made a frat that rates high at the University," she said.

He glanced out of the window at the lake in the spring night. He looked at Lucy. He wanted to put his arm around her.

"You weren't at the last Zeta dance?" she asked.

"What?"

She repeated the question.

"No," he muttered.

"You don't go to many dances?"

"Oh, once in a while."

"I see Dan. He does a lot of stepping out when he's in town," she said.

"I see Bill once in a while," said Studs.

"Bill, he was so funny."

"He still is."

"Say, Studs, have you a cigarette?"

He gave her one and smoked himself. It put him more at ease. He edged an imperceptible inch towards her.

"This is going to be a big dance."

"Fran talked about it enough."

"She works so hard for her sorority. I suppose Loretta will be there. She's gotten to be such a darling."

"She's a good kid," said Studs.

The bumping of the car pitched her against him. She stayed there. That perfume smell, and the smell of her clothes made him want to kiss her even more than he had been wanting to.

"With my sister and your sister grown up, I feel like the older generation," Lucy said.

"Yeah," he said.

He put his arm around her. He quickly and clumsily, on an impulse, kissed her.

"This is awfully public," she calmly said, completely disturbing him.

He looked at her, her face now vague in the cab.

"You work fast," she teased, pursing her lips as if she were waiting for another kiss. He kissed her again.

"You're fast," she said.

He tried to hug her more tightly against his shoulder. She stiffened.

He seriously puffed at his cigarette. Remembering the afternoon in the park, in the tree, swinging her legs, himself looking through the leaves at the park lagoon, neither of them speaking, swinging their legs, her singing *The Blue Ridge Mountains of Virginia*. It couldn't have been so many years ago. It wasn't all gone. He wished she'd sing that song now.

"They're having a hot Benson band tonight," she said, breaking his mood.

He was in for it, a chump. How in hell would he act? Jesus Christ. Already, he felt as if he were an entirely different Studs Lonigan from what he'd ever been, and they wouldn't even know him around the poolroom. They rolled nearer and nearer to the Loop, and he felt like he was being taken to his doom.

II

Entering the hotel, Studs tried to appear calm and natural, as if he belonged in places like this, and was the kind of a guy who could bust right into any kind of a joint, no matter how swell it was, and act like he belonged there and knew what to do. They passed across a pillared lobby that possessed an indefinite atmosphere of lacy ornateness. Studs felt that everybody was looking at him, ready to laugh if he pulled a boner. He knew that he was blushing. He walked by an old man lounging in a chair, half asleep, his somnolent face making him look like he was dead on his feet. He threw back his shoulders. He thought of himself as youth, and hoped the old man saw him and thought so too. He spotted several loudly dressed Jews, and they seemed to be looking at Lucy. She was worth looking at, and they should be envying him, but let them crack wise or dirty!

They turned to their left, and up a marble stairway with gilt banisters to the Blue Room.

"All the dances that count are being held here this year," she exclaimed.

"Yeah!"

He could just tell that she was able to see right through him, see that he was out of place and without confidence. Maybe she was just silently laughing at him, and later she would laugh and talk about him behind his back. If she did, let her, he thought, in a cursing mood. If she was that way, she could go plumb to ——. He wished it was over or that he hadn't been chump enough to let himself in for such a thing. He knew he would make a fathead out of himself. And he was too old for this cake-eater stuff. He determined that if trying could do, he would carry himself through it with . . . dignity.

A lanky, effeminate fellow, with blond marcelled hair, stood collecting tickets. Studs handed him the ticket, his face set in a challenging sneer. Let that sap bat out of turn. The fellow pointed to the right, and stated in an affectedly refined voice that the checkroom was in that direction. He started taking his coat off as he walked towards it. Placing it over his arm, he realized that he hadn't paused first to take Lucy's shawl. She handed it to him, and said that she would go and powder up. It was bull number one for him, bad way to start the evening off. Girls got sore when fellows pulled little boners like that; Fran always talked about them, and she didn't like fellows who were so dumb. All girls, he guessed, were the same way. After checking the wraps, he went to the lavatory. He shook his head with surprise. Building cans like palaces nowadays. Two fellows stood smoking by the washbowls. They looked like boy scouts to Studs. The kind of fake gentlemen that Fran would like. They all looked alike, and talked alike, and shook hands in the same Joe College way. Johnny O'Brien was getting that way too. They were all like a walking book of etiquette, and the only thing they needed was a good hard mash in the puss.

"Jake has a keen woman with him tonight," said one of the young fellows by the washbowl, as Studs washed his hands.

"I don't like her."

"What did she do, two-time you on a date?"

"That mama wouldn't two-time anything in pants. She's a tramp and anything from eight to eighty goes with her. If you ask me, Jake had plenty of guts, plenty of guts, bringing her to a dance like this, where there's all kinds of decent, respectable girls."

"Jake must be hard up if that's the case. Only whatever you or I say, I know I'd never kick her out of bed."

"I never could understand Jake anyway. He always does things like this."

"Yeah, he is kind of unconventional."

They passed on out. A white-coated shine started brushing Stud's suit. He was a pest. Studs handed him two bits and told him to lay off. Studs dallied over a cigarette, because he didn't want to face the crowd. Finally he shot the cigarette aside and walked out with the air of a guy who was making a big decision.

The groups, spread across the long, narrow, and gaudily upholstered lounge, disheartened him. They talked in muffled voices, strolled languidly up and down, stood and sat about. He was afraid of it all, afraid he might act like a clown. But it seemed warm, gay, because there was such a number, so many good-looking young girls. He was glad he'd come, and he wanted to, was determined to, become part of it. He went forwards as if he had nothing to do, hoping he'd recognize some friends. He'd never seen so many hot-looking women in his life; and he had one of the hottest ones of all here. His elation subsided as quickly as it had arisen. Hell, it was all artificial. They were all trying to put on the dog, show that they were lace-curtain Irish, and lived in steam-heat.

He waited for Lucy in a corner, near the entrance, feeling lonesome, watching more couples coming, envying the guys who came with laughing girls, because he knew they were going to have a good time, and he wasn't. He saw Lucy coming toward him and his mood vanished. Maybe she did like him. He noticed her high-heeled silver slippers, and the silver rose buds on her shoulder straps. He realized that she didn't see him, as she walked forwards, half-smiling, seeming very happy. He hoped she was that way, because of him. She was damn keen all right. Plenty of bastards were going to wish they were in his shoes tonight.

"Here you are. I've been looking for you," she said in a very friendly voice.

He said yeah. She babbled that the dance was going over big and would make money. It tickled her so that she could hardly wait to see Fran. Fran would be so thrilled because she had plugged so much for it and took such an interest in the affairs of the sorority. Studs listened, shifting his weight from foot to foot. When she finished chattering, he answered yeah.

"Everybody is here," Lucy said.

"Yeah," Studs said, wondering what the hell she meant by everybody, a lot of these goddamn two-bit jellybeans around the place.

The music started up. He suggested dancing. She nodded but said to wait until a few others went in. If she was one of the first on the floor, she'd feel like she was on exhibition. He put his hands in his pockets, and waited. He took them out, and let them hang at his side, figuring he guessed he might as well not put them in his pockets. She said he had a nice-looking suit on. He said it was the first time he had worn it. She said it was in good taste and in fashion. He folded his arms, self-conscious of his hands. He unfolded his arms and let them hang at his side.

They followed the other couples towards the ballroom. Studs was afraid he wouldn't dance well, and was too excited to say anything clearly to her. But he felt quite proud that others could see him with Lucy, see how well-dressed she was. A spine-shivering solo from the saxophone broke into his attention. It made him sad and want to be reckless. He walked down the steps with her, and saw the dancers inside, wheeling, and spinning on the glossy floor in dim lights.

The Blue Room was square-shaped, with French windows on two sides, a vaulted ceiling, and pillars in the center of the floor. The decoration was in a blue motif. He danced a little stiffly. The mere touching of her in the dance postures made him want to crush her to him, squeeze her against him almost to the point of breaking her bones, tell her that goddamn it, she had to be his woman, and there was no other side to the question. It made him gloomy. Some said a dose could never be cured, although his doctor said otherwise. Maybe even if she did love him and would marry him, he'd never be able to. A sudden vision of him ruining her for all times came to him like a nightmare. They swung into a patch of colored orange light, and then passed the tuxedoed orchestra, which was playing wildly on a dais. She let herself go against him, drew back. He wanted her close against him, wanted to feel her belly hot against him. He didn't have the nerve.

The lights brightened, and the music stopped. Following the example of other fellows, he clapped perfunctorily. A fat blond girl smiled at him. He smiled back, not knowing who she was. Must be a sorority sister of Fran's. It was pleasing, though, to have people he didn't know remembering him.

"Studs, you dance nicely," Lucy said.

He tried to take the compliment modestly, but wondered if she was only pulling his leg, the way janes always enjoyed pulling a guy's leg. He guessed, though, he did dance well enough to get by. And he wanted Fran, everybody to notice it. If he and Lucy went together, he'd learn how to dance as good as all the cake-eaters, even Rolfe. He saw Rolfe with Loretta at the other end of the room. Fritzie looked sweet in her new black velvet dress; too sweet for Rolfe.

The music commenced, and he tried to dance more swiftly, like so many of the guys did, and they got out of step and Lucy almost tumbled on the floor. She smiled, then laughed. There seemed to be a twinkle in her eye, the twinkle in the eye of the old Lucy, and he was reminded of the way she'd smiled at the party at his house on the night of their graduation.

"You trying to win a race or go to a fire?" she asked.

"We better not go so fast," he said with gravity.

He passed Rolfe and Fritzie, holding his head erect. His face was grave, and he nodded curtly. Phil smiled back at him, and then bent down to say something to Fritzie. She smiled sweetly at him.

"Penny for your thoughts?" said Lucy.

"I was just noticing my kid sister."

"Oh."

She turned and smiled at Fritzie.

"I'll bet she'd like to hear you calling her your kid sister. She's a young lady now."

He went outside of Carroll Dowson and Fran. They smiled at him; he nodded back.

"You know a lot of people here," he said to make conversation, noticing how many couples she greeted.

"Oh, you meet everybody, here and there," she said with intended casualness.

"Yeah, it's tough being popular."

"Now, don't you go getting sarcastic," she said, but not angrily.

Christ, he felt that he was acting and talking like a goddamn dingbat. Well, if it was so, he was only getting what he had bargained for. He looked into Lucy's face, and away, and felt again the desire to crush her to him.

Fran and Dowson joined them after the dance. She bestowed an approving glance on Studs and told Lucy that she looked lovely and darling. She said with enthusiasm that the dance was way over, and that they'd clear at least two hundred dollars on it.

"Thinking about playing any football this fall?" Carroll asked, shaking with Studs.

"Maybe," said Studs.

"If you do, let me know."

Studs asked Dowson how his brother was, and Dowson said all right. He was here some place with Gertrude O'Reilley.

They talked until the music for the next dance was heard. They again waited for others to go in first and then followed.

"Everybody is here," she said in a very natural voice, as if her body was not tight against him.

"Yeah," he said, looking at her, hoping she'd say something else, some hint about the way they were dancing, and that it meant something to her. Colored lights were played across the floor. Silly words were in his head. He was silent.

"Oh, there's Mike!" Lucy exclaimed.

"Mike who?"

"Don't you know him? Mike Crowley. He's such a cute boy."

"Hello, Mike," Lucy called.

"He's a darling boy," she told Studs.

Studs looked after him. He was a big, dumb, but decent-looking young chap, and the girl with him seemed eighteen or nineteen, a plain-looking girl with a wide, Dutch face.

"He's only a boy, but he's so darling. He's the captain of St. Ignatius football team, and everybody says he's a fine player and that some day he'll be a famous college football player."

"Oh," said Studs, looking again after Mike Crowley, wanting to meet him, wanting Lucy to remember that he'd been and still was a good player.

Studs told her he had just seen Dan Donoghue on the floor. He danced towards Dan, good old Dan. It made him feel better and more confident than he had all evening. Dan smiled with surprise, but Studs knew he was glad to see him, and said he'd never expect to see them together, and Studs liked it; particularly, because Dan linked him and Lucy together as if it was very natural and expected. After the dance, Dan and Studs walked off the dance floor together, and Dan's girl and Lucy strolled just ahead of them.

Studs asked how everything was going, as if it was a question of grave import. Dan said he couldn't complain, and asked Studs how it was riding, and Studs said he couldn't complain either. He asked about the old fellows, and Studs said he'd seen some, and he hadn't seen others. Dan said to tell them all he'd been asking for them.

They grouped together in the lobby. Studs felt as if he belonged, one of a talking group. Good old Dan. Dan was no cake-eater either, and if Dan could enjoy these dances, well, he could. He'd take Lucy to more of them. He looked at her as she laughed with Dan's girl, Catherine Marie Boylan. He envied everybody who knew her. He wanted the dance to be over, and the two of them to be alone in a cab, because it would mean the chance he'd been waiting for all his life, ever since they had sat in the tree. If he didn't make the most of it, win her, maybe he might never have another chance.

Studs and Dan exchanged dances. Catherine Marie was only a kid, but damn pretty, with chestnut hair, round face, blue eyes, athletic figure.

"I feel as if I know you," she said on the dance floor.

"Yes."

"Dan's spoken so much of you."

"We went to school together."

"I know, he thinks a lot of you."

"First down ten," Dan said: Studs had bumped Catherine Marie into him and Lucy.

Studs smiled, but his confidence was severely shaken. He danced rottenly and had nothing to say. Different from Dan and Lucy, they were talking so naturally. Some guys were just built that way, and could break into any new place. He wasn't and couldn't. Hell, he didn't belong with all these broads. They were not his kind. He couldn't talk about dances, and didn't know the people they talked about and knew.

"Oh, there's Perc Byrnnes," Catherine Marie said.

Studs said nothing, because after all, she was his old pal, Dan's girl, and he didn't want to make a snotty crack. They waited between pieces. A heavy but soft fellow with a thin girl in blue on his arm approached them. Catherine Marie greeted them effusively. Studs didn't like the way the punk seemed to have polish rubbed all over him, the way shoe polish was lathered on shoes. Catherine Marie introduced Studs to Perc Byrnnes and Vivian May Corrigan. Studs shook hands with the guy, feeling that he was holding a handful of crap.

"And how are you?" Perc Byrnnes said with a soft, solicitous voice, as if a negative answer would cause him irrevocable discomfort.

"I'm rarin', Perc."

The Corrigan girl asked if he were Loretta Lonigan's brother. He nodded. She said she knew Loretta.

"I must congratulate you the way your sorority has put the dance over. It's the most successful dance of the year," the Corrigan girl said to Catherine Marie.

Studs looked quickly at Byrnnes, and then back at the Corrigan girl.

"Isn't it gorgeous?" Catherine Marie Boylan said.

He was glad when the music started up again. All he wished now was that he was drunk with Slug and the boys and that they were all here. He had to smile at what they'd do.

"Oh, I'm sorry," he said, clutching her tightly. He had collided with a couple, and she'd almost been knocked off her pins.

"It was my fault," she said, laughing.

Returning to the lounge, he unobtrusively wiped his perspiring face. He wondered how in the name of Jumping Jesus Christ a regular guy like Dan could stand all this crap. Dan excused himself and said he'd see Studs later. He and Catherine Marie walked off. Studs watched them pause to speak with that Byrnnes clown.

During the next dance, Lucy told him that Dan was going steady with Catherine Marie. Her father was a broker on La Salle Street, and she rated. She was awfully sweet, but young, and in Loretta's class at high school. Dan and she were awfully attached. It made him wish that people would be saying Studs Lonigan and Lucy Scanlan were awfully attached to each other. At the intermission between pieces, they were joined by Phil and Loretta. Phil adopted an air of equality in greeting Studs, and asking him how he liked the dance. Studs ignored Phil and told Fritzie she looked nice. The music saved Studs' patience. After the dance, Fran and Carroll Dowson joined them in the lounge. Harold Dowson came up. He introduced his girl, a pug-nosed thing named Gertrude O'Reilley. She was the niece of

Joe O'Reilley, the lawyer whom Studs' old man admired so much. Fran stood watching him with studied approval. He didn't like it.

"You're comporting yourself fine. I'm proud of you. I never knew it was in you," Fran said, dancing the next one with him.

"Yeah."

"Now don't get nasty. I'm only telling you what's true. All the girls in my chapter have been saying nice things about you.

They were noticing him! He hoped Fran would tell that to Lucy.

"And you're dancing well. Only there's one thing. Please be careful about the way you acknowledge introductions."

"I can take care of myself."

"Now, please don't get bull-headed," she said.

He frowned sullenly. She accused him of trying to disgrace her on the floor.

"Cut it out," he said.

"Won't you please speak more loudly. The orchestra leader didn't hear you," she said.

"Well, I didn't ask you for any opinions."

"You're simply incorrigible."

In the lounge again he stood in a chattering crowd, feeling useless. Lucy whispered that she was having the next one with Frank Dolan, who was staging it. He watched Lucy walk off with Frank Dolan, a big broad-shouldered guy. He might be big, but, well, Studs Lonigan wasn't afraid of him. He could see himself whittling the big fake down to his own size.

"Jesus, how come you're here?" asked Fat Malloy with contagious good fellowship.

"My sister talked me into it."

"That's right. It's her sorority."

"Say, do those bastards call this a good time?" asked Studs.

"Well, it is in a way. I mean there's all kinds of fine girls, and it's swell. Most of the broads rate high, and I don't mean maybe."

"Well, Fat, I don't like most of the guys around here. They're fakes."

"A lot of them are. There's one guy here named Perc Byrnnes, and he's the biggest fake in the joint. He's got dough and his old man lets him have a big Lincoln, so he thinks he's the reincarnation of Jesus Christ!"

"I met him."

"Well, I'm gunning for that boy. The first time he cracks wise to me, I'm just going to up and let him have one. He's a foul ball! But say, Studs, come on in the can," Fat said, smirking.

"By the way, what girl did you take?" Fat asked in the lavatory.

"Lucy Scanlan."

"Say, she's a fine girl."

"Yeah," said Studs, proud.

"Drink," Fat said, pulling out a bottle.

Studs drank.

"Your dose must be better?"

"The doc says it's clearing up all right."

"Say, how did you get it?"

"I got it from a sixteen-year-old bitch named Nellie Cullen. I picked her up at Louisa Nolan's. I've met plenty of lowdown whores but she's the filthiest bitch I ever came across, and she's only sixteen."

"You ought to find her and crack her one in the teeth."

"I tried, but she never went back there while I was looking for her."

"Say, I heard about the scrap you got into at Nolan's."

"Yeah."

"You know, those lads around Sixty-third and Stony are plenty tough. Plenty. And I hear you made a hit with them."

"They're all white. I was around with them a couple of times. But you know, I'm not yellow, but hell, I don't go around inviting trouble. Christ, when they get drunk, they see a guy they don't like, and they walk up and clout him, or else if it's in a restaurant, they just toss a sugar bowl at his head. And Buddy Coen. . . ."

"I know Buddy."

"I like him, but, Jesus, he gets drunk all the time, and then picks out the biggest cop or dick he can find and pokes him. If I have to fight, I will, but that's too much," said Studs.

"They're tough hoods."

"Say, know a guy named Frank Dolan?"

"He's another one of these flannel-mouth Irish who thinks he's society stuff."

"Can he go?"

"A fart in a windstorm would blow him over."

"I didn't like his looks."

"We'll drink on that," said Fat.

They killed the bottle.

Studs and Fat walked back. Fat was only a punk, and he acted like an equal and old-time buddy of Studs. But Studs liked him. He was a godsend now.

Dolan walked up and thanked Studs, calling him old man. He nodded to Fat. Fat frowned. Studs was introduced to several couples but missed the names. He almost had to laugh when Fat Malloy acknowledged introductions the same way Byrnnes did. The dance suddenly seemed to Studs like a bunch of ten-year-old kids playing they were in a secret society. He looked at Lucy. Goddamn it, she'd got him. He looked at her hair, black curly hair, her face, round, young, always breaking into a laugh and a smile. They could talk and make up for all these years. He felt like a bum and a louse too. She was too damn good for him, him with a dose, all that stuff. But with her, well, she'd got him. Guys said love was all the crap. When a girl like Lucy got you, it was different. He wished, Jesus Christ, that things had turned out different after that day in the park, and all these years hadn't been wasted. He wanted to say something to her. Maybe in the cab, the time would be set, and the right thing would just come to him. He felt goofy, not at all like the Studs Lonigan everybody knew. He wanted the next dance to begin. He wanted to be just alone with Lucy. Lucy said that her old friend Morris Smith wanted the next dance. Smith smiled fatuously. Studs said all right. He watched them disappear, thinking how he'd like to take Smith and Dolan on together and lay them out cold. He didn't hear while Malloy talked half drunkenly. He watched a punk cooing with a little flapper. Silly. Goddamn it. Lucy had got him. When the dance ended, he anxiously watched the couples coming out. Fran Reilley bowed to him. Dan winked. Byrnnes gave a silly grin. Phil and Fritzie waved. They came, walking slowly, talking as if they were sincerely interested in each other. Studs' fists clenched. He was surly when Smith thanked him for the dance. Lucy seemed to notice it.

"You know, Studs, a girl likes to dance with different fellows. Variety is the spice of life," she said, during the next dance.

"I didn't say anything."

"I know that old dark look of yours."

He tried to smile. He wanted it to be over, and him and Lucy to be alone. He wanted to kiss her and love her. Waltz music and colored lights made him sentimental like a moon-calf punk. He could hardly wait to be alone with her.

III

Studs was glad when he and Lucy left a large group in front of the College Inn and got into a cab. He didn't mind the nine bucks he'd forked out at the place, but the people weren't his kind, and he was glad to be away and alone with Lucy at last. She babbled about how successful a dance it had been.

"I guess it made money," he said without interest.

"Didn't you enjoy it?"

"Oh, yeah."

"You certainly sound awfully enthusiastic."

"There were a lot of mopes there."

"Why, they were all nice fellows."

"Nice mopes, I say."

"I see that you're still a . . . tough guy."

He wanted to expand his chest and say yes, he was, and he was going to be tougher after seeing those dingbats at the dance. But he said nothing. He felt as if she was slipping through his fingers, and that he ought to say something to catch and stop her before it was too late. He looked at her, wanting her, all of her, and she was like something beautiful in a mist. She smiled at him. Maybe no, he wasn't losing her.

"You're just the same Studs . . . just like a little boy."

She edged towards him, patted his cheek, took off his hat, ran her hands through his hair. She kissed him. She was in his arms. Suddenly, he was french-kissing her. He dug through her dress and touched her breast. She froze up, turned her face away.

"I'm not that kind of a girl."

He tried, crudely, determined, unthinking, to pull her to him again.

"Please be careful," she said cuttingly.

He looked out the window. He saw the lake. He grabbed her hand. He kissed her. She opened her mouth on the next kiss. He felt under her dress.

"I won't hurt you. Come on," he said huskily. He didn't even think of his dose, all he had in mind was Lucy.

"I can't . . . no . . . not here. If mother isn't home, maybe. . . ."

"Why not?" he said.

"I can't . . . it'll be awful . . . I'll ruin my clothes . . . please wait till we get home," she begged.

He believed her. They kissed, and he felt her all the way home. She got out of the car rumpled, and rushed into the hallway. He paid the bill.

She opened the inside door, and stood holding it, blocking his entrance. She pursed her lips for him. They kissed. He tried to push open the door.

"No," she said.

She pushed his hat off, and when he turned, closed the door on him. He watched her go upstairs. She didn't look back.

He walked slowly out and away.

"That goddamn teaser!"

He felt that he'd been a goddamn chump, but realized what a bastard he'd been, trying to make her. He couldn't get her out of his mind.

XIX

July 19, 1924
Los Angeles Calif.

DEAR *Danny:*

Well O'Neill, I mean of course Danny old pal received your letter today and just think it took all that time from 18 to 28 to arrive to me I don't know what kept it so long Cause you know right well I would ans. it just as soone as it would arrive to me like I'm doing now I'm very sorry to hear that Arnold Sheehan die good old Arnold he was a card and wish to you to express my sincere sympathy to his folks for me because I always like them and I know how they feel because I feel the same way when I lose my father and he was the best man in all the world to me and there never a better father live anywhere You said you once had a pal name Andy but let me tell you still have that pal if I got anything to say about it. Acorse I sure felt kind of bad over you not writing figure I had said something in one of my letter that you didn't like so stop writing. So you might know how glad I was to hear from you first letter I received from any one in Chi for a long time indeed. So old Mike Higgins is back there again in one place then another thats hime all over with he sure has seen a lot of this good old United States let me tell you that we sure had a strange meeting know him the first time I saw him Can't forget that boy and blives me he has change in every way got a he mans voice and quite tall and take it from me none of the fellows there will make a full of him now and I don't mean maybe and I don't mean even the older guys like Stutz Lonigan. I never like them any way they always want to make a full out of us and I sure wouldn't let them try and make a full out of me anymore if I was back in good old Chi only Stutz now he was all right and work for his father and not like Red Kelly and the rest of them and I wouldn't maybe want to have any trouble with Stutz but if I was back in good old Chi and they others tried to make a full of me they sure would have a fight on their hand and I don't mean maybe Oh so Mike Higgins said I was setting on tope of the world Hu well not quit the tope yet Dan not untill I get to be a real saxaphone player get my shelf a nice little sport mondle Buick 1924 about six months ago and it sure is a dandy and I don't mean maybe had the Saxe for little over a year and I'm sure getting good even thow I say it my self playing now in a six peace dance Orchestra

do

and I sure ~~well~~ like it. I will start om a Clarnet in about two mor weeks and learne to play that. And then when I will be able to play about three insturments well then I can say I'm sitting on the top of the world there to stick Have not had any time for ball sence I've been going in the past year about forgot how to play. Glad to hear that you are still at the Con Ex and I want to say, you got the right kine of stickia a fellow never gets no where going from one job to another look at the time I lost doing that but never again fore me I haven't been in a pool roome sence I've been out here Cause if I was you know how har would be guess I don't have to mention it. And also Dan that's why I respec Stutz because he got stickia too like you only I don't think he ought to waste his time away in that old Greek pool roome the Greeks they only want to cheat you of your har earned money and make a full of you too Dan Well the White Sox lost to Pilly to day but they are still in first division and I expect to see them stay there and if they cant win the pennet why they sure can beat the Cubs thats there meat don't expect to the Cubs to be in second at the end of season doing good if they are in the fourthe by then. As fore me being a native son in a way I am and in a way I'm not but take it frome me you made a good guess when you said McAdoo I had McAdoo writen all over my face and sure did hate to see hime lose out frome now on I'm sopponting Daves I don't kno where you get that Wilson son in law at he is the best man of the lot and that is why they did not wan't him Cause he is for the labering man and my dad if he was alive would want the man that was for the labering man to get in and so do I and as for your pick Walsh is a good man I amit so is Ralston but this Underwood he is rotton as can be to much a raitcal and not a good enough American to suit me and I don't think very much of your Choce in mentioning him cause he can't compare with McAdoo and the rest good Americans And as for Woodrow Wilson why he is my Idee the graest Presendent the United State ever had like my dad said baring none But sence it is a over lets forgot McAdoo Underwood and the rest but Wilson and then saport Daves for the nex Presendent do you agree with me this time cause I don't belive you did the last time. Well old boy it was quite late when I got home tonight so I guess I better Close for the percsent Hoping I received a reply on the letter very soon I remain

your Pal

Andy Le Gare

P.S. Glad to hear all the folks are well as for me well I hope you can read this Miss Lady writing so small what say By the way when you see Stutz Lonigan do say I send hime my regards and hello because I like hime but not the other older guys By the way my new number is going to be R F D # 18 ½ or 869 Alhambra Calif
no not in the country the city Ha Ha.

Chapter Nineteen

I

HERE'S Shanty Irish Lonigan!" Barney Keefe said.

"Hello, False Face," Studs retorted.

"Hey, Barney, why don't you go to work?" Shrimp Haggerty kidded, as the gang commenced strolling over to Washington Park. Barney did not reply, and Shrimp smiled. Shrimp spotted a baby-faced thing with bobbed hair hobbling along on the other side of the street on high heels, and he declared that it was a pretty nice beetle.

"Yoo-hoo!" Tommy Doyle called.

"You dropped something," Les shouted.

Studs had an impulse to try picking her up, but he had been kidded so much because of what had happened the last time he had robbed the cradle and had made Nellie Cullen that he didn't. The sight of the flapper, the sight of any girl, even his sisters, drove Lucy back into his mind. Just before he had left the house, he had surprised Loretta in the hallway, when she dashed out of the bathroom in only a chemise, her left breast sticking out. Last week, by accident, he had seen Fran without a strip on. Such things were driving him almost cuckoo. He had just called Lucy up before meeting the guys and tried to get a date with her, and for the third time since the dance she had given him the go-by. All over again, he tried to convince himself that she was nothing in his young life. She did mean something to him. Goddamn it, he was going nuts without her, thinking of her all the time. He could see that she was only a teaser. It didn't matter what she was. He remembered dancing with her, talking to her, holding her in his arms, kissing her, their tongues touching, digging his hand under her dress and touching her breast. He loved Lucy. He wanted—yes—to marry her. Red asked Studs what was the matter, was he thinking hard, worrying about his dose, what? Studs said there was nothing and that the dose was cured. Red congratulated him. Shrimp suggested getting a bottle and celebrating. Les said it would be all right by him.

"Say, Les, don't you and Shrimp ever have the curiosity to find out how it would be to stay sober for one night?" Kelly asked.

"What the hell! All the tanks here couldn't get drunk on one measly bottle."

"Sorry, Haggerty, but the Alcohol Squad is A. W. O. L. this evening," Stan Simonsky said.

"It's swell out," Studs said, looking at the twilight sky, wanting to forget things by talking and looking at the sky; only the sky made him remember all the more. A song came to him. Blue and broken-hearted—Blue because we're parted.—There was a time I was jolly—You know the reason, I'm melancholy. The words only half-expressed his feelings. And he had had them ever since the dance. He had had them all his life.

"Say, you know, I think I'll join the Navy," Shrimp said, looking pointedly at Barney.

"Last week, Shrimp was joining the Marines," Doyle said.

"Hell, Haggerty, with that caved-in chest you got, and with your guts pickled in alcohol, and a leg and a half in the grave, the Navy wouldn't even take you for punkin'," Barney sourly said.

"I'm organically all right. I'm just tired of hanging around here, without any job, so I thought I'd join up, see the world, building myself up physically so I wouldn't end up with a balloon belly and false teeth like Keefe," Shrimp said.

"I'm laughing," Barney snapped.

Studs wasn't interested in the gassing and kidding.

"If I was like Studs now, with an old man who's well heeled, and gives him a good job, and has a business to leave him when he kicks the bucket. But, hell, all a guy can get is a thirty-five- or forty-dollar-a-week job. You won't find me wearing my can out that way," Shrimp said, giving Barney the eye.

"Yeah, you should be a painter too, and in summer time climb a ladder so much that your pants rub blisters on your tail, the way it happened to me last summer," Studs said. They laughed.

But Studs wished that Lucy would realize—see—that he could take care of her, give her things, make them . . . happy together. Why did he have to be such a goofy damn fool with sloppy feelings?

"Haggerty, better go back to that wife of yours, and let her take care of you. She might love you, even if her taste is all in her mouth," Keefe said.

"Shrimp is right. Now take me, what have I got to look forward to but always wrestling freight for the Continental Express Company?" Les whined.

"Will you bastards quit singing the blues? You're young, and there's plenty of gash in the world, and the supply of moon goes on forever," Simonsky said.

Studs wished he had someone to talk it over with. He had almost talked with Fran or Loretta. But he had never been able to talk about things like that with anyone. If only things were the same with him and Helen Shires as they used to be when they were kids. Then he could talk about it with her.

"Haggerty, if you get in the Navy, you'll end up like Mush Joss in the jug after deserting three times."

"Mush was always a bum anyway," Shrimp said, and he got the horse laugh.

"Mush was a funny guy. You know, he was a damn swell baseball player, and if he kept on he'd be in the big leagues now. He played a good game for one year with the Carmelites High School. Then he left school because the family didn't have the jack to send him, and he just went to hell," Red said.

"Studs, you know, I'm pulling Keefe's leg. The bastard thinks he's getting a job as sewer-pipe layer down at Grant Park. And today I spoke to a guy I know who's assistant foreman and he told me I could count that job mine. Watch me get him," Shrimp said in confidence.

"Yeah, I think I'll join the Navy. No flunkey job for me. If any comes along, Barney can have them," Shrimp said, looking at Barney; Barney whistled.

"Well, I been thinking I'd get into the political game," Doyle said.

"You goddamn Irishman. Because your brother is assistant precinct captain without pay, you think you'll be assistant to Brennan, or Barney McCormack, the state senator. Every election day they let you stand in front of the pools looking like Jesus Christ, and wearing a tag, begging everybody to vote for a bunch of Shanty Irish crook politicians, and you think you're an influence," Keefe said.

"Sic 'em, Keefe!" Kelly said.

They crossed over to the park. The trees and grass were deep green, and they made Studs think of the trees on that day as a kid, when he licked Kelly. People were walking, they seemed contented, as if nothing was bothering them. The only way he would have that feeling was if he could get Lucy.

"Lonigan, that rat Haggerty can't kid me! He's pulling his own leg. That bastard thinks he's going to be sewer-pipe layer, and I was speaking to a friend of mine who's an assistant engineer down at Grant Park, and he told me I got that job sewn up. That skunk ain't puttin' nothing over on anybody but himself," Barney quietly said.

Studs smiled. He wasn't able to appreciate things like he had used to. Goddamn Lucy! He shouldn't let her be bothering him; wasn't he young, healthy and tough, didn't he have something to look forward to, hadn't he even bought himself a couple of stocks that the old man said were hot stuff?

Only. . . .

"Well, what are we going to do?" Studs said, feeling restless.

II

Shorty Wolfson, a young chap the size of a bantamweight who worked as a lineman for the telephone company, boxed with Eddie Eastman on the grass in the park. He tore into Eastman and cracked his jaw. Eastman lay down white. Milt Rosensplatz, the referee, counted ten.

"You're pretty good. There's a yellow streak all the way down your spine," Studs said.

Eddie tried to justify himself, and they told him to get away with that B. S.

Wils Gillen and Swede Elston boxed like two clowns. Wils grimaced, swung, missed, fell on his face. He jumped up, rubbed his glove across his nose, hunched himself, cocked his hands. Swede toe-danced backwards out of danger. They missed haymakers, and clinched. They made faces at each other for a three-minute round and didn't land a blow. Studs told them not to box another round, because they were liable to break their hands on a tree.

Rosensplatz, the husky, flat-footed Jewboy, and Big Nose Jerry Rooney, from Johnny O'Brien's class at St. Patrick's, put on the gloves.

"Let there be light and there was light! Let there be Louisa Nolan's, and there was Three Star Hennessey! Let there be nose, and there was Rooney!" Young Rocky said.

"What battlers these boys are," Studs said, as they jabbed cautious gloves at one another.

"These punks are all the same. They can all fool around with fourteen-year-old girls, and not make the grade, but they got sawdust in their guts," Kelly sneered.

"Hey, Rooney, when did you get so good?" asked Doyle.

"I feel like I might go a round with one of the punks," Tommy said.

"Me too, but we don't want to hurt them," Studs said.

"A good stiff punch might wake 'em up, and they'll quit flogging the dummy," Doyle said.

"Hey, punk, I'll box a round with you," Red said.

"No slugging," O'Neill replied

Red and O'Neill boxed. O'Neill fought defensively, jabbing with straight lefts, blocking Red's lunges. He caught Red on the nose with a left jab.

"Think you're tough!" Red said, his nose bleeding.

"It was an accident," O'Neill apologized.

"Better cut it out, Red, you're getting sore, and you don't want to kill the punk," Doyle said.

"Think you can fight me! Think you're tough!" Kelly bullied, while Wolfson unlaced his gloves, and Studs held a handkerchief to his nose.

"We were just boxing," O'Neill said.

"You better say that," Red said, walking over to the drinking fountain by the boathouse.

"That isn't anything. Red's nose always bleeds easy," Studs said, thinking Red was slipping, remembering how he had given Red a bloody nose in their fight, feeling proud because he knew he was able to stand the gaff when Kelly couldn't, glad Red had been shown up.

Doyle boxed with O'Neill. Doyle rushed, and O'Neill again boxed defensively, jabbing with his left, blocking, trying an occasional jab to the guts with a right cross.

"Hey, for Christ's sake, I said I'd box with you, not run a foot race," Tommy beefed, stopping, hands at side, breathing rapidly.

"I am boxing."

"You mean you're trying to win a track meet," Doyle said, still winded, as he held his gloved hands up to be unlaced.

"Hey, I'll box with you!" Studs said to Rolfe.

"That's not my racket," Rolfe said.

Rosensplatz and Morgan were going to box next, but Milt acceded to Studs.

Jack Morgan was an unassuming, well-built, twenty-year-old kid. He waited calmly while the gloves were laced on Studs' hands. Studs felt good. He decided that he'd go easy with Morgan, and just show them that he wasn't through like Doyle and Kelly, but was the old Studs Lonigan. Just let the kid know he had the gloves on with Studs Lonigan.

Morgan faced Studs with hands out in the classical boxing stance. Studs crouched low, and waved his arms in Jack Dempsey fashion. He heard encouraging words from Fat Malloy, and it made him more strongly confident. He thought of himself a little like he imagined Jack Dempsey would be when going into the ring. He circled and swayed, pulled two feints, frowned for effect, set himself to let go with a left, and was stabbed in the jaw by a left jab.

"The boy's fast," Fat Malloy said professionally.

Studs lumbered in, and got stung with another left jab. He feinted, swayed, and let loose with a roundhouse right. Morgan stepped back and Studs looked foolish.

"Clever boy," Doyle said.

Studs didn't like the way Morgan looked at him, calm, unafraid, never changing his expression. He frowned to scare him. He feinted with a left, and got another sharp left jab, and before he knew it a right cross that gave him a headache. He momentarily saw wavering black dots. He forgot trying to box like Jack Dempsey. He rushed, and hit Morgan with a solid right. They clinched, and he tried to shove Morgan around. His arms were pinned, and he got a snapping short one in the ribs. Studs rushed again, took and gave a punch, they clinched. Breaking, he got Morgan with a wild right on the side of the head, and everybody was pepped up and yelled. Morgan's face was unchanged, and he waited, poised on his toes, left out, right cocked. Studs realized the kid could take it. No more giving him a break. He had to show some stuff, or be shown up. He rushed, and got four jabs for the punch he landed. Coming out of the clinch, he got an uppercut. Studs missed two rights, and received another stiff jab. He lost his temper, and slugged, not knowing what he was doing. Morgan slugged back punch for punch, until Rosensplatz said time was up.

"How about another round, kid?" Studs said, trying to hold in his temper and appear unaffected.

He wanted more. He knew he had been outfought and outboxed, and he had to come back. Everybody was pepped up too, but it was dark, and anyway, O'Neill had to take his gloves home. Studs shook hands with Morgan and said patronizingly that he'd been given a good workout. Morgan smiled taciturnly.

The older guys walked off. Studs was winded. His arms were leaden. His back ached. He had a headache and cuts inside his lip and jaw. He hoped they'd suggest sitting down on a bench or in the grass.

"There's all the difference in the world between sparring with gloves on and fighting with your fists. If I was using my fists and really trying, I'd have massacred that snotty little punk, O'Neill," Red said.

Studs agreed. Hated O'Neill for having taken the gloves home. Still he felt that he couldn't have gone another round.

"The punks took you guys," Barney said.

"So says you! You toothless, dried-up Irish bastard!" Red said with venom.

"That Morgan kid is clever. He could make a monkey out of punks like O'Neill," Red said.

"He slugged, too," Doyle said.

"He gave me a good workout. He's clever. I think I'll put the gloves on with him again. With a little coaching, he'll be a sweet young fighter," Studs said.

He waited for them to say he'd outpointed the kid. Well, he had, Studs thought, trying to lie to himself. One of his punches was worth six of the kids. Their non-committal remarks hurt him.

"I'm not in the best condition, and I think a few more workouts like that will do me good," Studs said.

"Yeah, he is good. He got in some nice lefts," Red said. He continued: "But I still say it's totally different, just boxing good-naturedly with gloves, and going to it with fists. That's why I told that snotty O'Neill so. I don't want him to think he can get tough now, because if he does, I'll slough him," Red said.

Studs agreed. Doyle said that if he had ridden a bicycle, he could have caught O'Neill. Barney sneered at them. Studs was glad when Tommy suggested they sit on a bench on the short walk near the boathouse. He brooded, and the whole thing about Lucy came back on him.

"You know, boys, the goddamn shines are getting too frisky coming around here," Red said.

"You Irish oughtn't to kick. You and the niggers can both look up to a snake," Keefe said.

"I came around the boathouse last Sunday, and it stunk with niggers. You know, it's so bad, that a decent girl can't walk alone here any more for fear a nigger might rape her. They ruin the park. When they come over here, you need a gas-mask if you want to stick around. . . . Why, you can tell they are inferior to the white race by the clothes they wear. Those goddamn loud clothes, wearing pearls in their bell bottoms, purple suits, pink shirts. They're worse than the Polacks. You know, you can tell an inferior race by the way they dress. The Polacks and Dagoes, and niggers are the same, only the niggers are the lowest. That's why I say we ought to get the boys together some night and clean every nigger out of the park. They're all yellow and if we do it once, they won't come back. We can get a few billies and clubs, and if they try to use razors, make them just wish they hadn't."

Barney told Red to hire a hall. Shrimp agreed with Red, and Barney kidded him, saying he'd run if he saw a mammy coming after him. Doyle said that it always turned out the same way. If you give a nigger an inch, he always took a mile. Studs wished there was something distracting to do, wished he could get Lucy out of his mind. He was pooped and felt that he was slipping because of what Morgan had done to him. The cuts inside his face hurt. Finally they walked over to the Bug Club.

III

They saw a crowd at the Bug Club near the hills by the Cottage Grove side of the park. There was one large circle, many smaller groups and numbers milling about.

"Well, I say that the world is coming to an end," Studs said, pleased when people from various groups frowned at him.

"The Bug Club will save the world, and drive everybody to drink or hell," Red shouted.

Smirking, they edged into a group, and saw, in the center, a well-fed, hefty, elderly, Jewish man shaking an Eversharp pencil at malcontent debaters.

"I should believe that. Rosenblatt here should tell me that I should think that. I should believe that Rosenblatt knows more than Einstein. I should think he can explain the theory of relativity in one sentence. Yah!" a sloppy fellow bellowed at the well-fed Hebrew.

"Friend, I shall explain the basic principle of relativity in one sentence that even you can understand."

"And I tell you I'm the traveling salesman that made Mary heavy with Christ. Yah."

"Relativity is a theory which assumes that, on a high basis of probability, there is no hitching-post in the universe."

Red lip-farted, and Slug said it all gave him a sharp pain in his royal rump. Studs said they were over his head. Red added that they were over the head of the human race.

"Friend, look at Orion up there in the sky. . . ."

"I should think maybe they got a hitching-post for mules like Rosenblatt up there."

"Finklestein, you're impossible!"

"Rosenblatt, get some monkey glands."

Jim Doyle brought them to hear Bishop Boyle in another noisy group. Bishop was a witty little Irishman, always kidding, and all right; he had a son a priest, and he was smart.

"Sure, Bishop, Jesus Christ was a bum. A hobo, with no place to lay his head. Why shouldn't he have been one when he wouldn't work and produce?"

"Arkwright, you're wrong there. Jesus Christ was the first communist."

"That guy talks like an atheist," Studs said, as Red emitted more lip-noises.

"He doesn't know whether Christ was crucified or killed with a second-hand book," Barney said.

"Sure, he's one of those liberal-minded fellows with no faith, who wants God to prove his existence by hiding behind every tree," Bishop Boyle said with a brogue.

"If I could see God behind a tree, I'd believe him."

"God made the tree; isn't that, my friend, sufficient proof? Or is the incomprehensibility in your anthropoid skull too dense to perceive that one fact of experience?" Bishop Boyle said.

"I'd like to see God. I'd like to tell him a few things. I'd like to say, 'God, why do you create men and make them suffer and fight in vain, and live brief unhappy lives like pigs, and make them die disgustingly, and rot? God, why do the beautiful girls you create become whores, grow old and toothless, die and have their corpses rot so that they are a stench to human nostrils? God, why do you permit thousands and millions of your creatures, made in your own image and likeness, to live like crowded dogs in slums and tenements, while an exploiting few profit from the sweat of their toil, produce nothing, and live in kingly mansions? God, why do you permit men to starve, hunger, die from syphilis, cancer, consumption? God, why do you not raise one little finger to save man from all the turmoil, want, sorrow, suffering on this human planet?' That's what I'd say to God if I could find him hiding behind a tree. But God is a wise guy. He keeps in hiding."

"You could make a better world, couldn't you, fellow?" Red Kelly yelled.

"Red, hell with him. He's a crazy radical," Studs said.

"Friend, if I had the powers attributed to Bishop Boyle's God, I certainly would not have created as botched a world."

Bishop Boyle tried to explain that the ways and purposes of God were mysterious, and that man suffered because of the fall of Adam. The atheist, a starved-looking little man, said it was disgusting, and walked out of the crowd. Red grabbed his arm.

"Fellow, are you healthy?" Red asked.

"I do not understand you, friend."

"If you want to preserve that health, lay off the Catholic Church."

"Yeah, keep your trap padlocked while you're all together," Studs said.

"You hoodlums cannot abrogate my rights of free speech."

"See this!" Red said, showing a closed fist.

"I'll have you arrested if you dare touch me!"

"It would be worth going to jail to punch in your filthy blaspheming mouth."

"Yeah, blow!" Doyle said.

The atheist slunk off. Red said it was the only way to talk with fellows like that. They had no brains, were ignorant and filthy-minded, and you couldn't argue with them. The whole human race should treat them the same way.

"I don't see why they let these radicals congregate here and speak like that," Shrimp said.

"The cops used to clean them out, but they got an injunction. I'd like to have been the judge. I'd have made them all go to work," Red said.

They listened in on a political argument. A Single Taxer was defending Davis, declaring that the Republican Party was corrupt, that La Follette was trying to destroy the Supreme Court, and that also, when the last war had been declared, La Follette had proven himself to be a traitor to his country. A six-foot-four giant was defending La Follette's progressiveness. A communist was saying, in a foreign accent, that La Follette was a class betrayer. Red got into the argument and spoke for Davis, but he didn't get tough because the communist and La Follette man both looked pretty big.

They wandered to another group. Jim Doyle said there was Father Kroke, who thought he was God. He pointed to a skeleton of a man over six feet, not weighing more than one hundred and twenty pounds, whose hollow eyes and face contrasted with a full Jesus beard and seemed ghostly.

"I suppose, Father Kroke, that you're the second coming of Christ?"

"Say, this guy's belly must have the same feeling for a meal that mine has for gin," Shrimp said.

"Hell, if he got a meal, he'd die of indigestion," Red said.

Father Kroke tried to say something, but stuttered so badly that no one understood him. Red told him to say it in Greek. Jim Doyle said the nut had taught himself Greek and nine other languages. Red countered that he'd never taught himself how to earn an honest dollar.

"I ask you to believe me because it is a revelation. I was an atheist, too, and talked as you do now. I did, until one night when the Blessed Virgin came to me in a vision, and her spirit flew through my whole body. . . ." Father Kroke said, stuttering on almost every word.

"She must have been pretty hard up, huh, Father Kroke?"

Father Kroke explained that mankind had been led away from the true Christianity by Anti-Christ, the Pope of Rome, and he had been called by God to guide it back to the simplicity of the early Christians, and to reestablish the Church of God on democratic principles. He has established the true church, calling it the American Church, because America was founded on democratic principles. The American Church was, in basic doctrine, the same as the Catholic, only priests were elected by the congregations, and the doctrine of papal infallibility was branded a lie. It had only a small membership but it was growing. Next Sunday, he would say mass in the park by a nearby tree, if one member of the church was able to procure the wine for sacramental purposes, as she had promised.

Slug remarked that the guy had plenty of marbles missing. A fellow at Slug's side said he was a paranoiac and also thought himself descended from Robert Bruce. Slug gave the guy a queer look. The fellow said, last Easter, Father Kroke had tried to say mass by a tree in the park, and that lightning had struck the tree. Red said it was an act of God. Studs said that nut thought he was the Pope and laughed. Jim Doyle said he was a real nut. Came from a good family, and his father would give him anything if he would work, and cut out all this insanity. But he was too far gone, and had let himself be disinherited. He lived by begging, and picking things out of garbage cans, and had no place to sleep. Sometimes, when he could get an extra dime, he walked downtown and slept in an all-night movie.

Studs goosed Father Kroke. He jumped and quivered. The mere touch of his bony body disgusted Studs.

"Father Kroke, the Holy Spook did that to you!"

"If the person who did that to me will step up, I shall be perfectly within my rights as an American citizen in slapping him," Father Kroke excitedly stuttered.

"Satan has his eyes on you, Father Kroke!"

"Yes, Satan tried to put obstacles in my path all the time, but God is behind me."

Father Kroke took up a collection, and four slugs and two pennies were dropped in his filthy straw hat. Father Kroke limped away from the Bug Club, a hunched living corpse in ill-fitting, hand-me-down clothes.

They went to the big circle. Jim Doyle told them about the chairman, Pat Gilroy. He was a corpulent, medium-sized, bald-headed man in white flannels and blue coat, and he had been running for Congress in the district east of the park ever since Noah put the Ark in slow speed. The Democrats let him run on their ticket because they didn't want to waste time and money on a certain failure. He'd pull off a hundred votes anyway, at the next election. Jim said he was also another crazy radical.

Gilroy declared that he was not trying to use the chairmanship of the Bug Club for personal aggrandizement by trying to get votes. He then told the crowd that the next speaker was a man they had been waiting to hear all evening, a man whose talks were always a delight and benefit, a man of solid intellectual integrity and conviction, who would have many interesting and original words to say on the question of race prejudice which they had been discussing and listening to all evening—John Connolly. Jim told them to listen because he was a brilliant fellow, and King of the Soap Boxers. Red sarcastically described it an honor. Studs suggested shouting him down. Jim said Connolly was tough.

Connolly stood in the center of the circle, a tall, handsome, physically impressive man with dark hair. He spoke in a deep, convincing voice remarking that the previous speakers all seemed to have been debating whether a Yiddish junk-man, a Pullman porter, or a flat-footed guardian of a hundred million city ordinances were the lowest example of the human ape. He did not propose to continue such inane blather. On the contrary, he would present certain aspects of urban growth which were relevant to the question of race prejudice in Chicago. These factors also were not mere hearsay, but plausible ideas presented by members of the Department of Sociology at the University of Chicago, and developed from the work they had already done on a community research programme. He explained that the City of Chicago could be divided into three concentric circles. The innermost of these circles was the business or downtown district, the Loop, where the principal stores, offices, and commercial houses were located, and where most of the high-class legal gypping went on. The second circle housed manufacturing and wholesale houses, slums, tenements, can houses and other haunts of vice. The outer circle made up the residential districts and it could boast of the most fog houses because the sky pilots and camouflage artists always found sweet pickings amongst the well-to-do whose gypping was high-class and within the law. When the city expanded, it expanded from the center. In Chicago, thus, expansion spread out from the Loop. The inner circle was pushed outwards causing corresponding changes in the other concentric circles. The Negroes coming into the situation as an economically inferior race, had naturally found their habitation in the second circle. Since they had located in the slums of the black belt, the city had been growing into bigger and better Chicago. The pressure of growth was forcing them into newer areas. Furthermore, some of the Negro booboisie had gotten into the big gypping process, and like their white brothers, they did not like to live in stench, and sandwiched in between a whore house and the junk shop of Isadore Goldberg. With their economic rise, the Negroes sought more satisfactory housing conditions. Besides, the black boys were happiest when engaged in the horizontals. That meant an increasing birth-rate amongst them, and another factor necessitating improved and more extensive domiciles. All these factors produced a pressure stronger than individual wills, and resulted in a minor racial migration of Negroes into the white residential districts of the south side. Blather couldn't halt the process. Neither could violence and race riots. It was an inevitable outgrowth of social and economic forces.

A young fellow booed.

"Some waffle pup in the audience is aching to get his puss slapped. Now the next one of you cheap wise guys who heckles is going to get the smile slapped off your mugs, and if any two or three of you want to try it, the same goes for you. If you want to go home with your snotty faces in a sling, just try getting wise. Otherwise, keep your traps closed like your mothers warned you to!" Connolly bellowed.

After the applause, he continued speaking.

"Slug, I'd like to see you tangle with that louse," Kelly whispered.

Slug said he had nothing against him, and liked a fellow who took nobody's sass. Red said he couldn't understand an Irishman being a nigger-lover. Studs supposed that the guy would let a nigger jazz his sister. The next speaker, a small, untidy Jew, monotonously said that according to anthropology, which was a new science they were studying at the University of Chicago, they had proven as a scientific truth that no one race is superior to any other race. Studs asked Red what he was trying to say. Red said he was trying to prove that a Jew was a white man. The audience called for time.

Excitement started outside the circle. The gang rushed to it. They found a cop arguing with a kid. The cop pulled a gun. Connolly, by a quick twist of the policeman's wrist, took the gun and warned him not to try shooting off more than his mouth. The cop barked loudly. Connolly told him to keep cool. He sent the kid away, handed the gun back to the cop, and told him to be careful or it would go off. He walked away, followed by an adulatory crowd.

IV

"He's a real guy," Slug said as they walked towards Fifty-eighth Street.

"He'll get his. Those wise radicals always do. You can't go against the human race," Kelly said.

"He's got guts," Slug said.

"He was in jail during the war for being a pacifist. And a few years back he went out to agitate at a coal strike in Colorado, and the police kicked out a couple of his front teeth. But even though I know he's wrong, he's a smart man," Jim Doyle said.

"If I'd been that cop, I'd have plugged him," Red said.

"He's just over the heads of you hoods," Jim Doyle said.

"Sure, he thinks he's too good for the human race," Red said.

"He isn't yellow," Studs said, thinking how big and tough Connolly was, and how small he himself was. He thought of how Morgan had baffled him. He admired and envied and hated the big fellow.

"All those guys read too much. When you do that you get lop-sided. Now I was reading some stories by a Frenchman named Balzac. . . ."

Haggerty punned the word.

"He was an atheist, and because he was, he wrote stories that are so filthy they make you want to puke," Kelly continued.

"Dirty stories?" asked Shrimp.

"And how," Red replied.

"Maybe I'll read them," said Shrimp.

"But, anyway, I suppose the French are a pretty filthy race, and that's why this guy wrote such stuff," Red said.

"Look at all the American soldiers who got the syph," Shrimp said.

"Me for Paris," Slug said.

"Boy, I'll bet that with a little dough you could get all you wanted there," Red said.

Tommy wondered how long it would take Slug to know as many whores in Paris as he did in Chicago. Shrimp said they needed some liquor. Studs wanted some. He couldn't get things off his mind, the humiliation he had suffered, Lucy. He wished he'd been a hero in the war or even killed.

When they got tired of hanging around Fifty-eighth Street with nothing to do, they got drunk on Jamaica ginger. Their drunken attention was caught by a passing Negro hot-tamale-man. They slugged him and took the wagon. Red wheeled it and they marched down the street towards the park. They each had a hot tamale and debated what to do with the rest. Red caught a passing shine. They tossed him into the fountain by the curve in the boathouse path. He struggled to get out of the slippery fountain, and was shoved back, and pelted as long as they had hot tamales. Studs passed out. He was carried home, and they left him to sleep all night on the back porch.

SECTION FOUR

1926—1929

XX

St. Patrick's *new church was a half block long, and several hundred yards wide. It was cruciform in shape, a squat box of dull red brick with a dome rounding out of the center. The nave was expansive, giving an illusion of tremendous size. It was segmented by impressive marble pillars, overhung by the hollowed dome of glass, and lined with oak pews. The floor was stone. The main altar, imported from Italy, was a huge slab of marble, set back in a hollow, and flanked by two altars that formed the horizontal sides of the cruciform. At the side altars, there were weakly conventional statues of St. Joseph, and the Blessed Virgin Mary. Above the altar were circular windows of stained glass with the half-distinguishable figures of Christ, Mary, St. Patrick and other saints, trumpeting and flying angels with the face of Donatello's "David," baby angels, sheep and retreating snakes. On the left towards the front, there was an altar shrine to St. Anthony with a marble statue of the saint. The stations of the cross dotted the church with cheaply emotionalized statuary representations of the suffering and death of Christ. The choir box, with a ten-thousand-dollar organ and gilded pipes, was overhead in the rear, and next to it, a small gallery with tiers of pews. The edifice was built in no specific architectural style. It was a loot of traditions.*

At eleven o'clock on the second Sunday in February, the year of our Lord nineteen hundred and twenty-six, the first services, a high Mass celebrated by his eminence, the Cardinal Archbishop, were conducted. Parishioners, former parishioners, visitors, sightseers, all attended Mass, and every pew in the church was occupied, with an overflow crowd along the side, in the aisles, and in the rear. In his eulogistic sermon, the Cardinal Archbishop described the occasion as the greatest day in the history of St. Patrick's parish. He lauded the untiring zeal, devotion, foresight, energy, and courage of the pastor, Reverend Father Gilhooley, and the unstinted loyalty, generosity, faith, and cooperative spirit of the good people of the parish. Years afterwards, this day of rejoicing and victory would be remembered by all who were so fortunate as to be present. For was it not a day celebrating the opening of a new and beautiful house of worship to God Almighty, the consecration of a church that would stand almost until eternity as a tribute of art and beauty to the lasting glory of God, and also as a memorial record of the religious fervor of the people of this parish. After the Cardinal Archbishop, Father Gilhooley mounted the marble pulpit, and expressed his own brief words of gratification, pride, joy, and appreciation.

It was a great day.

And standing in the rear of the church were four new and totally edified parishioners. Their skin was black.

Chapter Twenty

I

SALLY, a buxom human heifer, leaned forwards over the cashier's counter, and handed Dapper Dan O'Doul the autographed picture of Ramon Novarro, which she had procured by sending money and stamps. Her blue energetic eyes flashed, and she continued leaning forwards with the front of her dress sagging, permitting Dapper Dan to get an eyeful.

"Isn't he keen?"

"He's the nuts," Dapper Dan said, arranging his precisely-tied silver-and-red cravat.

"That bastard hangs around all night, peeping down Sally's dress," Studs said.

"Still raining. Christ, this weather," Red said, looking out the door to see the rain bouncing on the sidewalk like silver dollars.

"Say, will that broad come across?" Studs asked, resting his elbow on the radiator.

"Dapper Dan is sure trying hard enough," Doyle said.

"These young punks around here are worse than O'Neill, and that goof, Young Rocky, who went to New York," Studs said.

"They call O'Doul the Kodak kid. He hangs around the drug store all winter posing, and he kodaks on the beach in summer time, combing his hair as if he was having his picture taken, and never even getting his feet wet. He's a lulu," Tommy Doyle said.

"That goddamn rain," Kelly said.

A customer, hastening in hunched and wet, had to shove to get by the gang because they were choking the doorway.

"Hey, Dapper Dan," Studs called.

"Studs, it doesn't shave yet," Red Kelly said, as O'Doul stood before them.

"Listen, O'Doul, does she say you're handsomer than that movie actor whose picture she's got there?" Studs asked; the older guys laughed in O'Doul's face.

Sally heard, and laughed; Dapper Dan blushed. Red cursed the weather. Slug said O'Doul ought to wipe the milk from behind his ears with toilet paper. Studs sidled over to Curley and whispered to him. Curley looked at Studs, blankly.

"Go on!" Studs prodded.

Vinc pouted at Studs. He sulked over by Sally's desk.

"Say, Dan, Studs asked to ask you if you got that topcoat all paid for?"

"Vincent, you're not even as funny as a hearse," Dapper Dan said; the older guys laughed, and Sally gave them the wink.

"Studs, why did you ask me to ask that when you knew he would get sore, and he's my friend?" Vinc gravely said, causing another barrage of laughter.

"Vincent!" Sally coquetted.

"Hey, Cowboy, Curley's competition for you. Watch your step" Tommy Doyle said.

"Studs, is Curley becoming a lady-killer?" Fat Malloy asked.

"Vincent, won't you even talk to poor little harmless Sally?" she cooed.

Vincent said he had to ask Malloy an important question. Fat roughly asked what, Vinc said that with everybody all talking all at once he had forgotten it, but if he had a minute to think, he'd remember again. Studs yelled for him to beware of brain-fever.

"All right, Vincent, you'll be sorry some day, if you put Sally on the shelf," she tantalized.

Studs looked at the time: eight-twenty.

Malloy told Vinc to wake up, the girl was stuck on him. They shoved Vinc towards the desk.

"Vincent, you're perfectly horrid, you always act so high hat, and never even speak to me. Why, you treat me like I was a bug or something."

"When did I do that? I never said you was a bug."

"Hey, Fat, tell him to cut it out before we all laugh ourselves into a nut house," Studs said.

"I don't remember when I said anything like that," Curley said, twisting himself around the counter.

"Tell him to let it alone," Studs told Tommy.

"I'll bet if he had let it alone, he wouldn't have so many marbles absent from his brain," Slug said.

Studs suggested doing something. Slug said they might if the rain would stop. Tommy said they could go down to the poolroom at Fifty-fifth Street. Red said it would be nuts going down there in the rain. They said it was too bad that the Greek had closed up the poolroom.

"Here comes Society Brand, the Clothes Peddler," Fat Malloy said. Phil Rolfe entered, pulling down an umbrella. His greeting was ingratiating. He remarked that it was raining. Fat told him not to crap them, the sun was shining bright.

"Say, Society Kid, you look like the rage," sixteen-year-old, skinny Pete Webb said, as Phil unbuttoned his yellow slicker.

"Like the suit, boys?"

"It's the nuts, Phil," Pat Carrigan said.

"Listen, any time you need one, come down and see me. I'm at Sankey, Hatfield, and Cohen's, on Adams Street. We handle straight Society Brand stuff, give perfect fit, and have a reasonable budget plan. Here's one of my cards."

"Say, Phil, I was waiting to see you," Curley said, leaving Sally.

"Hello, Vincent," Phillip said.

"Want to go to the Michigan tonight?"

"Gee, Vincent, I'm sorry, but I got a date. We'll make it some other night."

He walked over to Studs, smiling. He ignored the grunted greeting he got, and mentioned that he was selling suits, had some swell buys, and suggested that Studs drop in on him the next time he was needing clothes. Couldn't get a better suit for the price anywhere in town.

"Leave it to the kikes," Tommy Doyle said, after Rolfe had gone over to the group around Pat Carrigan and Pete Webb.

"They're all the same. I'm your friend, fellow . . . but business first," Red said.

Studs looked at the clock: eight-twenty-seven.

"Jesus Christ!" he exclaimed, bored.

Slug mentioned seeing the girlies. Tommy said that after the last four nights, he'd had enough for a while. Slug kidded that he must be getting old. Studs said no more for him for a while. Slug kidded that you never could get enough of it.

"Say, I'll be damned, if the Jew isn't selling Curley a suit," Red said.

Tommy yelled for Vinc not to buy a suit. Phil protested that he wasn't selling anything.

"Oh, say, Davey Cohen's back," Red said.

"How is he?"

"He hasn't grown hardly an inch since he left, and he looks like hell. I tell you, if he hasn't got the con, I'll eat it on State and Madison at high noon."

"What'll we do?" Studs asked, observing that it was eight-thirty.

"What do you say, Doyle?" asked Slug.

"How about you, Kelly. Any bright ideas?" asked Tommy.

Slug called Vinc over and asked him if he wanted to go to a can house. It merited some more buffoonery. Phil button-holed Vinc again, and warned him not to let the barbers get his goat. Studs sneered, and moved more closely to them. He overheard Phil telling Curley that a new Sankey, Hatfield, and Cohen society suit would make a man of him, make him attractive to all the girls. Vinc said he'd think about it, and propositioned Phil again about the movies. Phil said he couldn't because he had a date with Fritzie Lonigan. Studs frowned and ambled back with Doyle and the guys by the radiator. Slug said that the punks had caused the poolroom to close, because they'd always hung around, and never spent any jack. Phil got razzed as he left.

Studs looked at the clock: eight-thirty-four. He watched the second-hand sweep around once. Another minute gone. Carrigan hurt the feelings of Dapper Dan O'Doul by telling him he could never succeed in outsheiking Phil Rolfe. Phil was the one and original.

"Jesus, let's do something. I can't stand the sight of these goofy young p——s and their goddamn gab," Studs said.

"Wait a couple of minutes, and if the rain stops, we'll walk down to the Michigan," Red said.

Malloy spoke loudly about the way Phil rooked in all the boys, telling them to come down, pay their first deposit, get the suit on the budget plan, and then not pay any more. He said that he got his commission anyway and didn't care. He had rooked Rooney in that way and Rooney could tell them how he had been dunned and forced to pay.

The store manager interrupted Fat, and asked the crew to leave because they were blocking the door and injuring business. They sulked. Everybody wondered what to do. It was still raining heavily. Vinc got in Studs' way, and Studs booted his tail. Studs looked at the clock in the window: eight-thirty-nine. Studs hated the manager, wished he'd clouted him. Getting kicked out of the store because of the punks!

Finally they went to the show. Coming back with the boys for coffee an', Studs noticed that Dapper Dan was still mushing around Sally. He laughed. He wondered out loud if she could be made. He consumed his coffee an' quickly and said good-night to the boys. He stopped for cigarettes, and asked Sally what she was doing after work. She said her boy friend came and got her every night. He left. Another goddamn night wasted, and the movie had been punk too.

II

After supper, Studs walked out of the dining-room with Loretta. He side-glanced at her, this girl, his sister. She was smaller than he, hardly more than up to his shoulder. Everyone said she looked like him. Well, she did. All four of them looked alike; they had the same broad brows, the same complexion, the same eyes. Only the girls had dark hair, and he and the kid brother had lighter hair, brown.

"Say, I saw Phil last night," Studs said, not knowing how to commence, feeling what the hell business was it of his anyway, but still believing that he ought to say something.

"Yes, I was to College Inn with him."

"Have a good time?"

"I had a perfectly grand time."

He couldn't but wonder how far Phil, how far any guy, could go with her. They said any girl could be made by the right guy, and maybe so, but, Jesus, he hoped that that kike was not the right guy. All those punks were always talking about making girls. He wondered how much of it was just crap talk.

Hell, for years now, he'd hardly spoken to her about anything much. He'd lived in the same house, seen her at breakfast and supper, talked a little bit now and then, but almost never about anything that was important. She was his sister, and she was a stranger. But goddamn it, she could find someone better than a cheap kike.

"It seems to me that you could find better fellows to go with than Phil Rolfe," he said, making his tone of voice doubly nasty because he felt that he was butting his nose where it didn't belong, and also because he didn't know his sister or know how she would feel or act about anything important to her.

Her mouth popped open; she was too surprised to speak.

"You're a good-looking girl and you could go with a lot of nice fellows, without having dates with a Jew."

"He's not a Jew. He's preparing to become a Catholic. He told me so last night," she said.

"They wouldn't let him in the Church, not a Jew like him," Studs said, losing his temper because of his lack of conviction.

"You have nothing to say about what I do or whom I go with," she said, her voice almost cracking into a sob.

"Well, if any guys like him start fooling around with my sister, I might show what I got to say," said he.

"You're a perfect beast. I hate you!" she said.

Her face relaxed; she cried. She turned and walked away. He was sorry.

"You leave her alone!" Fran yelled at him.

She talked with Loretta. Studs, passing back through the hall to the bathroom, heard Fran saying the same things as he had said, only in a different manner.

The father called Studs into the parlor.

"Bill, I know how you feel. I'm proud of you, proud that you would stand by your sisters. Only Bill, you know women are like a delicate instrument. You have to handle them with care. You got to be diplomatic," Lonigan said in preparation for an outburst of platitudinous parenthood.

"All right," said Studs.

"Bill, I had something else to tell you. Wait a minute. Don't go yet," Lonigan said apologetically.

"Yeah," Studs answered with annoyance as he half turned towards his father.

"I was thinking that maybe next summer I'll be taking myself and your mother back to the old country, and letting you manage things."

"All right."

"I got the business going fine. I just got that new hotel contract, and the way it looks, I'm gonna get that school contract. Of course, it's costing me a little. You know when you want a school contract, well, you have to see the boys you're getting it from. But I think I'll have that sewn up just as neat as you'd like in a week or two. Well, when those two are finished, I think I'll take a rest and let the mantle of responsibility fall on your shoulders."

"That's good. When will we start on that hotel?"

"In about a month. It's a hundred-thousand-dollar job. And that school one, there's going to be real gravy."

"How you getting it?"

"Barney McCormack and I came to a verbal understanding today. He can fix it with the right fellows who are letting out the bids. Of course, it'll only be fair to repay Barney for his favor, but I tell you, it's real gravy for us, Bill."

Studs left. His sister Loretta followed him out. He was conscious of her walking behind him, her heels clicking on the paving. She walked fast, flung her head proudly to one side, passed him. She kept a few yards in front of Studs. He was sorry he'd had the damn squabble with her. He was right, though, in trying to tell her but he hadn't gone about it the way he might have.

He watched her. She was a pretty kid, and decent. He felt as if always, even though they'd said little to each other, they'd had sort of a bond between them. Now that was broken, and he liked her and she was a pretty kid.

She walked in front of him as far as Fifty-eighth and Indiana Avenue. He wanted to talk to her, and tell her to forget it, but he could just see himself doing that.

She turned down Indiana. He walked on over to the corner. The contracts the old man had gotten would mean dough, but lots of work. He hated everything about the goddamn work. Sometimes he felt like taking all the damn paint he could get his hands on and dumping it in the river. But it meant dough and when the old man kicked the bucket, it would be his.

"Jesus Christ!" he said, expressing an unclean and sudden disgust.

From force of habit, he walked past the drug store on down to where the poolroom used to be. Looking at the empty, lightless place, he suddenly came to and realized that the poolroom was gone. He wished it wasn't. He went back to the corner of Fifty-eighth and Prairie.

III

Studs and Tommy Doyle leaned against the side of the drug store building, watching the punks. They were in old clothes and football outfits.

"Jesus, I'll bet they make a fine bunch of players," sneered Studs, wishing that he were in football togs.

"I'll bet they'll play that touch football so they don't get their hair mussed," said Tommy.

"If they get up against a good tough team, they'll be sweet," said Studs.

"Hello, Studs," said Phil who was in football regalia.

"What the hell do you play?" asked Tommy.

"I'm one of the halfbacks," said Phil.

"Sure, he's the All-American-Half-Ass," said Studs. Phil turned to say something to one of his teammates, acting as if he hadn't heard Studs' crack.

"OOPH!" Studs exclaimed, seeing Dapper Dan O'Doul in a football outfit.

"Jesus Christ, him too," said Tommy.

"You know they got their suits from Gorman. He's running for judge, and they're Gorman Boosters," said Studs.

"Well, they sure ought to make him lose the election," said Tommy.

"Here comes that kike pest," said Studs.

"Got a nickel or a butt, Studs?" Tommy mimicked.

"You got Father Abraham there down to a 't' that time," said Studs.

"Hello, boys," Davey Cohen said with ineffectual cheerfulness.

"Got a cigarette, Tommy?" said Studs. Tommy held out a pack and winked.

"Say, got another there, Tommy?" Davey asked.

Studs winked back. Davey took a cigarette.

"Boys, I saw Helen Shires," said Davey.

"How is she?" asked Tommy.

"Is she married?" asked Studs.

"I heard she's a Lesbian," said Davey, laughing sardonically.

"What the hell's that?" Studs asked.

"She's like a fairy only in love with women. I don't know if that's true, but that's what I heard," said Davey.

"Oh!" said Studs.

He remembered that show he'd seen at Burnham. He was disgusted. His disgust turned to a fierce but silent hatred of Davey. All his old liking and respect for Helen from the old days returned. It couldn't be true. It wasn't.

"Tell us the dope about her," said Studs.

"Well, I just heard it, that's all, that she was living with another girl, and that, well, a guy I know who knows her girl chum, he says he was up to their apartment, and that he saw plenty."

Davey bummed a cigarette off Studs and told Lesbian stories that he'd heard on the road. He was happy. And he hadn't been happy much since he'd returned. He had that cough. And the guys weren't the same. They didn't accept him as one of the boys. He knew it, and needn't kid himself. He was a little sick Jew now, a sick tormented Jew. He could see the way they looked at him, talked. And he was down, broke and sick. They weren't sick, and even the ones who hadn't any dough were able to raise more than he ever could. All he had was what he bummed. His kid brother had a good job, and once in a while gave him a half buck, but not often. Now, he was telling them stories that interested them, and he felt like it was the same as the old times when he was one of the boys, in with them, a battler who could go with the best of them; and goddamn it, he had been able to go with the best of them—once.

"That's queer, all right," said Studs.

"It ain't natural. They ought to take and shoot girls like that, they ain't natural, and they're a disgrace to the human race," Red Kelly said.

"I'll bet she must be awfully unhappy if that's true," Les said naively.

"That thing is against the natural law," said Red with unshakable self-conviction.

"Well, of course, I feel they can't help it. I think maybe they're born that way, or they are made that way because of something that happens in their life," Davey said, apologetically.

"B. S.," Red said.

"I suppose you'd like to kiss a girl like that," Tommy sneered.

"That's worse than having a nigger. Think of it, a girl comes from a self-respecting family, with a decent old man and old lady. She had a decent home, a chance for an education, an opportunity to meet decent fellows, and to become a fine, decent girl. And what does she do, but become worse than the hustler of a nigger pimp? And you try to say she can't help it! Why girls like that ought to be made to live with pigs," Red proclaimed.

"I wonder if much of that stuff goes on?" said Studs.

"Plenty, if you ask me. Only I said I just heard that," said Davey.

"She was always a tomboy as a kid," said Red.

"Yes, it wasn't natural for a girl to be like a boy," said Tommy.

"She was a swell pal as a kid," Studs said, nostalgically.

"Say what you want to, but the finest and most decent girls are Irish Catholic girls," said Red.

"No jane is decent if she meets the right guy," said Slug.

"Well, I don't know that I agree with you there, Slug," said Red.

"Say, it ain't a matter of what you call decency. It's all a matter of the right guy coming along at the right time," said Slug.

"No, sir, you get a good Catholic girl, who has a decent home, the right kind of parents, and fear of God in her, like Studs' sisters, and they're decent, they're fine, they're amongst the finest things you can find in life," said Red.

Studs felt proud of his sisters.

"And when girls don't, there's only two things to do. The old man to give her his razor strap, and the old man or brother or somebody to give the clouts to the guys that try and fool around with her," said Red.

"Well, boys, let's go to a show," said Studs.

"All right."

They walked off. Davey trailed after them, and asked if anyone had enough to lend him to come along. They didn't answer him.

"Studs, I can pay you back tomorrow," said Davey, half pleading.

"Sorry, Dave, all I got is enough for the show and coffee an' afterwards," Studs said.

Davey watched them straggle down towards Garfield Boulevard. He was sorry that he had returned. He had no pain in his chest, but he felt that he had. Only a poor sick Jew. He thought of Heine, whose poem he'd read in the Jamestown library.

"That Jew moocher," sneered Studs.

"Yeah," said Slug.

"Say, he's the kind, his kind, that sold out Wabash Avenue to the niggers. If it wasn't for the Jews, this would be a better neighborhood than it is. But anyway, with the new church, it will pick up," said Red.

"I know my old man is beginning to wonder if he ought to sell his building after all, and clear out," said Studs.

"Well, I tell you, once the kikes get in a neighborhood, it's all over," said Red with unanswerable argument.

IV

Davey Cohen bummed a dime off Joe Coady. He hung on Joe's neck talking, telling him about bumming, about anything, just to talk. Joe finally blew. Davey could see that he'd bored Joe. He suddenly hated Coady. Joe was only a punk. Once he'd been only that, and Davey'd been one of the big guys, and one of the toughest of the tough—well, he had—around the corner. Now, he was a little runt, cadging nickels and dimes off kids he'd formerly protected and been a hero to. He hoped, Jesus, some day—But it was pretty much crap to hope. He felt convinced that he had that pain back in the chest. He stopped in the Greek restaurant for coffee.

Christy, the waiter, was at the last seat by the counter, writing, with a book at his side. He came forwards, and said hello. Davey got a cup of coffee.

"Gee, I wish I was back in California," Davey remarked, putting sugar in the coffee, and stirring it.

Christy said that he'd gone to an American high school out on the coast.

"I like the climate. Jesus, it's a grand place," Davey said, wishing pathetically that he were there, forgetting that when he had been on his uppers in Los Angeles, he'd wished that he'd been in Chicago.

"It's nice out there," Christy said.

Christy was a tall, heavy-set, full-faced Greek in his forties. His hair was thinned out, and there was a bald spot on his head.

"The broads out there, they're thick as flies around a garbage can, and they're all like rabbits. Say, that place is paradise for a guy if he's got a little jack," Davey said.

"That's the movies," Christy said.

"Plenty of them are hot, nice."

"I know girls go there. They want to be like . . . like Mary Pickford. They are poor girls, no money. They get no jobs. They become what . . . whores. Yes," Christy said.

"I know it. Say, there's girls like that all right out there. They'll go the limit, do anything a guy wants for a meal. There's girls like that in any big town."

"It's this country, capitalism."

"I know how it feels to be out of work, in a strange town, stony," said Davey reflectively, taking a sip of coffee.

"And in Los Angeles, they have fanatics. Christians," said Christy.

"Sure. All kinds of bugs. There's more fake saviors there than any place in the world."

"Christians. Love your neighbor as yourself. Christians," sneered Pete.

"And what the hell did they do to get their God but steal him from the Jews," laughed Davey.

"And the Catholic Church. Yes. It has perverted the great philosophy of Aristotle."

"I don't like the Catholics none. They're hypocrites and idolators," said Davey.

"Jesus, He was great. Great man like Lenin and Savonarola and Socrates. Christians, they drag him in the mud. They don't love Jesus, or follow his example. They are afraid. They have a God of fear. That's religion . . . fear."

"The Irish made a shanty Irishman out of Christ," Davey said.

"Yes, Jesus was a noble man. The Christians, Catholics, they put him in a sink of superstition."

"Yeah, Christy," said Davey, kind of agreeing with him, feeling that agreement got him even with the Irish bastards like Lonigan and Kelly.

"And America, this great country. It's all cheap journalism, selling. Everything is sell, and what do people get? Things they can't use. Automobiles. Radios. Cheap clothes. The capitalists kill workers, pay them starvation wages, and why? To sell all these things, junk. America was a good country. It isn't now. America is capitalism. It bleeds the world."

Davey didn't know what to say. Maybe he agreed. Goddamn it, people didn't need as much as they had, when others, now himself, had to go without things, be sick, possibly die from want of care.

"America is a country for the parvenu rich man. No art, it's all journalism. America, you have one poet, you don't know him."

"Who's that? Longfellow?"

"Whitman. I'm translating him for my countrymen to read. Perhaps they will appreciate his greatness more than his own countrymen."

"Christy, what do you think of that German-Jewish poet, Heine?"

"A great spirit too, like Nietzsche. He was a great spirit, a great lyric poet."

"But wasn't Nietzsche pretty much of an anarchist?"

"Nietzsche was a great genius. Too great for people like Americans with Sinclair Lewis and all their journalism," said Christy.

Christy waited on another customer. Then, Davey told about how he had picked up the book of Heine when he was on the bum, and how much he'd liked it.

"Yes, he was fine lyric poet."

"You know, Christy, I like to talk with you, because, you know, hell, I never got a break. It makes me think there are things in life after all," Davey said, sentimentally.

"Yes, but the fine things in life, they are obscured in America because of greed. In America you have greed, capitalism. There are, boy, two countries in the world. Greece and Russia. Greece is the world's past, Russia the future of the world."

"You know, I wonder. Look now at all the things about Russia you read in the newspaper."

"Don't believe the newspaper, American journalism. That's the trouble with Americans. They believe the newspaper lies all the time. The newspaper is an American's Bible."

"The papers are pretty yellow."

"You want to read, read Plato's *Republic*. That's what Russia is going to become, maybe. A government and land of justice."

"Well, maybe bolshevism is not so bad as it seems," said Davey.

"Bolshevism is going to be justice for the workingman. He will no longer be a slave, work ten, twelve hours a day and have his children starved and underfed. He will have opportunities. Bolshevism will not allow greed, not allow capitalists to steal all the money to crush people, kill them in wars, to waste their toil on jewelry for silly women and silly wives. Russia is trying to make a decent world. America is trying to make a world for greed, capitalists, crooks, gangsters, criminals, and kill the workingman, make him a slave."

Davey sipped his coffee. He liked Christy, and maybe some of the things Christy said were true, but, hell, Christy was a Greek. He didn't get the idea about America right.

"In America what have you got? . . . politicians. Crooks and liars. You have that man in this city, Gorman, running for judge. What does he know of . . . justice? A noble word, and you make it like a whore in America."

"I guess Gorman is a shyster, but all the boys around here are for him."

"Yes, what do they know? Silly boys. They have no education. They go to school to the sisters." (Christy folded his arms, and made a face of mock piety.) "Sisters, sanctimonious hypocrites. They pray and pray and pray. Fear! Crazy! What can they teach boys? To pray and become sanctimonious hypocrites too. Silly boys, they grow up, their fathers want to make money, their mothers are silly women and pray like the sanctimonious sisters, hypocrites. The boys run the streets, and grow up in poolrooms, drink and become hooligans. They don't know any better. Silly boys, and they kill themselves with diseases from whores and this gin they drink."

Studs came in.

"Or else they are sent to the capitalist war and they get killed, for what? Like the last war, they get killed to make more money for Morgan and the bankers."

Studs looked quizzically at Christy.

"Why did America fight? Because of money, money for Morgan and the capitalists. Why, even the Kaiser in Germany, he had a better government, better laws for the workingman than America."

"I guess the war was for money all right, but I think Wilson was a great man, the greatest American we ever had."

"Why, then, did he want war to save the bankers, and why did he keep Debs in jail?" said Christy.

"Who's he?" Studs asked.

"He was a great man," said Christy.

"He was a socialist," said Davey.

"Oh, he was against religion and the home," said Studs.

"How come the boys aren't back?" Davey asked.

"Oh, they went drinking beer after the show. I thought I'd go home for a change. Jesus, I've been hitting the bottle too goddamn heavy lately," said Studs.

Davey hoped Studs hadn't heard much of the talk. He didn't want them to think him completely cracked.

Christy looked at them, two boys. He went back to work on his translation of Whitman into Greek.

"What the hell was that goddamn Greek talking about?" asked Studs.

"Oh, lots of things. He's radical," Davey said in a very low voice.

"Well, if he doesn't like this country why don't he go back to Greece or Russia?" asked Studs.

"He's a nice fellow, a white Greek. Only he's a little bit radical. He's a poet," said Davey.

"For Christ sake! I suppose he writes about the birdies and the stars, and my heart in love," sneered Studs.

A song of several years back jingled in Studs' mind, *Don't Bite the Hand That's Feeding You* . . . The first line kept returning to him:

If you don't like your Uncle Sammy . . .

The song hit the nail square. Stud had an image of Uncle Sammy in his brain, tall, thin, angular, kindly, a trifle bucolic, but with powerful Abe Lincoln or Slug Mason mitts. He had a picture of him steady in his mind, this thin, tall, kindly, bearded man in red, white and blue clothes, his eyes sad with sorrow caused by the ingratitude of all the foreigners who had come over here and been ungrateful to him. But he was a powerful man. He had licked the Kaiser and he could lick the world. It made Studs feel like saying to Christy:

"Why, you lousy Greek sonofabitch, get the hell out of a white man's country."

"Say, is that Greek an American citizen?" asked Studs.

"Yeah," said Davey.

"A hell of a lot of nerve he had, being an American," said Studs.

He had that image of Uncle Sam again, and it made him think of how, as a kid, he had used to see cartoons with Uncle Sam in them in the newspapers, and he used to wish that Uncle Sam was a real man, the same to America as God was to the world. It made him wish that again, and wishing that, he was wishing he was a kid again. He had a heartburn. He felt his stomach. Getting more and more of an alderman. He felt rotten. He wasn't sleeping so well, and some days, he got all pooped out at three or four o'clock.

"Say, remember the fun we used to have as kids?" he said to Davey.

"Yeah. It was the nuts. Jesus, wouldn't it be swell to be like that again, no responsibilities. Remember the time you licked Red Kelly?" said Davey.

"Yeah, and Paulie had that trouble in the piggy game with that punk, what was his name?"

"Young Dennis," said Davey.

"That was it."

"And I remember the day you licked Weary Reilley. That was a battle," said Davey.

"Were you there? I didn't think you were," said Studs.

"Yeah. In front of Helen Shires' house. Sure I was," said Davey.

"I didn't remember you there. But that was a fight, the hardest fight I ever had," said Studs.

"Say, Studs, could you stand me to another cup of coffee?" Davey asked.

"Sure."

Davey got the coffee. He asked Studs if a piece of pie would be all right, too. Studs said yes. He was thinking of the old days.

When Davey finished, they went outside. Hink Weber was on the corner, and he had a wandering look about him. Davey rushed up to Hink, put out his hand, and said hello. Hink didn't notice him.

"Hello, Hink!" said Studs, more ordinarily, feeling a sense of triumph that Hink had not batted an eye when the Jew had tried to put the rush act on him. Hink scarcely raised an eyebrow, but did not speak. He walked on, like a somnambulist.

"Jesus Christ!"

"Say, what the hell, Hink never used to be high hat like this, did he?" asked Davey.

"No. Jesus, he looked queer tonight."

"Yeah, he looked awfully strange. Did you catch that look in his eyes?" asked Davey.

"Yeah."

"He didn't look drunk to me. He looked crazy," said Studs.

"I wonder was he drunk?"

"Jesus!" exclaimed Davey.

"He's been acting queer of late," said Studs.

"Yeah," said Davey knowingly.

"He hasn't been around much of late, but when he has, he's been acting sort of far away," said Studs.

"That's too bad, all right," said Davey.

"I'm sorry, all right," said Studs.

"Me too," said Davey.

Studs had gas on his stomach from the coffee an'. He knew now he wouldn't sleep. It worried him.

"Well, I guess I'll be moving along," he said.

"So long."

"Poor Hink!"

"Poor Hink!"

"Say, I just thought: we oughtn't to say anything about it, huh?" said Studs.

"I guess so."

"So long."

Davey hung around, a bit chilled, waiting to see if anybody else would come. He hated to go home. He thought how swell it would be if a broad came along, and he met her, and they went to her room, and she warmed him, and ummmmm, Jesus Christ! He wanted a lot of things. Poor sick Jew! He wished the guys would come. They didn't. He tramped disappointedly home.

XXI

At the supper table early in 1927, Mrs. Lonigan sighed that she was glad because soon it would be time for Father Shannon, the missionary, to be coming back to the parish to conduct the first mission in the new church. And she was anxious to hear what he would say about it, and how surprised he would be, and pleased to be conducting a mission in such a magnificent house of worship. Lonigan reflected aloud that Father Shannon was as brilliant and as educated as any Jesuit.

Mrs. Lonigan, her hair graying, looked over her brood, her two stunning daughters and her two sons; Loretta, a fine girl with an excellent high school education at St. Paul's swell school for girls; Frances engaged to be married to that well-to-do Dowson boy; Martin, a growing boy, innocent and fine, attending the Carmelites high school, and, she hoped and prayed nightly to God, preparing himself to answer the call to the priesthood. She saw the day, in a mother's day dream, when he would celebrate his first Mass at St. Patrick's parish. There was only William, her baby. She prayed to God, too, that he would settle down. She was worried. Oh, God, would He only put grace into William's heart at this next mission. William was a good boy, with no harm in him. It was only bad companions.

"You children will have to make the mission," she said, covertly looking at William as he forked a piece of steak.

"Yeah," Studs mumbled, chewing.

"I like Father Shannon. He's a swell priest," Martin said in the changing squeaky voice of adolescence.

The father thought a better word than swell should be used to describe a great man like Father Shannon. Mrs. Lonigan said he was a holy man, and what a pride he must be to his old mother, if she were still living. Loretta said he was a darling. Fran said he was brainy. Lonigan told Fran that Father Shannon might say a word or two about those books by that man Sinclair Lewis that she was reading. She said she was not taking them seriously. She only read them because a couple of her girl friends who thought they were sophisticated were reading them, and she had gotten them to look at, only so they wouldn't be able to think that she was old-fashioned or not up to the times in things. Mrs. Lonigan said that some books were like bad companions.

"Please, mother!" Fran said.

"You're going to make the mission, William?" the mother said.

He said sure. Martin said he was also. The mother said she wanted them to because she and their father were going to make the mission for the older people, and if the whole family did the right thing, their home would be blessed by God.

"Sure, we'll take it in a couple of nights," Lonigan said.

She said every night they would. Lonigan said that missions were not meant for guys like himself who weren't sinners. She said he must set a good example for his children. He nodded, not to get her going. She was getting more religious every day, and it was a good thing, but she was filling the house with holy pictures and holy water, and hell, they weren't sinners, and did all their duties to God and the Church, and she didn't need to harp on it. He looked at Bill, with a father's love and pride. Only, he hoped, God, he hoped, that the mission would affect Bill, make him sort of settle down.

The daughters arose to get the coffee and dessert from the kitchen. Mrs. Lonigan told them how holy Father Shannon was. Lonigan expanded, rubbed his spreading belly, and agreed.

Chapter Twenty-one

I

"SURE, Father Shannon is regular. He won't jump three feet every time he hears a hell, and he doesn't try to scare people into loading their pants with any hell-fire and damnation sermons. He talks man-to-man, using psychology," Kelly said.

"I like Father Shannon," Les said, while Red frowned at some passing niggers.

"He seems to be working wonders with you hoodlums," Red said.

"Us hoodlums! What about yourself?" Doyle retaliated.

"I sure like him," Les said.

"He's certainly different from Gilly. He knows human nature. And he doesn't always harp for money. Still he gets it," Tommy said.

"The way Gilly harps on the dough, you'd think no one ever gave a cent. Like a couple of weeks ago, when he told people they should quit putting pennies and nickels in the collection box," Studs said.

"Of course, he has to, with the debt on the new church, and so many well-to-do parishioners moving out of the parish before it's up hardly more than a year," Kelly said.

"Hear Ye! Hear Ye! Hear Ye!" burlesqued Barney Keefe; they certified that he was sober by smelling his breath.

"Coming to the mission, Chu Chu?" Studs asked.

"Yes, but not with you hoodlums. The mission is for sinners and louses like you guys, not me. I'm holy," Barney said; Red frowned as two more niggers passed the corner.

"Listen to the bastard talk, when his war cry has always been: 'Let's get a bottle'." Red laughed.

"One of these days, I'm going to sue all you heels for defamation of character and slander," Barney said.

"Tell me, Barney! Is that the right spirit to have when you're making the mission?" asked Red.

"Get away from me. Woe! Woe! Woe! You're all the occasion of sin," Barney said.

"Seems to me you guys ought to be more serious," Stan Simonsky said.

"Of course, Stan, we're all Catholics here. If there were outsiders around, we'd talk different," Red said.

"Talking of people needing the mission, though, now this bastard Lonigan doesn't need it at all. Not after the way he went for that blond at the Rex last week," Doyle said.

"How about Les here? Drink isn't his temptation. He's a temptation to gin," Studs beamed.

"But, fellows, Father Shannon is showing us what's what," Les said.

"I know I wish I was as smart as he is," Doyle said.

"Remember Tuesday night, when he was talking about atheists, and said the Bible says that any man who says there is no God is a fool. And then he said that if anyone says there is no God, let him just go outside and look at the moon, and after looking at it, try to say that the moon made itself. Listen, if some of those atheists over around the Bug Club heard that, they would have squirmed in their seats, and if they aren't already too vain about their puny human knowledge, they'd come to their senses, and quit thinking that they were too good for the human race," Red said.

"Between us and that fireplug, I'll bet, too, that when he was young, he was no sissy," Stan said.

"Sure, he knows the ways of the world. He had his wild oats, I'll bet. That's why he knows so much about human nature," Red said.

"Oh, hello, Hink," Studs said.

"I just heard you guys talking about that priest. Sure he has his good times. All priests do."

"Say, Hink, I was hoping you'd be around. I wanted to ask you to come along with us to the mission tonight. Father Shannon is different from any one you ever heard speak, a brilliant, educated man, and he'll make you understand the Catholic philosophy," Red said.

"What do I care about the Catholics' side of it?"

"You wouldn't be so radical, then, about our religion," Red said.

"I'm not interested," Hink said snottily.

"Honest, Hink, he's the real stuff," Tommy said.

Hink walked away from them.

"There's something queer about Hink. He's not like he used to be," Studs said, and he offered one more of his many repetitions of the experience that he and Davey had had with Hink the previous autumn.

"And, Christ, nearly every night he's rolling all over the street drunk," Stan said.

"Hink is a white fellow. But there's something wrong with him. I think it's in the family. His brother Slew is in the sanitarium now.

Remember how he always looked first for the suicides in the paper, and remember how he would chase sixteen-year-old girls, and hang around the Bug Club, talk like they did over there, sit around the park all day stripped to the waist taking sun-baths. I tell you I think a brain disease like paranoia runs in their family. It's too bad," Red said.

"What the hell's that?" asked Barney.

"It's a brain disease that unbalances you, so that you won't associate with people, don't care about them or even yourself, think you're too good for the human race, and talk about people like Hink does about priests and the Catholic Church," Red said, causing doleful shaking of heads.

"Say, Slug, come on to church with us tonight. You don't want to miss it," Studs said, as Slug shambled up to them.

"You guys must want the pillars of the church to crumble," Barney said.

"Tonight, Slug, the sermon is going to be about guys who get nooky," said Doyle.

"I don't want to hear about it. I just like to get it. And I know all about how to get it," Slug said, with his Polack pronunciation.

"Come on, Slug!" Studs persuaded.

"Hell, I'd do everything the wrong way in church, and then when the priest was talking, I'd maybe fall asleep, and start snoring, and get thrun out of church on my tail," Slug said.

"You won't fall asleep when Father Shannon talks," Red said.

"Not me. Say, I wish it was over. I ain't had anybody to get a bottle with me all week," Slug said.

"Don't tempt us this week, Slug," said Doyle.

"Listen, you bastards, if you're making the mission, it means you should get there on time for the rosary that's said before the sermon. What are you trying to do, miss the rosary? Come on!" Barney said.

Slug nodded, watching them depart.

"Another black skunk," Red said, pointing to a young Negro ahead of them.

"Boy, they've been coming into the neighborhood fast, and so soon after the new church was built," Stan said.

"I see some at the mission every night," Studs said.

"They're ruining the neighborhood. That's why Jim and I have been trying to convince the old lady to sell the building before it's too late. Property values are going to pot here. You can tell it, when there's a saloon on Fifty-eighth Street, and beer flats all around, and flats and buildings being made into rooming-houses. And down on Garfield

Boulevard the other night, why a hustler even tried to pick me up," Tommy lamented.

"If we had a pastor like Father Shannon, instead of Gilly, that mightn't have happened. He wouldn't be the kind to build a beautiful new church, and then let his parish go to the dogs. He'd have seen to it that the good parishioners stayed, and that the niggers were kept out. He'd have organized things like vigilance committees to prevent it," Red said.

"That's what my old man has been saying," Studs said.

"It was the Jews who did it. And he would have settled those profiteering shonnickers. It's a lousy thing, if you ask me, Jews ruining a neighborhood just to make money like Judas did. It's all greed all over again, the greed of the Jews," Kelly said.

"Why don't the Jews all go back to Jerusalem where they belong?" Tommy said.

"And why don't you Irish go back and sleep with the pigs in the old country," Barney said.

"Chu Chu, you can't be serious for a minute," Stan said to Keefe.

"Speaking seriously, something will have to be done pretty quick if the neighborhood is going to be saved," Red said.

"It's too late now," said Tommy.

"What I want to know is this: Will the mission convert Doyle to work?" said Barney.

"No danger," said Les.

"He worked all summer warming his fanny in the boathouse," Red said.

"And don't think I didn't put in long hours," Tommy boasted.

"Say, fellows, I got a letter from Shrimp," said Red.

"That tb rat," Barney said.

"He's a good fellow," Tommy said.

"Yeah, a snake in the grass. I had a job as a sewer-pipe layer all fixed up a couple of years ago. And that louse queered it thinking he could get it. It was muscling in, and I lost it, and he just queered both of us," Barney said.

They laughed, and Red said anyway, Shrimp didn't like the navy at all.

"I hope he falls overboard into the mouth of a shark," Barney said.

"Say, by the way, did all you guys know that Rolfe has been converted, and is making his first Communion Sunday?" Stan said.

"That's the dope," Studs said.

"It was your sister, Studs, who did it," Red said.

"I suspect that guy. Him being a Catholic is too much for me. He's full of so much B. S. that I doubt how much he means it," Tommy said.

"If he gets your sister, Studs, he's getting a damn fine, decent girl. My opinion is that she's much too good for him," Red said.

"All right, you guys, step on it! You're going to church, not to an employment agency. You're too late for the rosary now, anyway," Barney said.

II

St. Patrick's Church was packed, and hushed. Father Shannon, a plump, bald-headed priest, emerged from the sacristy door on the right, pushed the back of his right hand to his mouth as he emitted a half-cough, genuflected, facing the altar, and proceeded to climb into the marble pulpit. He laid his beret beside him and faced the audience of young people, his soft, mushy, almost womanly face, half-distinct. He stretched his arms, and smoothed down his cassock. His bald head shone as it was caught in candle flickers. He emitted another cracked cough. In a quiet and confident voice, he said, while blessing himself:

"In the name of the Father, and of the Son, and of the Holy Ghost, Amen!"

He paused pregnantly, and dramatically. In a calm modulated voice, he exclaimed:

"My text for tonight's sermon is: 'Stand, therefore, having your loins girt in truth, and having on the breast-plate of justice, and your feet shod with the preparation of the gospel of peace.' Epistle of Paul to the Ephesians, sixth chapter, sixteenth verse.

"In the words, then, of the stern and austere Saint, Paul himself, I come and say unto you boys and girls tonight: 'Stand, therefore, having your loins girt in truth, and having on the breast-place of justice, and your feet shod with the preparation of the gospel of peace'."

His voice lowered almost imperceptibly:

"This evening, I shall have serious things to say, words of more serious import than those which have been, or will be contained in any other sermon or talk of this mission."

He smiled.

"Hence, I am constrained to ask that those of you who have the habit of sleeping through sermons, will kindly refrain from snoring. You know, there is a commandment of Jesus Christ, our Lord, which dictates that we must all love our neighbor as ourselves. Snoring, when your neighbor may be trying to hear what I say, or, God bless the mark, when he himself may be trying to sleep, is not what I call loving your neighbor."

He leaned on his arms, chest forwards, and smiled, while there were ripples of laughter.

"I stated that I have serious things to tell you. But don't, in the name of God, think that because I have said that, that I am coming here like a black-faced (he frowned dourly and hunched his shoulders) old man of gloom with crepe hanging from my shoulders. Because I am not (he smiled). I was young once myself, even though many of you may doubt that because of this billiard ball I have."

He touched his bald head; he waited until the self-conscious, restrained laughter subsided.

"I know what it means to be young. I know that Satan rides about through the night, like a witch in Sleepy Hollow, planning traps and temptations with which to beset the young. I know that when you are eighteen, nineteen, twenty-one, even twenty-five, you cannot be expected to live the kind of a life that a crabby, old maid aunt would desire you to live. I know that you want good times. I believe, uncategorically, that you should have good times. (His pitch rose.) . . . But I do say that they should be clean good times, clean fun, decent pleasures that will not rob you of your soul, your mind, even your body and your health. Thus, I want you to realize that I am coming here as your friend, attempting to understand you, and to be sympathetic with you in the problems you must face, and the temptations which you must resist."

He paused, permitting his eyes to rove about the church.

"I fail to see any sleepers. That, I take, as a good augury."

He waited again, while there was a quiet outburst of laughing.

"My young friends, modern youth (his voice became explosive) in that quest for joy and amusement and fun, which is the perennial quest of youth, has drunk deeply from the muddy fountains of sham sophistication. Modern youth, therefore—and I do not exclude many Catholic boys and girls of this nation—must, under the pain of serious and eternal consequences, eject this soiled, germ-ridden, sin-ridden sham sophistication from its minds and its souls. And the sooner young people realize that the only lasting purgatives to perform this task of spiritual catharsis are the Sacraments and teachings of Holy Mother Church, the better off they will be, the better off this great nation will be, the better off this world will be.

"Today, we live in a world (he sneered and his voice sharpened) that is debauched with paganism of the vilest kind. For in pagan Greece, and even in pagan Rome, there was a measure of spiritual and intellectual accomplishment that is lacking in our own times. We live in an age of growing laxity, of sin (his face and voice intensified), ugly sin that is the cancer destroying immortal souls that have been made in the image and likeness of God Almighty. Our modern jazz age of freedom and untrammelled unconventionality is characterized by immorality, vice, disease . . . spiritual cowardice. Today, there are afoot movements started by vicious men and women who philander with the souls of youth in order that they will receive their paltry profit, and their cheap, ephemeral notoriety. I refer to such movements as jazz, atheism, free-love, companionate marriage, birth-control. These, and similarly miscalled tendencies, are murdering the souls of youth" (he slapped his hand on the pulpit).

(His voice broke into lamentation.) "Oh, how closely, how closely, my young friends, does not hell yawn to the youth of America!

"'Weep, oh, weep for Adonais!' if I might quote that misguided poet, Shelley."

(His voice became calm and normal.) "I travel through this great, wide-flung country extensively. In the course of every year, I go from coast to coast. I contact these tendencies. I see their evil effects, the young people they ruin, the homes they wreck, the sadness they cause in the hearts of God-fearing mothers and fathers. I see how (his pitch rose) those seats of the godless—the universities—those iniquitous incubators of vice, cheapness, and trash—the movies; (he sneered) those imitation Anti-Christs, modern authors whose books perfume the vilest of sins—how all these take their toll in lives, in souls. In short, my young friends, I can perceive clearly (with dolorousness) oh, how clearly, Satan is making a powerful offensive, with all his artillery and machinery of strategems, bribes, craftiness, seductive lies and promises, upon this so-called modern world of ours.

"And speaking of books, what do I mean? (His tone sharpened.) I have no fear of naming names and titles, and condemning where condemnation is due. And if I met the authors of the books I shall mention, I should tell them to their faces (his voice rose, almost to a shout): 'Your books are vile. In order to make a sale for them, you fill them with spiritual poison, with all the resources of your filthy and putrid minds. For thirty pieces of silver, you sign your names to oozing immorality. You are worse than dogs! You are the vilest of the vile, the most vicious of the vicious, lower than snakes, you rats who write books to rob youth of its shining silvered innocence!' That's what I would say to them, if, God forbid, I were to meet them face to face. (He vigorously smashed his hand against the pulpit.)

"What books do I mean? For one, there is a scurrilous novel, *Elmer*

Gantry, a book that belongs in no decent household, a book that no self-respecting Catholic can read under the pain of sin, a book that should be burned in a garbage heap. In that novel, what does the author do? He mocks the most sacred profession that man can enter . . . the cloth, the service of Almighty God. Do you think I am afraid to tell you what kind of a man the author of Elmer Gantry is? (His voice grew in fearlessness.) Well, I am not afraid! I shall tell you. . . . He is a liar. I say (bellowing), he is a liar, and I am prepared to tell him so to his face!"

He paused, and surveyed a church taut with silence and interest. His voice dropped and he continued evenly:

"And in Denver, there is a puny little man, whose mind would have to be seen through the lenses of a powerful microscope. A man who has sullied the sanctity and justice of the courts . . . one Judge Ben Lindsay. And what does he preach? (He sneered.) . . . Companionate Marriage! Companionate Marriage, another of those masked fads that rise from a cesspool of spiritual cravenness (sneering). Companionate Marriage! That is his sugar-coated, seductive term. This little man, this human atom, this intellectual midget, what does he preach—at a profit (with rising voice)? I'll tell you in straight language without any fake pretence of those abused words, liberality and tolerance. In simple words, this human rat, like the anarchistic, atheistic Bolshevists in unhappy Russia, says (his arms flung out in a gesture): 'Away with the holy bonds of Matrimony!' Jesus Christ, (his head bowing), our Lord, said 'What God hath joined together, let no man put asunder!' Mother Church, after nineteen hundred years of tested wisdom and experience, achieved with the guidance of the Holy Spirit, Mother Church says that you must be married by one of God's annointed representatives, and that unless you are, you sin when you take unto yourself a man or woman as husband or wife. And Judge Ben Lindsay (with a sneer) says that this is all nonsense. It is not modern. It is old-fashioned. Away with it! (His cassocked arm swung outward in a demonstrative gesture.) He tells the youth of America to go out, flirt, taste sin, ruin their souls, experiment, and that if it does not succeed, try again. He advises young men to take a girl, a pure, innocent, decent, perhaps even a Catholic, girl, and live with her in violation of one of God's Holy Commandments. Try her out! Ruin her! And if she doesn't powder her nose the right way, or burns the toast in the morning, or you stub your toe getting out of the wrong side of the bed, and think she is the cause, leave her. You are then incompatible. Leave her a ruined girl, unable to look her mother or her God in the eye, unable to find a decent young man who would want her! Incompatibility! Another of those masked, ambiguous, lying phrases used to clothe the intent of Satan who sulks in the bottom of low and depraved mentalities, like that of Judge Ben Lindsay.

"And only recently, I conducted a mission in Baltimore. Baltimore, founded on principles of religious liberty and tolerance. Baltimore, that splendid city that was once the refuge of Catholics who risked death and exile for the sake of their faith. What books do you think the Catholic youth of Baltimore was reading? The books of that fake sage of Baltimore, that man who profits by telling youth to read Nietzsche. I refer to H. L. Mencken. Who is H. L. Mencken? He is a noisy, vociferous, and half-baked little man. What does he say? He says: 'Read Nietzsche!' That was what the ill-fated Leopold and Loeb read in this city, almost in this neighborhood. That is what the Germans who started the last war read. That is what H. L. Mencken says to youth. And they read him, and think themselves (sneering) smart. So I said to them from the altar of God: 'Do you think that smart? Do you think it smart to mock at all the things that are sacred to God and man? Do you think it is smart to blaspheme? Well, get it out of your heads! It is a cheap and easy sin! It is blasphemy! And woe unto him who is guilty of blasphemy! Woe!'

"The writers I have named are merely a few out of many. There are others, and amongst them, there is the biggest windbag of them all . . . H. G. Wells. That Englishman who preaches evolution, who says that man came from a monkey. And on what evidence do such false prophets preach evolution? On the evidence of science? That is a lie. I'll tell you the evidence. A slab of shin bone and a half a skull was found in China. These half-baked pseudo-scientists gave it a confounding and terrifying name—Pithecanthropus Erectus. Then they went to a zoo and saw a monkey eating with a fork. Because of that, and because of—pardon me if I mispronounce it—Pithecanthropus Erectus, they say that man came from a monkey and is only an animal. In their insane egotism, they think that all men are made unto their own image and likeness. (Snickers.)

"And the universities, miscalled seats of learning, temples of truth, are full of such men. Over here on the Midway, you have one such university. Recently, I conducted a mission in another part of the city, and a Catholic girl came to me and said: 'Father, what am I going to do? I'm given these kind of books to read in my courses, and if I don't read them, I'll be flunked. And they present fallacies contrary to my faith.' I told her what to do. I told her what every Catholic student should say in such circumstances. I told her to take the books back to her professor and say that Father said she should tell him this: 'I am a Catholic. I will not read these books and endanger my holy faith. They are full of half-truths, paradoxes, lies, and the men who wrote them are either ignorant, or else they are liars. You must put a stop to this sort of thing. You must stick to what you know, to the limited field which you have studied, and stop talking about or recommending books on morals and theology, because you are ignorant and biased.' That is what every Catholic student in a godless university should do.

"Another class of people contributing to the sham sophistication which I have mentioned is a bunch of snivelling old maids who do not care how many souls they ruin, as long as it permits them to get their hatched-faces plastered all over the newspapers as forward-looking women. And what do these snivelling old maids advocate to earn the dubious honor of being forward-looking? (A pause.) Birth control! The deliberate murder of human souls, in defiance of the laws of God and Nature. I'll tell what the birth control of these snivelling, hatchet-faced old maids means. It means this (he banged his right fist into his left palm): It means the legalization of sin, disease, promiscuity, the destruction of the Christian home; and the Christian Catholic home is the backbone of this, or of any civilized, nation. But what do such irresponsible old fools care? What do they care if they incite to the murder of innocent, unborn babes? What do they care if they turn this nation into a state of debauchery which would make pagan Rome look virtuous by sheer comparison? What do they care if all men live without even the decency of the beasts of the field? What do they care so long as their long, hatchet mugs are in the daily newspaper, with a description of forward-looking and modern, under the photographs?"

He paused, and slowly wiped his perspiring face with a large handkerchief. He coughed. He recommenced in an even voice:

"Ah, my friends, the mind of America is being ruined. For the youth of a nation is that nation's future. And our youth is being contaminated. And there is only one way, one method, of fighting this ruin and contamination. There is only one hope for America. That hope lies in the Catholic young men, the Catholic girls of this nation. They must be the leaders. They must offer the strongest resistance to sin and blasphemy. They must fight the untruths spread by these cheap little half-baked, second-rate Anti-Christs. When they, when you, meet someone defending birth-control, this must be said in answer: 'Birth control solves nothing. There is only one answer—that of the Catholic Church. It is not Birth Control that we need but . . . Self

Control!' When you meet someone advising you to read the latest book, you must say this: 'I am unashamed to say that I will not expose my mind and my soul to such trash. I read only good books, decent books, and no books by windbags and publicity-seekers like Sinclair Lewis, and H. G. Wells. I read books like those of G. K. Chesterton, the foremost living writer of this century. No, I don't read psychoanalysis, either. I read psychology, the true psychology, the rational psychology by the foremost psychologist in the world today—Father Maher.'

"For, my friends, your minds and your bodies are vessels of the Lord, given unto your keeping. They must not be abused. They are not tools for the indiscriminate enjoyment of what the world calls pleasure. There is one commandment which, above all, you must not violate. God says, clearly and without equivocation: 'Thou shalt not commit adultery!' If you do, the torments of hell await you for all eternity! That is clear and unmistakable.

"Today, sad to state, I come here as a priest of God, and I have to confess that the youth of this land neglects that commandment. On every side, they are encouraged. Books! Filthy movies. Newspapers. The doctrines in universities aimed to destroy morality. Men who cater to the purposes of the devil, and expose youth, tender girls and immature boys, to the danger of this sin, all because it is profitable, because a dirty, soiled thirty pieces of silver can be collected. Such men, I say, are worse than Judas.

"And what are the results? One result is this: today in America, there is a type, a class of young men, a recognizable young squirt. This squirt spends the money that his father earned and saved after long years of honest toil. He has an automobile. He has been miseducated at a godless university. He is fast, modern; he talks smartly, dresses smartly, acts smartly. He is always on the loose for a girl. He meets an innocent Catholic girl. She is pure and sweet and good, like Longfellow's Evangeline. But as young girls often are, she is attracted by his clothes, his talk, and his automobile. He has what they call a line. He gives her a lot of soft soap. So Mary has a date with him. He is pleasing, and spends money. She thinks he is a nice boy! Like the spider, he is weaving his web. He takes her out again, and drives toward the country. He pulls out a bottle and has a drink. He offers it to her. She demurs. He looks at her as if she were a zoological exhibit. He can't understand, because all the girls he knows drink. He laughs and asks if she is afraid. She shows her fear. So he tells her: 'Come on Mary, don't be a wet blanket. Once won't hurt!'

"Cursed phrase; 'Once won't hurt'. That first time seems so harmless and so easy. It seems to have such little effect. And it leads straight down the road to perdition and ruin. With it, he plays on Mary's vanity. He convinces her with soft-soap talk that once won't hurt. Then, he takes her to a roadhouse. There, they meet other couples. It is what they call a wild party. Everybody but Mary drinks. She is teased, and told not to be a kill-joy. Once hasn't hurt her. Once more won't, they tell her. Rather than spoil the party, Mary takes a second drink. Before she knows it, she is drunk. There is dancing, immoral animalistic dancing and petting. Then, there is another automobile ride. Mary goes home, pillaged of her most precious treasure, robbed (he smacked his right fist into his left palm) of that gift which is a girl's finest possession—her virtue, her honor, her chastity.

"This is not an exceptional occurrence. Pray God that it were! It is ordinary, and happens every day. It is the way in which Catholic girls, girls like those of you here, girls like the sisters and sweethearts and old schoolmates of you lads here, are ruined, and dispatched along a path that can only end in misery, both in this world and the next. You girls who are now listening to me! If you have not already met such temptations, you will. And, you fellows, your sisters will meet them. For if these squirts had their way, there would not be a decent girl left in this country.

"And when you girls do meet with this temptation what are you going to say? Are you going to agree that . . . 'Once doesn't hurt?' Or are you going to say: 'See here now, what are your intentions? I'm a decent Catholic girl, and I do not intend to fling myself away on any rat because he has a funny-looking suit of bell bottoms and an automobile. Before I ride in any automobile of yours, I want to know why you want me to go, what intentions you have, what kind of a person you are?'

"And you fellows, if you find some cake-eater trying to take advantage of your sister, what are you going to do? Are you going to shrug your shoulders, and say that you are not your sister's keeper, or turn your head the other way to avoid trouble? I know of one such case. It happened in Marion, Ohio. The sister of a young Catholic fellow was ruined, and died giving birth to an illegitimate baby. And the spineless brother answered my questions this way. He said: 'Father, it would have been such a mess. Father, I believe that each person has the right to live their own life.' Well, let me tell you this: God won't agree to such a principle on the final Day of Judgment.

"If there is an ounce of decency and red blood in a young fellow, he'll not do that. When any one of these jazz-age drug-store cowboys starts trying to fool around with his sister, he won't mince his words.

He'll say: 'See here, now, what do you mean, trying to ruin my sister?' That's what he'll say. He'll tell him to get out and stay out. And he'll punch his yellow nose in for him. Because that is the only kind of treatment these wise young squirts merit.

"Why, if I had a sister, and one of them started monkeying around with her, I'd grab him by the coat collar, and I'd say; 'See here! You're not honorable! You're not decent! Are you going to let my sister alone?' And then I'd let him have one."

Father Shannon paused, and again mopped his face. He glanced from face to face in the church. He spoke with calmness again.

"Remember these words! Years ahead, I want you, when you're my age, and I'm dead, to pause and think, to remember what Father Shannon said in his missions at St. Patrick's. And I want you to remember this statement particularly. . . . Sin doesn't pay.

"And I am willing to bet anyone here a hundred dollars that then you'll nod your head, and think that, yes, Father Shannon told you the truth. And of all sins, that which pays the least, is a sin of the flesh. Ah, you boys and girls, you don't want to ruin yourself, body and soul. You don't want to disease your body so that a decent person will shun you as he would a leper. Your bodies are young and strong now. You don't want to wreck them with disease and over-indulgence. There is nothing as fine as the sight of a good strong boy or girl, whose body and mind are clean, pure, decent. And the ideal of retaining such a body, and such a mind is both noble and practical. It isn't as hard as sin. I know, because I've seen hospitals where people were rotting away with disease as the result of their sins. One day, my young friends, they had bodies like you had, and the chance that you still possess. And they forsook that ideal. You want to remember the words of Thomas à Kempis: 'For they that follow their sensuality, do stain their own conscience, and lose the favor of God'.

"When the devil tempts you, as he tempted such people, you want to say to him: 'Satan, No! No! No! you cannot have my body and my soul!' You young fellows, you don't want to be fools, and go skulking, like thieves in the night, into brothels, consorting with the lowest kind of human beings, exposing yourself to diseases that can ruin your lives, and blast the chances of a successful and happy marriage with that sweet little girl whom you love. Ah, no, you don't want to do that. Because it doesn't last! And it doesn't pay. It's not pleasure. It's not fine. It's not decent! It's not manly. You don't want to be that kind of a fellow. If you do, you're not choosing the brave course. You're being a coward and a fool.

"And you girls! I know many of you. I know your fathers, mothers and brothers. And yes, some of your sweethearts too. I know that I've never met finer girls than you anywhere. That's why I'm saying that you don't want to be riding around in automobiles with fast young fellows, petting and necking, drinking, smoking cigarettes. You want to preserve that fine chastity you have, those fine, beautiful bodies God has given you, and later on when you marry that decent boy you love, you'll go to him clean and honorable. Worthy of the love he offers you, worthy to be the mother of his children, just as your own mothers were worthy of Dad."

He paused.

"And there's one thing all of you should not do, if you want to avoid these evils. That's drink. Once does hurt. Once starts you off, and you're in grave danger. Drink destroys character and will power, and stultifies the voice of conscience. It is the precursor of all sins. It poisons the body. Today in this country there are scores and hundreds of young people in every city whose hearts, livers, stomachs, vital organs have been ruined by drink. They are dying in their prime. Why? Because they didn't believe that once would hurt. You know what Shakespeare, the greatest genius who ever lived, said of drink; 'Oh, God, that men should put an enemy into their mouths, to steal away their brains.'

'You don't want to do that. Because it is you, your kind, your class, to which America looks. And if America is to avoid that drastic, terrible fate which befell the proud and mighty empire of Rome, it is you, and others like you, who will have achieved the victory. I can't save America. My generation cannot. But yours can. That is why Mother Church counts on you. She knows that today she must fight one of the greatest battles she has ever fought. She faces a world where materialism drives out the laws and will of God and Nature, where sin is rampant, where money is poured into the coffers of vice, making it rich and powerful, where great industries are built up only to pander to lust, where books, theatres, movies, universities, are all aligned on the side of godlessness, and where all these forces together constitute a mighty propagandistic effort to take her sons and daughters from her and give them into the hands of Satan. And her fight is your fight. . . . (A pause:) Now, how are you going to fight? What are you going to say?

"Unless I am wrong, you're going to say this: 'Get thee behind me, Satan!' You're going to be manly and womanly, clean, upright, decent, and you're going to stand four-square in the front line trenches of Mother Church in her ceaseless war against the world, the flesh, and the devil. You're going to be soldiers of righteousness, and you're going to say: 'Jesus Christ, my Savior, has walked down the aisles of time, a white-robed figure of virtue and strength. And His Church has followed Him and His doctrine. With it, I take my stand. I shall not bargain away my soul, my honor, my right to be a member of that holy Church for a paltry night's pleasure, for filthy pieces of silver. I shall not be another Judas!"

He wiped his face.

"Shakespeare laments: 'Oh, that we should with joy, pleasance, revel, and applause, transform ourselves into beasts'. You're not going to do that. No! I know it. I know that the young men and the young women of St. Patrick's parish are going to stand defending the gates of Truth and Righteousness, armed with Grace.

" 'Stand, therefore, having your loins girt with truth and having on the breast-plate of justice, and your feet shod with the preparation of the gospel of peace.'

"In the name of the Father, and of the Son, and of the Holy Ghost, Amen!"

There was rustling and straining in the pews.

"And now, I want to ask you all to follow me in a prayer to Mary, asking her protection and aid in the struggle of the Catholic youth of this land for the triumph of virtue."

He recited the prayer slowly, and the young people sing-songed it after him, verbatim.

"O Victorious Lady! Thou who hast ever such powerful influence with Thy Divine Son, in conquering the hardest of hearts, intercede for those for whom we pray that their hearts being softened by the rays of Divine Grace, they may return to the unity of the true Faith, through Christ, Our Lord! Amen!"

He climbed down from the pulpit, genuflected in front of the Blessed Sacrament, and disappeared through the sacristy door. An altar boy came onto the altar, cassocked, and lit the candles for Benediction of the Most Blessed Sacrament.

III

"Say, wasn't that a sermon!" Les exclaimed.

"It was a knockout," Studs said, watching the people gush from church, looking at the girls coming out with an attitude of almost futile hope and expectancy.

"It was even better than the sermon he gave Tuesday night," Red Kelly said.

"Sure it was, if it only teaches you guys something," Barney said.

"People who live in glass houses shouldn't fling bricks," Stan said.

"Me, I'm an old man. He was talking to youth, and you bastards might still technically classify as youth," Barney said.

Studs scanned the faces. Maybe that girl would be coming out, but it seemed that she had moved away. Lucy. He wanted them to see him there, calm, nonchalant. But he realized that he wasn't so much to look at any more. Getting fatter all the time, had an alderman, was twenty pounds heavier than when he'd taken Lucy to that dance. Then he had been a damn good-looking guy, and he hadn't danced so badly either.

"I like what he said about these bastards monkeying around with a guy's sister. Like the time at Nolan's, and that bastard, Guy Bain, was trying to lay it into my kid sister on the dance floor. Remember, Studs? Well, I got him," Weary Reilly said.

"He knows his apples," Les said.

"He didn't hand it to the sheiks much, did he?" Tommy said.

"And neither did he to those people who think they are too good for the human race like Young O'Neill who goes to the University. He knows better than make the mission. He'd get his ear full," said Red.

"Isn't he making the mission?" asked Studs.

"He's an atheist," Red said.

"I always thought he was goofy," Studs said.

Studs watched for a girl. Still plenty of them in the parish. He hated guys with a girl. Goddamn it, he needed a girl, he wanted the feeling a guy would have, having a girl that was his only. He edged over to listen to the punks razzing Curley, because he wanted to get closer to the crowd. He listened with a supercilious expression on his face. The razzing suddenly turned on Jerry Rooney because he had a big nose. Studs touched his own nose. . . . Well, Rooney's was bigger. Young Horn Buckford rushed to Studs from another group, and said he would let Studs prove it. Studs curtly asked him what?

"Listen, I was telling these dumbbells that there's a fellow named Cardigan who beat Locke of Iowa running backwards. Remember you told me about it. This Cardigan beat Locke in the hundred yards, running backwards, and he made a backward dive over the tape to nose Locke out. Remember you told me, Studs?"

"You heard Father Shannon, didn't you? Well, for Christ sake, leave it alone before it's too late."

"Hink wouldn't have a leg to stand on after that sermon," Tommy said, as they trailed back to the corner.

"He sure laid it on thick," Les said.

"That's the only way to do it," said Red.

"Well, then, let's see if you guys cut out the bottle after the mission is over, and quit adding to the revenue of whore houses," Barney said.

"Say, Barney, at a time like this, when we're all making the mission, there's no place for kidding. I know we all done things, but the flesh is weak, and that's why we're making the mission. It's to help us be more decent. We all know he told us the truth, and we all know that at times we've been pretty filthy bastards. But we're going to try not to from now on," Red said.

"Yeah," Studs added, as if with deep reflection.

"He didn't tell you nothing I ain't been telling you for years," Barney said.

"This is serious," Red crisply said.

They had coffee an' in the Greek restaurant. Coming out, Studs told about hearing Christy talk with Davey.

"Why don't he go back to Ireland where he belongs," Barney said.

"I think we ought to boycott the restaurant until Gus gets rid of him," Red said.

"We'll make the punks do it too," Studs said.

"We don't want radicals like that in this neighborhood. Father Shannon showed just what they are," Kelly said.

"Well, finished with religion yet?" Slug asked, coming towards them.

"Gus is not there now. But I'm going to speak to him tomorrow. If he wants our trade, he'll get a Greek waiter in there who isn't radical," Red said.

Slug told about the beer he had in Colisky's saloon down the street. Barney said all the boys would be back having it on Sunday night. Red said not this time, and asked the boys how about it. They agreed. Slug said that for him, seeing was believing, and that he had never given that religion stuff a go because you couldn't live up to it.

Red was still trying to explain religion to Slug when Studs started home. He saw Phil kissing Loretta in the hallway, and walked back towards the corner. It was a clear fall night. Even the Jew had a girl to kiss. Aw, hell, it was all the bunk. He turned back from the corner and took his time. Phil came along, whistling gaily. Studs started whistling in a don't-give-a-damn manner.

"Say, Studs, wasn't it swell? He's the best speaker I ever heard," Phil said.

"You got what he said, didn't you?"

"Sure. Why?"

"Well, now, don't try any monkey business."

"You know I wouldn't, Studs. You know I think too much of

Loretta, and she's too fine a girl. If I did, she'd probably give me the gate. And anyway, I wouldn't because I think too much of her, and I'm not a sonofabitch."

"You got your warning," Studs said, walking on.

IV

"I saw Gus last night. He gave that radical bastard his pay when he came down tonight, and he's through. There's a new man in there. I told Mike we'd boycott the place, and that if that wasn't enough, wreck that bastard," Red said.

"Good stuff," Studs said.

"How was the church tonight, boys?" asked Slug.

"Not so good. Father Shannon only gave the short talk tonight, and his partner, Father Kandinsky, gave the sermon. He's a bit dull," Red said.

Slug muttered an "oh," as if he understood. Tommy remarked that there wasn't as many as last night, and that no priest drew them like Father Shannon. Les said Father Shannon was an artist.

"Whenever he gives a mission in this town, there's a lot of people, particularly girls, who are Father Shannon fans, and travel all over the city to hear him," Studs said.

"He's worth hearing," Tommy said.

"Notice how the girls and women go for him," said Red.

"My old lady thinks he's a saint," Tommy said.

"Mine too," Studs said.

"Speaking of women, I know a new girlie that sure can guarantee to keep the sailor warm when it's zero outside," Slug said.

"Save it, Slug," Red said.

"Jesus, you guys must have got religion," Slug said, shaking a puzzled head.

"Studs went to confession," Red said.

"Yeah, Foul-Mouth Lonigan has got to keep his mind pure until Sunday morning. But then, I'll bet the bastard makes up for it," Barney said.

"Nix, Keefe," said Red.

"Sure, go ahead. I'll tell all of you, you have such filthy minds that I'm risking my immortal soul associating with you," Barney said, getting laughs.

Slug said he hadn't gotten the dope about Studs straight. Red explained that Studs had confessed his sins, and that he had to keep his soul in the state of grace by not committing any new sins between now and Sunday morning when he received Holy Communion.

"You mean he told the priest about all the parties we have been having?"

"Yeah."

"Wasn't the priest jealous?"

They tried to explain it to Slug, but he finally went back to the saloon for a drink. Red said that Phil Rolfe had meant things and was really baptized. Studs said sure, he went the whole hog. Stan said he was sweet on Studs' sister. Studs nodded, frowning. Tommy said he hadn't realized Phil was so intelligent as to really accept the faith. Red said to wait and see how much he accepted it before tossing bouquets at him. You should never trust a Jew.

"For Christ's sake, Fat, where you been?" asked Studs.

"Hell, I moved out of this nigger neighborhood," Fat Malloy answered.

"Where you living?"

"Out near Sixty-seventh and Stony."

"My old man's thinking of selling the building, and buying one out somewhere south," Studs said.

"You belong in a white man's neighborhood," Fat said.

"What you doing, Malloy?" asked Doyle.

"Down at the water works with my old man."

"I been thinking of going into the political game myself," said Tommy.

Fat pulled out a poem about gonorrhea. Studs said he went to confession. Fat said he was sorry. The other boys looked at it privately. It turned Studs' mind to girls. He started home to avoid the occasion of sin. He stepped on sidewalk cracks to keep his mind off women. Christ, he wanted one. He remembered how, as a kid, he used to count the cracks on a sidewalk as he walked. Those days. A girl walked ahead of him. Young. He liked young girls, something about them when they were just budding, when they were the age Lucy had been that day the punks had had the tin-can fight, the age that that bitch, Nellie Cullen, had been. But it had been nice with her, even if he had been dosed. Jesus, he wanted a girl that age again. Like the one in front of him. He would take her over to the park, kiss her, gradually work her up, pat her head, kiss her hair, her eyes, nose, mouth, ears, neck, feel her back and her boobs on the outside, stick his hand inside her dress, french-kiss her, grab under her dress. . . . He came to realizing what kind of thoughts these were. But he hadn't done it willfully. They had been temptations, not sins. They had come on him without his being aware of them. A sin had to be a grievous matter and have sufficient reflection and full consent of the will before it was mortal. He hadn't thought of having these thoughts or willed them. They had just snuck up on him. He couldn't keep his eyes off the girl. He wanted to swear, do something. And he had to keep himself in the state of grace all day tomorrow, until Sunday morning. He counted his steps, and avoided landing on the cracks in the sidewalk.

V

On Sunday morning at the eight o'clock Mass, St. Patrick's Church was jammed with young people. Father Shannon, in his brief sermon, said it was an edifying sight indeed to see how successful this mission had been, to see so many young men and young women doing the honorable, courageous thing by marching up to the altar to receive their God. It was the kind of demonstration that made himself and Father Kandinsky, and also Father Gilhooley and his assistants, take renewed heart and courage, because they realized that they did not labor in the Lord's Vineyard in vain, did not sow seed on fallow ground.

Three priests and over twenty minutes were required to give out Holy Communion. Studs went to the altar rail with a free conscience. He had gone back to confession again on Saturday, even though everybody had kidded him. He was certain that way that he was in a state of grace, after the thoughts he'd had Friday night. All the hoods received and Phil Rolfe knelt amongst them receiving his first Holy Communion.

In the afternoon, the church was crowded for the formal closing of the mission. Father Kandinsky delivered a short sermon, lauding them for their good works and intentions of the past week, and telling them about the mission collection that would be taken up before they left the church. He followed it with a short exposition of the sins in violation of each commandment, but he said little exciting about the sixth commandment. They lit their candles, and followed him, word by word, in a renewal of their baptismal vows. They received the Papal Blessing and Plenary Indulgences, and Benediction of the Most Blessed Sacrament followed. After it, the mission was over.

On Sunday evening, the boys gathered around the corner. Slug suggested a drink. They refused. They hung around, gassing, and smoking, looking at the drug store clock, wondering what the hell to do. Again they refused to drink with Slug. They hung around. Slug kept insisting that one beer wouldn't hurt them. They went down the street to Colisky's saloon and had a beer. They had another. Before they realized it, they were drinking gin. They got drunk and raised hell around the corner. They hung around until Slug talked them into going to a new can house, a small place. They went and had the girlies, and gypped them out of their pay. It was a big night.

XXII

A DISTURBING *sense of loneliness caused Danny O'Neill to close the copy of* The Theory of Business Enterprise *which he was studying for one of his courses at the University. The elation of intellectual discovery and stimulation, the keenness of feeling mental growth within himself, the satisfaction of having uncovered additional proofs to buttress his conviction that the world was all wrong, which he had derived from his reading, suddenly eased.*

He looked out of the window of the Upton Service Station on a corner of Wabash Avenue in the black belt where he worked. He felt as if he were in a darkened corner of the world that had been trapped in a moment of static equilibrium. The light on the corner seemed only to emphasize the dreariness of the scene. Across from him was the box-like carburetor factory that stood now darkened like a menace of gloom.

He had gone to services one night during the mission last week, and afterward, he had waited for Father Shannon. He had asked the priest if he could talk with him about the faith, because he was a University student who had lost his religion. Father Shannon had curtly replied that he was, for the present, very busy. The incident had crystallized many thing in Danny's mind. It had made him feel that it was not merely ignorance and superstition. It was perhaps not merely a vested interest. It was a downright hatred of truth and honesty. He conceived the world, the environment he had known all his life, as lies. He realized that all his education in Catholic schools, all he had heard and absorbed, had been lies.

An exultant feeling of freedom swept him. God was a lie. God was dead. God was a mouldering corpse within his mind. And God had been the center of everything in his life. All his past was now like so many maggots on the mouldering conception of God dead within his mind. He jumped up, and went outside to stand on the gravel service-station driveway, and shook his fist at the serene and brilliant March sky.

He opened his book, but after a few more pages, closed it a second time. He was too lonely, too aware of almost complete rootlessness to study. Everything of value, all his ambitions, had turned, churned on him, curdled. He remembered himself as a boy, one of the neighborhood goofs. Around the corner he was now more of a goof than ever. His nostalgias for past experiences in the neighborhood seemed to have died too. He hated it all. It was all part of a dead world; it was filthy; it was rotten, it was stupefying. It, all of the world he had known, was mirrored in it. He had been told things, told that the world was good and just, and that the good and just were rewarded, lies completely irrelevant to what he had really experienced; lies covering a world of misery, neuroticism, frustration, impecuniousness, hypocrisy, disease, clap, syphilis, poverty, injustice.

He tried again to study. He envisioned a better world, a cleaner world, a world of ideals such as that the Russians were attempting to achieve. He had to study to prepare himself to create that world. A few more pages, and he again closed the book.

His sense of loneliness seemed to grow upon him. The air compressor behind him suddenly whirred, and he jumped with that fear that is caused by unexpected distraction in a moment of over-sensibility. He sat down again. He opened a book of readings in English literature, and read The Garden of Proserpine. *His realization that death was the end terrified him. Then he was lulled, and he imaged a world when the last human had died, a world of tall grass over the gravestones of humanity, with winds sweeping the grass, through which the sunlight spread to reflect colors perceivable by no eye. Death seemed like a sensuous falling into sleep. But it was not so. It was the last slap in one's face, a final defeat, disgusting, disintegrating, insensate. His courage ebbed. Who was he to dream of doing things? What did he know? What had he accomplished?*

He wanted to be a writer. He didn't know how. He wanted to purge himself completely of the world he knew, the world of Fifty-eighth Street, with its God, its life, its lies, the frustrations he had known in it, the hates it had welled up in him. The mere desire gave him a sense of power. Without his having seen the man enter, an old Negro, hunched, the weary price of work in his creased face, stood before him holding a gasoline can. He bought four cents worth of kerosene. They talked.

"You all is white and young. You is not black, you all has a chance in dis worl'."

"Someday you will, too, maybe."

"Ah, no, not in dis worl', son!"

He watched the Negro slowly leaving, a wistful snapshot as he crossed the station driveway, and turned down Wabash Avenue. He was returning with the kerosene for the lamps. He lived in one of the hovels along Wabash Avenue. He gave O'Neill a sense of the misery of the world, perhaps the unnecessary misery in it.

It would all go in a newer, cleaner world. He seethed with sudden dizzying adolescent dreams and visions of this new world. He, too, he would destroy the old world with his pen; he would help create the new world. He would study to prepare himself. He saw himself in the future, delivering great and stirring orations, convincing people, a leader, a savior of the world. He became aware of the clock. It was fifteen minutes past his closing time. He hurriedly closed up the station, and walked to the elevated at Twenty-sixth Street. Riding home, tired, he felt that people didn't realize they were riding home with somebody who was destined to do big things. His dreams again collapsed on him like a tire gone suddenly flat. He repeated and repeated a line from Swinburne's poem:

"Even the weariest river winds somewhere safe to sea."

He was a disillusioned young man.

He wanted to get coffee in the Greek restaurant. But he might meet some of the guys. He hated them. He didn't want to see them. And Christy, whom he had always talked to in the restaurant, was gone. He didn't know why. The new waiter had just said he had left. He walked home, carrying a brief-case full of books. Studs Lonigan, Red Kelly, and Barney Keefe passed on the other side of the street. They called him goof and told him to leave it alone. He didn't answer. Some day, he would drive this neighborhood and all his memories of it out of his consciousness with a book. He swerved again from disillusionment to elation.

Chapter Twenty-two

STUDS and his father stood in the parlor and the early morning sunlight glared through the unwashed, curtainless windows. They looked around at the covered furniture. The room had an appearance of disruption.

"Bill, I'd rather let the money I made on this building go to hell, and not be moving," Lonigan exclaimed, with wistful regret.

"Patrick, are you sure all your things are packed," Mrs. Lonigan said.

"Yes, mother," Lonigan said, very gently.

It seemed to Studs that his mother wiped away a tear. She turned and went towards the back of the house to ask the girls if they had all their things packed.

"Hell, there is scarcely a white man left in the neighborhood," Studs remarked.

"I never thought that once they started coming, they'd come so fast."

"You know, Bill, your mother and I are gettin' old now, and, well, we sort of got used to this neighborhood. We didn't see many of the old people, except once in a while at church, but you know, we kind of felt that they were around. You know what I mean, they were all nearby, and they all sort of knew us, and we knew them, and you see, well, this neighborhood was kind of like home. We sort of felt about it the same way I feel about Ireland, where I was born," said Lonigan.

Studs didn't like the old man to let himself out like that because how could he reply? The old man and old lady were taking it hard.

"Yeah, it used to be a good neighborhood," said Studs.

"Well, Patrick, we're going to have a new home," Mrs. Lonigan said, returning to the parlor.

"Yes, Mary, but no home will be like this one has been to us. We made our home here, raised our children, and spent the best years of our lives here."

"Sunday in church, I watched Father Gilhooley. Patrick, he's getting old. He's heartbroken, poor man. Here he built his beautiful church, and two years after it's built, all his parishioners are gone. He's getting old, Patrick, poor man, and he's heartbroken."

Studs stood there, looking at nothing, feeling goofy, vague, as if he was all empty inside.

"We're all getting old, Mary; it won't be long before we're under the sod."

"Patrick, don't talk like that, please."

"Goddamn those niggers!" Lonigan exploded.

"I guess it was the Jew real-estate dealers who did it," said Studs, believing that he ought to say something.

"Mary, remember that Sunday, a long time ago, when we came out here in a buggy I rented, and drove around. It was nearly all trees and woods out here then, and there wasn't many people here," the old man said.

"Yes, Patrick, but now are you positively certain that you're not leaving anything behind?" Mrs. Lonigan said.

"Nothing, mother! And remember when we bought the building over on Wabash. That was before you were born, Bill."

Studs walked over to the window. He saw two nigger kids twisted together, wrestling in the street. They went down squirmingly. He remembered how, coming home from St. Patrick's every night, they used to wrestle and rough-house like that, and Lucy and the girls, not meaning what they said, would call them roughnecks, and then they would go at it all the harder. Funny to think that was all gone, and here he was twenty-six, actually twenty-six, and next fall, he'd be twenty-seven. He lit a cigarette.

"Out there there'll only be about ten buildings in our block, the rest's all prairie," Lonigan said.

"It'll be nice, though," the mother absent-mindedly exclaimed.

"Mary, you know it's not like it used to be. We're not what we used to be, and it'll be lonesome there sometimes."

"It's a shame. This was such a beautiful neighborhood. And such nice people. A shame," Mrs. Lonigan said.

"Well, there'll be nice people out there south, too," said Lonigan.

"I wish they'd hurry up," Fran said nervously, as she joined them.

"They ought to be here any minute now. The movers said they would be here at seven-thirty. Let's see now, it's seven twenty-five, no seven twenty-six," Lonigan said.

"Well, I wish they'd come. OOOOh, I can't stand the sight or thought of this place and this neighborhood any more. OOOH, to think of all those greasy, dirty niggers around. Every time I pass them on the street, I shudder," Fran said.

"Yeah, they look like apes, and, God, you can smell them a mile away," said Lonigan.

"Dad, they're coming in here, aren't they?" said Studs.

"Yeah, a shine offered the highest price for the building, so I let it go. But he paid, the black skunk."

"And this is such a beautiful building," Mrs. Lonigan said.

"Well, they can have it, only I hate to see how this building and the neighborhood will look in about six more months," said Lonigan.

"Yeah, I guess the damn niggers are dirty," said Studs.

"I know it. Did you ever look out of the window of the elevated train when you go downtown and see what kind of places they live in. God Almighty, such dirt and filth," said Lonigan.

"Sometimes, I almost think that niggers haven't got a soul," said Mrs. Lonigan.

"There's quite a few were in church last Sunday," Lonigan said.

"Yes, and coming out, did you see how they were trying to talk to Father Gilhooley, and he trying to edge aside from them. Poor man, he's heartbroken, simply heartbroken," said Mrs. Lonigan.

"Well, well, well! How's the little fairy queen? Is she ready to move too?" Lonigan said. Loretta smiled back at her dad.

"Dad, Phil is going to come over and help us move," she said.

"Now, that's fine of him. You know he's Jewish, and I always made it a point to never trust a Jew, but I finally am convinced that he's one white Jew, if there ever was one. And accepting the faith, well, I suppose we oughtn't to call him a Jew any more. He's on our side of the fence," said Lonigan.

Loretta smiled.

"He's a fine boy. He's got manners, and he was willing to be an usher in the church," said Mrs. Lonigan, looking at Studs.

"Yes, Father Gilhooley, I guess, is proud he's made a convert," said Lonigan.

"And he is so polite and thoughtful. Every time I come into the parlor when's he's here, I notice that he stands up. And before he smokes in my presence, he asks my permission. I think he is a fine boy," said Mrs. Lonigan.

"Well, it's seven twenty-nine, they ought to be here," said Lonigan.

"Martin, now you're only a boy. Don't you go trying to lift and carry any of those heavy pieces," said the mother.

"No danger," said Studs, smiling at Martin, who was now a tall, skinny, awkward young boy, a trifle loutish in appearance.

"I'm all right," Martin said in a falsetto voice.

The bell rang. Loretta rushed to the buzzer and pressed it. In a moment, she came back with Rolfe, who was dressed in old clothes. He politely said hello to everyone.

"Well, Phil, we're all set," said Lonigan.

"Yes, Mrs. Lonigan, I see that you are, and it's a fine day for moving too!"

"Phillip, it was awfully nice of you to come and help us," said Mrs. Lonigan.

"It wasn't any trouble, Mrs. Lonigan, I was glad to help you."

"Here, I must get you a cup of coffee," said she.

"Please don't, Mrs. Lonigan, I had my breakfast. I'm not at all hungry."

"It won't be any trouble, and I can fix it in a jiffy," she said, rushing out, as Phil graciously protested.

"I suppose you're glad to be moving, Mr. Lonigan."

"Well, Phillip, as I was saying, we're getting old, Mrs. Lonigan and me, and we kind of felt we'd rather not live with a bunch of damn smokes."

"Yes, I know how you feel. They ruined the neighborhood," said Phil.

Mrs. Lonigan called him from the kitchen.

"Yes, I wish they hadn't of gotten in, and they wouldn't have, if all the property owners got together. But I'll tell you this much, they'll never get out where we are going. That's certain. It's nice out there, too."

"Phil, Mother is calling you for your coffee," said Fritzie.

"Hi, there, Martin. All set?" smiled Phil, turning to go out to the kitchen.

"Say, Bill, he's a good, decent, clean-cut boy," Lonigan said.

Studs nodded.

"Dad, the movers are here," Fran called.

"Well, let's go."

The movers commenced taking things down. Studs took a large rocker, and carried it slowly downstairs. It was tedious work. His arms and back got tired. When he set it down in the alley, he was breathless, and all pooped out. Jesus Christ, and he was only twenty-six. Goddamn it, he felt rotten. In rotten condition. He touched the soft, unnecessary flesh about his abdomen and stomach. Goddamn it!

He walked slowly back, wishing the moving was done. Upstairs, the old man, mother, and two girls were standing in the parlor.

"Well, mother, take a last look around and say good-by," the old man said.

"Yes, Patrick."

"Now, you and the girls go ahead out there."

"No, Patrick, I'm afraid you'll forget something."

"Not on your life."

"I had better wait until everything is moved."

Studs picked up a lamp. It was lighter. He carried it down towards the back. Loretta and Phil followed him. He paused at the kitchen sink, and got a drink. Turning, he noticed Loretta squeezing Phil's hand, and telling him not to hurt himself lifting anything big.

He walked downstairs with the lamp. Yeah, he was kind of sorry to be moving. So were they all. Well!

XXIII

IT WAS A *Saturday night. Husk Lonigan had the dough from the first pay he had earned since starting to work for the old man. He, Pete McFarland, Crabby Konetchy, and a couple of other fellows from their old gang at St. Patrick's wanted a woman. But they were leary about going to a can house. They stood around the corner of Sixty-third and Cottage Grove, telling each other how they wished they would pick up some broads. Husk finally got bored and suggested some liquor. They chipped in and bought a quart of moon. They walked down to Jackson Park and sat on a bench drinking it, talking about girls, each trying to pretend to the other that he had already lost his cherry. They followed two girls and couldn't make the grade because of their lout-like approach. The booze gave them more courage and they took a taxi down to Twenty-second Street. They walked around lost, but feeling romantic and adventurous. A pimp picked them up, and took them to a can house. It cost two bucks, and the women wormed two bucks extra out of Husk, who was afraid and unable to talk. It was over quickly, and they were disappointed, because there didn't seem to be hardly anything to it.*

Riding back to Sixty-third Street, they acted like men, and with bravado and hard obscene language, minutely discussed their experience. They killed their stuff, and, scarcely able to walk, they bought another pint of cheap moon and staggered back to Jackson Park. They coughed as they drank the bitter stuff, but would not be outdone. Husk suddenly pitched forwards, bawled like a baby, and muttered prayers. He passed out, still mumbling prayers that were interspersed with incoherent curses. They carried him around, and once, he started coughing and spit up some blood. They let him sleep on a bench for about half hour, and still they couldn't bring him to. They soaked their handkerchiefs in water, and sponged his face. Konetchy went over to Sixty-third and Stony Island and came back with black coffee in a milk bottle. Trying to pour it down Husk's throat, they spilled it all over him. Finally, they rushed him frantically to a hospital. It cost ten bucks to have his stomach pumped. The doctor said he would have died if they hadn't brought him. Husk was left in the hospital, and the gang departed, humble, but still with a feeling that they were adventurous and the real stuff.

Chapter Twenty-three

OOPH, the last of the Mohicans! Studs thought to himself, as he came out of the Fifty-eighth Street elevated station and saw Sammy Schmaltz.

"Say, Schmaltz, who won the ball game?" asked Studs.

"Studs!"

"You're still around, I see."

"Yes, I'm always here."

"How's business?"

Sammy shrugged his shoulders, and said he sold some papers.

"All the old people are gone, huh?"

"Doyle, he still lives around here. Oh, one or two."

"They hang around?"

Sammy had to turn and sell a racing sheet to a nigger.

Studs walked towards Prairie Avenue. In the cigar store on the right-hand side of the elevated station, he saw a group of niggers hanging around, talking with a sweaty brown-looking, sporty bastard who leaned forwards on the counter. He saw pearly white teeth flash in a coal black smile.

Niggers passed him on the sidewalk. They nearly all looked alike, as if they were the same person. The corner, their old corner, looked like Thirty-fifth and State. A gang of young niggers were gathered around the fireplug talking, kidding, laughing. He tried to frown. Suppose they should get snotty or try to mob him? He suddenly thought of himself fighting ten or twelve niggers, standing with his back to the wall, swinging, laying them down one after the other with a punch, as guys sometimes did in the movies.

He went into the drug store. There was a pretty, white girl at the cashier's desk. He walked over to the soda fountain to get a coke. But the niggers used the same glasses. His stomach almost turned as he thought of himself using the same glass as a nigger did. He bought a package of cigarettes, and stepped outside.

A loud, irritating Negro laugh struck him, rubbed him up the back. He turned to see a dude, with baboon lips, twisting and bending forwards as he laughed.

"Hi, there, Mistah Morgan!" a loose-jointed, middle-aged Negro said to another passing Negro.

"Hi, Brother Jones," the second replied.

A handsome, light brown, well-built girl passed. Studs looked at her. So did the Negro lads on the corner. He wondered if she was a whore. He'd like to have her. He remembered how a couple of times he'd been to nigger can houses, but the girls he'd had had been too black and bony. One like that was nice, even if she was black.

He felt uncomfortable on the corner, and walked west towards Indiana Avenue. The street was changed. There was another chain store in the block. The garage was still at the corner of the alley. There was still a dry goods store where the old Palm Theater had been. He remembered how they'd used to sneak in the side doors, years ago when he'd been still in grammar school. He tried to remember some of the pictures he'd seen, with Maurice Costello, Fatty Arbuckle, John Drew, Broncho Billy, Charlie Chaplin, Mary Pickford. He couldn't remember them well, except for Charlie Chaplin.

He lit a cigarette. Hell, it hardly seemed that they had moved five months ago. Now, too, there was no place to hang out. Sometimes he went to Sixty-third and Cottage Grove, and sometimes to Sixty-third or Sixty-seventh and Stony Island. No other corner would ever be the same. Christ, and what wouldn't he give to have just one more night, with all the guys back again, and Arnold Sheehan too?

There was a greasy-looking Jew in the drug store at Fifty-eighth and Indiana where Levin had been, and where once, on the day he'd licked Weary Reilley, Helen Shires had treated him to a chocolate soda. He looked north down Indiana Avenue, and slowly crossed the street and walked down, past the vacant lot, past the three-story building where Red O'Connell had lived. Red was a skunk, a no-do, no-work, crapping sonofabitch. He'd used to hang out down at the poolroom around Fifty-fifth the last Studs had heard of him, and he and a bunch of guys like him would be there, shooting their mouths off, selling the buildings around there and even real estate out in the lake with their line. He passed the wooden house, set back from the sidewalk where the O'Callaghans had lived. On past the apartment where the Donoghues had lived. He stopped at the gray stone brick, Lucy's old house.

He had stood there that summer night, and she had blown him a kiss, and he had gone home carrying his handkerchief, as if he kept it there, and never again had things been the same, and funny, time had passed, and here he was, and Lucy was married. He hoped to Jesus Christ she'd get fat as a pig, have ten kids, and a husband who'd kick the Christ out of her, dose her, and blow out. He looked at the house, with lights behind shaded windows. Niggers now lived in it, and the house was probably stinking because niggers always stunk, and it was dirty because niggers were dirty. He tried to whistle. He heard some vague sounds, and stood convinced that they were human voices, and somehow he felt as if he was hearing Lucy, and Dan and Helen Shires, and all of them talking once again.

He turned back towards Fifty-eighth, cut through the vacant lot, where they'd all played, into the alley, out on Fifty-eighth Street and over to Michigan. He crossed Michigan and looked at the playground, dark and gloomy, with the school building half visible. It was misty, an autumn mist, a night like many nights he'd known around the neighborhood, when they'd all get together in the poolroom or at the corner, Slug and Red, Tommy and Les. And they'd goof around, listen to the punks, or go to a show, or get a bottle. He turned around, and walked back. The same railing stood by the grass plot, in front of the corner buildings at the northeast corner of Fifty-eighth and Michigan. Sometimes as a kid he used to jump back and forth over it. He vaulted over it. He vaulted back. He put his feet together to make a standing jump over it. He looked at the railing. He didn't jump, might not make it that way. He was stiffened up, heavy on his feet. He felt his belly. Jesus, was he going to get a belly like the old man?

He walked back to Indiana. On the east side of the alley between Michigan and Indiana, there was still that row of shacks. Poor people had lived there. He looked in and saw a dirty, disrumpled Negro home, lit by a kerosene lamp.

A buck nigger came along. Studs took his hands out of his pockets and tried to look tough. The nigger passed, singing.

He wondered where the guys were. He turned and walked south along Indiana towards St. Patrick's.

He started singing:

"Gee, but I'd give the world to see
That old Gang of mine,
I can't forget that old quartette,
That sang 'Sweet Adeline'."

Good-by forever, old fellows and pals. . . .

He stuck his hands in his pockets. He took them out, and swung them at his side. He lit a cigarette. The night was swell, that mist, the moon, just a little bit damp, all like some mystery or song or something. He thought of Lucy, and of that girl he'd knelt next to at Mass. Wonder what had become of her. Was Lucy happy? Hell, things were all funny. He guessed he, too, might as well get a girl and marry. What the hell else was there to do? Red Kelly had his girl. Sooner or later a guy married . . . if he could find somebody to marry him.

Ahead of him, he saw the lights of an elevated train appear, disappear. He heard the echoes from the train.

A long time ago, he had walked along the same sidewalk with Lucy. He stopped under the elevated structure, just south of Fifty-ninth Street. A train rumbled overhead. Sometimes they'd played shinny, or had fights here. He moved on past a row of apartment buildings. In his time, they'd looked new and modern, with lawns and trimmed bushes in front of them. Now they seemed old. The niggers, all over again, running down a neighborhood. He heard a victrola record going:

I hate to see de evening sun go down,
I hate to see de evening sun go down,

An elevated train blotted the song out momentarily, then he heard it again:

St. Louis woman, wid her diamond rings. . . .

He walked on. Niggers living in all these buildings, living their lives, jazzing, drinking, and having their kids, and flashing razors at each other.

He crossed Sixtieth, and, quickening his pace, he saw the sisters' convent, and the east side of the church grounds, with a bare flag-pole half distinct, in the center. And the school building. He looked at it, a long, low building, now like a shadow, its shape distorted because of the night. Christ, how many times had he come here? They used to play pompom-pullaway in the yard at lunch hour. He'd run through, stiff-arming anybody who came near. They were afraid of him. Damn tootin', they were. Studs Lonigan had been something to be afraid of. And one day, he remembered Battling Bertha giving TB McCarthy the clouts. He remembered TB covering his face and yelling to be let alone, then thinking suddenly that she was finished, he'd raised his face, and she'd been bringing her clapper down, and it had got him in the nose. He had yelled like hell, and his nose had bled. And in all those days, he'd sat in the chalk-smelling room, looked up at the desk where Bertha sat in the right hand corner of the window, he'd watched the sun coming through the window, and it would seem to come in lines, and show up all the dust. And the way Bertha would say with respect: William Lonigan, now perhaps you can diagram the first sentence. He'd had a drag with her, and she usedn't to give him the clouts as much as she had the others, because his old man always give the sisters a turkey at Thanksgiving and Christmas. He still sent one to the sisters.

He passed along the iron picket-fence. He noticed a light in the sisters' convent. He looked at the old building, from the front, the steps leading up to the wide wooden doors. He'd stood here, too, after Mass on many mornings.

He was still doing it. With this building here, looking the same, things couldn't be changed, and it couldn't be so many years ago, it couldn't. This building gave him confidence. Everything was all the same as it used to be, and he wasn't fat and worried about his health, and it couldn't be different, and all that couldn't be gone. He stood in a trance.

A street car passed. An old nigger in overalls walked wearily by him. He looked to his left at the new church, standing now huge and high. He remembered how the parish had talked of it. And it was a goddamn beautiful church, and what was it for now—a handful of black bastards.

He turned and walked away. At Sixtieth and Calumet, he paused to watch two young nigger kids wrestling. Three classily-dressed young shines minced past him. He walked right along behind them.

"I swear, ah'll tear your eyes out, Gloria, if you all start making those oogle eyes at my big man."

"What does I care for that big black bastard you got?"

For Christ's sake! He followed them. They slackened their pace. He walked by them, and one of the fairies said hello. A second one said he looked lonesome. A third asked if he had any chickens on the block. He was momentarily tempted to take a chance out of curiosity. Self-disgust rose, changing his mind. He turned and told them to blow. They laughed, and he walked on, hearing their voices and laughter behind him, feeling that he was being talked about. It was almost as if he were being humiliated, undressed, in public, and he hastened.

Automobiles were coming in all directions at Sixtieth and South Park. He wanted to get across the street. He dashed in front of the cars, dodged, and just landed safely on the other side. He was out of breath, but he was proud of himself. It had been taking a chance. His guts were still there, and he was still the old Studs Lonigan, ready to run risks. If he hadn't had guts, he wouldn't have taken the risk of his life, dashing in front of the cars. Damn tootin', he was! He drifted through the park. The wind was powerful, and he heard it beating steadily through the empty trees, scraping and rustling the dead leaves. It was dark, with scarcely a star in the sky. Dark, lonely in the park. It had used to be his park. He almost felt as if his memories were in it, walking about like ghosts. He turned to go and look at the lagoon.

Ahead, he saw a stout, squat fellow searching on the ground, repeatedly lighting matches. The sight was funny, almost like a shot from a movie comedy. He suddenly imagined that the guy had lost a valuable ring, money. It was perhaps something happening in real life, like one of the detective stories he had been reading recently. Studs Lonigan the sleuth would find it.

"Lost something!"

"Lonigan!" the fellow said with a curious lisp, as he looked up.

Studs laughed at Barney Keefe who faced him, wearing pyjamas and a bathrobe.

"The sonsofabitches!" Barney said.

"You drunk?" asked Studs, perceiving that Barney did not have his false teeth.

"No!" snapped Barney.

"Well, what the hell's this?"

"I'm sick!"

"You look worse. What the hell you doing out here in that outfit?"

"Oh, Doyle and them bastards came around, and I was sick, and they said come on, they'd take me for a little ride, because Doyle has his old lady's car, and they promised to give me a drink of some bonded stuff. And the wise bastards left me here and threw my false teeth some place around here. But there's nothing funny about it," Barney said, because Studs had to laugh.

Studs found the false teeth. Barney cursed all the way back to the park exit. He hailed a cab, and gave Keefe the fare.

He walked back, because Barney had said that the boys always met by the stone bridge in the park. He knew they'd be back. He found them seated on a bench. They all laughed when he told them how he'd met Barney.

"The jiggs drove us over here," said Tommy.

"How's everything been going?" Studs asked.

"Oh, so-so. You heard about my cousin, Les?" asked Tommy.

"Why no, what happened?"

"He's in a sanitarium."

"How come?" asked Studs surprised.

"Oh, drink. His heart is on the kibosh from that bum gin he's been guzzling," said Tommy.

"Jesus, I'm sorry to hear it. Is it serious?"

"It almost was, but I guess he'll be all right."

"Les ain't drank his last yet, thank God," interjected Joe Moonan, the dick.

"But Shrimp is in a bad way," said Tommy.

"Yeah? Where's he at?"

"He was dishonorably discharged from the Navy and he's down in Fort Wayne. That's where he comes from, you know. Yeah, he's dying by inches," said Tommy.

"It's too bad. What's up with him?"

"Con. I guess he got it from too much carousing around."

"Jesus, first Paulie, and then Shrimp."

"How you feelin', Studs?"

"Pretty good," said Studs, wishing he wasn't worried about his health.

"You're looking good," Tommy said, although it was too dark to see how Studs was looking.

"Slug been around much?" asked Studs.

"Sure. He's always around. He'll be here tonight."

"I'd like to see him."

"You heard about Hink, didn't you?"

"No?"

"They put him in the nut house."

"Jesus, I'm sorry to hear that. Christ, that's too bad. He was kind of queer, though. I remember seeing him several times when he didn't act like he was all there. But say, Joe, how are you these days?" Studs said.

"Oh, I'm all right. Since Thompson got elected again, I feel better, because that goddamn Dever wanted the force to be honest," Joe said.

"He made the boys work for their dough," kidded Tommy.

"Wait till your brother Jim gets on the force, Tommy. He'll work. They'll make a flatfoot out of him goddamn quick."

"When you getting yourself a jane, Lonigan?" asked Moonan.

"Hell with that crap," Studs said.

"Come to think of it, Studs, you never ran around much with girls," Tommy said.

"Jim's getting up in the world, huh?" said Studs.

"Yeah. He'll be on the force in a month," Tommy said.

"Seen any of the other boys?"

"Red. He's still around. He's out with his jane tonight. He's been going around with her more than he used to. I think he's already put the ring on her finger since he's got to be a bailiff in Dinny Gorman's Court," Tommy said.

"That stuff's crap," Studs said.

Tommy said also that Davey Cohen had just come out of the county hospital and he looked bad; lungs.

Slug came around. He and Studs greeted each other.

"Say, listen boys, it's getting late, and this ain't no place to be hangin' around all night. What you say we go to Cooley's saloon, huh?"

"Sounds like an idea," said Tommy.

"Gee, things are changed," Studs said, getting into the cab.

"Yeah, the old neighborhood is shot."

"The boys are all getting separated."

"You know, I was thinking, it might be a good idea to get all the boys together, and have a blowout party, say, New Year's Eve. Red's been thinking about it, and he's willing to make the arrangements and collect from the boys," Tommy said.

"Count me in on it," said Studs.

"How you like the car? My mother finally put out and bought it."

"Pretty nice."

"The Doyle Cab service," Moonan said.

"Well, I'll tell Red to call you up," said Tommy as they drove to Cooley's saloon.

Studs got the blues from gin. He suddenly left the boys. He staggered back to the park, and over onto the wooded island. He looked for the tree where he and Lucy had sat on that afternoon so long ago. He couldn't find it. He staggered about frantically, and finally got out of the park at Cottage Grove. He fell asleep on the car and rode out to South Chicago. He didn't get home until three o'clock. He felt lousy.

XXIV

LES' old man, and his sister, Mrs. Doyle, went to the midnight show at the Prairie Theater on New Year's Eve. He was a wizened man, with a bloodless, wrinkled face, humped shoulders, and quivering hands. She was a full-bodied woman, who breathed in gasps when she did much walking.

"Well, Mike, sure and another year's passed," she said.

"Ah, yes, Margaret," he said.

"There won't be many another year for the likes of you and me, Mike."

"Ah, no, Margaret. But God forbid that we should be dead before next New Year's."

"Well, Mike, I only have one more boy to see married to a nice girl, and it's me baby Tommy."

"And Les is my only worry, Margaret. He's a hard-working boy, but after him being so sick, I hope he doesn't drink tonight."

"And I do be worried about my Tom. He's a good boy, only it's bad companions. Now that my Jim is on the force, and Tommy has his job with the city, he might be settling down."

"Sure, Margaret, let us hope. It's the New Year."

At Prairie, Nate Klein staggered up to a passing white stranger, and told him to go take a pee-pee-pee for himself in his hat. Nate told the street that he was going to the party.

"And Lord bless me, I was afraid for a minute that that was me Tom."

"Ah, and I thought it was my Les."

She walked rheumatically across Prairie Avenue, holding onto her brother's arm.

"I do be worried because my Tom has the car, too. That car has a curse upon it," she said.

"Now don't worry, Margaret," Mike said.

At the midnight show, they saw sixth-rate vaudeville, and a weeping, five-months' old movie.

Coming out, they yawned, and complained that it was too late for people their age to be up. They walked home slowly.

"Mike, I hope that my Tom is all right. I have a feeling."

"Now, Margaret," he said, without conviction.

Chapter Twenty-four

I

A VOICE within Studs, that wasn't his voice, and that perhaps maybe might have been the voice of conscience, said reiteratively, as if in a hoarse accusing tone:

You're nothing but a slob. You're getting to be a great big fat slob. Nothing on the ball any more. Slob! Slob! Fat slob! Double slob!

"I'm drunk. Happy New Year. Whoops!" Studs yelled loudly: he staggered backwards and forwards with the utterance of each syllable.

Slob! Slob! Double Slob!

He looked at the street. It seemed familiar. What was the name?

The voice said:

You don't know your fanny from a hole in the ground!

He ran to escape that voice that kept hammering at him, in his heavy, heavy, twirling head. He ran, thinking he was running straight, and with form. He halted after about a hundred yards and thought that he'd run a block.

He knew the street as well as he knew his name. His name was Lonigan, the great Studs Lonigan.

Slob Lonigan! that voice said.

He stared bleary-eyed up and down the street. There was a light mist, and the street lamps seemed lopsided.

An automobile passed. Studs eyed it intently.

"Hey, where's . . . fire?"

He looked at three-story buildings. They seemed like he knew them and had seen them before. Where, oh, where is my wandering street tonight? Where, oh, where can it be?

The street rolled under him like a ship in a storm. His head spun like a top that was in perpetual motion. The street went up, whoops, and slow, slowly, evenly, it went down, whoops, just like a see-saw.

He shoved his hat on the back of his head.

He stared across the street, and it went up, whoops, and it went down, whoops, and the building came towards him, whoops, like a railroad engine coming forwards on a screen, growing nearer and nearer. Whoops! The building stopped. That was funny.

You're drunk, you clown, drunk as a lord.

He walked, like a paralytic, head down, his body loose, his nervous control deadened. He raised his feet high, as if in a caricature of Germans in a movie comedy doing the goosestep. He halted, threw out his chest, tossed back his head, and almost fell over backwards. His hat slipped to the sidewalk. He turned around in a circle, wondering where, oh, where was his wandering hat tonight.

He saw the hat lying as big as a balloon on the sidewalk. He pulled out a stick that had somehow and somewhere been stuck in his overcoat pocket, and held it over the hat as if it were a fishing pole. He jerked with both hands, like a man dragging in a huge fish, and he tottered backwards for about three yards before he gained a precarious balance. He looked at the end of the stick. No fishee, no hattee! Whoops!

He laughed, and tossed the stick away. He snuck up on his hat, tiptoe, shshing his right index finger to his lips. He circled, continuing to shssh his finger to his lips. He quietly snuck three feet from the hat. He dove for it, clumsily, like a green football player falling on the ball. He lay on the sidewalk. It was cold. Struggling, and by degrees, he achieved his feet again.

Slob Lonigan! Slob Lonigan! You're no goddamn good any more. Got an alderman. Alderman on your gut, and couldn't even get yourself a decent girl. Slob! Slob! Double Slob!

"Who's a slob?" he shouted.

You're a slob, the voice said.

He hauled off on the air, and went for a head-first dive in the hard, cold dirt by the walk. He lay there and looked at the world go around. The buildings spun about as if on a swiftly propelled merry-go-round. An automobile coming along went uphill and then downhill. Whoops! He arose, and ran around in circles in the middle of the street, trying to catch the buildings.

A taxi came skidding along. It stopped.

"You goddamn fool, get off the road!"

Studs uttered some inarticulate sound which seemed like uuuuhhhh.

The driver jumped out, and asked what did he say. Studs cursed him. The taxi driver pushed Studs back over the curb, and drove away. Studs fought to his feet, and rushed in the middle of the street, yelling after the vanished taxi.

Studs staggered, and draped his arms tightly around a lamppost. He vomited.

"I'm sick. I want Lucy. I love Lucy. I want Lucy. I want Lucy," he cried aloud, a large tear splattered on his cheek. The vomiting caused a violent contraction and pressure, as if a hammer were in his head.

"I'm sick! Lucy, please love Studs!" he cried.

A light flurry of snow commenced. Studs tenderly kissed the cold lamppost, which suddenly seemed to be Lucy.

"I always loved you, Lucy!"

Tears rolled down his drunken, dirty face.

II

Weary Reilley went to Trianon to get a pickup to take to the party the old boys from Fifty-eighth Street were throwing. There was a huge crowd at the dance hall. He moved about, and danced with several girls. One of them wouldn't sock it in. Another couldn't dance well enough to please him. A third laughed as if she were an idiot. The fourth girl was pretty in a chubby way with brown eyes and a quiet manner. He guessed, though, that here was a case of still waters running deep. She was his meat. She weighed about a hundred and twenty-five pounds, nice figure, got a guy hot just looking at her, straight, small hard breasts, nice legs, meat on them and on the thighs. Just his speed! He danced three successive times with her, and she seemed to like him. At first she drew back when he got her in the corners, but then she laid it right up to him, and they socked it in plenty. That made him sure that she was what he wanted. She had everything. He was going to give it to her like she'd never gotten it before. Dancing with her, he thought of what he would do to her, direct, crude images of brutalized sex.

"You're a pretty good dancer," she said.

"You're keen too," he said, working against her. "Shake that thing," he added.

"That's not . . . nice," she said, blushing as her eyes dropped.

"Come on, sister!" he said, aggressively.

She smiled, and let herself go against him.

"Do you come up here often?" she asked, hanging on his arm, and walking off the floor at the conclusion of the dance.

"I haven't got time for it," he said.

"Umm. Swell people. I suppose you go to the South Shore Country Club."

"No. There's too many pigs, and no-do's around here."

"Am I to take that as a compliment?"

"You're the real stuff, girlie."

"You'd be surprised."

"Meaning which?" he said, looking unflinchingly into her dark eyes.

"Maybe I'm not."

"I can take care of that."

"You're not confident, are you?"

"I pick my women, baby."

"Just like that! You're not what they call an . . . egotistical."

"Listen, want to go to a party?"

"Oh, I couldn't."

"How come?"

"Why, I don't even know you?"

"Come on, never mind that. This damn joint is too crowded. There's too many no-do's here. Come on, baby, and can the stalling. You don't want to be wasting your time with these imitation Valentinos up here."

"But what will my girl friend say?"

"Hell, she can find some guy to look after her, and if she can't, that is just tough."

"But. . . ."

"Listen, Irene. You know you want to come, and you're just playing around before you say yes. I don't like that stuff."

"You're a frank fellow, I see," she said.

"Come on," he said, grabbing her arm. They walked down the stairs to the cloak rooms.

III

The party was held in a suite of three rooms at a disreputable hotel on Grand Boulevard in the black belt.

"Here, Pat, have a drink of my stuff," Red Kelly said to Carrigan, as they stood in a corner of the crowded room.

After drinking, Pat Carrigan coughed and grimaced. He smiled that broad, happy, good-natured, chubby-faced smile of his.

"Ah, good stuff," he said, rubbing his belly.

"Damn tootin'."

"Where'd you get it?"

"Never mind. It's good stuff."

A jazz record was put on the portable victrola.

"Here now, Red. Have some of mine," young Carrigan said.

"Don't care if I do."

Pat handed Red the bottle, and Red took a big drink. Pat tried to take as big a drink, but couldn't. He put the bottle aside, coughing and sneezing.

"You'll learn how to take it in time," Red said.

"Say, I had too much already. Jesus, I'm drunk as a loon. I'm drunk, Kelly. Drunk," Carrigan said.

"Sure, I know how it is."

"But why shouldn't I be drunk? Ain't it New Year's Eve," argued Carrigan.

"Don't crap me now."

"Hey, Leach, commere."

"What the hell you want, you drunken Irishman?" Shorty Leach sourly asked.

"What day is it?"

"What's this, a joke?"

"I'm trying to tell Kelly here what day it is, and he won't believe that it's New Year's Eve."

"Jesus, that's tough tiddy. Give me a drink," said Shorty.

"Sure. Happy New Year," said Carrigan, handing him the bottle.

IV

"Don't say that I'm not a lady, you bastard," the exotic dark girl said.

"But say, kid. The ladies do it, and so do the birds. Don't you know that song, I love the birds, and the bees, and the trees, because they all do it too," Wils Gillen said.

"Well, don't say that I ain't a lady," she said.

"You know what I think you are?" said Wils.

"What?" she muttered, slobbering over the small glass of gin she had in her hand.

"I think you're a man."

"Look at me, then!" she said, laughing raucously.

"I'm from Missouri, kid. Show me!"

"Goddamn you, I will!" she said.

She ripped off her clothes.

"Now, you sonofabitch, do you believe me?" she shouted.

"Yeah, I guess you are."

"Now, you goddamn dirty skunk, show me that you're a man."

"I always aim to please."

"Come on over here, and show me. I had plenty, and I'm particular. Particular, I said. You got to prove it to me," she said, looking him over with a sneer.

"You got the right telephone number this time, girlie."

V

"Hey, Swede, don't. Lay off that bitch. She's got a dose."
"Listen, you ain't a man till you got it," Swede said.
"Well, don't say I didn't warn you."
Swede took the pig into one of the bedrooms.

VI

"Say, Dan," said Vinc Curley.
"Yeah," said O'Doul, as he stood in a corner, sheiked out, and unrumpled.
"Want to go to the Tivoli tomorrow afternoon?"
"For Christ sake, hop in the bowl."
Dapper Dan turned his back. Vinc looked puzzled.

VII

"Say, kiddo, listen! Give Doyle here a break!" Slug commanded.
"You know. I can't," Slug's blond jane protested.
"It ain't nothin'."
"I don't mind you, dearie, when I'm this way because I love you, but nobody else. That goes!"
"Come on, kid. I won't hurt you," Tommy Doyle said, his drunken face full of lust.
"No!"
"Go ahead, and do it, or it's the gate!" Slug said, shoving her.
She looked at him with eyes of meek protest.
"Hear me!" snapped Slug.
She went into a bedroom with Tommy.

VIII

"I'll tell you why I'm drunk," Shorty Leach said, letting the tears stream down his cheek.
"Sing 'em! Sing 'em!" Joe Moonan said.
"You didn't know my girl, Pearl. Well, I love Pearl. I love her."
Joe vanished. Shorty buttonholed Les, who looked thin and pale.
"Here, kid, have a drink and brace up," said Les.
Shorty took the bottle and drank.
"I love Pearl. And she's out with Jack Morgan tonight. Now

Morgan stole my girl. He's a nice guy, and I always liked him, but he's out with Pearl, and I'm crazy about her."

"Sing 'em, kid!"

"Have you ever been in love? Well, I have. You know I was out riding with Pearl. And she took and held my head in her hands and she looked into my eyes, and she said: 'There's something about you that makes me crazy.' That's what she said. And I tell you, if you've never been in love, you don't know how it felt. And then I looked out at the moon, and she did, and Jesus, I've never had a feeling like that before. And I thought she was straight, and now she went out with Morgan."

"Here, kid, have a drink, and brace up. The first hundred years is the hardest."

Shorty drank.

"But I tell you I wouldn't be drunk if I was with Pearl because I love and respect her too much. I love that girl," sobbed Shorty, putting his head on Les' shoulder.

IX

"Whoops!" yelled Studs, standing in the doorway.

They wished him Happy New Year. Slug handed him a bottle, and said bottoms up. Studs drank. The New Year bells rang. Everybody drank, and shouted, and a naked girl rushed from one of the bedrooms to kiss everyone. They had to hold Vinc while she kissed him.

"Whoops! It's 1929!" yelled Studs, raising an empty gin bottle with an unsteady arm.

X

"Where you going, Joe?" asked Red.

"I can't telephone here with this noise, and I want to call my mother. I do every New Year's."

"Wish her a Happy New Year for me," said Red.

Moonan went out.

XI

Vinc heard a moan. Then, he heard a girl sobbing. He rushed through the opened door of a bedroom, and turned on the light. He saw Benny Taite and a girl.

"Is there anything wrong?" he said, breathless and embarrassed.

"For Christ sake, who let you in, monkey face?" the girl asked.

"You goddamn idiot!" said Taite.

Taite went at Vinc. He socked Vinc. Vinc lost his temper, and rushed Taite like a bull, socked him, knocked him down, and stood over him, yelling:

"Come on! Come on!"

A crowd gathered. Some of them laughed. Red dragged Vinc off, and told him to get the hell out of the place.

"But he hit me!" said Vinc.

"I told you to blow!"

"He hit me. And I paid my money. I won't."

"Will you shut up, you bastard?"

"Gimme my money back, or I'll call the police," whined Vinc.

"Let me handle the mutt," said Slug.

"Listen, seal your trap and there's the door," Slug said.

"I'm gonna tell my mother!" he said, surlily from the door.

Taite sat in a corner nursing a shiner.

XII

Mickey Flannagan slept in the corner with a stupid expression on his face. He snored. Barney Keefe folded his hands, and placed a soggy Merry Widow in them.

XIII

"Daddy, you're a man. What a man! Daddy!" the exotic dark girl said to Wils Gillen.

"As Napoleon said, don't give up the ship," Wils said.

XIV

The blond girl rushed from the bedroom yelling that she'd been raped. She opened a window, screamed that she'd been raped, and threatened to jump.

Red pulled her back. She stood looking about the shocked group, her face distorted and insane. Tommy appeared, asking what the hell was eating her.

"He! He! He!" she shouted, missing Tommy's head with a gin bottle; it ricocheted off the wall, and hit Mickey in the bean. He continued to sleep.

Slug walked over to the girl amidst a tense silence. He slapped her face. She cowered.

"One more bat out of you and you won't have to jump!"

XV

Shorty Leach sat fully clothed in a bathtub of water, droning:

The pal that I loved, stole the gal that I loved, and took all my sunshine and joy;
Nobody but he was a buddy to me, since we played on the floor with our toys.
I just can't believe my old pal would deceive. Gee, but I'm heartsick and sore,
The pal that I loved, stole the gal that I loved, that's why we're not pals anymore.

XVI

"I shouldn't be drinking. I'm sick. I just came out of the hospital, and the doc he says to me, 'Les, cut it out, or you'll be picking daisies!' "

"Shut up, fool!" Barney mocked.

"But I don't care. There ain't nothin' in life for me. I'm just a goddamn expressman for the Express Company. I ain't got no future."

Tears rolled down his thin, red face; he drank.

"Listen, heel, what's the idea of holding out?" said Keefe.

"Here, pal!"

"Barney, I had a vocation to be a priest. I should be a priest. And look at me! Look at me! Look at me!" Les said, while Barney guzzled.

"I am looking!"

"Ain't I a wreck?"

"Sure, you're the Wreck of the Hesperus."

"Barney, I might be dead next New Year's. The doc said so. He said: 'Kid, lay off the liquor.' But why should I? I'm nothin'. a goddamn teameo for John Continental. Here, gimme a drink," he said, snatching back his bottle and drinking.

Les sneered, looking at a lamp.

"That goddamn thing, I don't like it"! he said.

He kicked it over.

Barney pulled out a little bottle and raised it aloft, saying: "To myself; good men are scarce."

XVII

There was a sharp rap on the door and a command to open up. Two burly, monkey-faced cops entered.

"What the hell do you call this?" one said.

The other drew a gat. A girl fainted.

"Call the wagon," said the cop, holding the gat on them.

"Who's running this party?" asked the other cop.

"We all are," said Carrigan.

"All who? Speak up, you birds!"

"What the hell, Officer. It's New Year's. We're just havin' a little party," Slug said.

"Yeah, so I see," said the cop ironically.

"Pipe down, you!" said the cop with the drawn gun.

"Me?"

"Yeah, you!"

"Say, what's the idea?" Slug asked.

"Stand back, or I'll shoot."

"Drop that gun, and talk!" Slug commanded.

"Just a minute, Officer," Joe Moonan said, appearing, and flashing his star. Red followed, showing his bailiff's star.

He and Red talked to the officers, and Red told them his old man had been a sergeant.

"Sure, this is just a party. You know, all the boys having a good time," Joe said.

"Well, we got a complaint, and we had to come."

"Want a drink, Officer?" Red asked.

"Sure."

Red gave them a couple of drinks.

"And say, listen, you know Moonan, kind of ask the lads to pipe down on the noise. We don't like to be gettin' calls like this."

"Sure."

"Here, take this along," Red said, handing one of them a bottle of gin.

XVIII

"Say, Slug, that goddamn broad in there has made a wreck out of me. Jesus, I'm a wreck. Christ sake, please help me out," Wils said.

"Sure thing, kid," said Slug disappearing.

"I just wanna lay down and die," Wils said, dropping on the floor.

XIX

"Come on, let's play football," said Nate Klein, squatting.

Red yelled to cut it out.

"Sixteen, nineteen, twenty-four, Fifty-eighth Street. Cardinals hike!" he yelled, springing against the wall.

Red and Weary grabbed him from behind, and told him to cut it out. He struggled free, squatted, flung himself at the wall again. He bounced back, moaning, holding his hand. Red took him into the bathroom to soak it in hot water.

XX

"Come on, it won't hurt you," Weary coaxed.

"I better go," she said.

"Irene, come on. Don't pull that stuff," he said sharply.

"No. I've never drank. I'm not that kind of a girl."

"Listen! Don't kid me!"

"Please, I'm afraid of you," she said, drawing back.

He took her in a corner, kissed her, pushed her head back, and poured the gin down her throat. She coughed.

"Please, take me home!"

"Come on, we'll dance."

He dragged her, half-willing, to the victrola. He put on a record and yelled for them to pipe down. They danced, and Weary shimmied. She stood in the center of the floor, an abandoned look on her face, her abdomen pressed forwards, her arms loose, her head flung backwards, shimmying.

XXI

Mickey Flannagan lay in a corner, still out.

XXII

"I got mine from that broad," said Mahoney.

"I thought she was a virgin," said Fluke.

"She was!"

"Well, how did you do it?"

"I got her blind. She's out."

"Where is she?"

"She's in the second bedroom. She passed out, and I carried her there. She's out like a light."

"Mind if I try my luck?"

"Go to it, Fluke," said Mahoney.

XXIII

"Come here, bitch!" Studs said to one of the pigs.

"After a while," she said.

"Come on, bitch!" said Studs.

He pawed at her. She gave him a shove, and he was so drunk that he stumbled backwards. Taite laughed at him. The girl ran into the bathroom. Studs staggered to the door, and tried to open it. It was locked. He pounded the door.

XXIV

"Listen, Irene is my broad. Don't you be monkeying around her," Weary said to Dapper Dan O'Doul.

"I was only dancing with her."

"Listen, rat, you're all together. If you want to stay that way, don't monkey around her," said Weary.

"I'm sorry."

"You heard me!"

XXV

Barney crawled on his hands and knees looking for his false teeth. Slug gave him a slight boot in the tail. They laughed. Barney cursed. Everybody laughed again.

XXVI

"Let's drink this one for poor Shrimp Haggerty," said Les.

"Yeah!" said Studs.

"Poor Shrimp is dying in Fort Wayne. I'll be dead, too, maybe by next year," said Les.

"Yeah!"

Les raised the bottle. Tommy Doyle grabbed it, and told Les he'd better lay off.

"All right, Tommy, but will you and Studs drink to poor Shrimp, our dying buddy?"

"To our buddy Shrimp, may he be guzzling with us next year," said Tommy, drinking.

"Yeah," muttered Studs, taking the bottle.

He raised the bottle and drank, most of the gin pouring down his chin and shirt.

"Studs is so drunk we'll have to hold his head while he drinks," said Tommy: he laughed.

XXVII

"Jesus, Joe, let's get some of these guys out of here. This is getting to be too much of a goddamn mess. If we don't, something's going to happen," said Red.

"Yeah," said Joe.

"Hey, punk," Joe said.

"What's the matter?" O'Doul asked.

"See the door? Blow!"

"But I ain't doing nothing!"

Red told some other punks to blow.

"Some goddamn thing is gonna happen if we don't get some of these drunks out," Red said.

"Tommy, can you get Les out? He's sick and needs air, and we want to cut it down. Then you and him come back," said Joe.

"Sure. Les is my cousin. I stick by my cousin Les."

"All right, do it, Tommy."

XXVIII

Three of the girls staggered away drunk.

XXIX

Studs floundered over to Irene like a listing ship.

"Come on, bitch!" he muttered, clutching her arm.

"All right, Lonigan, hands off!" Weary commanded.

"Aw, gimme the bitch!" Studs said.

Weary socked Studs in the eye with a right. Studs went back against the wall, and bounced off, his eye swelling. Weary caught him in the nose as he rebounded. He grabbed Studs by the coat lapel with his left, smacked him in the eye with his right, and then gave him a last one on the button. Studs sagged to the floor, and lay there, his nose bleeding profusely.

XXX

"Please let's go. Everybody else is gone," Irene said.

"He's here," Weary said, pointing at unconscious Mickey Flannagan.

"Please?"

"Have another drink!"

"Then will we go?"

"Sure!"

"Promise me?"

He nodded. She sipped from his bottle.

"Now get my coat," she said, shrinking, as she saw the expression on his face.

"Oh, please! Please! Please! I'll scream. . . ."

"Commere, goddamn you! And shut up!"

She cowered with fright. He tried to kiss her. She fought off his thrusting mouth with her hand. He knocked it aside, and pressed his lips against her shaking forehead. He encircled her with his arms, and dragged her towards the bed where Mickey lay. He flung her towards the wall, and rolled Mickey off. She ran to the door. He tackled her.

"OOOH, my ankle!" she sobbed.

"Will you come across now," he said, towering over her, while she sat on the floor, holding her ankle.

She screamed. He grabbed for a pillow slip, and tore a strip off it. She hobbled out of the room on her sprained ankle, screaming. He caught her from behind, and as she twisted and tore, he got the pillow slip tied around her mouth. She raised her hand to tear it off, and he twisted her arm. He could see the pain on her face:

"Will you come across?"

She nodded.

He released her. She tore the rag off her mouth. He smothered her scream with his hand, and she hit and scratched. He gave her an uppercut, and she toppled to the floor. She started to rise unsteadily, and he was on her, holding her mouth, using his other hand to ward off her scratching hands. She slumped back limp, breathing heavily. Her hair was down. Her dress was torn.

"Please. I never done it before. Please, lemme go. Please!"

"I won't hurt you. For Christ sake, cut out the stalling."

"Honest to God, please, I never did this. Please. . . ."

"Can that! You're comin' across if I have to kill you!"

"Please . . . you might act like a . . . gentleman."

"Come on, for Christ sake!"

He half smothered her scream. He stuck his knee in her stomach, and slapped her viciously with his left hand.

"Oh, you will, will you!" he said, punching her jaw after she again flashed her teeth.

He carried her unconscious to the bed.

XXXI

Her face was black and blue, and her coat thrown over her torn dress. She winced with each step, sobbed hysterically, shook all over.

"Now don't try that game on a guy again!" he said, shoving her out the door of the suite.

He left the bloody sheets soaking in the bathtub. Coming from the bathroom, he saw Micky Flannagan stagger out and he smiled.

He was awakened by the cops, who had been let into the suite by the night clerk.

"This is gonna be a tough rap to beat for you, fellow!"

"You ain't got nothin' on me."

"No! She's beat up pretty bad!"

"She was drunk and fell down!"

"Maybe you can prove that alibi."

The other cop came from the bathroom with the dripping, bloody sheets and asked what about them.

"I don't know nothin' about them."

"Where did you get your puss scratched?"

"I had a fight."

"Yeah!"

"Yeah!" said Weary, challengingly.

"Listen, everybody isn't a helpless girl. Watch the way you talk."

"Listen, they sent you to get me. Here I am. Call a cab, and I'll pay the bill. But don't try pullin' nothin' on me!" Weary said with clenched fists.

"Shall I let him have it, Joe?" asked the other cop.

"Don't soil your mitts on him."

Weary sneered. He walked out with them. As they went through the door, he made a gesture and said:

"She ain't got no kick. She only got that much!"

XXXII

The dirty gray dawn of the New Year came slowly. It was snowing. There was a drunken figure, huddled by the curb near the fireplug at Fifty-eighth and Prairie. A passing Negro reveler studied it. He saw that the fellow wasn't dead. He rolled it over, and saw it was a young man with a broad face, the eyes puffed black, the nose swollen and bent. He saw that the suit and coat were bloody, dirty, odorous with vomit. He laughed, the drunk stirred as the Negro said:

"Boy, you all has been celebratin' a-plenty."

He searched the unconscious drunk and pocketed eight dollars. He walked on.

The gray dawn spread, lightened. Snow fell more rapidly from the muggy sky of the New Year.

It was Studs Lonigan, who had once, as a boy, stood before Charlie Bathcellar's poolroom thinking that some day, he would grow up to be strong, and tough, and the real stuff.

XXV

THERE *was an inward, selfabsorbed expression upon the black face of woolly-headed, fourteen-year-old Stephen Lewis, as he walked along Fifth-eighth Street. He thought of an awkward black girl named Eliza May Smith. He spotted a tin can on the sidewalk, and kicked it, thinking that he was the hero of a high school soccer game, and that Eliza May Smith, pretty as a picture, was watching him. Suddenly he paused, fearful. He couldn't remember now, gosh darn it, whether his mother had told him to get butter or sugar. He stood as if petrified, with his eyes popped open, the whites showing. He scratched his head. He proceeded slowly, racking his brain.*

At the corner of Fifty-eighth and Prairie, he stopped to watch some older fellows shooting craps. He listened to their language, watched the dice, gazed large-eyed at the money. Some day, he would be big enough to stand on the corner and shoot craps for real money, and he'd win and buy something pretty for Eliza May Smith. He went on because he had been instructed to hurry home. In the chain store, he ordered sugar. A clerk left a half pound of butter on the counter, and continued to fill an order. Stephen copped it; he had both butter and sugar. He paused a few more minutes at the crap game. He went on, kicking a tin can, imagining himself to be the hero of a high school soccer game, while Eliza May Smith, pretty as a picture, watched him.